BILL MC NEIL

Voice of the Pioneer

Pioneers of all sorts—
prospectors, scientists, homesteaders,
teachers, bush pilots, and many others—
tell their fascinating stories here,
as they have told them on
Canada's best-loved radio program

MACMILLAN OF CANADA
TORONTO

TO EILEEN, RUSSELL, BRETON, AND DAWN
*who entered my life, captured my love,
and enriched my being.*

Canadian Cataloguing in Publication Data

McNeil, Bill, 1924-
  Voice of the pioneer

"Pioneers of all sorts—prospectors, scientists, homesteaders, teachers, bush pilots, and many others—tell their fascinating stories here,
as they have told them on Canada's best-loved radio program."

ISBN 0-7705-1730-7

1. Canada—Biography.   2. Interviews.   I. Title.

FC25.M333   971.06′092′2   C78-001537-1
CT288.M32

Printed in Canada for
The Macmillan Company of Canada Limited
70 Bond Street, Toronto
M5B 1X3

Contents

Author's Preface

THIS BOOK is the result of a lifetime interest in people who are senior to me. Even as a child I remember being fascinated by stories of people who had lived through times and events that had taken place before I was around.

At this time the light of my life was Granny Walsh, my mother's mother. A Newfoundland outport woman, she was full of stories of terrible winters, ships' disasters, drownings, and hard times and she relived all those adventures for me as I sat spellbound at her side. There had been that awful winter in Little Bay when the community was completely cut off from the rest of the world; food and fuel had run out and people froze or starved to death. Somehow most did manage to hang on, including my Granny Walsh, but that winter in Little Bay became a symbol of desperate times all over and even today if you say to some older residents of Newfoundland "hard times in Little Bay" they'll know what you mean.

When I was thirteen Granny Walsh moved out of our house to live with another daughter. I would visit her every day after school to hear the old stories and just before I'd leave she would say, "Pass me me purse, chile, and I'll give ye a bit o' change." I'd dutifully give her the purse and she'd root around and pass me two of those old English pence and a couple of religious medals. And while I put the old purse away for her I'd slip the coins back. Each day the ritual would be repeated.

One day Granny's bed was empty. My red-eyed aunt put her arms around me and that was the end of that. Alone in her empty room for a few minutes, I picked up the purse and removed the coins for the last time, slipped out the door, and walked home. Hard times in Little Bay.

The Cape Breton of my boyhood was still steeped in the great tradition of story-telling; the men would gather on selected street-corners in the evenings and exchange stories and almost every home had a grandmother or grandfather living in. Although I didn't know it then, listening to these people was the best training I could have had to prepare me for my future at the CBC. I joined the CBC in 1950 and thanks to the patience and perseverance of Barry MacDonald, the station manager of CBI in Sydney, I managed to get enough experience under my belt by 1953 to feel that I was ready for Toronto. It was there that I met Harry Boyle, the great man behind CBC *Wednesday Night* and a host of other programs. We worked together for several months on the concept of a magazine show and just three weeks before it was due to go on the air Harry asked me to be the host. He told me I would have to leave staff and go on contract and that was a hard decision to make for someone who had worked long and hard to get into the CBC in the first place. But I couldn't say no and in October 1956 *Assignment* went on the air. It caught on immediately and my first thirteen-week contract went on for fifteen years!

Assignment was basically an interview show and I was in seventh heaven because I was fortunate enough to be doing what I loved—talking with the most amazing variety of people: fishermen, farmers, lumberjacks, prime ministers, poets, musicians, writers, and labour leaders. But through it all the most interesting to me were always the aged—those with the look of a life lived, in their eyes and on their faces.

In 1967 Dick Halhed of the CBC asked if I would be interested in producing a show which would feature the voices of Canadian pioneers. That great Canadian radio pioneer J. Frank Willis was to be the host. I readily accepted and we went on the air with *Voice of the Pioneer* in 1968.

After Frank's death in 1969 I was asked to take his place on the air. And although I took the job with misgivings—it's damn hard to replace a legend—I soon realized that you don't replace someone; you just continue and do a completely new job.

"Where do you find your pioneers?" is the question I'm most frequently asked. That has never presented any particular problem; there's not a week goes by that I don't receive suggestions from listeners from somewhere in the country. Sometimes it's somebody's mother, or father, or uncle, or just somebody in town "who tells wonderful stories". I have a file with at least a thousand letters like this, and if I happen to be in a particular part of the country, I dig out my file, and pay a visit to the people who've been suggested in the letters. I'll phone them up, tell them who I am, and ask if I can come over for a visit.

If I'm driving through a town where I've never been before, I'll just ask about the community's senior residents at the local gas station. Sometimes a rare gem will surface this way. Usually we sit in the kitchen with a pot of coffee and gab away, sometimes for hours. I take special care to use the smallest tape recorder I can find, because I've found that equipment tends to intimidate people. The one I use now is not much larger than a cigarette package and before long its presence can't be felt at all; the memories come out like a flood.

Perhaps the most astonishing thing is that I've never met a pioneer I didn't like, and that includes the one-hundred-year-old lady in Penticton who absolutely refused to talk to me. "Get outa here and take that darn fool contraption with you: I wanna watch the hockey game!" She turned her back, switched on the set, and that was the end of that. Somehow I think she would have been great.

There's no trick or particular skill involved in the interviewing process, you just have to be super-curious, and a good listener. And since I really am curious about people and why they do things, it all happens very easily. I want to know about the girl or boy who once existed inside the person I'm talking to. I want to know what were they like, why they did what they did. How, for instance, did they feel when they first saw the land they were to homestead, covered with rocks and trees? How did they cope with the forest fire that destroyed everything they had built up over the years? What was it like at the moment of discovery: of something new in medicine, or some new natural resource? What were the frustrations and the hardships or the moments of joy? Questions just come naturally, and grow out of the responses to earlier questions. "Interview" is probably the wrong name really, because these are just conversations with people who soon feel like old friends. In fact, some of them do become friends, and I've had many pleasant exchanges of letters over the years with some of "my" pioneers. And I always feel a deep sense of loss when the letters stop.

Editing and selecting the material that I have gathered in my talks with the pioneers is the next step, and that can sometimes be difficult. How do you boil a person's life down to just one or, at the most, a few short programs? There's no formula; you just do the best you can, and think of the story in terms of the country as a whole, and maybe some similar stories you've done before. You try to vary them, both in terms of geography and experience, while recognizing that no two experiences are totally alike. Two people can go through the same disaster, but their memories will be very, very personal. I remember one man telling me that after a forest fire had destroyed his town he felt joyous because so much of the bush land was finally cleared. Talking about the same fire, a woman told me that her thoughts had only been of the friends whose lives had been claimed by the walls of flame.

I'd like to say a few words about the photograph on the cover of *Voice of the Pioneer*. Ed Plant, who originally came over from Ireland and now works out at Black Creek Pioneer Village just outside of Toronto, gave generously of his time to help us capture the perfect photograph for the book's cover. And as far as I'm concerned, in this photograph he epitomizes everything that the book and the people inside it stand for: strength, honesty, courage, and a sense of humour that all combine to create an attitude to life that embraces hardship and challenge and thrives on it.

Because of the ephemeral nature of radio and because I never really thought that one day these interviews would be turned into a book, I've been unable to include a complete and up-to-date list of the addresses of the pioneers whose stories are featured here. I hope that perhaps in future editions we will be able to include such a list and I would be grateful for any information from readers. I apologize if I have misspelled any names.

Putting this book together has been a labour of love for me and I've enjoyed every minute of it; my only regret is that for reasons of space often only a portion of interviews has been used and, of course, not all the interviews that I have done over the years could be included.

I would like to thank all those pioneers who gave so willingly of their time and their memories; the listeners from all across Canada who wrote to tell me about these people in the first place; the CBC for giving me the opportunity to do what I love for so many years; and the people in radio archives whose consistent advice and encouragement was invaluable. I would also like to thank Doug Gibson at Macmillan, who believed the interviews could make a book; and Charlotte Weiss, my editor, who worked so hard to make it so. My wife, Eileen, burned the midnight oil typing most of the original manuscript and the Ontario Arts Council and the Canada Council were generous in their help; my thanks to them and to all those other friends, including Norma Cox of Regina and Cy Strange of Toronto, who've been urging me to do it for years.

BILL MC NEIL
Toronto, Ontario
July 8, 1978

JESSIE TYREMAN

Mrs. Jessie Tyreman was ninety-four when we talked at her daughter's home in Calgary in 1973. A happy woman, she looked back on a family well-raised and a life well-lived. Her father was a Scotsman who pulled up stakes in Ontario back in 1882 and heeded the call of the West. He packed up his wife and eight children and made the long journey across the Prairies and up the Saskatchewan River to a little town of promise called Prince Albert. The West was just starting to boom. Things were fairly quiet, although Louis Riel was even then, in 1882, preparing to change that.

The Scouts Were Out Every Day

"I WAS JUST THREE when we came up the river to Prince Albert in a Hudson Bay boat. It was quite a luxury boat for the times. Prince Albert was a busy little town of about 500. It was building up. We had two flour mills, a big brickyard, and a strong trading post where the Indians brought their furs. The trading post was a Hudson's Bay store; they had two stores in the town, one down in the east end and one uptown, and it was just simply a case of buying the Indians' furs. They'd come in in the spring of the year to dispose of their winter's catch, have a holiday, and then go back.

I wasn't scared of them, but I think my mother was a little nervous. I guess I probably didn't have sense enough to be afraid. They were quite a reasonable people and they seemed to want to be friendly. They had their hair in long braids, painted their faces up a little bit, and wore Hudson Bay blankets wrapped around them. They bought most of their wearing apparel from the Hudson's Bay Company, and they loved bright-coloured things, the brighter the better. Of course, we did have the Rebellion, but I think probably it was more the half-breeds that were responsible for that than the real Indians. They always came to our homes and just walked in and sat down; we were expected to give them

1

refreshments. But everybody knew that and nobody was offended. They'd take a cup of tea or just anything you gave them. If you gave them more than they could eat, they'd take what was left over home with them.

One thing I remember particularly was how careful they were about being out after dark. Soon as the sun got low, away they went home. I think it was a superstition among them. In the early days our mothers used to employ the Indian women for doing the rough work, washing and doing floors. And no matter what job they were at, if the sun started to get low, they just dropped everything and went. They seemed alarmed at being out after dark. They were very peaceful and quiet.

There was no actual fighting between bands of Indians and bands of white men, as you see in the movies—at least in Prince Albert, there wasn't. Duck Lake was the nearest we had to that. That happened early in our stay in Prince Albert. But, on the whole, we considered the Indians a friendly, gentle people. If you were kind to them, they seemed to respond. They told some weird stories about what they did in the States, but then that didn't apply to us.

I was six years old in 1885, the year of the Riel Rebellion. I remember it, of course, the way a child would remember. We were quite disturbed by this fight at Duck Lake between Louis Riel's half-breeds and the Government troops, 'cause we knew practically every one of the men who were killed as well as some of them who had been imprisoned in the cellars down in this part of the country. And of course the townspeople were very much alarmed, because we'd see the soldiers with guns, and the scouts were out every day, from dawn till dusk, and nobody was allowed on the streets. I remember we smaller children being sent to bed, and then being hustled out again and sent over to the Presbyterian Manse. They had built a stockade around the Manse with the cordwood from everybody's backyard. We had all been told to go to this stockade as soon as the church bell rang. I remember sloshing through the wet snow in my stocking feet. The Manse was full of people. The soldiers came in and told us that if we heard any shots we must lie flat on the floor. A group of nuns came in; they seemed more disturbed than most of us. We children sat under the dining-room table. They were expecting trouble, really. And they did tear down some houses, thinking that the Indians might get inside and shoot from the windows at us. Our parents thought we'd all be killed.

2

There we all were inside a stockade made from the cordwood we used for fuel in our homes; it was just piled lengthwise, not too close to the building. It was our fortress, as poor as it was. The men were there with their guns in the yard, waiting to see if anything was going to happen. The church itself had been torn down because people thought it would be a place for the Indians to get in and shoot through the windows at us. My mother was making herself useful looking after those people who were ill upstairs in the Manse. The rest of us just seemed to be sitting around the floor in the dining room or living room, any place where there was room to sit down. And, of course, the men were milling around outside and everybody was very excited.

In the morning it was all over. Nothing happened. The alarm had started because some nervous person saw Indians approaching the town on horseback, and he sounded the alarm. There was nothing to it at all really. We all went back home in the morning.

The battle of Duck Lake happened just before that. I remember a man who was Captain in a detachment from the East came in the very early morning to our house; he left from our place with the others to go to Duck Lake. He was very excited. He was the captain of the group, and he was killed in the battle. There's a plaque in the Presbyterian church in Prince Albert with all the names of the men who were killed. There were a few Mounties shot down and several civilians we knew very well; that brought it pretty close, you know.

The interesting thing is, most of the settlers were fairly sympathetic with the half-breed movement and many of the farmers didn't even bother coming into town for protection in the stockade. They just stayed on the farms, because they weren't afraid of the rebels.

We children took it all up as a game and later, if our mother missed her broom she knew it was being used for a gun out in the backyard. We played that way long after the Rebellion was over. We felt we were playing cowboys and Indians for real, challenging everybody that went along past to advance and be recognized. When they hung Louis Riel nobody seemed to be making a fuss about it; I think that most of them felt it was the thing to do. At the same time, he *was* respected by a great many people because he didn't seem bitter or cruel. And nobody thought he was insane. Those people who knew him never said that; that kind of talk came only after he was captured. I think that Riel felt he was just doing the right thing. He was out to help his people. There were quite a few French half-breeds in several districts up there at that time. Some people today say they were treated as second-class citizens, but I don't think so. They were the same as any other working man."

JAKE STEWART

When Jake Stewart's father left Ireland and landed in Ontario he had a wife and children, but nothing else. They were building the CPR at the time, and those railway construction jobs were hard, grinding work, but for Jake's father, a job was a job, and there were mouths to feed, so he grabbed at it and headed into the Ontario bush.

Here in the Ottawa Valley

"WHEN DAD GOT HERE IN THE OTTAWA VALLEY, the CPR was built to somewhere between Pembroke and Petawawa. He got right in there, and worked with the pick and shovel, and did everything there was to do. He told me it was fearful hard work. Tough, tough work—they had to dig and chop, and blast the whole way. By the time they got to Thistle's siding, my father had been there about five years, and by this time he was with the dynamite gang. This fellow Thistle was a lumberman and he had oxen drawing his squared timber out of the bush, where it was cut and hewed with a broadaxe. The oxen drew it down to the Ottawa River, and it was floated from there to Quebec. I think that was where Dad got his first look at the lumber business.

He stayed with the railway for a little while after that, and then he quit to go prospecting with a fella named Sam Bromley, from down Pembroke way, and they prospected for years, and one of the claims he staked was sold for half a million dollars. All my father got was a dollar a day for prospectin', and fightin' black-flies.

Oh boy, the flies in those days. Just like a black cloud. There was no such thing as fly dope then; you used salted pork rind, rubbed it all over yourself. I think the flies got a taste for it after a while, and they'd go lookin' for a guy who had pork rind smeared on him.

Back in those early days, some of the pioneers here in the Ottawa Valley held title to land that the Crown wanted later for something else, and the Crown would try to buy the land back. But these people wouldn't want to go. After all, *they* were the ones who cleared the land, they built their houses, and it was their home; so naturally, they didn't want to go, especially for the kind of money that was being offered. They'd come to you and buy your property for say, twenty-five hundred. Well, they'd come back in two weeks, and tell you that price wasn't satisfactory to the King, or the Queen, or to whoever the hell was running us at that time. Then they'd give you another offer that was about three or four hundred dollars less! Well, you'd accept that, and I guess those Crown fellas kept the difference, eh? Those guys were stealing from the settlers.

Well, they came along, and bought my father's property for three or four thousand dollars, I forget the actual price. But then they came back in two weeks with one of those lower offers, and Dad, who was a hot-tempered Irishman said, 'If this is satisfactory to them, it sure as hell isn't satisfactory to me.' They said, 'We'll look after you! We'll sheriff you out.' Old Tom Dixon, one of the Crown men, said something else to Dad, and Dad let him have it and knocked him down on the floor. I can see him yet . . . Constable Tom Dixon lyin' there on the floor, and poor Mother runnin' to him with a glass of water. It was a hell of a time.

Anyway, all the other farmers sold out, but not Dad, and we were there for three years in that area all alone. We didn't even have a school to go to because they closed it up. We were the only kids left.

One day old Alex Morris, the Sheriff, come up driving a covered buggy. Dad knew him well—they prospected together, and so on. This particular day, Dad was seedin' some grain by hand, when this buggy came up along the fence. Morris shouted at Dad, 'You got any haywire?' Dad thought they broke the buggy or something, so he jumped the fence to see if he could help them. Soon as he jumped the fence they jumped out of the buggy and arrested him.

Dad started back for the house with these fellas draggin' after him, and he hauled them behind for a good 150 yards before they stopped, and it's a good thing for them he did. He was tryin' to reach his big number 12 shotgun, that he had kept loaded for three years sittin' in the corner in case they tried to force him off. Then about six or seven wagon-loads of soldiers rushed in, and I can see my dad yet, covered with blood, lyin' on the grass. I had a little dog then, a long dog with short legs, and he was helpin' Dad. He bit a half a dozen of them. Finally, Mother pleaded with Dad to go with them. She was scared they'd kill him. So he did, for her sake.

When they were crossin' the bridge, as they got into Pembroke, he asked Morris where he was takin' him. Morris said, 'We'll have to put you in for tonight.' Dad said, 'There's not enough damn men alive in Pembroke to do that.' And he jumped out of the buggy, and he took off.

He stayed that night at Alex McAdam's, a friend of his from years and years back—came from Ireland too. The next morning, he was back home. When they finally got him to court he asked what was the fine. They said it was ten dollars for hittin' the constable. He threw down the ten dollars, and another ten with it, and he swung around and hit Tom Dixon, and broke his nose in two places. Right there in court! Geez! He was tough!

Dad switched over to the lumber business after a while, sometimes workin' for somebody else, and sometimes he'd take a contract and work for himself. He had me and some of my brothers with him by this time. Beans and salt pork was what we'd eat, what we used to call 'sowbelly'. It was just the fat of the pig, with no meat on it. Pork and beans, pea soup, too—that was the lumberjack's diet, and if anyone made any kind of a remark about the food, the cook would drop everything and quit right on the spot! The cook was the absolute king of the camp, and nobody ever argued with him.

Another important man in a camp was the sandhill man. See, the sleighs had to haul down the hill, and it was winter, all ice, and they had to put sand on the hill to keep the sleighs from running into the horses. If there was too much sand the team would stick to it. If there wasn't enough, they'd get what was called 'run on the hill', and maybe kill the horses. A good sandhill man was hard to find, but he knew just how much sand to use so that the teams could walk down like it was the middle of summer.

Now these sandhill men used to get their sand by digging in the side of a hill, and as the winter went along, and they'd be digging away, after a while they'd have a real home in there—it *was* like a home, for God's sake. There'd be about two feet of frozen ground over them for a roof, and they'd have some hay in there and when the teams weren't coming, they'd have a snooze, and they'd boil a pot of tea in there.

And, oh boy, those sandhill men didn't want to change holes. Oh no! What they used to do was cut firewood for their hole one winter, and have it nice and dry for the next winter. Now you couldn't very well take a sandhole from them when they cut a cord of wood for it, could you? I knew fellas who were in the one hole for seven years.

I remember one time, we had a greenhorn Englishman here, shipped down in the car with the horses, and the lads got him fixed with clothes and stuff. He knew nothing at all about drivin' horses. They got the wagon ready for him with a good 'dry-arse'— that was a bag of hay for sitting on, so you wouldn't be sittin' on the cold logs. Anyway, he sat up there, just as if he knew what he was doin', and he said to the horses, 'Go forward.' Now, any man would say, 'Giddup,' or some damn thing like that, but this silly bugger said, 'Go forward.' After a while the horses went forward, and this fella was goin' like blazes before he hit the sand on top of the hill, and that old team just shot down the hill, missed the curve, went right over the sandhole, and piled up there with him in it. The fellas in the sandhole tore out after this guy, and the last I seen, they were chasin' him down the road with an axe. But they never got 'im. Oh my, I thought I'd split my pants laughin'.

Anyway, he was fired that night. We took him out to Bass Lake, and let him go. You couldn't have a greenhorn in the bush. He might kill himself and everybody else around him.

In these camps with maybe 150 or 200 men together in the bush, every Saturday night, they'd have what they called 'the buck set'. See, there was no girls, so it was all 'bucks'—men. They'd have five or six fiddles, and three or four windjammers— that's what we called accordions. Then there might be a dozen mouth-organs and maybe a flute, and when they got that all goin', they'd dance a buck set. Have a hell of a time. Everybody was the best of friends—the very best of friends.

Boy, we had big pine in those days, and we had lumber companies like Booth's, McLaughlin's, Thistle, and so on. Those were the big companies then, cutting all over this part of Canada. So they had to have a bark mark on the side of each log, and a hammer mark on the end, to show which company had cut that particular log. The reason for the two marks was that when you couldn't see the hammer mark, you could turn the log over in the water, and see the bark mark.

I remember one time, during the First World War, we got

8

word that this big shot—his father was a big shot in some pulp company—was coming over from Ireland or England. I guess to keep him out of the trenches, they were sending him over to manage a mill in Canada. So we got word to arrange a 'sorting' boom, because this fella wanted to see how those logs were sorted. So he landed with a brand-new pair of Cort boots, and all brand-new work clothes. I guess he thought that made him an expert! Anyway, we were sortin' the logs there, and he'd keep yellin', 'Turn that log over, turn that over! Turn that one! That might be ours. Let me see the bark mark!' Oh, I guess we kept at that for twenty minutes or half an hour, when he said, 'That's enough, boys. That's enough. I'm President of this Upper Ottawa Improvement Company now, and I'm going to change all this. There'll be no more of this next year. I'll have them logs come down the rapids next year *with the bark mark on top.*' And the bugger meant what he was sayin'. How the hell he meant to keep a log from turnin' in the rapids, he never said. My God, I'll never forget that. It was sure hard keepin' a straight face, I'll tell you. I don't know whatever became of that fella. Maybe they sent him to the trenches after all.

The boys in the woods put the bark mark on with an axe, and it was quite a skill. If the mark wasn't on there right 'from the heart to the bark' as the contract said, they'd be deducted when they went to settle up. There were five men in a gang: two logmakers, a roller, a trail-cutter, and a teamster. The roller would maybe be the one who stamped the logs. These marks were important, because after the log went into the river, on the way to the mill, it joined all the other logs, so they had to know which company owned it.

To take the logs down the river we'd use tow boats, and those tow boats were big—125 or 150 feet long, side-wheelers. After that we got big steel boats called 'Alligators', powerful sons o'guns. I seen one of them pull a load down here with a raft of 25 or 30 thousand logs. They were wood-burning engines, too. The farmers all along the Ottawa River would cut wood in the wintertime, split it, and pile it on the shore for the Alligators. That was extra money for the farmers. He'd do his winter chores, and maybe put three or four hours in the bush. He never got much money for it, but it was a help.

I remember one spring a new fella came up here to work on the spring drive. It was his first, and he was askin' me all kinds of questions. I told him the only thing he was to watch for was these big Alligators in the river. I never said they were *boats*. Well, his eyes opened up about a foot, and that was the end of him. We never saw him around after that.

Another way the farmers made a little extra money was with moonshine. Boy, that moonshine! That was the stuff! There were 'stills' all through the woods here. When I was runnin' some of those election campaigns an old fella up here used to make me up about ten gallons for every campaign. There was a hell of a lot of votes picked up with moonshine! You'd go to a fella with a bottle in your pocket, and while you were talkin' to him, you'd shift it from one pocket to another, so's he'd see you. He'd be rollin' his eyes, and lickin' his lips, and then, when you'd be leavin' his house he'd follow you right out the door. That's when you'd give him the little drink or the whole bottle. He'd never ask, and you never said anything. It was just understood. And boy, if they said they would vote a certain way, you could trust that they would. Anyway, everybody knew which way everybody else was votin'. I never went near anybody I knew wasn't a Conservative. I'd be just wastin' my time—and his!

I never drank or smoked in my life. The only time I ever tasted wine was on Communion Sunday. I never had time to learn. Too busy, too busy. I made a lot of money and I lost a lot of it. I had a good family, every last one of them. I had fourteen boys, I think it was, at last count, and not a bad apple in the lot, and when I was hirin' men, I never figured they were workin' *for* me, they were workin' *with* me, and if they weren't, I didn't want them anyway. There were hundreds of them, over the years— hundreds! All good lads. But now, the camps are gone and the men are scattered all over the country."

DR. CLUNY MC PHERSON

Cluny McPherson was born in St. John's, Newfoundland, in 1879. His grandfather came over from Scotland on a fishing boat in 1804 to try his luck in the waters off what was then Britain's oldest colony. He also set up a small office in St. John's where, on a part-time basis, he looked after the business of a Scottish firm that had fishing schooners working on the Grand Banks. Grandfather McPherson was an ambitious young man and he was able to combine the two pursuits quite easily until the War of 1812 started.

The war finished the business but the family stayed on in St. John's as merchants and young Cluny McPherson grew up to the sound of horses and wagons in the summertime and sleigh bells in the winter.

The 1892 St. John's Fire

"I GUESS THE THING I BEST REMEMBER and the one thing I'll never forget was when I was thirteen years old. The city of St. John's was almost completely destroyed by fire. Everything was built of wood then, wooden buildings all packed closely together, and fire was always everybody's big fear.

The year was 1892 and I was out walking in the woods that surrounded the city in those days when I smelt the smoke. I ran back into town and got there just as the Methodist College caught fire. I went into the Protestant Academy next door, the top part of it was the Masonic Temple, and helped to save a lot of the Masonic regalia. Then I went across the street into Fort Townsend and worked on the hydrant practically all night. People were carrying buckets of water trying to save the parade roof. They were worried about that because right behind it was the powder magazine. This was on the outskirts of town.

In the downtown area it was bad. Everything was burning but, do you know, the fire stopped at my father's premises. The

11

firemen had ordered Father out of his office because of the ammunition in Bowring's Hardware Store which was practically next door to him. But the mob didn't mind that. They rushed into Bowring's and looted the whole place. It was about 4:30 in the morning when they were able to stop the fire right at my father's front door. I remember somebody coming up to where we had gone to wait the fire out and they were yelling, 'We saved the shop, we saved the shop.' Father and I made our way down and saw that the whole place had been looted. The mob took what they wanted and threw everything they didn't want all over the place. Afterwards the insurance companies wouldn't pay; they said things hadn't been burnt, they'd been stolen. Father went to the Supreme Court over that and won it. That was a terrible, terrible fire. Half the city went up in flames and we came very close to losing all of it."

LILLIAN GROSVENOR JONES

In answer to the question, "Where was the telephone
invented?" Alexander Graham Bell once replied, "It was
conceived in Brantford, Ontario, and born in Boston,
Massachusetts." With that answer he hoped to put an end to
the controversy that did indeed last long after his death in
1922. But the invention of the telephone is only one aspect of
this great man who was a humanitarian first and an inventor second. All of his work was directed towards helping
mankind. In fact, he always considered himself, first of all, a
teacher of the deaf. It was Edison who had invented the gra-
mophone, but it was Bell who developed it into a superb de-
vice that could help the deaf to hear.

Alexander Graham Bell was a medical scientist who developed surgical probes that were used before the invention
of the x-ray. He was a pioneer in the treatment of cancer
with radium. He experimented widely with manned flight
and with marine vessels, one of which, the JD-4, was, for a
time, the fastest boat in the world.

Dr. Bell was born in Scotland in 1847. At the age of
twenty-one, he moved with his family to Canada, to Brantford, where he overcame the tuberculosis that threatened to
take his life. It was in Brantford that he launched the great
scientific career that led him to teach in Boston, where he
met and married Mabel Hubbard. Bell became an American
citizen, but he lived nine months of every year on the Island
of Cape Breton, in his "Benn Bhreagh" (beautiful mountain)
at Baddeck. This is where he established his laboratories,
and this is where he did most of his work until his death in
1922. His granddaughter, Lillian Grosvenor Jones, remembers him well.

Much More Than the Inventor of the Telephone

"ABOVE ALL, Grandpa loved to be called a teacher of speech to the deaf. All his life, he considered that to be his primary profession. Of course, he was grateful to have been the inventor of the telephone, but his lifelong interest was in bringing these deaf children out of the isolation that silence imposed on them. So many people were writing to him for information about their children that he realized there should be some sort of a central bureau to answer these requests. With the thirty thousand dollars that he earned from the sale of the phonograph record patent to the Edison Company he set up this information bureau, which he called the 'Volta Bureau'. Now that name came about because he had won the Volta Prize from France for the invention of the telephone. It had been his first international honour, won when he was a young man of about thirty, and he expressed his appreciation by naming the Bureau after that prize. He was a member of the Board of the Volta Bureau for twenty-five years, and he was connected with it for fifty years.

My grandmother was Mabel Hubbard. Her story was quite a dramatic one, and Grampy used to often tell us about it.

The Hubbards had this little girl, you see, who was four years old. She talked, she sang, she ran around, and then, suddenly, after an attack of scarlet fever, she lost her hearing. And her parents were told that within a few months she would lose her speech. In those days, this meant that Mabel would be confined to a very limited world, because, of course, nobody had yet found a way of having these children retain the speech they already had before going deaf. But the Hubbards wouldn't accept this. They were deeply religious people, and they worked with the child daily, and they managed, by using some of the language that she had, to keep building on it. They were fortunate in having enough money to be able to get a girl to work full time with her. Of course, there weren't any speech teachers for the deaf then, so this girl would no doubt have been the first, through her work with Mabel Hubbard. Anyway, they succeeded in having her keep her speech, and they always kept her with her brothers and sisters, who talked with her, and made her talk, and when she went to school, it was a school for *hearing* children.

Grandma's speech couldn't be considered *perfect*, but *we* grandchildren had no problems understanding her. She was a marvellous lip-reader. She went everywhere, and did everything. Grampy was devoted to her, and it was from her and the Hubbards that he got this tremendous interest in helping the deaf. He always believed that no deaf child should be allowed to grow up mute, without the most persistent efforts being made to teach that child to talk.

One thing that most people don't realize is that Grampy played a large part in the story of Helen Keller. He found her first teacher. Helen Keller was brought to Grandfather Bell when she was three or four years old, and she said later that he was the first person whose warmth and sympathy she felt. He took her on his knee, and she felt his watch. She could feel the vibration of it through her fingers. He sent her parents to the Perkins Institute for the Blind and they got Annie Sullivan there. We have endless letters, stacks of letters, from Annie Sullivan to him, and one of Helen Keller's very first letters, written when she was only five or six years old, was to Grandpapa. Somehow, he had managed to instill in this little girl the desire to speak or make her presence felt in some way. He often said that he learned more from her than she ever learned from him. He had this hope that, as far as possible, deaf children could be kept at home, and could go to day schools, so that they would always be with speaking people.

No matter what Grandfather was working on, it was always something that had to do with people in some way; he was always helping people overcome what were then considered to be their limitations. He dedicated his life to what Helen Keller called 'the penetration of that inhuman silence, which severs and estranges'. He was much more than the inventor of the telephone. *That* was while he was still in his twenties."

LEWIS MCLAUGHLIN

Lewis McLaughlin was born in Edinburgh at a time when the British Empire was at the height of its glory. British troops were spread out all over the globe, maintaining the Imperial presence in the far-flung colonies. Every schoolboy had an uncle or a cousin or a brother serving in India and the military was the ever-present dinner-table conversation at home. This was the atmosphere that shaped the young Lewis McLaughlin when he finished school and headed for the frontiers of North America long before the turn of the century, in search of adventure.

I Knew About This
North West Mounted Police

"I WAS TRAINED IN EDINBURGH as a first-class horse-breaker, so when I came to North America first, I landed in Cheyenne, Wyoming, and became a cowboy. There was a lot of people like me that came to North America just for the adventure, to see the buffalo and the wild game that was still available on this continent. The Indians had only killed what they needed for themselves and there wasn't any anxiety about the survival of the buffalo, musk-ox, and moose, that I can remember. Mr. Busby, the man I worked for, told me about the mounted police in Canada, and I thought that might just suit me fine. I had seen all of the United States I wanted to see by 1897.

I left the cowboy business, and I learned to become a first-class hobo on the trains, travelling all over the place, getting kicked off, and waiting for another train, and so on. I got pretty good at that before I tired of it. So I knew about this North West Mounted Police, and I thought I'd try to get in. The force at that time was full of men who'd tried everything, looked at everything, gone everywhere, and still weren't satisfied. There was rumours of wars with the Indians, and all that kind of thing, so I soon found myself in Edmonton, which was the capital of the Hudson's Bay Company's domain at that time, and I joined the NWMP there. The man who swore me in was Sergeant-Major Griesbach—he was one of the original members of the force when it was formed in 1873.

The first thing I learned on the force was that the Mounties felt a lot more sympathy for the Indians than they did for most of the white men there. They felt the Indians were getting some pretty rotten deals from the Government, and just because these white men had jobs with the HBC didn't mean they were pillars of society. The Indians could be trusted, where a lot of the white men couldn't. Law and order in that part of the West was pretty flimsy then, and some of the big companies were taking over big tracts of land and treating them as if they owned them. They didn't, of course, so it was one of the duties of the mounted police to let them know where they stood.

We were getting fifty cents a day, plus our room and board and our uniforms. That was real good at that time. We were about the only ones who had any money at all. If you tried to get change for a fifty-cent piece, you were out of luck. Nobody had that much money on them!

We were the only law west of Winnipeg in those days. There wasn't a whole lot of crime. Mostly drunk, or supplying liquor to Indians, things like that. I can't remember that there was much cattle-rustling, if any at all. I guess I made hundreds of arrests, but my gun seldom left its holster. One time, though, I was in a scuffle and I shot a man in the collar of his shirt, which seemed to discourage him from any further resistance.

I think the greatest thing we did was just to be there, to be seen. People knew we were the 'law', and that was good enough to keep them from breaking the law. We arrested people, and sometimes acted as the magistrate, or one of us would. We looked after our own horses, and even made the shoes for them, and we did carpentry work too. Sometimes we were even called on to 'doctor' somebody, or be a mid-wife. We were 'Jacks of all trades, and masters of none'. But it wasn't the Indians who gave us our problems. They were all right. We respected them and they respected us. I can't say the same for the other people there at that time."

ARCHIE MCINTYRE

Archie McIntyre of Glace Bay, Cape Breton, was born in 1900. Twelve years later he went underground to work his first day as a coal miner. That was to be his life for the next fifty-three years until he retired at the age of sixty-five. He was seventy-five when we met, extremely spry and active, and very proud of the part he played in the union movement of Cape Breton.

Fighting the Mine Masters

"MY FIRST JOB was what they call 'trapping'. It had nothing to do with animals, although we had lots of rats in the mine; I opened the doors for the horses and the driver to go through. These doors had to be kept closed most of the time because they formed part of the ventilation system in the mine. Those were the days before child-labour laws, so I never really had a childhood and, as you can imagine, I didn't have much of a school career either. I was in the mine before my twelfth birthday, working twelve hours a day with an open-flame light strapped on my head.

The coal miners in them days used handpicks and of course we had horses, used mainly for pulling the coal boxes. Most of the miners had to walk to their places of work in the mine and I remember the first day I worked I had to walk three miles underground before I got to my work and three miles back after I finished my twelve hours. I got $1.05 for that.

Three weeks after I started the boss came and said, 'We're going to promote you.' I was overjoyed at the news. The next day when I came down, the mine official took me to an underground stable and showed me one of the biggest horses I ever seen in my life. He says, 'Archie, from now on you're going to be a driver and you're going to haul the coal from the men because we've hired on another boy to be a trapper in your place.' He put his hand on my shoulder and said, 'Your wages will be increased five cents a day.' I suppose he thought I'd be happy but I wasn't because that was one of the toughest jobs in the mine and you had to be careful at all times. Drivers were always getting killed by runaway boxes of coal and those open lamps went out very easily.

But those horses were wonderful. They came from Saskatchewan and Prince Edward Island, and they were better in the mine than we were. The minute the lamp went out, the horse would stop and then you would get on the box he was pulling, or he'd wait till you took hold of his tail, and then he'd lead you right out to where you could find one of these lighters to get your lamp lit again. I never seen anything in my life that could sense duty as much as a mine horse. Some of those animals in that mine I was in had been there for over twenty years without ever seeing the light of day. Many of the miners will tell you this, that the companies gave more consideration to the horses than they did to the men. They had to buy the horses but they got all the men they wanted for *nothing*.

There was no such thing as compensation for injury in those days either, and there was no such thing as the old age pension, or the widow's pension. When a coal miner died or got killed in the pits, the Company had no responsibility. That's why some of the boys started to work so young. The father got killed and the nine-year-old was forced to become the breadwinner for the family. A personal friend of mine, Allie McKenzie, went in at nine years of age. You see, there was no compulsory school attendance at this time and Glace Bay was a Company town. The mine managers had terrific power. They should have been called 'mine masters'. They were managers by day and magistrates by night. These same men who bossed you in the mine were the ones who also ran the courts. So, even for minor things like, say, getting drunk, they could get at you for it in the mine and they could fine you or throw you in jail when they got you in court, which they did with great relish.

You know all this trouble and unfairness started way back when kings could give away big slices of the New World to some noble or other who did him a favour. You take the Duke of York. He ran up huge bills buying jewellery for all of his girlfriends. I read about this, and to get him out of trouble his father, the King, gave him Cape Breton to do with whatever he wanted. He gave him not the whole island, but the mineral rights in certain parts of Cape Breton, and it seems to be that this fellow owed those jewellers a huge amount of money. They went to the King and told him. The King gave the Duke Cape Breton and he in turn gave this Company the land for a certain amount of money. The Company took over an engineer by the name of Richard Brown and he looked around and saw what a treasure it was. So he went back to England and Wales, and took back young miners from there to get things going. The Company supplied these miners with beef and rum and those long row houses and for a while things ran along fairly well, until the early part of this century. But you can only treat people like animals for so long before they wise up.

It was on August 7, 1879, that the Company brought out the straw that broke the camel's back. They offered the men a reduction, so the men gathered together in secret meetings, so they wouldn't be blacklisted, and they formed what was called the Provincial Workers' Association—the PWA. The problem with this union was that it was never 100 per cent organized. A minority of the men were very strongly in favour of a union but they weren't in favour of Company stores, which the Company wanted in return for allowing the men to have a union. You see they would deduct from the wages all the things bought in the stores. The men didn't want that. They said, 'We'll buy things in your store providing you leave us pay it ourselves. The time may come,' the men said, 'that if we start getting everything on credit from you, and then there's no work, or, there's trouble with the Union, you'll threaten us by cutting our credit off.' See, those men knew exactly what the Company had in mind. Along with that, the Company had a 99-year lease on the land so that no other Company was allowed to come in and start a secondary industry. In this way, because there was no other place for a man to get a job, the Company would always have a steady supply of young men for the mines. The Company had no thought for the people at all, at all.

The PWA was a poor excuse for a union though. It was just a Company union, sponsored and favoured by them. But the United Mine Workers, the UMW, a *real* union, was trying to get in and replace the PWA. That was a tough fight. It went on for thirty years.

There was a young man come over from Scotland about that time, 1902, and his name was J. B. McLaughlin. He was in the PWA for a while and saw all the discontent and all the things that were wrong, so he got into the fight to bring in the UMW. There were two other fellows with him, a couple of Cape Bretoners by the name of Jim McLennon and Dan McDougall. They started holding secret meetings here and there and enough men joined them so that they could form a union. But the Company wouldn't recognize them by taking the check-off. That's where the union dues are deducted from a man's wages.

The president at that time of the International UMW, a Mr. Mitchell, arrived in Glace Bay. Meetings were held in Sydney Mines, and Waterford, and all over the place, and a huge meeting was held at Alexander Rink in Glace Bay, and the result was that a majority of the men decided they wanted to join the UMW. Lo and behold, that's when the real trouble started. The Dominion Coal Company blacklisted many of the men who favoured the UMW. Things went from bad to worse, until the clergy and other prominent people said, let's have a referendum, let the men decide themselves.

On August 7, 1908, the vote was held in Sydney and the UMW was chosen by a majority of 548. Then the Company said, 'We can't accept the verdict.' The Government of Nova Scotia said, 'We have a hands-off policy and we will do nothing.' The Company said, 'We want those men to honour their contract with us.' You see, they didn't want a real union in there that would be really working for the welfare of the men. And that's where we come to the strike of 1909, one of the longest, and bitterest, most vicious strikes in the history of Canadian labour.

I was nine years of age at that time and I remember it well. We saw our father walking in what they called the 'picket line', first time it was used down here. The Company hit back right away by cutting off credit at the Company store and evicting the striking miners from the Company-owned homes. Then they brought in 'scab' labour, a dreadful word. They brought in men from all over Canada and other parts of the world to fill the places of the UMW men who wouldn't join the Company union—the PWA. Neighbour turned against neighbour until one morning we all woke up to find that all the mining towns in Cape Breton were turned into an armed camp. They brought in the soldiers all right, and along with them 650 provincial police from Halifax. So much for the Government's 'hands-off' policy! We knew now whose side they were on.

The soldiers and the police strung barbed wire around all the collieries. They put machine guns up and defied any of the picketers to interfere with any of the scab labour coming in. Well, all hell broke loose. The coal miners said that regardless of the price,

21

scab labour wasn't coming to those mines. Men were shot, families were turned out of their homes in the coldest part of winter. The people were hungry, and there was no help coming from *anywhere*. After ten months the miners went back beaten, and there was a lot of bad feeling between those who worked and those who didn't, exactly what the Company wanted. But, despite everything, those men kept on their fight in secret to bring in the International Union.

Although the strike was lost, it was kind of a victory too, because gradually all the PWA members realized how much the Company really cared for their workers by the way they treated those who were on strike. So they started to come over, one by one, to the UMW, which still wasn't recognized, and by 1917 the PWA passed out of the picture.

For a while there was no union. They had what was called the N.S. Amalgamated Coal Miners, but it didn't amount to anything. Then on May 1, 1919, District 26 of the UMW was organized. I was one of the first members. Things started to get a little better. The eight-hour day was starting and being compelled to join the Company store passed out of the picture and laws were passed that little boys would not be used as labour in the coal mine. The struggle continued until the infamous strike of 1925.

What triggered this one was a move by the Company to cut the wages of the miners. We were already so underpaid it was a struggle to keep food on the table. Shortly before Christmas in 1924, the Company offered a reduction in wages of 37½ per cent. They told us they couldn't survive on the low level of profit they were making. The UMW asked to see the books but the Company said, 'No.' You see, the whole problem was that this company was owned by people who lived in other countries. Many of them never saw Cape Breton, and the only interest they had in our island was how much money they could make out of it. They didn't care about the people, or the communities, or how we lived. You see, the Dominion Coal Company was a syndicate that had gone to the Nova Scotia Government in 1893 and made a deal to buy out the companies then operating, and they paid the Government for this 99-year lease which prevented any other company coming in there to do any kind of business, without getting the consent of the Dominion Coal Company. The Government, in turn, was to get a royalty on every ton of coal. So the Company was in fact made the complete masters of Cape Breton and everybody who lived there. They supplied the only work; they rented us our houses; they sold us our food and clothing at the highest prices; and they kept our wages at rock bottom. From outside Cape Breton they imported the kind of bosses who were experienced at whipping people into line. One fellow, I won't mention his name, was known to the miners as 'Roy the Wolf'. As soon as he came in he said, 'We'll start making this thing work by cutting the miners' wages.' The 1925 strike was on.

It was the worst strike up until that time in the history of Canada. The Company and the Government were together in calling the UMW a foreign organization, a communist union, which would bring about turmoil. It was the hardest, the hungriest strike ever. It was the most bitter winter in memory. It was the cruellest time we ever went through and I pray to God nobody will ever experience anything like it again. The Coal Company started by closing the Company stores so there was no food. There was another big strike going on in the United States, so John L. Lewis, head of the UMW, sent word that there was nothing the Head Office could do to help. It was like 1909 all over again—people thrown out of their houses, children too hungry to go to school. Martial law was brought in again but now it was worse. They had what was called 'the Dragoons' on horseback and the machine guns were mounted again. Our president of the UMW was a man named Dan Willie McDonald who also happened to be Mayor of Glace Bay, and he tried to set up meetings with the Government, the Company, and the Union, but he didn't get anywhere.

The Coal Company put their own police force on horseback and they gave them guns. The miners were holding a demonstration at a power plant in New Waterford, about seven miles from Glace Bay, and the Company police rode in among the men on horseback and in the violence that followed, a wonderful man, a miner who was a veteran of the First World War, was shot dead. His name was Bill Davis. The men went wild and now it really was war.

The Company stores were packed to capacity with food, but they were closed to the hungry miners, who were desperate by now. The stores were raided and the soldiers came storming in and instead of the 1,500 they had in 1909, they had 3,500 soldiers, armed to the teeth, to bring the miners under control. It continued like that for months until once again the miners were forced back to work, beaten. This time though, they won the big battle because they were 100 per cent organized and they had the power they never had before to fight the Company on equal terms. There never could be again anything like those cruel strikes of 1909 and 1925. The Company stores were finished and men could never again be kept in bondage to the Company because of debt. Other merchants came to town and there was competition for the miner's dollar. For the first time men started to own their own homes and miners' children started to get education and become something other than coal miners like their fathers before them.

But the sad part about all of this is that by the time things started to improve, the coal-mining industry had died in Cape Breton, and there are very few mines left today.

They can take the mines away but they can never erase the history of those men who fought so hard to bring about justice for themselves and the whole Canadian labour movement."

JOE DOYLE

Joe Doyle was a blacksmith in Dublin, Ontario, "as Irish as Paddy's pig", but as fiercely proud of being a Canadian as anyone you're likely to meet. His ancestors came to Canada in the middle of the nineteenth century looking for a new way of life in a brand-new land of promise. Behind them in Ireland they left starvation, famine, corruption, and revolution. For them, the chance for a new beginning on land they could call their own was more than they could ever hope for. They called their little villages Dublin, Armagh, Newry, Enniskillen, building a new Ireland in Ontario.

All They Had Was an Iron Pot

"THE FAMINE IN IRELAND was in 1846, '47, and '48. That's the time that most of them came around here to this part of Ontario. The population in Ireland went down from eight million to four million in three years. Half of them—two million—died from starvation. Over there, you see, the lords owned everything and they could put you off the land anytime they wanted to. They'd drive out a whole village, just put them out on the road. The villagers would say to the lord, 'Where can we go?' He'd say, 'You can go to Hell or Connaught.' That was an old saying in Ireland. Connaught was some county that was low down and there was nothing there. You couldn't farm it. That was what brought the Irish out here. They wouldn't have come up to this cold country except for that. And the saddest thing was, their parents would never see them again, because they could never get money enough to come back.

One man was telling me he was down at this dock when he saw a woman kneeling down there and she was throwing holy water on her son who was getting on the boat. He was the seventh son that was leaving her, and he turned to his sister and said, 'Look after Ma.' He was going to Australia and he would probably never see his mother again. That was the way it was. The same when they came out here. They never had money enough to go back.

If you were ever in Ireland and saw the farming conditions there and how small the farms were, and the hills on most of them, and then you come out here and see this country with all the space, you'd know how they felt.

But when they landed in Southwestern Ontario first, all they could see was bushland. It was parcelled out to the settlers and it was called the 'Huron Tract'. They walked all the way into this bush and from down around Toronto, carrying the few things they needed. Maybe all they'd have would be an iron pot to cook the meals in. I heard my grandfather say some of them only had half a pot; they got it broke in two in some way. But for the first time in their lives they had a piece of ground they could call their own, for the first time they could say, 'This is mine'. All they had to do was cut those trees down with an axe, and dig the stumps out and haul them out with their own power and burn them. Half our good timber around here was just burned, but they had to get the land cleared. How they ever did it, I don't know. They had to cut their own roads themselves—all that big timber: maples, rock elm, and beech. How could they cut those things down with an axe? For years after they came here they didn't even have a saw. It was all work from sunrise to sunset. No wonder when they got old they were all bent and twisted.

There were no doctors, of course. There was one up around Stratford or Goderich but he wouldn't have known how to get to your place anyhow. It was all trails with marks on the trees. My grandmother told me about the time she was pregnant with her thirteenth child. Her husband was out somewhere cutting down trees and it came time for the baby to be born. There was no doctor close enough but even if she could've found one, there was no money to pay him. Somebody down two miles and a half—a Protestant woman—a spirit told her that my grandmother was in trouble. Well she came into that shack just in time and did the doctoring. Well I'll tell you, my grandmother thought that was a godsend. This woman walked that two miles and a half through the trees because the spirit told her to.

But, little by little, the farms grew, and the villages prospered and became towns, and the towns became cities. Those poor people from all around here produced some of the best people in this country today. Just look around for the Doyles and the Boyles, the O'Learys, the O'Regans, and the Flanigans. Look for the Irish . . . anywhere in Canada. They spread out all over the place, leaders in everything. Some of them don't even know where they came from but if they took the trouble to trace it back they'd find it all began on a poverty-stricken farm back here, and before that during the potato famine in Ireland."

THOMAS WILFRED MURPHY

Thomas Wilfred Murphy of Vancouver was born in 1892. His father was an Irishman who accepted the Government's offer of free homestead land around Parry Sound in Northern Ontario. Mr. Murphy recalls now that "it should never have been opened up for farming. It was gravelly and rocky; no good for farms, but good for timber." So the boys in the Murphy family were expected to follow their father's example, helping to scrape a living out of subsistence farming by working part of the year in the woods.

Working in the Woods

"MY FATHER just cut a little homestead out of the woods there, with a lot of other people who were moving into the Parry Sound area at that time. When he went in the pine grew up to about four feet in diameter, which is a pretty big tree. There were a few larger than that, but the average was around thirty inches. These were all taken out for square timber. They hewed it with a broadaxe.

Our homestead was on the river, where they used to drive these big square logs down. The river men had to wear rubber boots for jumping around on those big rafts, made up of the logs all chained together. The railroad had just come in to our little town, and all these big square timber were loaded on the cars. It went from there down to Quebec, and it was shipped to the old country, just as it was hewed out of the woods. Of course, these were all selected trees, nice and big, and straight—the best of what we had up there. I imagine the customer over there specified just what he wanted. I don't know why they wanted those timber squared like that, unless it was just that they wouldn't have to be hauling any of the waste around and, of course, after it was broadaxed, you could see which was the really select timber—the very best.

28

My father was a broadaxe man, and broadaxing a tree was a very select skill. The broadaxe man was the top man in the woods at that time. I remember our barn was built with broadaxe lumber. The framework was all 4 x 4, or 8 x 8 wood. It was a big barn too, about 40 x 50, and Father hewed all those pieces with a broadaxe. All the shingles on the roof were hand-split, and shaved with a broadaxe. All pine, too. It was a tremendous amount of work for Father, who built it, after all, in whatever spare time he had. I remember going back, after about fifty years, and the shingles had started to come off in chunks, four or five together. The shingles were still pretty good, but the old square iron nails had rusted off, but the barn was still standing, and in good shape too.

They used to have 'bees', y'know. A bunch of the settlers would all get together after a man would get his timber all hewed out, and pulled into place by the horses. A 'raising bee', they'd call it—getting all the framework erected, so that one man could handle all the rest of it himself. The women would come too, and there'd be big meals, and generally a lot of fun and hard work for the one day it usually took to get the frame up. The barn was big enough so that you could put those first little thrashing mills on the floor. It had to be good and solid, because the mill was on the top floor and the livestock was underneath.

All those settlers up there in Northern Ontario had to do the two jobs. Their farms would just provide enough potatoes, and stuff to raise the family on. It was too far north to grow wheat, but you could grow peas and potatoes, and raise a few hogs to keep you in pork all winter. The early frost meant that farms didn't have any produce to sell. That's why they all had to work in the lumber woods besides.

When a boy got old enough, he was expected to leave home and go someplace. To a lumber camp in the winter, and maybe go on river drives in the spring. I left when I was seventeen to go on as a 'flunky' in a lumber camp. A flunky was a cook's helper—a chore boy. He washed dishes, peeled potatoes, split wood, or anything else that needed to be done. It was nice if you could get work within reach of your own home, but usually the jobs took you a far distance off. You usually stayed in the lumber camps all winter. You never had time to be lonesome because work was ten hours a day, and maybe more than that. You'd get absorbed in this new life, and you were seeing new country, and new things. After the first winter you came out a man, so it was good training.

29

That set the course too, for the rest of my life, because after I left the Ontario woods, I went out to the west coast in 1913. That was everybody's dream at that time . . . to go West! My brother had already gone on one of those 'Harvest Excursions'—that's where they'd fix up a boxcar, and everyone could pile in that to go out and help the Prairie farmers take in the harvest. A lot of them would stay out West once they got there, especially the single men.

Two of my other brothers and myself went out on the regular train to Vancouver because we knew somebody working there in a wood factory who said he might be able to get us a job. It was a very different kind of logging on the west coast to what we had seen in Ontario. They were still using oxen in the woods to pull out the logs, and they were just beginning to use steam donkey engines. It wasn't a big industry then at all, but there was timber growing right down to the coast, from Vancouver right up to Alaska. They could fell them right into the water, but the best timber was always in, away from the salt water, in the inlets.

One of the big differences on the west coast was that the camps closed in the winter, when the snow came, for a month or two. In the East, that's when most of the woods work was done. The food in the camps out West was better, too. In the East it was all pork and beans, because that was easy to keep; they didn't have potatoes or vegetables because they would freeze and spoil. Out here, on the west coast, we had everything because the weather was different. All kinds of meat and potatoes, pies and cakes, and bread. The food was always excellent in all the camps. The thing I noticed most, though, was the size of the trees out here at that time. It was *nothing* to see a tree four feet across!

There were a lot of Swedes and Irish working in the woods when I got here . . . some French Canadians, and a lot of Ontario men. And the one thing that most of us missed out on in the kind of life we led was a chance to meet people of the opposite sex. We were in the camp all the time, and there were no women *there!* When we'd come to Vancouver, there were very few women to meet there, because not many were on the west coast at that time. Lots of men, but hardly any women. After the First War, quite a few families started to arrive, but even at that time, I would say ninety out of a hundred men had no families to go to in Vancouver. It was, for most men in the camps, a very lonely kind of life. Even when they came to town they were lonely because they just had each other there. They'd go to the beer parlours, and talk with the same men they worked with in the woods. A lot of those young men never did get married and raise families of their own, because they never had the chance. That's probably the biggest regret of my own life, because I never married either. I would love to have grandchildren to talk with now."

JAMES GRAY

James Gray spent his youth in Manitoba, and saw first-hand the struggles of the homesteaders trying to get started on the rough and barren land. He was deeply moved by their plight, and the fight they had to just stay alive. It was frontier country, peopled by the young. Freezing to death was common, as was starvation, and many watched helplessly as their own children drifted into prostitution, the only way open to them to earn a living in the "big" cities of Winnipeg and Brandon.

Booze and Red Lights on the Prairies

"THE FIRST SETTLERS of Western Canada came out here from Ontario in the 1880s. They were predominantly farm people from the Galt–Kitchener–Guelph area, the old farm-settled areas of Ontario. They were young farmers' sons who came out here to make a start for themselves. There was what was called 'the Manitoba Fever' in Ontario, and a lot of shysters were selling land to these young people at greatly inflated prices. In 1880, '81, and '82, there were something like forty thousand Ontario people moved out to Manitoba and settled on farms; some of them, not many, went to the cities. Then the boom collapsed, and it never took hold again till after the Sifton immigration policy took place. Sifton and the CPR went out to sell Western Canada to settlers. The CPR went down to the States, and they lured up hundreds of thousands of settlers from down there. The Canadian Government went to Europe and to England, and they brought people out from there, and they still brought a great number from Ontario. The people from the Bible Belt in Ontario came out and established another Bible Belt in Manitoba.

There was a great conflict of achievement over all this shortly after the turn of the century. In Winnipeg and Brandon everything was wide open as far as booze and prostitution were concerned, and they were closed tight as far as everything else was concerned. The Sabbatarian influence was so strong among the Methodists and Presbyterians from Ontario, that in Winnipeg, for example, nothing happened on Sunday . . . nothing! No streetcars moved; they didn't deliver milk or bread; and no store was open. There was no amusement of any kind permitted, and one minister in Winnipeg even preached a sermon against the holdings of concerts of sacred music on Sundays because he felt that might lead to the opening of Sundays to other forms of entertainment. Now you can imagine what kind of situation *that* was for all these single young men out there at that time. There were something like 250 or 300 thousand more men than women coming to the West during that great influx between 1905 and 1915; and remember, they had to come to the cities first, and they were away from home, some of them for the first time.

All these young men had to find a place to live, and they crowded into the most incredible, congested rooming houses and hotels, and the only recreational facilities that there were in Winnipeg were bars, and poolrooms, and brothels. At that time Annabella Street had fifty houses of prostitution; there were two hundred women employed there and on Sunday afternoons, when there was no other form of entertainment permitted in Winnipeg, these young men would go for a walk down to Annabella Street, with the result that that street was crowded with hundreds and hundreds, and up in the thousands, of sightseers, and there wasn't a farm boy in all of Manitoba from 1915 to 1925 who didn't know about Annabella Street, or similar streets in the other cities of the Prairies. In Moose Jaw, it was River Street; in Edmonton, it was Kinesteena Street; and in Calgary it was 9th Avenue and 6th Avenue, and Nose Creek Hill. In Lethbridge it was 'De Point', as they called it. These areas were accepted by the police departments of Western Canada. They approved of them, and in fact, when, in 1910, Winnipeg had a civic election, and segregated prostitution was the issue, the people voted overwhelmingly for it. The Annabella Street area of prostitution was established, and it existed for thirty years after that.

The girls for those houses of prostitution were often farm girls from God-fearing parents who came into Winnipeg or into the other cities. Maybe they got pregnant and were thrown out of the house by their parents. You see, in those days, there were few ways for a woman to make a living. She could be a charwoman, a schoolteacher, or maybe a nurse. The Catholic orders had the nursing profession pretty well monopolized, so that left Protestant girls out of that. There was honestly very little that a woman could do to make a living in those times, and many were widows with small children. A lot of them would go into the brothels and they would work there for a while. Eventually some man would come along. They would fall in love, get married, and disappear.

A lot of these girls came up from brothels in the United States as well—girls who had come from slums, and whose only way out was the brothel and then marriage. Some of these marriages, a lot of them, turned out extremely well. The man was lonely, and needed a mate; the woman was doing what she was doing only because she had to survive. They both knew the realities of the situation, and they were able to put it all behind them. They usually went to a different part of the West, and life started all over again. A lot of people in Western Canada today, many of them prominent people, could, if they had a mind to, trace their beginnings to a brothel."

HARRY MARSH

Harry Marsh was born in 1892, in England, and by the time he was eighteen he found himself in Canada with nothing in his pockets, but with a desire in his soul to succeed, and a willingness to work at anything at all. He was going to need those virtues in the years ahead, plus a lot of faith.

Talk About Your Hard Times!

"ONE OF THE FELLAS I WORKED WITH migrated to Canada and he did his darndest to persuade me not to come. It was a terrible place, he said. Well, I thought he wanted the whole country for himself, so I came.

On the immigrant train going West, I had no idea where I was gonna get off. Something about the name Qu'Appelle attracted me. I don't know why, but it did, and I decided I'd go there. It was known as South Qu'Appelle in those days. I got off the train, and I met a man who asked if I wanted a job, and if I wanted to learn about farming. I said, 'Yes, I certainly do.' He didn't mention money and neither did I but naturally I assumed I had a job and would be paid. We went up to the farm and I started to work and everything went along fine. Then one morning, there was one heck of a snowstorm came along, y'know.

Well, the man who hired me got very talkative, and he said, 'This is a terrible morning. I wouldn't turn the horse out. Don't turn the cattle out. I wouldn't turn a dog out on a morning like this.' Then he thought a little while, and he said, 'Harry, you can go out and buck wood.' Well, you know what that old bucksaw is, sawing up the stuff for firewood. Like a darned ass, I went out and I bucked wood till noon. I came in wet from the ears to the appetite, and I reminded him of what he said. 'Now,' I said, 'if *I* don't rate any better than the dog, I think you and I better part company.' Well, you won't believe it, but his response to that was to ask me for the money for my farming lessons. I figured I'd be

35

getting money from *him* for the time I spent there, and here *he* was, demanding money from *me*! Well, I won't tell you what I told him, but he didn't get any money, and neither did I! I found out later there was a lot of that going on at that time. These fellas would hang around the railroad stations looking for greenhorns. I chalked it up to experience, packed my bag, and left.

The one thing I wanted to be was a homesteader. One day this fella I was workin' with told me about a wonderful homestead up in central Alberta. He said it had a windbreak of trees all around the outside, and the rest of the land was just bare prairie. It intrigued me so much I took the train up there. After I got off at the station I started to walk, and walk, and walk . . . until finally I got there. There were a few settlers in there and a couple of them came along with me on horses to find this place, and we did—but this so-called 'windbreak' covered most of the 160 acres, and the only open land was a bit of a hay meadow in the middle of the damn thing. In fact, the timber was so thick the horses couldn't get through and we had to walk in. So that ended my search for a homestead in central Alberta.

Harvest was coming on so I went down to Qu'Appelle again and had no difficulty getting a job as a fireman on a thrashing machine. I worked there that fall, and we thrashed. We thrashed, and we thrashed, and we *thrashed*, and when it was through, and all stacked up, the fella said to me, 'Well, Harry, there's the wheat. Take out enough for yourself to pay your wages.' I took a wagon load and I headed in to town where the elevator was. The man looked at it and he said, 'This stuff is worth seventeen cents a bushel.' I said, 'Open the doors, I'm taking it back home.' 'Oh,' he said, 'I'll give you nineteen cents.' Well that was better, so I dumped off the load and he gave me a cheque. I went over to the store, and I got a pail of syrup, some tobacco, some oatmeal, and prunes, and that was all the cheque would buy. In other words, that's how much I earned for that whole fall's work. I took the stuff back to the farm, and gave the whole lot of it to the fella and his family and lived there with them that winter.

Imagine though, seventeen cents a bushel, and possibly you could get at the *very* best ten or fifteen bushels an acre. Talk about your hard times! We chopped wood, and hauled wood, and did anything we could find, just to stay alive, and we made it through until spring. The one thing I still had though was my ten-dollar bill tucked away, so I could file on a homestead when I could find one. I also had to find out how you went about getting it. I *still* didn't know!

In the spring, I met an old chap by the name of Cyrus Ezra Booth, a real old sourdough who had prospected all over the country, and he gave me the location of the piece of land I eventually filed on. So I went to Moose Jaw, fished out my ten dollars from its hiding place, and was *finally* a homesteader! I also got a pre-emption and agreed over a period of years to pay this large amount of three dollars an acre for it. So that was my start in this country, in the winter of 1908. Well, there isn't much you can do with a homestead in the winter, but I met this man who was going to England with his wife, and he offered me twenty-five dollars a month to look after his farm while they were away. He said he would make arrangements at the store so that I could get all the things I would need while I was there. This seemed fair, so I drove them down to the train. They left, and I went over to check in at the store. He had made *no* arrangements at all, and here I was, stuck with his farm, horses, cows, pigs, chickens, *everything*, and almost no money. So I looked around, and I found a small engine and a chopper which this farmer had for chopping up his cattle feed. Well, I stuck my shingle out on the road—'Chopping Done Here'—and do you know, I made my winter's grub out of that darn thing!

That's the way things were in those days. You had to tackle any darn job that came along in order to exist."

MRS. CARL TELLANIUS

The pioneers who homesteaded in Western Canada were a hardy lot. The men grew old before their time with back-breaking work in the fields, and the women, without whom the men could not survive, did everything else. There were few chances for these lonely ladies of the plains to dress up and look pretty, but when a rare occasion did come along, nothing was going to stop them.

The Woman on the Prairies

"WE WERE AWFULLY POOR, and a friend of mine had given me an old hat, white with some flowers on it, but it was very dirty and all bent out of shape. However, we were going to a picnic, and I didn't have a hat. In those days, you wouldn't *think* of going without a hat. *Everybody* had to have one. So I washed this old hat, and I put it on the fencepost to dry, but it turned out just *awful!* The rim turned all curly, and the front went up like a peak. I didn't know what I was going to do, and I was heartbroken, because it was the only hat I had, bad as it was. Anyway, I took it in the house again, and I wet it, and laid it out on the table. I put weights all around the brim, and I took hold of that peak, and I pulled it out just as far as I could get it, and I put a weight on that too. When it was all dry again, I put a little bunch of forget-me-nots all over the peak part, and I washed and ironed the ribbon, and put that on. That afternoon, when I got to the picnic, everybody was saying to me, 'Oh, Mrs. Tellanius, what a nice hat!' I felt so good! Just like a queen. It was a *wonderful* picnic.

In those days, you just had to make the most of what you had. We had no money at all, and if we wanted something, we'd just have to look around, and see what we could make it from.

The woman on the Prairies had to be able to do anything! I used to spin all my own wool, and knit all my family's sweaters, and their stockings, and their mitts, and all that. We had no deep-freeze of course, so we canned all the vegetables and the fruit and that. We canned the meat too. No matter how hard times were, we seemed to have enough to eat.

With the clothing, that was something else. I patched till my fingers were sore, and tried to make things look different by re-modelling all the time. We just kept using and using things, over and over again, for one thing or another, until it was gone! I mean *really* gone! Until it wasn't any good for anything, except maybe a floor cloth, or a duster. Even then, when a floor cloth was all fall-ing apart, we used to dry it out, and roll it up into little balls, and use it in the fire, or to stuff up cracks in the walls of the barn. Nothing was wasted. We couldn't afford to waste anything!

I did most of my sewing by lamplight after I put the children to bed. I bought a second-hand sewing machine in 1909, and I still sew on it. It was a Singer, and it still works good. I sewed in the nights till my eyes would sting. Then it was time for bed.

'Course, you couldn't make food out of something else! You either had enough, or you didn't. It was as simple as that. But you learned to make the most out of what you *did* have. I remember, just after school had started in the fall, Ernest, my oldest son, brought a note home one day which said that the School Inspec-tor and another man would like to come and have lunch. I thought, 'What in the world will I do! What will I give them?' It was Monday, and I had given all the bread to my husband, who was doing some work about three miles from home, putting up hay. So I said, 'Ernest, you've got to run out, and catch two or three of those old roosters.'

Away he went, and before I knew it he did the whole thing himself! He caught them, and chopped their heads off; he took all the feathers off, and washed them, and cleaned them. He was so proud when he brought them to me, and so was I! Anyway, we only had a few hours before the men would come, so I hurried and got the roosters ready for cooking. I fried them in butter, and made hot biscuits, and had it all ready when they arrived. I served them some wild strawberries and cream, and, oh, they were so pleased! They said that it was the best meal that they ever had.

After they were gone, we found a dollar bill under one of the plates. That would be like *ten* dollars today! It was wonderful! Of course, if I had seen it before they had left, I would never in all the world have taken it from them. I guess they knew that, and so they hid it under the plate. Anyway, we could sure use that dollar!

Fire was the thing that we were most scared of. You see, there was just about nothing we could do about the fire if it came. The barns and the house were all wood, and as dry as could be; just as dry as the prairie grass that caused the fires. Our school had opened in 1919, and it was so dry that year that it just burned night and day. One day the teacher sent all of the children home, and closed the school, but most of them came to our place because they couldn't get home. The fire was cutting them off. Every man that could was out fighting fire to try and save our school. Well, it got on to four or five o'clock in the afternoon and no one had come to our place so I went up to the school. I was getting really worried. When I got almost to the school, I could see that the fire was coming across the neighbour's wheat field, and heading straight for his barn where I knew he had these four horses tied. And there was a haystack on the west side of the barn as well!

I don't know whatever caused me to do it, but I turned around, and ran back home, and told the children to fill every pail and pan they could find with water. I yelled at a couple of them to come with me. 'We must get those horses out, because the fire is almost to the barn.' When I got there three work horses and the big stallion were there, pulling at their ropes, and kicking. They were terrified! Well, before I left the house I had picked up this big butcher knife to take with me. I'll never know to this day why I did that, but it's a good thing that I did. When I got to the stallion to try and untie him, he wouldn't let me near him. I cut the rope, but he still wouldn't come out. By this time, the haystack and the barn was on fire, so I grabbed this pitchfork standing by the door, and I stuck him! He took off out through the door, and he jumped over the fence to our place where the other horses had already gone. I wasn't long getting out behind him either, because the barn was really burning now!

I don't know what I must have looked like! They told me later that I looked a mess! My hair was down, and my face was black. I didn't even have time to wash because we had to go to another neighbour and carry water and throw it all over his haystacks, and his barn. We saved his place though. I was pregnant at the time.

One of the worst things then was the loneliness. You couldn't even see the light of a neighbour's house. The nights were very, very long in the wintertime and, of course, there were no radios or anything like that. I used to sing a lot. The harder I worked, the more I sang, and every night I sang my children to sleep with a song about the lily that lived alone in the woods; and even today when they come to see me, they ask if I'll sing it again, and I always do, in the Scandinavian language we still were speaking to each other at that time.

We knew it was a hard life, but, oh my, it was a happy time too."

MAY APPLEYARD REDMAYNE

"What's a nice girl like you doing in a place like this?" That pretty well sums up the story of May Appleyard Redmayne, who found herself leaving an upper-middle-class home in England in 1911, to settle down on a homestead in Western Canada, with all of the hardships which that kind of life entailed. Why would you trade a home full of servants for a cookstove on the Prairies? That's easy. The man you loved and wanted to marry had asked you to, that's why.

The Happiest Days of Our Lives

"NORMAN AND I had been sweethearts since we were very young, and I was actually engaged to him before he came out on his own to take up a homestead grant. But I'm quite sure that if he hadn't been Norman Redmayne of a well-to-do family, my parents never would have allowed it. They knew that Mr. Redmayne had left a good deal of money when he died and I would be well looked after. So the family relented and I was allowed to marry Norman when he came back after two years in Canada. The wedding was a glittering affair, with lots of fine but not very practical gifts for a young couple preparing to leave for a home in the Canadian bush. Things like a piano, and a sterling-silver tea service.

It was a very bad crossing and we decided it was better to get off at Halifax rather than to go to Saint John where we were booked for. We thought we'd make better time on the train. I wish you could have seen that train. I'll never forget it as long as I live. Garlic and everything else. It was really something, the smell of it. They were all foreigners, you know, with their heads covered up with shawls. Oh, they were having a high old time dancing and everything and they went to the end of the train and cooked their meals on the stove and made coffee and sang all night long. It nearly drove you crazy. There we were, knowing nobody, sitting on these hard wooden seats and feeling very far from home.

In the middle of the night one of these immigrant women came over and said she was sick. She came to my husband and said, 'Will you take me to the toilet?' So Norman went up with her and she took his arm and off they went. That put us in pretty good with everybody. I think they rather resented our being there a little bit before that, you know. They thought we were snobs I guess because we hadn't crossed on the boat in the same class as they'd crossed in. They had come steerage and we came first class. But once we got to know them and them us it was really quite something. They tapped and wheeled and sang as we went along. And that was my introduction to Canada!

Finally we got to Montreal, were taken off and put on a train westbound to Edmonton. So there I was, just turned twenty, sitting on a train, rolling across the Prairies, the white smoke from little farmhouses going up into the sky. It was all absolutely strange but I think that I was so very much in love with my husband that I didn't care where I went. We were going together and there was no thought of money because money was something that I knew very little about. I mean, everything was always looked after at home for me and I knew that Norman would do the same, because after we were married his mother insisted upon him making a will which left me the interest of his money.

It took days on that train but finally we got to Strathcona. The steel didn't go into Edmonton then. We got off one early morning and got onto a sleigh and it went down the banks, and across the frozen river. Nearly all the people on this sleigh were men with big fur caps and huge coats, and they had icicles hanging on their eyebrows and noses. They looked awful.

We stayed with Major Griesbach, the friend who had first interested Norman in homesteading, and then set off in a lovely little white cutter on the last lap to our new home. When we got to the stopping place or whatever you'd like to call them, that was a bit disastrous. We sat down for dinner with all these men, awful looking, beards, and dirty. There was a huge table full of food, just screaming, really, with food, and no one passed you anything, you just had to grab it. That is where that expression 'the Canadian long-arm' came in. Nobody stood on manners there at the stopping place. They just gawked at you, just looked at you and spit in the spittoon, you know. Ping, in it would go.

Just before we went to bed my husband said, 'Would you like to go to the little back-house?' And I said, 'Yes, if you'll come with me.' I was sure if I ever put my foot outside a bear or an Indian would get me. And of course, Norman wouldn't go out with me. I realize now what a fool they would have thought me if he'd walked out with me. So we went up to bed without me going to the out-house. That was a mistake. The bedroom was just one big room, and people were sleeping on the floors. They put some blankets around a little corner where we slept. And it just got after a while that I *had* to go, and that was all there was to it. It was impossible to wake everybody up, you know, so something had to be done. So my bonny lad said to me, 'Well, there's a dirty shirt, if you think you can use that.' So I used his shirt. And the next morning when we were getting ready to leave, I didn't know what to do with the shirt 'cause it was frozen. Well, at that time I carried a big muff, so I bent the shirt as small as I could and shoved it in my muff, and we went on our way in the sleigh towards the new home I hadn't yet seen.

Every time we passed a farmhouse I'd say, 'Is our place anything like that?' The only answer I ever got was, 'Well, wait and see.' So this went on until it got to be quite a joke you know, and finally we came across this slough, and into this clearing and there was my home . . . the little shack that Norman had built on his first trip out. Norman had left a hired man to look after it when he went back to England for me, and there was this man coming out of the shack door. He must have known we were coming because of the bells on the horses. I was introduced to him, and he barely acknowledged it, he was too shy. Then Norman took me into the shack, and I never saw anything like it in my life. The floor hadn't seen a broom for goodness knows how long. It was the most terrible, poverty-stricken place I've ever seen in my life. I couldn't believe it.

Norman went outside to check on what the hired man had done or what he hadn't done, and I stood there, and I didn't know what to do. I looked at everything, and I was getting colder and colder and I was just paralysed and frightened. Then Norman came in and he seemed surprised I hadn't lit the fire and made a cup of tea, or taken my things off. Well, that was just enough for me! I just burst into tears.

So he made a cup of tea and we went to bed that night and the next morning I got up with determination. I had decided that this was my lot and I was going to make the best of it. So I cleaned the house, and scrubbed it, and Norman came in and helped. And then he brought in a few of the things from the unfinished bungalow that he had put in there before he went away. That was it. Everything happened from then on.

Life in Canada was starting. The house had to be finished, the fences built, the land cleared, and the crops planted. And I was expected to do my share. I'd sit on the plough to make it heavier— and suddenly it would hit a stump and I'd fall off. It was a strange life for a girl from the kind of background I had come from.

We didn't know it then but we were living the happiest days of our lives . . . especially the day we moved from the shack into the new house. Oh, it was an occasion. I had been working, trying to get it sorted out, more or less. I went over in the morning, quite early; Norman took the bed over and what else had to go over and I told him that he wasn't to come near it until dinnertime. And then I wanted him to come at six o'clock, dressed as I'd always seen him, not in farm clothes. Anyway I had put my very best dress on, and it was a pretty one, blue with a chiffon top and all the rest of it. And I went over to the shack, and Norman was there waiting for me. And bless his heart, he was shaved and sweet and nice and lovely. So we went over together. We went into every room, and I can so well remember him taking my hands, and saying, 'I've never in all my life thought I'd have a home like this in the bush.' Then we had dinner, and after dinner, Norman made the tea and he carried it in in the silver teapot and the whole works—it had been a wedding present. And there were these thick brown cups alongside this beautiful silver teapot because that was all we had. But we brought this in and put it in front of the fire. We sat talking and we discussed our life, what we hoped for, and the family we hoped we would have. I think we sat talking till the early hours of the morning and went to bed very happy. Our bedroom looked so clean and sweet.

Perhaps it paid to be young and in love, because I needed all of that to swallow the life we had, living in that shack, waiting for the home to be built, helping to burn the bush, to cut the trees, and pile up rocks in an attempt to get farmable land. It was a hard life for a girl with soft hands. I remember when we fenced the 160 acres in with barbed wire. I was at one end and Norman was at the other, and he would walk so far and nail it up and then we'd walk a bit further. And we just did everything.

After two years of roughing it, the farm was gradually taking shape. And the house was starting to look like a home. The fences were built and the crops were growing in the field. A small stranger was added. Just Norman and me and little Bobby, or 'Bobbums' as we called him, made three. Things were going well and we were very happy. It was early autumn in 1913 and we had special plans for the first real harvest from the farm, a load of grain, and Norman was taking it to Clyde. It meant being away overnight. The money from it was to be the start of our baby's bank account. We saw him off; I had Bob in my arms and we waved and waved until he was out of sight, and I wondered what I could do as a surprise for him when he came back. We were quite pleased and happy about things. And just as I was thinking about getting dinner ready, a strange man drove up and he said that my husband had had an accident and he thought I should go to him. So I pushed Bob over to my friend, Mrs. Hill, who lived in our shack, and I told her where I was going. They took me to a place called Dusseldorf, and there my poor darling was. He knew me; he could talk to me. But the thing was, he was on his way home and he looked behind and saw a drunken man trying to drive a team and a wagon through a barbed-wire fence. Norman loved horses and this was just something he couldn't stand. So he pulled off to the side, and got off and went to the horses' heads with the idea of tying them behind our wagon and bringing them home. Well, just as he got to the horses and got them on the road, this man—he was very drunk—raised up and threw a bottle of whiskey. It hit the horses and they bolted and knocked Norman down and they went over him. Practically every rib was broken.

Somebody, I don't know who, got an ambulance from Edmonton. I went in with him, and he died there. It just proves how quickly our world can fall apart. In the morning, we were full of plans for our baby's bank account, and by night, I'm a widow with a baby on a homestead in Northern Alberta, wondering what to do and who to turn to.

To cut a long story short, I went back to England and my parents looked after me and Bob. They made us very comfortable for the next four years, but I couldn't stop thinking about Canada. I couldn't adapt to the old life . . . the tea-parties and the theatre. Not after the homestead and the dreams we had. As soon as the war was over I told Mother and Father I must go back, at least just to see it again. I came over and sold the farm and visited around with the Hills and different people. Then I decided I couldn't go back, living the life in England. It was certainly not the free life that I had been used to in Canada. So I stayed."

NELLIE PRYOR HOOD

Mrs. Nellie Hood of Victoria was the wife of Colonel F. G. Hood, a son of the 4th Viscount Hood of the Royal Engineers. Her father was Colonel Edward Pryor, Commanding Officer of the 5th Regiment of Canadian Artillery. Later, he became aide to two Governors General, Lord Stanley and the Earl of Aberdeen. In 1902, he was Premier of British Columbia, and later its Lieutenant-Governor.

Victoria, before the turn of the century, when Nellie Pryor was a girl, bore no resemblance at all to the rest of Canada. It was just as settled in its ways, just as elegant and proper, as the England of the reigning monarch, Queen Victoria, after whom Sir James Douglas had named the city when he started construction in 1843. It was a time of grandeur for those of privilege. Sailors would come to wax the floors for the "right" families before a dance, and little boys and girls from those families would get to see a very different side of Sir Matthew Begbie, the hanging judge, from the one displayed to tough miners in his courtroom. The sun never set on the British Empire, especially on Victoria.

And Dear Queen Victoria Was on the Throne

"FATHER WAS A YORKSHIRE MAN who came out to Nanaimo, where he was appointed British Columbia's first Inspector of Mines, but we came up here to Victoria after a time. Ah, it was smelly in Victoria then. I don't know if it was the clamshells or what, but Victoria was noted for the awful smells that would come up sometimes, with the different winds.

I remember when the Royal Navy was here in Victoria. They were always so gay and full of fun. One day I remember we looked out the window and saw four naval men and a buggy there. These young men had decorated the horse and the buggy all over with sunflowers, and they were all holding sunflowers when they arrived at our house.

We used to have all sorts of dances on the ships, and lunch parties, and often after the tennis parties we'd go down and have dinner at one or other of the big houses. I remember, after one party the Navy people said, 'Oh you *must* come back to dinner.' We said we'd *love* to, and there was one pier there called 'Fluster's Pier' that all the Navy people used, and we all got in wearing our best clothes, and while we were rowing over to the ship, a salmon jumped out of the water, right into Lady Perry's lap, and all of her beautiful party dress was *ruined*! Oh, I'll *never* forget it! The salmon just rose up *beautifully* out of the water and landed right in her *lap*!

The Navy people were always doing kind and nice things. If we were giving a dance, some of the officers would send some of their 'blue jackets' up with canvas all covered with candlewax. These 'blue jackets' would drag this canvas all over the floor with weights on it and if we were there we'd say, 'Oh, may we sit on it?' And they would drag us all around the ballroom floor. Oh, we loved it! But that waxed the floor for the dance, you see.

We used to have regattas, of course, and Indian races. The regattas were *simply* wonderful! Hundreds of people used to line the shores, and there'd be big parties at all the houses, with the sailors there, helping to run it all. The Big Canoe people used to come down from the Queen Charlottes for the Indian races. The Chinese came, too. They used to race in the old days, and they would carry different coloured banners in their boats. It was very pretty. Later on, in other years the Artillery and the Engineers would always put their boats in. There was great rivalry, you see, with the Navy. In those days the Navy would come out here from England for four years. They were able to bring their families out and there were rows and rows of houses down at Esquimalt for the naval officers' families. It was after that that the Engineers and the Artillery came. They brought their families out, and they'd stay for four years too. We were considered to be the end of the world here in Victoria. *Uncivilized*! Oh my!

We used to go down to San Francisco and Los Angeles every winter, and spend a few weeks there. We used to go, too, to watch the poor dears going off to the Gold Rush. They were so full of hope. 'We'll bring you back a diamond tiara,' they'd yell from the ship as it left. There was a big shop down on Wharf Street where they got all their sleighs and their ropes and their picks, you know, and they'd go with great excitement. But do you know, you had to keep your dogs tied up, or hidden, because they *stole* all the dogs in Victoria for their sleighs. And they took a lot of horses too, poor dears. But they didn't last long up in that cold. It was *awful*, trying to keep your dog from them!

Oh, the Gold Rush went on for a long time. It was pathetic! Some of the Mounties used to stay with us sometimes, and they'd tell us the most *terrible* stories. These young boys used to go out y'know, and they thought if they had a coil of rope around them and a pickaxe and a fur coat, that they could just *walk* there. Well, of course, they never came back! You see, it was an expensive job, getting all the things they needed, and they'd die without those things.

We used to go out on *beautiful* picnics, because that's all we had to do, you see? Picnics and tennis parties. In those days, everyone had tennis courts, often two or three of them. And then there would be huge parties at Government House.

Then old Sir Matthew Begbie used to give the most *delightful* parties, and he used to ask the children to come down too, and there'd be all sorts of games for them. Then one day, he said to Mother, 'Do bring Nellie down because the cherries are ripe and delicious.' When I arrived there with a lot of other little children we found that Sir Matthew had picked all the cherries, and put them in little muslin bags, and tied them to the trees. So his idea was that we should each have a little bag of cherries, and we could say that we had *picked* them off the tree. Oh dear, poor Sir Matthew!

There were two characters I loved especially. They were old Indians, and one we called 'Laughing Jinny' and the other, her husband, 'Jimmy Chickens'. They lived on an island in Oak Bay called 'Jimmy Chickens' Island'. They used to come to our house, and pick weeds off the lawn and maybe have a meal, but most of the time, I think, they'd be in jail, because when I went down to school in the morning, I'd often meet the chain gang, and there would be old Jimmy with them, smiling and waving, 'Good morning, Miss Pryor. Good morning.' There would be about twenty men chained together in twos and a man would be behind them with a rifle. They used to come up to Government House to work in the garden, and tidy up, you know. You could hear them coming from the longest way off. Clink, clink, clink. Poor old drunks, they were.

One day I went into the pantry, and Laughing Jinny was there, hiding. She was a huge woman, and she said, 'Jimmy, he beat me. He beat me.' Now I don't know how Jimmy managed that, because he was just a tiny little man, but they were always being 'had up' by the police for something or other. They were real characters in Victoria, and everybody knew them. Eventually, their little cabin burned down, and they just went away somewhere.

One of the worst things that happened when I was young was when the Ellis Bridge went down. It was the 24th of May, you see, and they were having a big review down at McAulay Point with the Army and the Navy and everything. People started going down there at ten o'clock in the morning. Father took his regiment down about twelve o'clock, and just as they got to the bridge, somebody said that it wasn't safe, so Father examined it, and said, 'No, I don't think it is.' So he made all the men break up before they went over. Well, we came after that, about one o'clock. We just got to the bridge, just on the first board, and everything started to shake, and the wagons and people on the bridge went through. Then there was a loud noise, and everything let go, and the whole thing came down. People were screaming, and it was the most awful thing. Well, we couldn't do anything, so we just stood there looking at all this, just horrified! Many, many people and horses were drowned. Oh, it was ghastly!

We always had the grandest Christmases. The shops and the churches would be decorated and the butchers would hang all their beef and pigs outside. There'd be rows and rows of carcasses with little bits of holly and coloured flags on them.

We always went out to our uncle's. They had a nice old stone house, and an old-fashioned kitchen, and oh, what meals! We'd go early in the afternoon, and come back about three o'clock in the morning, tired little children, full of good things to eat, and loaded with Christmas presents. The next day, we'd go to visit the Chief Factor of the Hudson's Bay Company, and we'd have another Christmas there! They were good, old-fashioned Christmases, you know, with huge big turkeys, plum puddings, and umpteen things to drink. How the table would be loaded down! We all used to go to church and sing the carols. It seemed that almost everyone could sing in those days, and play the piano too. Entertaining was simple. Somebody would throw back the rugs; somebody would sit at the piano, and play a military schottische or a polka. We

might have a little claret, or lemonade, and a few little sand-
wiches.

Ah, it was all such a lovely time, so nice and elegant, and
dear Queen Victoria was on the throne."

ELIZABETH GOUDY

Elizabeth Goudy was born in the Labrador. Her father was a trapper and when the time came she too married a trapper. From the very beginning she was used to the idea that life was no bed of roses. You had to work for everything you got: the food you ate, the water you drank, and the clothes you wore. And the children were expected to help with every-thing.

'Twas the Trend of Life in Labrador

"MY FATHER WAS A TRAPPER. He trapped in winter in the valley of the Hamilton River and he'd leave home in September so he could get in over the ponds and lakes that was between him and the trapping grounds before everything got frozen up. It was won-derful to see all the trappers come home safe and sound in the spring. We always prepared what we called 'our best food' to give them a treat. They also came home once during the winter, for about a month, for what they called a 'January break'. This was so they could prepare more wood for us and do all the other things that the family would need done. Then they'd be gone again till about the middle of April.

I suppose I began to be a grownup in earnest around the age of twelve. You had to learn to use your hands just as soon as you were able so that you could help your parents out. And everyone had to do their share; there was no such thing as sitting back and letting somebody else do it. No sir. I can still remember the first job that my father gave me: fixing Mother's breakfast at six o'clock in the morning! It was usually the same: a pot of salt fish or stewed trout. Sometimes there'd be rolled oats. We used mo-lasses in our tea and we didn't have coffee. On special occasions like Christmas or Easter we'd get milk and sugar; I used to be some happy when I saw that coffee can come on the table. Apart from that though, we lived completely on the land: on meat, fish, and berries. Some might say it was a hard life but I never stopped to consider that at all. 'Twas the trend of life in Labrador and we all accepted it. Our neighbours were living the same and some had it harder than we did.

In Labrador man was the provider, the mighty hunter who spent almost as much time away from home stalking game as he did with his family. Mother stayed home looking after the house and children and kept the fires going. She made all the clothing and did a thousand and one other jobs that made survival possible in that hard land. Recreation was a word we had never heard of and leisure was something she never thought about. In Labrador the 'Life of Riley' was measured in simple terms, like living on the shore of a fresh-water lake instead of a salt-water ocean; by the lake you could simply get your water with a bucket, whereas by the ocean you had to melt snow. It made a big difference. When I got married we lived at Mud Lake for a time and it was wonderful; all I had to do was cut a hole in the ice and fetch the water in buckets. I had to put snowshoes on to get there of course; the water was a couple of hundred yards away, but that was nothing.

I was really proud of the way I protected my children from getting into an accident or causing a fire or scalding themselves when I was out fetching water. I'd take a blanket and spread it over the top of the kitchen table and set the ones that could get into mischief on that. The table was by the window where they could see me and, most important, I could see them. The baby, if I had a baby at the time, would be shut up in the bedroom. This is what I had to do to bring my water in! There wasn't a moment of the day when you couldn't be thinkin' of the children because every movement that caused you to be out of their presence for a while worried you. I was lucky though; some Labrador women had to cut, stack, and store their own wood as well as do all their other work, but my husband always saw to it for me.

Most Labrador homes were the same. You had a big kitchen, no livin' room, a couple of bedrooms, and a big back porch to store some wood, your snowshoes, or sleds, or whatever you needed for winter. Then you had a big forty-gallon water barrel. You melted snow in that. I remember at Father's home it used to take my brothers and sisters all day Monday to get this barrel full of water. Then my mother would do her laundry, her cleaning, her baking, and her cooking all in one day on that barrel of water.

53

Then the next day we'd start out and do the same thing all over again. This was when we were livin' by the ocean where the ice was salt so all you could use was the snow that fell on the top of the ice, not the ice itself because that was salt. In the summertime we had a well and we dipped our water from that. Summer was great in so many ways, no snow to melt, and about six weeks of nice warm weather. Best of all Father would be home with us. He'd go out fishin' or choppin' wood for the winter but he was home most nights and he'd tell us stories about the wolves and the polar bears he trapped during the winter.

My husband was very much like my father in many ways. He was a trapper and he could turn his hand to anything. We moved around Labrador a lot but wherever we went to live he always built a house—by himself.

I remember one time in 1929 we moved back to my father's place at Mud Lake. We were down and out and as low as we could be without starving and my father took us in with him. In the fall my husband went up the river and got a supply of food that would put us through until he returned from his first trip to his traplines on the height of land. We were all waiting for him when he returned at the January break to see how many skins he'd have. A trapper never knows himself how many skins he's got until he gets home because as he traps them he keeps putting them in these skin bags; and even if he did know he would never tell anyone because he wants the family to see first. Then after-wards, everybody around the neighbourhood comes in for a look and to say what nice furs and find out how many and just gener-ally to rejoice about it all. It's a high point of the year.

So anyway, when my husband returned I was so anxious to see what he had. The furs were all packed into bags and lashed to the sled but I could see he had a good lot. I felt so thrilled and hoped there would be at least five or six hundred dollars' worth of fur so we could build a house. I knew that five or six hundred dol-lars would be enough because it would be all our own labour. The logs were always cut from the woods and the lumber for the floors and the roof was ripped out of logs at the mill and nailed right away same as they came from the rough saw. The women and the girls that were big enough got down on their knees and scrubbed that floor with sand and cork until it was smooth. After a month or two of doing this the floor would be nice and clean and white and smooth as anything—no splinters at all. So anyway, when my husband's furs were counted and sorted he had about seven hundred dollars. We were all so happy because now we knew we'd get that new house."

ALFRED BARNES

Alfred Barnes of Toronto was born in 1886, and while he was still a boy he was apprenticed to the carriage-and-buggy industry. There were no assembly lines in those days and everything from the iron-and-steel work to the carpentry, painting, and upholstery was done in the same small factory. Each man was a specialist, but they all worked together on each individual carriage until it was as perfect as they could make it. Mr. Barnes was eighty-eight years old when we had this conversation.

Our Company Built a Nice Buggy

"I WAS WHAT THEY CALLED A 'TRIMMER' with the Canadian (Cone) Covered Carriage Company of Palmerston, Ontario. I was learning my trade in trimming, and I worked at all the upholstery work on buggies, cutters, and carriages. I did all the leather work for the cushions, the backs, and the tops of the buggies.

Our company built a nice buggy, and we had a good hundred people workin' in the factory at Palmerston. They had blacksmiths, painters, woodworkers, and trimmers of course, as well as the assembly men who put it all together. It wasn't an assembly-line operation, like you see today. Oh no. Each man had his little job to do. For instance, at the blacksmith shop, they'd make all the ironwork for the engines and then they'd take that from there to the woodshop. The man there would build the buggies and carriages and then send them to us for the upholstery and trimming. Then they'd go off to the paint shop, and after that the varnishers would finish them up.

Oh my, the pride we all had in our work. The painters would use twelve and fourteen coats of paint. Before they even got to the paint of course, the woodshop men would have sanded those bodies again and again. Then they'd 'rough-stuff' them. That was a coat of paint. Then fellas would come along and rub that all down till it was right into the wood. After that, in the paint shop, one fella'd put on a coat of paint and another fella would come behind him and put a different coat on, and they'd rub each of these coats down till they were smooth as glass, and they'd keep on doing that till there was maybe fourteen coats on her. Then they'd varnish her. There was 100 degrees of heat in where they did that and the varnish would be a foot high on the floors from the drips. They might put seventeen coats on before they were satisfied. You could see your face in her, when she was all finished. Gee, they were a nice job, and every man was proud of it when she rolled outa there.

We trimmers used to do the cushions and the fancy backs inside. I'd take great pride in that. I never got to learn the fancy backs until I was there three years at the business. You worked up gradually from all the other small things to the cushions and finally, to the fancy backs. Then we could go on 'piece-work', so much for each one we did. We could make two dollars a day then, and that was real good money! Trimmers, painters, and varnishers were considered very, very skilled workers. Those buggies and carriages were real works of art. They were beautiful! They were wonderful!

I moved from the carriages to the automobile industry in 1904, when I went with the Packard Motor Car Co. They had a sign up over their building then that said, 'Ask the man who owns one.' That was their slogan. They were great cars—one of the best! Them and the Pierce-Arrow. All the same kind of care that we used to put into the making of the carriages was put into the making of these cars. You see, they didn't do 'Duco' in those days. They used all paint, and the result was really wonderful. It was nothing at all to have fourteen or sixteen coats of paint on it before it was finished.

There were lots of companies making cars then, and lots of them didn't survive. The Maxwell didn't survive. I don't think Pope-Hartford ever survived. Mercedes didn't survive, but they're back in business now. Then there was the Hup—the Hupmobile. There was the Grey-Dort. That was made in Chatham, Ontario, after they went out of the buggy business. There was the odd Rolls-Royce around too. I worked on them. There was a lawyer here had two of 'em, and he used to come down to me for a set of slip-covers or to fix up some of his trimming. It was all leather in those days, no imitation, and we had all the time in the world to trim a car then, too. Especially up at Packard. When I first went there and got the carriage shop, I thought it was wonderful. I'd be working on a cushion or a back, and the rest of the boys would come down and say, 'Don't do it so fast.' Oh boy, that was lovely leather we used.

I worked for Packard a long time and I left there to go to Cadillac. I never would work on Fords. At that time they were too cheap. I used to get the special work on Packards and Cadillacs when they were sending them to the big shows in New York, and they'd have them all trimmed up in a special kind of leather: maybe a green, maybe a pigskin, maybe a nice red. I don't care if I do say it, I was really a good trimmer, and I got the special work.

I didn't own a car myself then. That was too much money for any worker to have, but we sure admired them. I didn't get one until I started in business for myself in Toronto. Then I got a Model-T—one of the old brass ones. In the mornings you used to have to go out in the cold weather, jack that thing up, and crank your head off to get it to go. We didn't have any anti-freeze then, and you'd have to drain all the water out at night, and then the next morning, you'd get boiling water and then crank 'er up to get 'er goin'. That crankin' could be dangerous too. You could easily break your wrist if she kicked back at you. You had to be very careful. Those cars were really more trouble than they were worth.

When I started my business I had two or three boys working for me, and I used to pick 'em up in the mornin' and take 'em to work. We had what we called 'engine hood covers' to help keep the engines warm. I used to make them out of asbestos, wadding, and flannelette and then put imitation leather over top of that. All quilted in diamond shapes. Those young boys were pretty proud to have this Model-T stoppin' at their front doors! In the evenings I used to make sure to remind the boys to be sure to run the water off the car. But the odd morning I'd come in, and she'd be froze up!

I was a great sports fan then, and we used to nip over to the ball park in Detroit whenever we had a chance. Ty Cobb was my big hero, and Honus Wagner too. They used to play a lovely game of ball, especially Cobb. Cyclone Taylor was the best hockey player I ever saw, even better than Howie Morenz. He was the fastest one I ever saw, and he was the highest-paid player when he went to Renfrew to play. He got $5,500 for eleven games.

We had a little baseball league in Mount Forest. I was the catcher for our team and a friend of mine was the pitcher. We called our team 'The Barnes Battery'. We played at Mount Forest, Listowel, Palmerston, and Harriston, and after work we'd all jump into one of the company carry-all wagons and drive to the games. We played pretty fair bush-league baseball too. I never wanted to get professional though. I never had the desire to be a star. I liked the car trimming too much, I guess. The bodies on those cars were made as good as it was possible to make them, and all of us took a real pride in our work. You just wouldn't want to turn out a bad one."

DAN J. MCDONALD

The early days of coal mining in Cape Breton, Nova Scotia, produced many disasters. Working conditions were unsafe, and in many cases, primitive. Death in the pits was almost a commonplace occurrence, and the disaster whistle blowing short, loud blasts brought off-duty miners and their families running to the pithead. Dan J. McDonald worked in the Glace Bay mines for fifty-two years, from the age of thirteen to sixty-five, and he told me he had experienced "much more darkness than light" in his lifetime. His father, Neil, was an early fighter for a union, and Dan himself has also been a lifelong battler for better conditions for miners.

Death in the Pits

"DISASTER IN A COAL MINE was always looked after by a crew of 'draegermen'! They were specially trained and equipped to go immediately to the scene of an accident underground. They would have with them too a crew of trained miners to assist them. But, of course, when miners on the surface hear those short sharp insistent blasts on the colliery whistle, they know something is wrong, and no matter where they are, they rush to the mine to see if they can get down to help.

In every coal mine there is a combination coal miner and stone miner. They are called 'brushers', and play a very important part in accidents where the stone roof has collapsed. It's their job to clear everything away and to get to where the trapped miners may be. As long as those men are in there, hope is *never* given up. The only time we ever concede that there is a dead body is when we see it. I remember during the Springhill Mine disaster, a man was trapped alive in a standing position for eight days with no light or food or anything. Everybody everywhere outside the mine had given up hope, but those miners just kept diggin'. They felt there might be somebody alive in there, and they wouldn't stop till they were sure! And they were right! After eight days, they found him alive. Even the miner who is trapped never gives up hope because he knows his buddies won't stop till they find him, dead or alive.

The lights a miner carried in the old days were very, very poor. They gave almost no light at all, and it took very little to put them out. When that happens there is total darkness—inky black! The horses were uncanny, though. They could make their way in that darkness, pulling a two-ton box of coal, and they'd never miss a step or a turn. And some of the best horses we had down there were stone blind in both eyes.

One time, I was down the mine later than all the other fellas and I suddenly realized I was there alone; just me and the horse. It was the weekend, and there'd be no other shift coming on until Monday morning. So anyway, just as I started to put the horse back in his stable, my light went out. There was no way to light it again, and I started to panic a bit. I happened to reach out, and I grabbed hold of the horse's tail. Soon as I did, she started to move, and I said, 'If you can go, I can follow!' She just kept movin' ahead in the dark for maybe a mile till we came to the bottom where the shaft was, and the 'cage' to take me to the surface.

The drivers in the mine built up a great pride in their horses, and woe and behold to anyone who came along and said anything bad about a man's horse. He'd probably find his teeth down his throat. I saw a fella come along, and spit tobacco on a driver's horse once, and the driver just hit him as fast as he did the spittin', and he wound up minus a few teeth.

I was just a boy when I first went down in the pits. I never thought much about it one way or another because it was natural for all the miners' sons in those days. You just followed on. The conditions were bad, and the pay was poor, and some of the miners were secretly trying to start a union. My father, Neil McDonald, was one of these, and he suffered for it. He was persecuted and thrown out of work. He was fired and the family was destitute. There was eight of us, and we didn't have a red cent! No food, nothing to fall back on! The operators had put such fear in all the miners that even the close neighbours were afraid to give us any help in case they'd end up fired like my father! There was nothing else to turn to, no other jobs of any kind.

After about two days of no food, my father went out at night to a workers' secret meeting. There was a rap came at the door, and there was a black man there. He said, 'Mrs. McDonald, I know that Neil is fightin' for what is right. Would you be insulted if I gave you some money?' With two days of hunger behind us, Mother certainly wasn't going to say no, so he handed her a ten-dollar bill. That was a *lot* of money in those days. He said, 'Please, don't mention this to nobody.'

People lived with a *real* fear of what the Company could do to them. For example, they could throw you out of your house on a three-day notice because *they* owned the house. This happened to us when the 1909 strike was declared. Company police would come and viciously toss a family and whatever furniture they had right out on the street. I even saw them put women out with brand-new babies. During the 1909 strike, the International United Mine Workers was trying to get places to put the miners and their families up because so many people were homeless. They partitioned the basement of the Catholic church and put a lot of families in there. Children were put wherever there was a place for them.

The neighbouring town of Dominion had a mine, but the miners there, most of them, didn't go on strike in 1909. My mother sent me there on the streetcar to stay with an aunt. Well, I missed the stop, and I was wandering around, and this young fella who was bigger than I was, came over and started to talk and he asked me, 'What does your father do?' I said, 'My father's on strike.' Well, he never paused for a minute, he just let me have it right in the face, and knocked me flat on my back and jumped on top of me, and started to *pound* me! Luckily my cousin, who was out lookin' for me, came along and pulled him off. But see, that's the way it was; some of the miners were out on strike, others weren't, and they were divided! And that's the main reason we were beaten in that strike!

The company was really *vicious* in that strike. They electrified the fence around the mine, so the strikers couldn't interfere with the scabs they brought in. Well, it kept the strikers out but one of the young fellas playing around there one day grabbed hold of the wire and was electrocuted. They also recruited a bunch of thugs from around the waterfront in Montreal, put uniforms on them, gave them guns and batons, called them police, and turned them loose on the miners. Those guys had no scruples at all about beating a man half to death.

The strikers decided to hold a meeting in Dominion to try and persuade these other miners to join the strike, and the army threw up a barricade at the town line. They set up a machine gun on the steps of Bridgeport church while the strikers were forming the parade, which was how they intended to come to Dominion. It was set up like a real war operation, with army men on top of the hospital, signalling with flags and so on. But the strikers fooled them that time; they heard about this big military operation, and they called the parade and the meeting off!

The company starved the men. They *downed* them in *every* way that they could, and after ten months, the men went back, beaten. But the strike *did* serve to show the Company that in spite of all the power they held over the people, there were those who would *always* resist. The secret meetings continued, and many years and another bitter strike later, the miners *got* their union, and the dictatorial power of the Company was broken!"

MRS. MARGARET INNIS

The Canadian nation was only fifteen years old when Margaret Hamilton was born. She grew up in a politically active family in Nova Scotia where dinner-table talk was always made lively with political discussions.

That Joe Howe

"MY FATHER WAS A NEWSPAPER MAN IN HALIFAX by the name of Percy St. Clair Hamilton—he was called 'Peace and See' for short —and my grandfather was Pierce Stephens Hamilton, who charted many of the early plans for Confederation.

My childhood was a very exciting time. All the talk at home was about the Whigs and the Tories doing battle on the floor of the Nova Scotia Legislature—and of course Father and Grandfather continued the battle on the pages of the newspaper—and just about everybody who came to dinner at our house was a politician. They had great fights while dinner was going on and I enjoyed every minute of it. About the only thing these people agreed on was that Grandfather had been cheated out of his right to be a Father of Confederation. They said he should have been, and whether Joe Howe had anything to do with it, we don't know. Sir John A. was certainly a personal friend of Grandpa.

When I was about four or five years old, we moved to Yarmouth, Nova Scotia, for a few years. A nice little town with lovely people, muddy old Yarmouth was full of those funny old sailing ships in those days. They put up that Grand Hotel while we were there, and it's still there today. We were so proud of it. A big modern brick hotel in little Yarmouth. But oh, they ran it so beautifully; the sparkling linen, and the silver in the dining room, and the waiters always 'just so'.

Outside, on the lawn in front of the white church, was the bandstand. The bands would be playing and the people all just strolling around in their Sunday best. It was a place like no other.

The nice cool breeze would come in from the ocean and in the summer the sweltering Americans would flock in there to cool off and eat lobsters and clams.

I married an Englishman named Innis, and would always brag to him about Yarmouth. It was during the First World War that he had a chance to go down there. He laughed at Yarmouth, but he loved it too, at first sight. He said he understood why I was always talking about it. I asked him why he laughed, and he said he thought it would be much bigger from the way I had been talking. Although we were only there for a day, my husband talked about Yarmouth for the rest of his life.

All the people in Nova Scotia were proud of Grandfather, and they were resentful of the fact that he was not made a Father of Confederation. The papers were full of it. He was a very outspoken man, especially when it came to Americans, and he was very much against all the American influence. Funny thing too, his daughters all married Americans. Grandfather would visit America and he always had his American in-laws down for visits in the summertime, but when he spoke about America there was always a bit of sarcasm in his voice and a twinkle in his eye. He loved to tease them. There's just one thing I'd like to find out before I die and that is who it was that kept Grandfather from his rightful place as a Father of Confederation. *I* think it was that Joe Howe."

BARNEY WILLIAMS

Barney Williams of Alert Bay, British Columbia, spent his whole life in the newspaper business. His father was an Eastern publisher who could have provided his son with the security of a good job, but by the time he was twenty, Barney could no longer control his wanderlust. There was a big country out there, and he wanted to see it. The West was calling.

A Printer's Devil

"I WAS BORN IN THE OTTAWA VALLEY, at Arnprior, in 1882. My father was a newspaper publisher, so it was natural for me to get into that business too.

My favourite childhood memory goes back to when I was eight years old. My father was running a newspaper in the Eastern Townships of Quebec, and it so happened that he was very well acquainted with Sir John A. Macdonald. Anyway, Sir John A. asked my father if he would call on him in Ottawa. The elections were approaching, so I presume it had some connection with that. So Father got me all dressed up, and took me down with him to Ottawa, and we went straight into Sir John's office. He was pretty well up in years at that time; in fact, it was the year before he died. He called me over, and I stood there between his knees talking to him, you see. He said, 'I suppose when you grow up you'll be a newspaperman like your father.' I said, 'Yes sir.' Then he said, 'Suppose you were interviewing me, what would be your first question?' I looked up, and said, 'Sir John, what makes your breath so bad?' Well, he laughed, and after he stopped he said, 'My boy, when you get to be my age, your breath will probably be as bad.'

I never liked school very much, and after I had one year of high school, I decided that the road to higher learning would never feel the touch of my shoes. Father put up a terrible fight, but

The graves of soldiers who died in the 1885 Riel Rebellion. (The Public Archives of Canada)

The men who found Louis Riel guilty. "Riel *was* respected by a great many people because he didn't seem bitter or cruel. And nobody thought he was insane." Jessie Tyreman (The Public Archives of Canada)

St. John's lies desolate after the fire of 1892. "That was a terrible, terrible fire." Dr. Cluny McPherson (The Public Archives of Canada)

A member of the NWMP with a Plains Indian. "The first thing I learned on the force was that Mounties felt a lot more sympathy for the Indians than they did for most of the white men...." Lewis McLaughlin (The Public Archives of Canada)

Troops marching in Springhill during the

Twelve-year-old miners, like
the one at the left, were
common in the mines of
Cape Breton. Boys like
Archie McIntyre worked
alongside older miners and
in the same conditions (*top*).
(The Public Archives of
Canada)
The domination of the mine
masters was resisted in a
series of bloody and violent
strikes. Mining towns were
turned into armed camps
full of police and soldiers
(*above*). (Postcard courtesy
of Allan Anderson and Betty
Tomlinson)

(*Left, above*) Homesteading on the prairies was like homesteading anywhere; it was team work. "Without a good woman most men wouldn't have stood a chance!" Alex Burnett (The Public Archives of Canada)

(*Left, below*) Looking east on Winnipeg's Main Street around the turn of the century. "In Winnipeg and Brandon everything was wide open as far as booze and prostitution were concerned, and they were closed tight as far as everything else was concerned." James Gray (The Public Archives of Canada)

(*Above*) While most others were struggling to survive, a few privileged people in Victoria, B.C., lived in houses like the one above, held parties, played tennis, and went on picnics, Nellie Pryor Hood recalls. (The Public Archives of Canada)

Margaret Innis still blames Joseph Howe, the well-known Nova Scotian publisher, journalist, and politician, for robbing her grandfather of his place in history. (The Public Archives of Canada)

1918 Ford trucks similar to the ones Alfred Barnes worked on as a trimmer for the early makers of automobiles like Ford, Packard, Maxwell, Mercedes, and Rolls-Royce. (Ontario Forest Industries Association)

Newcomers on Kensington Avenue in Toronto. "We had immigrants from everywhere, ... every religion and all the colours of the world too. ... you'd hear a dozen different languages being spoken." Arthur Cohen (The Public Archives of Canada)

Sir John A. Macdonald was still Prime Minister when Barney Williams asked him why his breath smelled so bad. (The Public Archives of Canada)

KING COBALT SILVER MINE, COBALT, ONT.

J. J. Byrne remembers the incredible story of the discovery of silver in Cobalt, Ontario, by a prospector named Fred LaRose. (Postcard courtesy of Allan Anderson and Betty Tomlinson)

he finally gave in, and I started as an apprentice in the family newspaper.

I was a printer's devil—which means that I set type, learned the job-printing business, helped to get out the newspaper, and was general roustabout. Later on, I went down to Montreal, and worked on the *Montreal Herald*.

In March of 1902, I hopped on a train for Vancouver. Now, my father was also a very good friend of old Sir William Van Horne, who built the CPR. He had given Father a complimentary pass so that anytime he wanted to go anywhere, he could travel on the train free. I thought I would like a free ticket too so I tried to get in contact with Sir William. Let me just say that I ended up buying my own ticket!

It took six days to get out on that particular trip because when we got to Winnipeg there was one of those Prairie storms on. We stayed there about thirty hours. Then after we left Calgary, we began to get into very deep snow, and the train was running in a trench most of the way with these walls of snow on both sides. I remember that trip being cold, but when we arrived in Vancouver all the embankment there by the CPR track was covered with flowers. Well, that was really something for all of us on the train. We thought Vancouver was God's country.

Around 1903-4, on one of my first jobs as a reporter, the newspaper sent me out on the CPR to the Rogers Pass. They were digging a tunnel through the mountain there so they wouldn't have to use the switchbacks, which were very dangerous. Large gangs of men were digging the tunnel from both ends of the mountain and the trains were running in empty and coming out loaded with all this rock and dirt which they'd use to build up an embankment somewhere else. The CPR was double-tracking at that time, and they were using a lot of this material for that down around Albert Canyon and Revelstoke.

At that time Vancouver was really only a village that covered the area of the city that's called 'Gastown' today. In 1902, when I arrived, the only *real* street was Cordova. That part of the city had been built up after the big fire. There were a few cars, but it was mostly all horse-and-buggy stuff. We had lots of mud and wooden sidewalks and big forests surrounded the town on three sides. It was still the frontier.

Quite a number of buildings were being torn down, so they could put up new buildings under the single tax. This single tax meant that buildings were exempt from taxation. For a while there was a tremendous development in buildings all over the place. Well, they found out after a couple of years that buildings dominated the financial situation, and in order to save the city they had to revert back to the double-tax situation.

About 1912, there was a very decided land boom. The result of this single tax was that all the commerce of the city shifted over from Cordova Street to Hastings Street, between Main and Granville. Cordova was practically abandoned, and Vancouver really started to grow and develop into the big city it is today."

DOROTHY MCLAUGHLIN HENDERSON

Robert McLaughlin was eighty-five years old when he died in 1921. In his lifetime, he built from practically nothing a carriage factory that was the finest in the British Empire. From his factory emerged the McLaughlin Democrat, the McLaughlin sleigh, and the McLaughlin carriage. Later, when the motor replaced the horse, there would come the McLaughlin Buick and still later the cars that are General Motors products today.

Robert McLaughlin's father came to Canada from Ireland. He was a cobbler who was looking for a better life for his family and who found it on a homestead in Ontario. His first son founded an empire and his children carried it on. Dorothy McLaughlin Henderson revered that first son, her grandfather Robert McLaughlin, a kindly man who always had time to play with his grandchildren.

One Grade Only and That the Best

"I WAS TWENTY-ONE YEARS OLD when my grandfather Robert McLaughlin died so I remember him well. When I was a child he was a companion and friend: he treated me as an equal, which is a rare compliment.

Now, of course, I see him through different eyes. I see a man who never gave in though his whole factory burned to the ground and he lost everything; I see a man who was a friend to those who worked with him and for him and whose business was not the end and the aim of his entire life. He was a great community worker; he started the Gravenhurst Hospital for consumptives by inviting to his home people powerful enough to get out and work for it. And he was one of the first people to help the Salvation Army when it was far less respectable than it is today.

It's really funny, you know, how the McLaughlins got involved in this whole business of making automobiles. It started well before the motor car was invented of course. One day, when he was a young man, grandfather saw a picture of a sleigh in a catalogue. He wanted one, but he needed the money for other things, so he decided to build one for himself. It was so good that his neighbour paid him to make another one for him. Well, pretty soon one order followed another until McLaughlin sleighs and carriages were famous throughout the British Empire. The young farmer from Durham County, Ontario, the son of a homesteader, had become an industrialist, almost without knowing it. Then he had to make a choice between manufacturing and farming, and in 1869, at the age of 34, he set up his factory with a staff of one journeyman, one carpenter, one apprentice, and himself as designer, painter, and manager. The McLaughlin Carriage Co. was born, and out of it, many years later, would emerge a much larger company called 'General Motors'. One of the things that helped make the McLaughlin Carriage Co. a success was the carriage gear which my grandfather invented. It increased the safety and comfort of the carriages and, in those days, anything that made the carriages more comfortable was bound to be a success!

The motto of the McLaughlin Carriage Co. was always 'one grade only and that the best' and that wasn't a lie, either. It was something that my grandfather insisted they live up to. He wouldn't stoop to using poor metal or anything just because it was cheaper. I don't know what he'd be like if he were alive today. I don't know if he could compete if he insisted on remaining honest. One thing I do know, though, the McLaughlin Carriage Co. lived up to that motto while my grandfather was alive, that's for sure.

When they were old enough, my grandfather's sons, Sam and George, became very involved in the business. Colonel Sam, as they called him, was a very dynamic man and he was the engineer. My father, George, was the quieter one. He was the company salesman who travelled across Canada; in fact, he was the first man ever to drive a motor car across the Canadian prairies. Looking back now on when I was young, it seems that I was always waiting for my dad to come home from work. In those days people worked very long hours. They worked Saturdays too, you know. Anyway, my dad would go to the factory at 7:00 and then at noon the whistles would blow. That meant the factory was closing for an hour. As soon as I heard that whistle blow, I would go to meet my dad on the wooden sidewalk. And I would wait until I figured out which man walking up the sidewalk was him and then I'd meet him and walk back home the rest of the way with him.

Every Christmas we'd have parties for all the employees of the factory. This big old room where the finished carriages were stored would be cleaned out and decorated with holly wreaths, evergreen wreaths, and, of course, a magnificent Christmas tree. My father would let me go and we would dance all sorts of old-fashioned dances: the schottische, and the Lancers, and everything!

One thing I remember very clearly about my grandfather is how important hobbies were to him. He was ahead of his time in thinking that, as he was in so many other things. Nowadays people are beginning to realize that everybody should have a hobby for their own mental comfort, their interest in life, and also for the real success of their business. When his sons were signing the final papers that meant that the company was going into motor cars my grandfather was in a separate office, at his easel, painting. All that legal business didn't interest him; he knew his life was done as far as the carriage and motor-car business was concerned, but he was happy. Because he'd had a hobby all his life he was quite willing to relax and leave the business to his sons. He knew they would carry on the way he would want them to.

They all tried very hard to keep this business Canadian, to have the motors and everything made here. But, well, everybody knows the story today, it just wasn't possible. It's too bad too, because Grandfather worked so hard in those early days in the carriage business."

DEWEY NICKERSON

The salt Atlantic Ocean that batters the shores of the Maritimes and Newfoundland produces a special breed of men, men of great determination and independence who literally tear a living from the sea. The Atlantic fisherman is more than just a man; he's a tradition that goes well back before Columbus and John Cabot to the Vikings, and no doubt before that too. He has a love/hate relationship with the sea, but given the choice of any other kind of job he would take the sea every time.

Dewey Nickerson of Cape Sable Island, off the shore of Nova Scotia, is one of these men. He was crawling along the deck of his father's Cape Island boat—a fishing boat specially developed by these Atlantic fishermen—before he could walk.

These Waters off Sable Island

"THIS CAPE ISLAND BOAT is an art all by itself. It ain't like a car, there ain't no model--there's a change from one boat to the other. It's all done by eye. If I want her bow off a little more, or her stern changed—whatever I want those men will do for me. Every boat is different because every man who has one has put a little bit of himself in it. That's what made them so famous. All the fishermen down here have experimented with them—something different here, something different there. This boat, you see, has developed over the centuries and she's the perfect boat for our needs in these waters off Sable Island. It's pretty treacherous off here if you don't know the waters. It's known as the graveyard of the Atlantic and with good reason too. It's all shoals under that water and if you don't know where they are—too bad. Then, with the bad storms off here, there's always ships going aground.

I started out in the fishing boat with my father before I could walk—just the same as he did with his father. I grew up listening and paying attention to everything he had to say. I used to go to the grocery store and all the old fellows would be sitting around gabbing about sailing ships and sailing boats. I was all ears. Those old fellows had the knowledge and the wisdom; they had spent their lives fishing the same grounds that I had to fish, and anything they had to say was important to me. It might save my life some day. When they went out in those boats they were on their own—just themselves against the sea. A gale of wind might come up—we called them the 'August twisters' in them days—they'd come up suddenly and the best you could do was make for shore as fast as you could. You *had* to know that water and every inch of shore like the back of your hand. There was no electronic equipment, not even a weather forecast. There was only yourself and what was inside your head. Sometimes I didn't know if I was gonna make land or not. See, the mainland of Nova Scotia might be eighteen or twenty miles away when one of these sudden gales would come up and there would be no way we could make it back. That's when we'd have to turn in to Sable to land our boats. If we didn't know the waters there, that would be the end of it.

Of course, we had accidents too and men were lost. I was aboard of my boat once and she exploded. I had my two boys with me. There was a thick fog and we were all smoke and flames and the only thing we could do was bale water into her as fast as we could. The nearest boat to me was four miles and, do you know, he happened to see me through a break in the fog. So he raced over and came alongside and we started with these old fire extinguishers. They did no good—so finally we got her full of water and got the fire out. We got on his boat and towed mine into Clark's Harbour. She was pretty well burned but all the boys got together and fixed me up so that I could get to work again, because it was the lobster season and you couldn't afford to lose a day. Well, I did lose three or four days that time—but if it hadn't been for my friends pitching in I might have lost the whole season.

That's the way those boys were. No matter how hard they had to work themselves, they always had time to help the other fellow. If you wanted a boat hauled, or if one of the fishermen died and there was a funeral, everybody stayed out of their boats till that was done. They all went to the funeral and they all chipped in to help the other fellow if he got into a mess. I remember, in the wintertime, we'd come home to Clark's Harbour when the season was done; we'd sing out 'Haul boat' and the men would come from everywhere. They'd drop whatever they were doing and get around that boat to get her out of the water.

We only stayed on Sable while the season was on, and we enjoyed ourselves. There was families there, and cookhouses, and in the evening we'd all gather in the cookhouse to tell yarns and play cards and sing.

My people were always fishermen as far back as anyone can remember, on and around Sable and Seal islands, off the shore of Nova Scotia. We always had it warm and comfortable. We used to cut our own wood. We'd have a barrel of flour, a bag of sugar, and a bucket of lard—the necessities of life. We might come to the Mainland on weekends to get some salt or something, but we stayed on there for twenty years, the wife and I. The light-keeper was on there, and the first radio beacon on the Atlantic coast was on Seal Island. See, it's the turning point of Nova Scotia, and the entrance to the Bay of Fundy. The ships coming up from Halifax or from wherever she's come, she'll make straight course up the shore, till she gets to Seal Island. If she's going to Saint John, or Boston, or New York, she's gotta alter her course.

That's as good a fishing ground as there is anywhere, and the boats don't have to get that far from the Mainland, 18 to 20 miles. That's all. We'd just take those fish in, and salt 'em, and split 'em, and put 'em in hogs and tubs, y'know—hogsheads and small wood tubs—and then come October we'd take 'em and sell 'em to different buyers in Yarmouth or Clark's Harbour. I was on there when forty boats went to the west side of Seal Island. Today there's only five.

A lot of people wonder why we stay here on Sable Island. I suppose it's not much of a place for anybody, looking at it from the outside. It's really just a long strip of sand—twenty-two miles long—no trees or anything like that, and the weather can be gosh awful—gale winds, storms, and that—but we love it! Lot of Scotch people here. Originally, they were shipwrecked here—the Irish and the Scotch. They claim the Nickersons came from Cape Cod ... migrated across the Bay of Fundy. But most of the people here are here because of shipwrecks. The sea throws everything up on the shore: people, wood, bones. I remember in the old rum-running days we used to pick up the odd keg of rum or whiskey that washed off the decks of those boats. You see, Seal Island was kind of a station for the rum-runners. They'd all come in their boats from St. Pierre, and lay here till they got their orders, and they'd come over when they got the word that rum row was clear. We'd go aboard and give them the odd mess of lobsters in exchange for rum. I remember one wintertime, I was going along the shore with Orville, my oldest boy. He's fifty-three now, but I don't think he was more than four years old at the time. I looked down over the bank and there was this keg. I went down and rolled it up on the bank, took my knife, and opened it up; it was a keg of malt whiskey, thirteen gallons. We were staying down with the light-keeper that winter. I just went back and got a jug, and that winter we just used it up as we needed it.

In the olden days they'd go out there from Barrington Passage and Yarmouth in whale boats. They'd row out and gather up the debris from the shipwrecks and they'd bury the dead there on Seal Island. They found a petrified woman one time—just solid stone, boy. She was washed ashore there and people used to come from everywhere to have a look. Finally they moved her over to Mud Island, and buried her in this man's field. Even there, people used to come and dig her up—just to have a look. Finally, the man who owned the field said he'd shoot the next man who came to dig her up.

The old light-keeper used to save a lot of stuff. He had shin bones of humans that he picked up around the beach, but after he went all that stuff disappeared! But all of these things gave us something to talk about on those dark nights. There was two families of us lived on the west side of the island. We had a baby, and there was another man and his wife. We used to play whist, and we'd keep a score for the whole winter. We were happy as long as there was enough to eat, and a few rags to wear, and a boat so we could get out and catch the fish. What more does a man want?

I get kinda lonesome for all that today when you see the boats go out and you don't go . . . but we have a ship-to-shore right here in the house because the wife worries about the boys, and we keep listening in all the time to know they're all right. I could go out, mind you, but I stay around here on the shore and help the boys rig trawl, and I find fault with them. For instance, last year, I went with one of my boys to help him set lobster traps. I said, 'Ralph, here let me do that.' He said, 'All right, old man, you do it. You sink the traps, you know where to go!' So I went and lined them up the way I thought; the holes and the places where I caught lobsters in my day. Anyway, he hauled them up after I set them two or three times, and finally, he said, 'There's no lobsters there.' I said, 'Ralph, there's going to be some, just wait. If there's none here, there'll be none nowhere.' This went on for a few days, until finally, he shifted the traps out of where I put them. Then one day he came in with a pretty good haul of lobsters. I said, 'Where did you get them?' He said, 'Well, I got them where you said and I wish I'd kept them there in the first place.'

See, I put those traps where *my* father had them, and his father before that. Now, *my* sons will do it, and most likely the others who take over after him. They're starting to find out that you *can* learn something from the old-timers."

DOROTHEA MITCHELL

Dorothea Mitchell was born near Manchester, England, and did a lot of her growing up in India, during the days of Empire. Her parents were wealthy, and Dorothea was part of a minority.

When the fortune disappeared, and her father died, Dorothea was in her twenties, but work had not yet soiled her hands. Nevertheless, the family's destiny was suddenly her responsibility, and the plucky Dorothea decided that Canada in the early 1900s was a land of opportunity. She came, she saw, and she conquered; as you'll find out in this conversation, recorded when she was ninety-four.

The Thing to Do

"I CAME OUT TO CANADA in 1904 at the age of twenty-seven to test the country for the rest of my family. The reason I came to Canada in the first place was that in England, around the turn of the century, it was very much the thing to do. Everybody was talking Canada, and I suppose it was friends, more or less, who interested us in coming. I didn't know what to expect, but I was determined to make the best of anything that came along.

One of the first jobs I got after I arrived in Toronto was as manager of a large boarding house on Jarvis Street—I think it was 314, but I'm not certain. When I knew my mother was coming out, I was sure she wouldn't want to live in a place like that, so I nosed around and found a rooming house that I could rent that had quarters for the proprietor. As soon as I had made the arrangements to take it over, I got a wire from Mother saying she wouldn't be coming because my sister was ill. So there I was, stuck with this ten-room boarding house on Church Street. But I ran it the best I could, and it worked out all right.

One time, this very nice couple came, and they wanted to rent two rooms, one for themselves, and one for a friend of theirs.

They moved in, and they were very good, looked after the rooms themselves, never made any fuss over anything. Then, one day, a man came to the door and asked if he could talk to me for a moment. He said, 'Do you notice anything about these people you've rented the rooms to, anything strange?' I said, 'No, not particularly, except they're in all day, and out all night, but that's all.' He said, 'Well, we've been watching the house for days, and they are the leaders of the biggest drug ring in the United States, and we've come to arrest them.' I was flabbergasted! I had to go to the station with them to make sure that they didn't have anything of mine in their luggage. I don't know what they could have had, because I had nothing in those rooms worth taking. I told the police that, but I had to go anyway. Afterwards, I was advised by the policemen to visit all the newspapers in town and ask them not to mention my name or address in the story. So I went around to all six newspapers, and not one of them ever mentioned me or even the name of the street.

I got tired of the boarding house after a while, I wanted to do something different. That's when I went to Silver Mountain in Northern Ontario, and bought a little general store, and a little later, a small sawmill. The First World War happened while I was there, and there was quite a shortage of men. It was mostly local people that I employed in the mill, but even they were inclined to take advantage of the fact that, if I fired them, I couldn't find anybody else to take their place because so many of the young people had gone off to war. A few times, I *had* to fire somebody, and I ended up taking the job on myself. One time I was the fireman/-engineer for three months. My gosh, it was hard work. These boilers had to be fired up with nothing but wood and I had to make up the fire every twenty minutes, and carry the wood from the cross-cut saw to the boiler. That was really hard work, but at one time or another, I did all the jobs at the mill.

One thing I'm proud of is that I never wore men's clothes even though I was doing men's work. A lot of the women in the bush did, but I had a riding skirt, kind of a divided skirt, and I'd wear that, but never trousers! That's where I drew the line.

There wasn't much in the way of recreation in Silver Mountain, except once in a while when they'd have dances. If the train ran off the track and it was delayed, somebody'd put on a dance, and somebody else would go around on horseback, telling everybody in the district that there was a dance on. I thought the country dances were awfully funny, and I'm afraid I disgraced myself at the first one by laughing when I heard them calling off the dances. Half the time, I couldn't make out what the man was saying anyhow, and it seemed so ridiculous to be told what to do when we'd been taught to dance from the time we were very young, and we knew what to do!

I enjoyed lumbering very much, and I learned to do all the jobs, from cutting the trees to making them into railroad ties and lumber, but after a while, I began to feel it was time to move on to something else. So I sold my sawmill, and I went to the Lakehead, the twin cities of Port Arthur and Fort William (Thunder Bay), where I took this course at the business college. After I got through they asked me to stay on for the summer and take the place of the teachers who were away on vacation. Well, I'd been only there for a few days, when one of the regular staff came over to me and said, very snippy, 'Don't work so hard.' I told her I wasn't and she said, 'You must be. The girl who had that job before you took a day and a half to do it, and you're through in the middle of the afternoon, and looking for something more to do.' So I said, 'Perhaps it's because I don't talk.' I don't know if she liked it or not, but I didn't care. What she was calling working hard was nothing at all to me after my years working in the bush.

After that job ran out, I got a job at a very stylish women's tailor shop down on Queen Street. They supplied all the wealthy women in town, and they had engaged a mademoiselle somebody from Paris, to be in charge of this dressmaking. Even in those days they didn't make anything for less than $200. I'd been there for, I don't know how many weeks, when we got our pay cheques. I saw this elderly woman who did the fancy work quietly weeping over in the corner so I went over and asked her what was wrong. She said, 'Look at my cheque! I haven't got enough to pay for the next week's living, and I have a sister who's an invalid.' I looked at her cheque and said, 'What is the usual amount?' So she told me, and there was a whole day's pay cut off. I said, 'Well, why's that?' And she told me it was because Monday was a holiday and they'd cut the full pay off for that. Well, I wasn't going to put up with that, so I started off down to the office to tell them what I thought about it. Well, there was nobody there; they had all skipped before anybody had a chance to look at their pay cheques. I never went back again.

I worked at Eaton's for a while then, and the girls working

behind the counters were getting $2.75 a week. A week, not a day! Those girls were usually crowded into some rooming house where room and board was $2.25 and they had to share the room with one or two others girls. That left them 50 cents to spend on everything else. Can you imagine? That just goes to show you how hard it was for women in those days. I was one of the lucky ones."

ARTHUR COHEN

Arthur Cohen was born in Toronto in 1880, the son of a Jewish immigrant from Poland. Arthur grew up to study law at the University of Toronto, and he went on from there to become Canada's first theatre-chain operator, a fully fledged show-business tycoon in the early days of motion pictures.

Ladies and Gentlemen, Mr. George Bernard Shaw

"MY FATHER WAS BORN IN 1847, and his name was Rappaport. The young United States Immigration Officer couldn't spell that, so he said to my father, 'Your name is Cohen.' My father worked in the States first, and he used to say that he had been in the lumber business there. Actually, he sold matches on the street! Then he came to Toronto. I was born upstairs in a shoe store at 59 Queen Street West.

I remember when I was a boy, the streetcars were pulled by horses, and every place there was a hill they used to keep two extra horses to attach to the other two, so they could make it up the hill. Then they'd unhitch them, and take them down to the bottom to wait for the next car. In the winter, the passengers used to get out and push to help the horses. I can remember, too, when the tracks were laid for the new electric railway, and the wires were put up overhead. Our city roads were mostly macadam; they were made of dirt and chopped stones. The prisoners used to have to chop stones when they were sent to jail, and those stones kept the dirt from becoming mud.

Queen Street then was one of the main business streets, just as good as Yonge Street today. It was paved with blocks of cedar. The sidewalk was made of big slabs of wood. I remember when they tore it up us kids used to stand there to grab the pennies that had fallen through the cracks.

In 1900 I had a chance to go to London, England, on a cattle boat. At that time, George Bernard Shaw had never had any of his plays performed in London. Somehow or other I got a copy of his *Plays Pleasant and Unpleasant*. He had written them, you see, but couldn't get them published. There was *Candida, You Never Can Tell*, and *Mrs. Warren's Profession*. Anyway, I brought them to the attention of two of my professors at the University of Toronto. They said they had never heard of Bernard Shaw, and they were delighted with his plays. For years after this, whenever they lectured on Shaw, Professor Alexander and Professor Keyes always said they were introduced to Shaw by Arthur Cohen of the class of '03. That was nice of them, because what I really wanted to be in life was a writer and a playwright.

As far as I can remember, there was no anti-Semitism in downtown Toronto when I was a boy. In the neighbourhood where I lived, we had immigrants from everywhere, and we had every religion and all the colours of the world too. Just walk down the street, and you'd hear a dozen different languages being spoken. I never ran into it in school, or university, but I *did* come face to face with it when I got out in the business world.

When I graduated in law in 1906, I won the first prize, and I was a gold medallist in law. And do you know that I couldn't join the Lawyers' Club? They didn't admit Jews! Well, I thought that was funny. I never experienced it in the poor neighbourhood where I grew up, or in school, but here I was, barred from belonging to a Club by supposedly educated and enlightened men."

GEORGE M. ROBINSON

George M. Robinson was born in Halifax, Nova Scotia, in 1871, and this conversation with him took place in 1963 when he was ninety-two years old.

As a boy, George did most of his growing up around the livery stable run by his father, and very often he found himself pressed into service as a coach driver when some visiting celebrity came to town. One of the favourite people he met this way was another George, the Prince of Wales, who later became George V. The Prince was with one of the warships in Halifax Harbour as a midshipman, and suddenly young George, the stable boy, found himself coachman to George, the Prince!

The First Sight-seeing Service in Canada

"IN FACT, the first time I drove the Prince, I said, 'Pardon me, Sir, I'm not in the habit of driving royalty. I don't know how to talk to you.' He said, 'My name's George.' 'Well,' I said, 'I have no intention of calling you George.' So I settled on 'Sir': Yes Sir, No Sir. Like that.

We got very friendly during the two years I was drivin' him around here. One time we were on a fishin' trip and he was a very heavy cigarette smoker y'know. He said, 'You don't seem to be smokin'.' I said, 'No, I never got started.' He gave me a package and said, 'Oh, a little cigarette smoke will never hurt you.' I smoked them all before the day was over, and boy was I sick!

I found him very very nice to talk to. There was no airs about him at all. On one trip we went out to a club on the St. Margaret's Bay Road, about twelve miles from Halifax. He had a little fore-and-after peak cap, a shootin' cap with the ribbons on the top, y'know. He said, 'How about swappin' hats?' I said, 'You're quite welcome to this one, Sir.' I had a larger head than he had so he put newspaper in mine. And I was goin' round all day with this little hat on top of my head. So about six o'clock, we climbed back up, and he took the reins again. He drove it out himself y'see, and he drove it back too. I'd be just sittin' there beside him. When we got to the dockyard, he says, 'If it's all the same to you, I'll keep your hat, and you keep mine.' Then he marched aboard the ship with my old straw hat on. His hat was no good to me at all.

Well, I knew he was goin' away the next day and, since I had done considerable drivin' for him, I was more worried about not gettin' paid than anything else. So I made out the bill, went up to the ship, and went to the boatslip, which was next to the dock-yard. I should have got a man to take me, but I just took the boat and rowed out, and there was a half a dozen ships out there, so I called out, 'Where's the *Thrush*?' They said, 'Oh, she's in at the dock coaling.' So I rowed in to the dock, tied the boat up to the rope ladder, and climbed up onto the ship. Sometime before that there were a couple of suspicious characters around town, and the detectives found that they had a lot of explosive stuff in their quarters on Barrington Street, so the rumour was that they were goin' to blow up the Prince's ship. So, anyway, when I got aboard I saw a note there that nobody would be allowed on without a pass. But I wanted my money so I walked past, and went right on, till I found the Prince's quarters. I knocked at the door. The secretary came out. I said, 'I got a bill here for the Prince.' 'Who let you aboard?' he says. I said, 'Nobody let me aboard. I just came in over the side.' Well, he sure was surprised! 'Came right in over the side of a warship?' So I said, 'I don't know anythin' about naval rules, but that's how I came.' He called the guards and gave them a bawling out and then he ordered them to cut my boat adrift and put me ashore. I felt like givin' him a punch!

In later years when he died, he was George V by then, I sent a letter of sympathy to the palace in London. I got letters back from, I think, all the Kings, Queens, Princesses, and Princes—I must have got about twenty-five different letters.

We used to have some bad fires here in Halifax in those days, and I remember that the Union Protection Corps was a salvage unit in the Halifax Fire Department. Everything then was volun-teer. The UPC boys had a wagon of their own and we used to sup-ply the horses for them and keep it at our stable. Every time the bell rang in my bedroom, I or somebody else would have to jump up and get the horses, and go to this fire. One morning the fire alarm came and I was the first one to get there. I got down to South Park Street, and the smoke was comin' out the top windows and there was some old ladies up at the top of the house. Me and Joe Fulse went up and got these old ladies out and one woman said she had some money and wanted to get it. I said, 'You got no time to get it.' The smoke was so bad I grabbed somethin' and put it in my mouth to keep from chokin' and we carried the two ladies out. By the time I got down a big crowd of people was there with torches and one thing or another. Everybody started to laugh, and I didn't know what they were laughin' at. I carried the lady next door and the laugh started up again when I came back out. Someone yelled, 'What you got in your mouth?' I pulled it out, and it was the old lady's bloomers!

There was no pay for anybody in the UPC, but it was such a famous company that almost every alderman was a member. They never went to a fire, these fellas, and every fire they missed, they were charged fifty cents and that's the money that kept the company goin'!

I made a trip to New York in about 1900 and they had those big double-decker buses there, with teams of horses pulling them, taking people around to see the sights. I was quite impressed, and when I got back home I hitched a team up to a five-seated buckboard, and started showing people different things around the city. That was the first sight-seeing service in Canada!

When Lord Stanley, the Stanley Cup man, was Governor General of Canada he came here on an official visit. He sent word up to our stable that he'd like to get a carriage, so I went up and got him. He wanted to see Sir Frederick Fraser, the head of the first blind school in Canada. I knew Sir Frederick very well so I drove Lord Stanley down to the Blind School to visit. Then I drove Lady Stanley down to visit a friend in the south end, and we had Lord Stanley's big coachman on the carriage. Big fella, who weighed about 200 pounds. We both had beaver hats on, y'know. I left Lady Stanley at the house and she said to come back in an hour. Well, I thought the coachman, who had never been here before, would like to see something of Halifax, so I took him down by Pine Hill to show him our Natural Park. We drove down the Serpentine Drive and got off, and when we got back the carriage wasn't there. The horses had ran away and all of Lady Stanley's stuff was in the carriage with them! So I started running up the hill, and I hauled off the coat and the beaver hat, and I flung them down in the bush, and kept goin' in my shirtsleeves. I met a boy with a couple of cushions, and I said, 'Them's my cushions. Leave 'em down here.' I kept on, and I met up with the carriage on Barrington Street. Then after I got *it* back it took me about twenty minutes to find the coachman. He got lost in the woods. When I found him I got some grass and wiped the sweat off the horses, got my hat and coat on, and drove back to get Lady Stanley. Just as I drove up she came out the door, pulled out her watch and said, 'My, you're right on time.'"

J. J. BYRNE

J. J. Byrne was a prospector in Ontario who found what he was looking for, and, unlike so many others, managed to hold on to it.

When I met "J. J." he was eighty-eight years old, living in a posh Toronto apartment, and still going every day to the offices of the mining development company that he founded.

To Whom It May Concern— This Is Cobalt

"My father and my uncles, two of them, were into mining and that's about all they ever talked about. Listening to them, I developed a tremendous interest in mining, even as a child. That's the thing about miners; when they're not actually doing it, they're *talking* about it!

My parents wanted me to finish school and go on to university, but no sir, I couldn't wait to get goin'. Just as soon as I was sixteen, I told them that was it! They argued and everything else, but finally they broke down and said I could have a year off, but I'd have to go back to school after that.

A job was found for me as a timekeeper at a new mining site in Sudbury. They were calling this new mine 'the Creighton', and they were sinkin' a hand-steel shaft on the north rim of one of the biggest ore bodies, I guess, in the whole damn country. You never know what you're gonna get, but as it turns out, that Creighton mine was a real winner; it's still goin' today and it'll be goin' for a long time yet. And as a matter of fact, I helped bore the auger holes for the first headframe that was built at the Creighton mine. A man named Ritchie was the framer, and he would spot the holes with one of those long-handled, old-fashioned augers with cranks on 'em, and I'd sit on the timber, and bore these holes. I was also the timekeeper, but I could do all that part in three hours.

87

Then I hit the boss there for a job underground. He just laughed, and said, 'We haven't got very much room down there yet. We've just finished the shaft down to 60 feet. We're cutting a station, and getting ready to drive across the ore body to the foot wall.' 'Well,' I said, 'that'll be a good place for me to help on one of the machines.' Well, anyway, my dad came down to visit me on a Sunday, and he and Uncle Bob must have got their heads together and decided to teach me a lesson. Uncle Bob called me and said, 'We got a job for you, underground. Ten hours, and if you stick your head up over that collar there before those ten hours are up, you'll be fired. That's the rule here.' I said that suited me fine.

Well, my father thought that workin' underground for a while would drive me back to school fast. It didn't! It just gave me an appetite for the whole business and I stayed there, underground, till 1904. I was twenty, by this time, and a full-fledged miner, and I wanted to explore other fields.

Right at that time, Sault Ste. Marie was just starting to open up, so I boarded the train and headed out. The Canadian Sault had about two thousand people in it at that time, and Queen Street was one long, muddy mess. Now the Sault, at that time, was the headquarters for one of the most exciting, and visionary men that this country had ever seen, or ever will see again! His name was Francis Henry Clerg and he was a real Northern tycoon. He was building railroads like the Algoma Central that would open the country up. He had gold mines, iron mines, sawmills, and lumber camps. The fact was, he *was* Mr. Northern Ontario. *Everybody* up there depended on Clerg. Everything revolved around him. But wouldn't you know that the very year, 1904, when I arrived at the Sault, the bubble burst, and Clerg went bankrupt! It caused a terrible panic. People weren't able to get their money, and they began to riot. It got so bad the Queen's Own Rifles had to be called in from Toronto to quiet things down.

While all this was happening, Mr. Smith, who was the MPP for the Sault, was pleading in the Legislature for money to rescue the situation. But because he belonged to the Opposition nobody on the Government side was very sympathetic to him. But Smith put on a filibuster that went on for days and finally the government came through with two million dollars. That was enough to pay all the wages that the men were owed, as well as all the merchants who were owed money. I can remember when Smith returned from Toronto; he was carried on the shoulders of half a dozen men, and then he was put in a carriage and driven down Queen Street. Everybody was callin' for a speech, so he got up and, boy, was he a good orator. He was the hero of the day. You could pay off a lot of people in 1904 with two million dollars!

Now just about this time, in another part of Northern Ontario, a prospector named Fred LaRose was searching around without too much luck. The way the story goes, this fox came sniffing around where Fred was, and wouldn't go away. So Fred threw his prospector's pick at him, and when he went over to get it, he noticed it had hit this rock, and made a big scratch on it. When Fred examined the scratch, it showed a heavy concentration of silver. And it was from that scratch that the big silver boom started, and the town of Cobalt was born in 1904.

The area didn't even have a name then. There were five or six men there, including the McMartins and the Timminses, Willet G. Miller, the provincial geologist for Ontario, and another fella by the name of Cyril Knight, who I knew very well. Anyway, all these fellas were trying to pick a name. The reason they finally decided on the name 'Cobalt' was because you could see this mineral, cobalt, all over the place and they decided to call it that. Somebody got a couple of boards and nailed them to a tree, and Noah Timmins grabbed some coal from the fire and marked on the board: 'To whom it may concern: This is Cobalt.' And that's the true story of how Cobalt got its name.

I got into the prospecting myself after that, and I had a lot of success with it. There's something about discovering something, and then following it through till it becomes a mine, that gives you a real sense of having done something worth while. I'll say this: I'd much rather be up there in the bush with a pickaxe, than goin' down to an office every day in Toronto."

SUE LOWTHER

Isolation from the Mainland has always been a blessing and a curse for the people of Prince Edward Island. Too easy access by outsiders would have the effect of destroying the island's pastoral tranquillity while, on the other hand, easy access to the Mainland makes life easier for those who bask in their island paradise. Communication with the outside world by modern technology was first established on December 11, 1852, when an underwater telegraph cable was connected to P.E.I. This is an important date to Mrs. Sue Lowther, for it was on this day her mother was born, and her mother would grow up to marry the man who operated the telegraph station. Sue herself was born at that station at Cape Traverse in 1874, and by the time she was eight years old, her father had taught her and her brother how to operate the telegraph key that linked P.E.I. with the outside world.

A Little Bit of Everything

"THERE WAS ONLY FOURTEEN MONTHS between me and my brother. We grew up like twins and whatever one did the other had to do, so we both started using the telegraph key at the same time. The operators at the other stations thought nothing of the fact that the messages they were getting came from seven- and eight-year-old children. They were used to us. They knew we were always around the office with our father anyway. We practically grew up in there. We opened at eight o'clock in the morning, and closed at eight in the night, and we'd be practising all the time. We caught on to the code very quickly—the dots and the dashes—and we got real good at it too.

At times when we were visiting other places by train, I would sit near the telegraph key at the railway station, and listen to all the messages coming through and going out. I always knew everything that was going on. Of course we were sworn to secrecy, and we couldn't tell anything.

We weren't paid of course, but my father got thirty-five dollars a month, and he had to be there all the time from the time the station opened till it closed—twelve hours. We used to spell him off at the key, and send and take the ordinary messages, but he had to deal with all the important things like the stock market and so on. We had nothing to do with the stocks at all, because if there was just one letter astray, it would be just too bad for him. We were allowed to send out business messages though, as well as news of receptions, births and deaths, and marriages. A little bit of everything.

When the ice boats were going across in the wintertime, we'd send a message to the other side saying that they left at, say, eight o'clock, and they'd expect to make the trip all right, the ice is good, and the wind is in their favour. Then we'd tell them how long they were expected to take—two or four hours—if they don't meet with too much ice. What they'd have to do, you see, was pull the boats over the ice parts and then when they'd come to the water, they'd jump in, and row, then jump out again, when they came to more ice.

There'd be three boats leave at a time, and they always went with the tide. Six men to a boat and they'd have straps over their shoulders for pulling, you see. The boats would have the mail, some freight maybe, and a few passengers. When the boats landed on the other side in New Brunswick, the men would stay overnight and then they'd make the return trip the next day. I never made the trip myself but my father did, many times. He was in charge of the service, you see.

Our office was closed in the summertime, because they didn't think it was needed then. I kept on there until 1904, when I was thirty. My father died at that time and that was the end of it for me, because T. C. James, the Superintendent in Charlottetown, said he didn't want any women working in that office. He wanted all men. Well now, in Crapeau there was a lady there who was an operator but there was nothing said about that. I never bothered making a fuss though, because I had decided to go into training for a nurse.

I stayed in training for five years, and then worked around Massachusetts for the next fifteen years or so, and I didn't come back to P.E.I. until they sent for me at home. My mother was alone by this time, and I made up my mind to stay nursing around where we lived at Cape Traverse, so I could look after her. I wasn't married, you see, so that was all right.

I was engaged when I was a lot younger. I was nineteen. The boy was twenty-one, and he was a telegraph operator. He wanted to get married then, but I said no. I wanted to wait until I was twenty-one. So he went away and married someone else and I didn't get married until I was in my late sixties. I didn't really want to get married all those years, though, because I didn't think I could be a very good nurse if I did. I always thought more of my patients than any of the young men I went around with.

There was an awful flu epidemic broke out here in P.E.I. one time, and people were dying with it, and everything. I nursed right through that, and I never caught it and this is why. One of the doctors said to me, 'When you come off a case, go out and have a big beefsteak dinner. Go home then, and take a bath and go straight to bed and stay there till the next morning.' I did what he told me, and I never caught it. I forget the year of that epidemic. I think it was after the First World War.

We had wonderful doctors then. They'd say, 'You know what to do. Go ahead and do it.' I never lost a mother, and I never lost a patient except those that were pretty nearly dead when I got there. I was a midwife too, you see. My grandmother was, and so was my mother, but they didn't have the nurses' training to go along with it. Nursing seemed to be in my blood. I didn't give up nursing till I was nearly eighty. I just couldn't refuse anybody who was sick.

I'm ninety-seven now, and I feel good. I could still send a tele-graph message if I had to. It's like your ABC's. You never forget."

CAPTAIN EDWIN MCWILLIAMS

The men who go down to the sea in ships are a special breed of men. There's something that sets them apart from those who spend their life on land. They are tough and gentle at the same time; cheerful and optimistic on the one hand but fatalistic and realistic on the other. They live every day as though it might be their last ... and well it might be for those who take their living from the fickle sea.

Captain Edwin McWilliams was born in 1884 on Prince Edward Island and the sea has always been his life.

Thin Ice

"LIFE WAS PRETTY GOOD in the days before the big ferries went back and forth to the Mainland. We were isolated, I guess, but most of us managed to take our families across to the Mainland every once in a while. In the winter though it was tougher. When the Gulf was clogged with ice, we had what we called 'ice boats'.

Now these were really something; these boats were specially built to be hauled across the spots where it was all ice and then to go back into the water where there was no ice. It was a real prize for a man to get a job on these ice boats, and the day he could qualify he was presented with his harness for pulling. It was like getting a diploma and was a cause for real celebration. I got my harness in 1905. There was an election that year and my father had always voted Conservative. I was working for him and when election day was coming along he said, 'Will you come up and vote?' I said, 'I ain't got a vote.' Anyway, when the day came I went up. It was an open vote then, no secret ballot. You just went in and they asked you who you were going to vote for and you told them. When they asked me I said, 'I'm voting for Captain Joe Reed.' They never said, 'Aye, yes, or no.' That was a Liberal vote I cast even though I wasn't entitled to a vote. You see, they had promised me a harness if I voted for them. The harness—or strap

93

—was put over your shoulder and it was tied back to the boats and you hauled on it just like a horse. When they gave you the harness that meant they were giving you the job, so it was really something. That winter I started hauling the boats.

When I started first there was three men to each side of the boat. The captain went ahead to pick out the way. There would be five boats in a party, and the captain, so that made thirty-one men altogether. Then it went up to eight boats and forty-nine men. It was the same thing over at Tormentine, on the New Brunswick side; eight boats going one way and eight boats going the other. The next day we'd go back and they'd go the other way. We stayed overnight, of course. We got our meals and our bed over there for seventy-five cents and it was even cheaper than that when I started in 1905. I don't know how they did it but they fed us good.

The last winter we crossed, the captain of the other team was lost. He wore glasses and shouldn't have been on the boats. The first day he went across was fine. Going back the ice was thin and the boats were breaking through. That day the captain was in the centre of the boat; there was always one man on the bow, one on the stern, and one in the centre. The tide was squeezing this broken ice together and the ice caught him and his strap got caught on this ice as it came together. It pulled him right down out of sight, and there was nothing we could do.

The ice boats themselves were wonderful rigs. They were made of wood wrapped in metal, and were as good in the water as they were on the ice. If we struck a good long lead of water we could do the fourteen miles across the strait in about two hours and forty minutes. Sometimes, though, we had a lot of ice and this broken-up stuff and it'd take eight hours. We did that six days a week.

The big ferry boats were put into service in 1917 and the ice boats weren't needed any more, but you know, I've still got one of those boats stowed away up the beach there. Her wood and the metal wrapping is in good shape and it wouldn't take much work to put her back on the ice again. I'd like that."

JULIA BREWSTER

Julia Brewster was a teacher in those far-off days when the teacher was the undisputed figure of authority in her classroom. Her word was law, not only for the students, but for the parents as well. Her career was in small schools, some of them one-room, and she feels they were better than the huge consolidated schools of today. Miss Brewster was born at Dorchester Crossing, New Brunswick, and she taught for thirty-five years.

One Woman That I Can't Boss

"IN MY DAY the teacher was respected and very often loved. I'm in my nineties now and it's many years since I taught school, but there's never a summer goes by that I don't have some of my old students come to visit me. They sit and we talk over what we did and relive those days. I remember one summer in particular that this boy came and we had a great long talk and he said, 'I certainly remember one of the punishings you gave me.' I said, 'Yes Walter, did you deserve it?' He said, 'Yes I did, Miss Brewster.'

There was that about it. You didn't give the punishment until the person deserved it, and then when I gave it I didn't just pat them on the hand like that. I had a little strap and I didn't want them to want that strap again.

There was one case when I was teaching at Riverside. I had grades one, two, and three there. It was reported to me that this boy was stealing apples from a neighbouring orchard on the way home. I didn't punish him or anything. I just said, 'You're to stay in a half-hour till the whole school is gone, until we get this stealing problem fixed up.' And then, the second afternoon that he was staying in, I heard a great big thump on my door. I answered it and there was a great big man with a great big whip in his hand and he said, 'You're keeping Weldon in?' I said, 'Yes, Mr. Collins, I am.' He said, 'I want him to come.' I said, 'Well, that's just too bad. I don't. He's been stealing apples and he's being punished.' He said, 'Well, I need him at home and I want him to come now.' I said, 'Well, that's just too bad because he isn't going now, and he isn't going the rest of the week.' We looked at each other straight in the eye for a while. Then the man turned away and walked out the door.

After that I never had better supporters at that school than that man and his family. He said, 'I guess I've struck one woman that I can't boss.'

I think there was an awful lot to be said for the small schools. Many of our greatest people have come from the small schools. I can think of an awful lot of boys and girls that I taught in my life who lived from a mile to two miles from the schoolhouse. They lived and flourished and got their professions by walking to school every day.

The only thing I'd like about teaching today is the money. You see, in my day, the teacher was looked upon by those who had to pay for it as something of a necessary evil. My first school in Elgin was a poor district and I remember that at Christmastime after teaching for four months and after paying my board, I had only ten dollars left over. But it was the first and the best ten dollars I ever earned. They get as much now for a week as I got in a whole year. We worked long hours with no equipment, only a blackboard, a box of chalk, and our imagination. You paid for all the little extras out of your own pocket or made them out of cardboard or whatever.

You know, people were very serious about religion in those days. For my first job, I had to go into an almost 100 per cent Catholic district. When they'd asked me my religion I said, 'I'm a Methodist.' The lady on the school board said to me, 'You go right ahead, Miss Brewster, and do just as you were taught. I've got a little boy in that school and I'll risk you doing him any harm. It'll be good.'

Do you realize what a wonderful thing she did there—for those times? It was unheard of then for a Protestant like me to be hired by a Catholic school, or the other way around for that matter.

When I went to sign my contract a man came into the room and asked me, 'Are you the new schoolmarm?' I said, 'Yes sir, I am.' He said, 'Are you a Protestant or a Mickey?' I said, 'I'm a Protestant. I'm a Methodist.' He said, 'Aren't you afraid that we'll murder you up here among the Catholics?' I said, 'No sir, I'm not one bit scared.' Then he took to laughing and said, 'No, no, no. We wouldn't harm you.' Well, when I went back I told Mr. Carty—I was boarding at his house—and he went down to that man's house the next day and said to him, 'Miss Brewster is different from the rest of us. She's had a different bringing up and I want it understood that while she is here, if there's one single word or deed to bother her in any way, that person will answer to me.'

The Cartys were Catholics—very nice, very wise people."

JEFFREY EDWARD BLAKE

Jeffrey Edward Blake joined the old North West Mounted Police in 1903 when he was twenty-one years old and he stayed with the Force all through those years when the West was being settled. By the time he retired he had attained the rank of Staff Sergeant. The early West of Canada was not the West of the movies perhaps but it was the Frontier and there was a need for law and order. That's what the NWMP provided.

The Ounce of Prevention

"THE FORCE GOT A NAME CHANGE IN 1904, the year after I joined. We were just the North West Mounted Police up till then, but in that year the Royal was added—RNWMP—and it stayed that way till 1920, when it became the RCMP. Back when I joined, once you had taken your oath of office and your oath of allegiance to the Sovereign and had signed the document, you were earning the princely sum of fifty cents a day.

We had a lot of dealings with the Indians out there and I always found them trustworthy. If they said they'd do something, they always lived up to their bargain. I couldn't say the same for the white men who were on the wrong side of the law. We had cattle rustlers and thieves . . . the whole lot. It didn't pay to turn your back on them for a second—they'd as soon shoot you as not.

I remember in December one year there was a break from the Calgary guardroom of a man who was under sentence of death for murder. We were at the barracks in Macleod at the time, and that night another constable and I were on duty. We were the men who had to go to any emergency that came up. Just about nine o'clock we were having a beer in the canteen—five cents a schooner then—and the Corporal rushed in and told us of the break from the guardroom. He ordered us to get our horses and told someone else to get down to Calgary and clean the rest of the

Force out of the bars and get them back here on the double. We had our horses in no time and set out on separate ways.

I wasn't out long when a storm came up and I got completely lost. About 4 in the morning I landed at the back door of Corporal Gegin's outpost, and he hauled me inside. Everything I had was frozen solid on me. We got the clothes peeled off and he stuck a bottle of rum in my face and said, 'Take a drink.' I think that was the longest drink of rum I ever had in my life. It hit me like a club and I was out and I didn't wake up till late that day. Needless to say we didn't get our man that day, or for a while after.

One Sunday, though, they decided to put a big sweep on in Calgary—they searched every building for him. In one empty barn they found evidence that someone had been lying in the haystack recently, so they went into the house and Corporal Biggs started down into the cellar. A bullet slammed into the frame where he was going down, so he got back up fast. The rest of the men closed in then and smoked him out and took him alive.

The funny thing about that one is that in all this excitement the house went on fire, and there was a lot of damage. The owner put in a claim for damages and he ended up being charged for hiding an escaped convict, and was sentenced to something like two years. If he had kept his mouth shut there probably wouldn't have been anything said. The escaped murderer was brought back to jail and hanged the following Monday week. So that was that.

A constable's horse then was his most important asset, and although it was supposed to be impossible for one man to have his own horse—the horses were detailed to you—there was one horse, Dandy was his name, that I really liked. He had an aversion to civilians. When they were around he went wild, but with a man in uniform he was as calm as could be. So after a while Dandy was put out for auction, as all the horses were after a certain time in service. When the civilians came over to look at him he'd tear the stall apart, so they didn't want anything to do with him. I was able to buy him for a very good price.

It was easier to get a horse for yourself than it was to take a wife. You had to apply for permission to get married and in your application you had to apply for double rations, because how married could you get on fifty cents a day? But it was very much an unmarried Force anyway, when I joined first—mostly all single adventurous young men who lived in barracks. Most had gone

West in search of excitement. This was the frontier, after all, and it certainly wasn't much of a life for a woman to be mixed up in.

We had an epidemic of smallpox that hit the barracks in the winter of 1903-4. It hit just two of our Indian prisoners, but the whole place was put under quarantine and the men who were on duty at the guardhouse were ordered to stay there till it was over —and they were under canvas, in winter. The sick prisoners meanwhile were taken to the pest-house outside of town where they were kept nice and warm while the guards stayed where they were, shivering under canvas till it was all over. Every community had a pest-house in those days. There were no such things as isolation hospitals.

Eventually, in later years, I became a Staff Sergeant and that's what I was when I retired. It's been a grand experience for me. We were the law of Western Canada at the time, and if I do say so myself, we did a good job. Hollywood may have over-romanticized what we were—there weren't too many of us riding around and singing on horseback—but they did one thing, they made the Mounties' name known around the world. There were good times and bad times, exciting times, and long stretches where nothing happened at all, but the North West Mounted played a very important role in the settling of Western Canada. We were there and we were visible. You might say we were the ounce of prevention."

DR. MABEL RUTTLE

Dr. Mabel Ruttle was born in Boissevain, Manitoba, in 1896. She was a sickly child with a desire for education. Her father believed in her ambitions but her mother was sure that such thoughts were nonsense for girls, whose main purpose was to help out around the farm, to get married, and to have children.

Queer Little Country Girl

"BY THE TIME I WAS TWELVE YEARS OLD, I already had gone through double pneumonia, nephritis, and tuberculosis. I managed to get through these things, but when I was fifteen and in high school I developed the nephritis again, and was out for another while.

My father was a wonderful man. My mother had no understanding at all. She couldn't accept the fact that I couldn't do anything, while they all had to work so hard. There'd I be, sitting around reading, while they never stopped working. I was weak with the tuberculosis, and needed all the fresh air and sunshine I could get. Mother couldn't seem to realize this, but Father did. He was building a roof on the barn at that time, so he got me up there with him every day to hold the nails for him. I guess that satisfied Mother for a while. At least I was holding nails. It took me ten years to get through high school, but finally I did and I went to Normal College and taught for a few years.

Well, the teaching wasn't enough. I just had to get to university. I was able to save a little money after a few years, and I got down to the University of Toronto, where one of my teachers was Miss Addison, a marvellous woman. My application had written on it by somebody that I had tuberculosis, and shouldn't be in college, and that girls had no business being there anyhow. Miss Addison saw this, and her fighting instinct was aroused. She found a room near the campus for this queer little country girl. She took care of me that year and found a very good doctor for me.

I had, in the meantime, developed trouble with my appendix and the doctors wouldn't touch it because they thought it might be tubercular. She said, 'Look, there are two chances. One is that you do have tuberculosis of the appendix, and if they open you up, you will probably die. The second, is that you may not have it at all. It may just be a true appendix problem. Those are the choices. What will you do? You can probably live as you are, dragging yourself around, or you can get it out and be a person. What do you want to do?' I said, 'Let's get it out.' I did, and I was all right. I went on to get my PH D, married a medical doctor, and had two fine children. But, you know, it was very very difficult for girls to go on to advanced education in those days. It was fine for them to be teachers or nurses, but if they wanted to go beyond that it was felt that they had no business doing it. A woman's place was supposed to be in the home, having children and all those other things. Being a teacher or nurse was okay, because they felt that this was just a little extra training for being a mother. I was bucked every step of the way, and so were all the women at that time who wanted to do something out of the *ordinary*.

At home, I was resented because I could do nothing. Other people thought I was strange or queer, because I wasn't just like them. The history of women who became educated despite the barriers imposed by their working-class backgrounds is one that has to be told, and told with the understanding of the positions taken by both sides in those times. Later, I could understand how my family and those other people felt about me, even if they had no comprehension of why I was the way I was. One of my teachers one time was teaching us a history of the Franco-Prussian War, which she reminded us was written by a German. She told us that she had studied in France, and had studied a history of the same war written by a Frenchman; it hadn't seemed like the same war. Two different points of view, you see."

ELIZABETH POPOFF BASSIOVE

Life in a new land can be a pretty frightening prospect for anyone, but when the language is different from your own, and the people regard you with suspicion and even fear, the outlook is dim indeed! That was the Canada that a lot of Doukhobors came to in the latter part of the nineteenth century. They were on the run from Russia, where life had become intolerable for them. In exchange for opening up the West, Canada promised them the freedom to live the way they wanted to live and to worship the way they pleased. They asked for nothing more. The Popoffs came with their group to Saskatchewan in 1899; baby Elizabeth was born when her parents were fashioning a house with a few sticks, and a great deal of mud.

All the Other Doukhobors Were Farmers

"MY PARENTS CAME ACROSS THE OCEAN under terrible circumstances. My mother was pregnant with me at the time, and they were on the boat for twenty-seven days; and then, when they were unloaded in Quebec, they were quarantined for a month because there was smallpox. There were over two thousand on the ship. Mother was very sick, but Dad stayed all right. They had to do their own cooking and the water was rationed. They were jammed in like cattle, and in fact, it was a cattle boat they were on. They just made up bunks down in the hold, and that's where they stayed most of the way over.

When they got out of quarantine, they split up into groups, and followed their different leaders. They took any kind of work they could find. That was when they built the huts out of sticks and mud and straw.

Oh, I remember the mud houses so well. They were made of logs and sticks, plastered with mud and whitewashed. Summer fallow was put on the roof instead of shingles, and the rain ran off just fine.

Once we got our own homestead we all took part in the work: the thrashing and stooking and milking. It was very hard work, real pioneering. That's what I remember most about my childhood—hard work.

I must say though, that it wasn't really good when I was young. I didn't know why at the time, but now I *do* know. The other children, and even the teachers, seemed to try to make us feel out of place. You see, my parents had no money at all, so we weren't dressed as good as some of the kids, and the kids, along with some of the teachers, would look down on us. Our parents were looked down on too, because they were Russian immigrants and had customs that the others didn't understand. We spoke Russian, of course, and we had no English at all when we started school. The teacher wouldn't look at us at all! She just couldn't be bothered! Our parents dressed different too, and because they only had time enough to work they couldn't, of course, know what the fashions for clothes were in this country. So Mother would just make us a dress the same way she had always done and we had to wear it even though it didn't look like the dresses the other children were wearing. And because she had no time for buttons and buttonholes, we just used safety pins. The teacher would say, 'Well, sew it on yourself,' and we'd try, but the button-hole was usually too big for the button, or it was in the wrong place or something. We must have been a mess!

In Blaine Lake where we lived and where my father had a blacksmith shop and a small mill as well as his farm it wasn't just Doukhobors. We had the English and French, Germans, Ukraini-ans, and everything. I had more of a chance to mix than most of the Doukhobors because they pretty well stayed to themselves on the farms, while Dad's blacksmith shop threw us in with a lot of people. I can speak Ukrainian just as well as Russian or English. Our parties were a mixture of everything: square dance, schot-tische, heel and toe, and *everything!* Boy, they *really* were the good old days.

Like I said, all the other Doukhobors were farmers. The taxes were low then and they had cows and chickens, and lots to eat, so they were happy in Canada—happier and better off than they ever had been in Russia.

The big day of the year for them was always St. Peter's Day.

That's the day they celebrated the time in Russia when their fore-fathers made the decision to burn the arms of war, and embrace peace forever. There'd be a great feast with home-made bread, all kinds of meats and vegetables and fruit, and singing. It's the big-gest day of the year for us, St. Peter's Day, the burning of the arms, but it is a strictly religious day too, with church services, and different people making speeches about our past, which is a pretty sad one when you think of Russia.

We had a very simple religion; no big churches or anything like that. We just had our services from house to house. We'd take turns. The word 'Doukhobor' means 'spiritual wrestler for the bet-ter of your soul, your heart, and your mind'. It's too bad that over the years, the only thing you'd see in newspapers about Doukho-bors was naked parades, house burnings, and children being kept out of school. That's not most of us, that's just one radical sect, and we too consider them fanatics. The trouble is, they wouldn't let their children get educated so that when some fellow with a bit of education came along he could twist them to his way of think-ing very easily.

I went back to Russia a few years ago to see the land of my parents. It's better there for my relatives who didn't get away when my parents did, but they're still a long way from being as well off as the Doukhobors who came to Canada. The early days were a terrible struggle, but it was worth it."

THOMAS PATRICK MURRAY

The Irish were among the first settlers of the Madawaska Valley of Ontario. They were poor people from the old country who felt rich when they got here because they had land of their own, warm and cozy log homes, enough food to eat, and clothes to wear.

Thomas Patrick Murray was born in one of these log homes in 1880, near where the town of Madawaska is today. When this interview took place he was ninety-two years old and still going to work every day at the lumber company that he founded himself. He looked back on a life of hard work on the railway and in the lumber camps, and was content to think that maybe, in his lifetime, he did a small share to make Canada a better place to live. He had even found time to take part in the political affairs of his country when, for a period of sixteen years, he served as an MPP in the Government of Ontario.

Out of the Cedar Shanties

"THERE WAS SEVEN OF US IN THE SHANTY and I was about five years old when I first started to think we were pretty well off. We got four meals a day and we slept in a feather bed. There were no schools or churches, and no doctor, but we had sheep, and there was a flour mill at Combermere. As far as we were concerned, we had everything we needed!

Around 1894, when they were building the railroad through here, I got a job as water boy. The railway comin' through was a godsend for a lot of people who came in from all over the countryside off the farms to make a dollar. They worked hard, too, for them dollars. It was all done by hand—no trucks or things like that that they have now to build those grades—just picks, shovels, scrapers, and wheelbarrows. Hard, hard work! Others came in to build the telegraph line and the railroad fences. It was a hard work time. All of it.

I remember there was one fella there, by the name of George W. Leith, who used to pull a scraper. I was water boy on the gang next to the one he worked on. The next time I saw him was years later when he was President of the Northern Temiskaming Railway. I had an awful time tryin' to stay sober; he kept sayin, 'Pour another one for the water boy.' George sure went up in the world. A lot of those people did. James H. Sanderson, who became a Member of Parliament, was another one who came out of there. He was a big Irishman, a section foreman in 1894. After that railroad job Jim Sanderson and his brother went back on the farm and they became the biggest cheese exporters in Canada.

Another fella there was John Wesley Dafoe, who became one of Canada's wisest men. He was a big red-headed boy who got his education in a shack in the Madawaska Valley. The teacher we got there was one of the old, wise Irish schoolmasters and he had a box of books with him that he had brought over from Ireland. When he died they buried him near the church. His shack was there for a long time, and when they tore it down, Dafoe got into this box of books, books written by Cobden and Bright, and all those great writers, *The Way to Build Up a Nation*, and all that stuff, and he studied them from cover to cover. He taught school here for a year and then at Bark Lake. After that he went down to Montreal and got into the newspaper business. In 1923 Mackenzie King took him to the great Imperial Conference, and it was Dafoe who changed the whole setup of the British Empire. The papers at the time said that the man who got his education in a shack at Madawaska was too much for the Oxford scholars.

You just wouldn't believe the kind of men who came out of that stretch of woods in the Madawaska Valley of Ontario—out of the log cabins, and the cedar shanties! But don't get me wrong! We had other kinds too. Not all were great just because they were born in a log cabin!"

PHILIP SCOTT CAMSELL

Philip Scott Camsell was born in the Northwest Territories in 1883, the son of an Englishman who came to Canada as Chief Factor of the Hudson's Bay Company. His mother was a Winnipeg girl who quickly acclimatized herself to life in the harsh northland, and who was quite happy with only an occasional trip to the outside.

Samson

"THE FIRST TRIP TO THE OUTSIDE I remember making was when I was two years old. Actually it was the trip back that I recall best. We came back a different route—up the Mackenzie River, across Great Slave Lake, up to Lake Athabasca, then up to Fort McMurray, which was at the junction of the Athabasca and the Clearwater rivers. Then we came East by York boat to what was called 'The Long Portage', which was the dividing line between the waters flowing into Hudson Bay and those flowing into the Mackenzie basin. This was a twelve-mile portage and the voyageurs used to have to carry these hundred-pound bales of fur across this portage. A load was two of these, two hundred pounds! I've forgotten how many trips they had to make, but it always took them a couple of days to do this twelve miles.

Looking back on that trip with my mother, I don't know how she ever did it. We were coming back from Winnipeg through country like I just described, portages and everything, and she had all of us kids with her, six of us, and we must have been an awful nuisance!

Many years after this trip with my mother, I was on the survey with one little Indian, about five foot nothing, who we called 'Samson', of course. We were doing a three-mile portage, and that was tough enough! We'd carry the stuff a half-mile and then we'd go back for another load. Well, the last half-mile, I was lying down having a rest when Samson comes along. He leaned over and said, 'Are you tired?' I said, 'Well, I have all this oil here,' and before I could do anything he trots off with my load and his, two hundred pounds! He wasn't any more than five feet, but he was strong and very good to me.

Travelling along like that, we always had trouble finding water because we were usually on salt water. So I asked him one day, 'Samson, how far is it to a river?' 'Oh, about five miles,' he said. So when we got up to five miles I said, 'Where's the river?' He says, 'Oh, just about a hundred yards over there.' So I got a pail out and then he said, 'You'd better take a cup. It's a very small river. You gotta dip it out with a cup.' Well, you know, it turned out to be just a spring. You see he didn't make any distinction in his mind between a river like the Mackenzie and a creek, it was all just water to him. But the real point is, he knew exactly where that little spring of fresh water was in all that wilderness.

I was really just a baby when I came out to the Territories on that first trip—and I never came out again till I went back to St. John's College in Winnipeg for the purpose of getting an education. Winnipeg was known as 'Fort Garry' in those days and that's really just about all it was—little more than a fort. It was just one of the Hudson's Bay forts. On our first trip we didn't stay in Fort Garry but we went down to the lower fort which had been built in 1820. It was comparatively new in relation to Fort Garry, and was built by Sir George Simpson for the accommodation of his new wife, Lady Frances Simpson—but she didn't stay very long. She stayed about a year and she hightailed it back to England. That was the last of her as far as Sir George was concerned. But you have Lake Frances, Fort Frances, and all kinds of Franceses named after Sir George's wife, and he was a tough old bird but a very capable administrator. He had charge of all this great territory when he was in his late twenties. He knew nothing about the fur trade because he was in the Hudson's Bay Company office in London. They brought him out here, but their judgment was right. He always travelled with a piper, and I knew the piper's grandson. He lived at Fort Chipewyan. His name was Fraser and he raised a large family, a mixture of Frasers and Cree Indian."

MARY ANN DUGGAN

Mary Ann Duggan was a great trouper and entertainer in the early part of this century in St. John's, Newfoundland. She was everything: singer, dancer, and actress! And there was plenty of entertainment then in St. John's, lots of plays, operettas, and musicals. One of Mary Ann Duggan's favourite people of that era was Johnny Burke, who gained immortality as the author of one of the all-time favourite Newfoundland songs, "The Kelligrew Soiree".

Good Entertainment in St. John's

"THERE WAS GOOD ENTERTAINMENT in St. John's in those days. The big opera companies used to come to town and they always went to the convents and picked twelve or thirteen girls for the parts in the chorus and things like that. Well, one year I was picked as one of the twelve and that's what gave me the taste. After that I was always on the stage. I didn't care about anything else but the theatre.

By the time I was sixteen I had been in chorus lines a lot but I'd never had a real stage part. Well, they decided this one night to try me out by myself because, I suppose, I was kind of a comedian backstage. After the performance, Mr. Power came down and I heard him say to someone, 'See if you can get her.' The lot of us went on down to Burke's, that was kind of a place of meeting for the stage crowd, and everybody was singing and dancing and I was carrying on too when someone said, 'Book her, book her.' Well, I didn't know what they meant, but the first thing I knew I was appearing on the stage with Johnny Burke in *Captain O'Grady*. Then there was *Captain Kidd: The Pet of the Mining Camp* and *H.M.S. Calypso*—we did it down on the docks!

Then Mr. Power, the man who had the theatre, asked me to play in *The Runaway Girl*. The theatre seated about five hundred people and for eight nights we had a packed house! So then we took it to Broad Cove, and the Mechanic's Hall, the Irish Hall, the Queen Theatre, and even on board the big ships. That's when I really got to know Johnny Burke. I'd met him before, of course, down on Water Street. We had kind of a little sideshow there. He was a fine, distinguished-looking man with grey hair, and a lovely smile. I don't think he ever spoke more than a word in his life to anyone but he'd smile at them, and he'd always have a bit of wit to say. He sold these little trinkets along with a little booklet with some of his verses; 'The Kelligrew Soiree' was just one of the hundreds of little verses that he wrote. And he had one of these phonographs there, and a lot of the people would stop and listen. We were good friends till he died during the 1930s. I always think of Johnny Burke when I hear 'The Kelligrew Soiree'.

After my first performance in *The Runaway Girl*, I got a bouquet of flowers presented to me on the stage. I never saw that happen on the stage before that so I didn't know what I was supposed to do. The surprise of it all, just as I was coming off the stage, and getting ready to go back and take my bow! There was this great big basket of flowers. I could hardly *lift* it, and when I came backstage, I was all flustered, and the others had to push me back on. I just started to cry, and I threw the audience a kiss. Well, the house just went up. They knew I didn't expect it, you see. That was a wonderful night. Oh, I'd give anything to live those days over again!"

ANDY MCFARLANE

The people who settled the Canadian North never thought of themselves as pioneers. They tackled that rugged country for many and varied reasons; some for adventure, some for the possibility of the riches that lay beneath the surface, and some simply because they wanted a job.

Shortly after the turn of the century, the solid town that is Englehart in Northern Ontario today was nothing but a mudhole in the spring, and a frozen wasteland in the winter. That's when Andy McFarlane headed North. He had his own reasons for going.

I Hope You Gave Him a Good One

"THE REASON I CAME NORTH is kind of a funny story. I was working for the old Grand Trunk Railway at the time, lineman, y'know. I had been climbing poles for the Bell all down through the East before that. The *old* Bell Company. We were putting in the first telephones. That's when we used to go 'round through the country with a horse and covered wagon. You slept in the wagon, and you got your meals anyplace along where you were working. A farmhouse or something like that. Well, I quit the Bell, and I started climbing on contract for the Grand Trunk. You know, you'd take so many miles for a certain number of dollars. God, I was spry in those days. I could fly up and down those poles in a flash. I was in great shape, and I don't mind saying it. I'm in pretty good shape now! But I was young then, about fifteen.

Anyway, I had been working with this fella at the Bell, and he kept riding the hell out of me, and I told him, 'If I ever meet you when I grow up, I'll make mincemeat out of you.' Well, dammit, y'know, I happened to meet him in Orillia, in the fall of '07 when I was twenty-three. He come in to the old Orillia House and I knew him the minute I seen him. So I spoke to him. He spun around, and started to stick out his hand to shake and I *planted* him one! So it was a ruckus!

They called the Bell Chief of Police. I knew the bugger, but never had any acquaintance with him. And by the time he got there, I had this fella down on the floor, evening things up with him a bit. I was beating hell out of him. I felt someone grab me by the back of the neck, and when I looked around, I saw the brass buttons. I thought, 'Hell, I never got in a mix-up like this, so I better get out of it.' I jumped off this guy on the floor, and I come up quick, and hit the Chief in the stomach with my head. He had quite a stomach, so it was hard to miss. He went arse over head, and I went out the back door, and headed fast for the railroad station. When I got there, blast if his brother wasn't there, He was an engineer on the old Grand Trunk, and he was in there picking up some cars. I knew him because I had rode in the engine a lot with him. That's the way you do on telegraph work, you ride in the engine a lot.

I jumped up in the cab with him, and I said, 'Which way you goin'?' He said, 'North.' I said, 'Me too.' 'What happened?' he says. So I told him and he said, 'I hope you gave him a good one.' We got a great kick out of that, and that's what put me up in this country.

I never regretted coming North; not at all. I got off in Liskeard first, because I figured nobody'll know me. The first damn man I met on the platform was Jim Kennedy. I knew him in Lindsay. He drove the bus there for years, and he knew me from there when I was with the CPR. I didn't want to see anybody who knew me because I figured that Police Chief would come and get me, so I hopped back on the train, and kept going to Englehart. Kelly, the telegraph superintendent, was on the train, and he offered me a job taking charge of putting in so many miles of poles. Well, when we landed, I took a look at this place, and what a mudhole! Something damnable! Shacks everywhere! And 3rd Avenue was just one shack nailed against another, all the way down. If you got yours up first all you had to do was hook on at the corners, and you'd save a wall. It was all Italians, Chinamen, and everything else. Boarding houses, laundries. It was a hell of a place, and the last place on the corner was the Elk Lake Hotel. It was one layer of boards, and one layer of tarpaper. I tried it for a month one winter, and I got out. Cold? Lord! There was ice on the tips of the nails inside all the time.

I drove team for a few months, and I put in a power line for Pete Farr, when he put power to his mill from the river, then I put in the electric-light line from Liskeard across to Haileybury, and then I was in charge of putting in poles for the telegraph again. By nineteen I had a little money saved, so I bought a little company out, and started in the transfer business, you know, handlin' freight for the town, movin' people. I had a team of horses, and a great big dray that'd carry about eight ton. I moved coal. I moved furniture, hogs . . . you name it. We hauled practically every damn brick and stick and piece of furniture in this town.

I think I did my part in makin' this a good place to live. I'm all alone now, and some of them are after me to retire down south, but to hell with them! I like it here!"

EVELYN ASHTON CAMERON

Evelyn Ashton Cameron was born in 1877 in the British Isles, but she spent most of her childhood in Norway and Sweden, where she not only learned the language but also picked up an accent which remained with her all her life. Her father was a wealthy man, a geologist with business interests all over the world. Young Evelyn had a scientific bent, too, so there was no doubt that she would follow her father into a similar profession.

Nothing There But Mud

"I WAS TWENTY-THREE when our family fortunes started to change. Suddenly I was a lady geologist looking for a job.

A Mr. McGrath in Belleville, Ontario, wrote over and asked if any of us would be interested in coming to Canada. Well, I thought I would so I closed the laboratory and I wrote to my father's firm in England, for whom I had been working. They asked me if I would be willing to come to Canada to prospect and give them an option on anything I happened to find. I said yes, and I signed an agreement for two years.

I came over here on the old *Lake Manitoba*. It took ten days to cross the Atlantic and we landed at Saint John, New Brunswick, in March of 1903. There was ice everywhere, just solid. I was so disappointed; I guess I wanted it to be different because I hadn't left Sweden and travelled halfway round the world for the same old ice I left at home! However, I accepted that as I had to accept some other things that I didn't expect in this brand-new world.

I remember the first night at the hotel in Saint John. I put my shoes outside the door to be brushed as we did in the old country. The next morning when I got up they were still there and just as filthy as ever. I rang for the bellboy and I said, 'They didn't brush my shoes last night. Would you please see that they get brushed?'

He said, very kindly, 'They don't do that here, you know. In Canada we have to brush our own shoes.' So I said, 'How do you do it?' He went out and came back with a bottle and a little sponge on a wire and he painted over the shoes for me, and he said, 'That's the way we clean our shoes in Canada.' That was my first lesson in becoming a Canadian.

Before long I had traded my shoes for boots and I was tramping through the bush of Northern Ontario. I couldn't find an outfit in any of the stores for a lady prospector so I had to design one myself. I had a very heavy cloth skirt with a jacket and a blouse, and bloomers in a lighter material but the same colour as the skirt, and of course those big stout boots. When I went to a mine, they'd put me in a bucket that they used to bring up the ore, and they'd winch me down into the mine. I'd get some samples and I'd get back in the bucket and they'd winch me up again!

In the spring of 1904, my third brother, who had been very ill, was sent out to me by my mother. Now I had met, on the boat coming over, a Haughton family who lived near Regina at a place called Tregarva. And as a result, I had been offered a job out there as a companion to a lady. So Albert and I set out for the West on the train and we had to get off at the little jump-off station, Tregarva. But when we arrived there was nothing there but mud, and I said, 'I'm not going to stay in this mudhole.' But my brother said, 'Evvie, this is a new country, and if we turn back for a little mud, we're not much use.' So I said, 'You're right,' and we got off the train.

We were supposed to have been met at the train but there was nobody there. We were standing around wondering what to do when a horse and buggy arrived from the ranch where we were to stay. We got aboard and drove through mudholes and ruts for what seemed like hours. The driver stopped at a ramshackle building that I thought must be a stable, or perhaps a bunkhouse. I knocked and a lady opened the door. I said, 'Could you please tell me where Mr. McKay's residence is?' She said, 'This is it.' Well, I very soon found out that I wasn't hired to be a *companion* to Mrs. McKay; what she had wanted was a *servant* to help her. I don't mind saying I was flabbergasted! If they'd asked me to analyse a stone I would have been able to do it. I helped Mrs. McKay for a while, thinking that I'd find some way to get back into mining. Well, it didn't take me long to realize that mining wasn't for the Prairies and the Prairies wasn't for mining, so I decided I'd better take up some other occupation!"

There is no one I've ever met who typifies the independent spirit more than Lorne Saunders. Lorne told me that he can't remember when he wasn't working at something or other. His life was always hard but he didn't mind it because he thought that's the way it should be. I call him a homesteader because that's what he did for the longest period of time, for almost forty years. But he did many things—from shovelling coal on lake ships to firetower watching in the North. He calls himself "a tough old buzzard" and if you met him you'd have to go along with that description. He is tough, the kind of toughness that comes from dealing with and overcoming the tribulations of life. But he's also compassionate—as you'll find out when you read this. He lives in a shack in Moosonee, Ontario, on the shores of James Bay. He could live in a nursing home if he wanted to, but he prefers his shack.

A Nice Clean Murder for Twenty-five Cents

"I HAD MY SEVENTEENTH BIRTHDAY in a lumber camp up on the Bruce Peninsula. While we were there one of the saddest things I ever heard of happened: a woman, a young woman, wandered out of the hospital in Owen Sound and clean across the town out eighteen miles to the Balaclava country near the Hog's Back. It was the wintertime. She was lost and she got cold. I guess she got to sweating too and got even colder. Well, they found her in a day or two sittin' on the ice near Sucker Creek on the shore of Georgian Bay, undressin' and lettin' her hair down. She was froze solid. She thought she was goin' to bed you see. It still makes me cry when I think about it.

After four years around the lumber camps, I packed up and headed for Western Canada to start homesteading near Morse,

Saskatchewan. It was sixty years ago this winter (1910) I was over on that homestead land. I had lots of feed for my horses and I rigged up my stable there without any money: old railroad ties and sticks and bits of board and stuff, and wires and flax straw for the roof. I got the horses wintered okay but I hadn't nothin' to winter on myself. I went to the Imperial lumberyard and I said to the manager, Lou Marden, 'Lou, I want you to gather me all the broken, twisted lumber, everything that's no good for nothin', everything that you can't sell to nobody and I'll buy it.' So he cleaned up his yard and I took the team and wagon in the next day and got the lumber—about a thousand feet for two dollars.

When I got home I started to dig on the level at the bottom of this hill. I dug twelve feet back and then I cribbed that up with lumber about four feet wide by six feet high. I put lumber on top and then I threwed dirt in around the sides and piled her in over the top. This was to be my tunnel to the main room. To dig that I went up on top of the hill and dug down eight feet square till I came to the end of the tunnel I built. I lined her all with the old boards, put some planks across for a ceiling, stuck my stovepipe through, and then threwed about five feet of dirt back on for a roof. So I had one big room and a tunnel into it, all lined with this lumber from Lou Marden's lumberyard.

Then I built a sleigh and I went all over the place gatherin' up cattle chips. That's the Sunday name for dried cow manure. Weekdays you can call it somethin' else. I had my stove in there and I moved into that place the first part of November and started burnin' cattle chips under one lid of the stove. The winter had come by this time but I was cozy. I had my bed and I had seven dollars and thirteen cents. I rolled my feet in bran sacks and kept them that way all through the winter. I even went into town with them on. I lived on wheat that I boiled over this one lid of the stove. Day and night that fire stayed on with cattle chips. They won't blaze y'know, but the fire gets red hot.

There was no work to be had anywhere. There was nothin' to sell. I went to town one day and the grain elevator man said, 'Lorne, how would you like to earn twenty-five cents?' I told him that I could do a nice clean murder for that twenty-five cents. Anyway, I moved a big carload of wheat and got me about five pounds of brown sugar, nice fresh brown sugar to eat with my boiled wheat. I never had any bread or meat but I never got sick a day that winter and never had a cold and the only fire I had was the cattle chips under the one lid of the stove. That winter lasted from the first part of November till way on in April. I was twenty-one years old.

At the age of sixty, my wife dead and my children gone, I returned to where I came from—Northern Ontario. When I got there I built a shack in the bush and got a job as a firewatcher in a tower where I'd be away for long periods of time. While I was away this time, Bell Telephone came along and they was gonna bulldoze my shack into the lake. They had already bulldozed my winter wood supply into a gully and covered it up. The Ukrainian at the sawmill came over and said, 'Hey, you can't bulldoze a man's house into the river like that. You'll get into trouble.' They said they could do what they liked because I didn't own the land and didn't pay taxes. They didn't push my shack in the lake though; they put it on skids and hauled it away.

All this happened back in the fifties when they were building all these radar bases. The Bell people had big contracts for that and it was all hush-hush. Anyway, some time after my shack had been hauled away by Ma Bell, I met this fella on the train. I knew he was a stranger, so I said, 'Hi mister. Where ya goin'? I'm goin' to Moosonee.' He says, 'I'm goin' a lot farther than that.' So I says, 'I bet you're goin' to Fort Severn.' 'No. No,' he says. 'Well,' I says, 'I bet you're goin' to Great Whale.' 'No. No,' he says, 'I'm not goin' there either. We're not supposed to talk about where we're goin'. We've signed papers.' 'Oh,' says I. 'Then you're goin' to that new radar station at Winisk. Those seven fellows in the next car are going to the same place.' Well! He got all red and flustered and didn't say anything else. It turns out that he was an engineer with Bell Telephone and when he got off the train he headed straight for the Bell office. An old Scotsman who was in there at the time said this engineer came in and was raisin' hell about this old fella with a beard on the train who knew all about what they were doin' and how much money they were spendin'—one hundred and fifty million by the way—and he was all upset. Well, I was the old fella with the beard, y'see. When the Scotsman asked me how I knew all that, I said I heard it on the news on the radio, where they were buildin' the radars and how much and so on. Military secret. Big deal. Anyway I had a great big laugh at Bell over that one and it kinda made up for them bulldozin' my wood in the gully and haulin' my shack away. Who ever hears about radar any more now? They might as well have gone fishin' and saved the money."

ROCCO TALENTINO

When Rocco Talentino came to Canada from Italy in 1901 he was fifteen years old and ready for any job that he could find. What he found was backbreaking work on the railroads that were then being built in the attempt to open up Northern Ontario. The Algoma Central was snaking its way from Sault Ste. Marie towards the northern town of Hearst and the Ontario Northland was moving towards Cochrane. It was dynamite, picks and shovels, and bull work all the way, with intense heat and cold and clouds of blackflies and mosquitoes. This was to be young Rocco's life for the next eight years. By that time he had grown to manhood and developed a fierce love for this country, but he still had the worst trial to come—the big Dome Mines fire of 1911, in a little mining community surrounded by bush that was dry as tinder.

Everything Around Me Was Burning

"AT HALF PAST TWELVE we were having dinner in the kitchen of the bunkhouse and the fire alarm rang so we all went outside. We knew the fire was close before that because we could see and smell the smoke, but when we got outside *everything* was on fire. You couldn't see ten feet ahead of you. I spotted a little opening of green bush and my friend and I made for it to try and save ourselves. We followed a trail in there with burning trees falling all around us and ahead of us. The fire was gettin' closer all the time, and all the time I kept holding onto my horses. They followed me just like a person, you know. The heat by this time was so bad that my boots were burning my feet, and I had to take a knife and cut them off. Then the fire swept over my head and burned all my hair off and my clothes went on fire so I had to tear them off too. Everything around me was burning, and I had to keep going and following this trail. There was nothing else to do. After a while, I don't know how long, I came to a pond, so I ran into that and pulled my horses in with me and I got down in the water and only put my nose up to breathe. The horses were all covered with the water too, with only their heads up. We stayed like that all night and the fire kept burning all around us. I never thought we would make it.

The next morning we crawled out and started back. It had rained during the night and a lot of the fire was out. I saw Charlie Dalton and as soon as he saw me he ran over and kissed me just like we were brothers. My hair was gone, and I had no clothes on, but I still had my horses. Charlie had some bread and sardines so we ate that and I continued on back.

It was terrible. Everything was gone! The mine buildings, all the homes of the miners, and the miners and their families themselves. There were dead animals and people all over the place! It turned my stomach and I had to stop and throw up. Everything was black and still smoking. The ground was all cracked from the heat and I had no idea who was dead and who was alive! Over at the mine—what was left of it—the men gave me some clothes and they told me that when the building with the dynamite caught fire it exploded and a kind of tidal wave came and drowned a lot of other people. It was the end of the world.

Finally I found a wagon that hadn't burned and I hitched up my horses and started collecting bodies. They were burnt so bad you couldn't tell who they were. Nobody knows for sure how many people died. For years afterwards people would come over from Europe trying to find out something about their sons and fathers and husbands who disappeared in 1911. But a few days after it was over the company had new bunkhouses built. They buried the dead and started rebuilding the mine buildings and everybody said, 'Well, boys, let's get going again.' What else could you do?"

EVA MARIE SWEENEY

Mrs. Eva Marie Sweeney of Victoria might be described as a "woman of the sea". Her father was a sailing man, and so was her husband, and she lived all her life within the sight and smell of salt water. She wouldn't have it any other way. And when she dies she would like nothing better than to have the sound of the sea drown out any sounds of sorrow. Her father came to Canada from Scandinavia and the story of how he got his Canadian name is an interesting part of Canadian history, like the stories she has to tell of the west-coast seal hunt.

The Grand Old Days of the West-Coast Seal Hunts

"MY FATHER'S ORIGINAL NAME was Homeland. And when he came out from Finland, like a lot of Scandinavians he took the first name, the Christian name, of his father and added 'son' to it. So he called himself 'Jacobson'.

He was a typical man of the sea, loving at times, often stern in his discipline, a tough man with a bull-moose kind of strength. One time when they were up in the Bering Sea a boom came and hit him and broke his jaw. And do you know he wired up his own jaw himself—bored it with a brace and bit and wired it up himself. That's the kind of man he was.

My father used to seal off the west coast of Vancouver Island. The seal herd was coming up from the California coast, going up to those islands in the Bering Sea. When that happened, we never saw my father for six months after that. He would be away six months sealing.

We had a ship called the *Minnie* that was Father's pride and joy. She could stand up to just about anything except a big gale like the one they had in 1908. She was carried right over this reef with all hands on board and there wasn't one of them lost. The

Minnie was wrecked, of course, and father wanted to build another *Minnie*, but a golden opportunity came along in the form of
a ship with a proud history called the *Casco*. Robert Louis Steven-
son chartered her and used her down in the South Pacific and he
wrote *Treasure Island* and a lot of his works on board the *Casco*.
Then he died and the *Casco* was brought up to San Francisco and
she laid on the beach there for about two years. Then somebody
got her and refurbished her and put on all brand-new sails and
brought her up to Seattle. In the meantime they had been told
about my father going to build another ship and they contacted
him and he went to Seattle and he bought the *Casco* for $4,000.
He brought his new ship into the sealing industry of the west
coast and made many trips up to the Bering Sea.

He used to recruit the Indians as crew from the different res-
ervations, around there from Dodges Cove, and up in the Nitinat
and all around the west coast. He used to pick up special hunters
that went with him every year, with their own canoes, Indian canoes, piled on the deck. There were two hunters and a boat-puller
in each canoe. One was a hunter, one was a steerer, and the other
one would have a rifle to shoot the seals. But the Indians weren't
allowed to handle the firearms so they used to spear the seals.
Many a canoe never got back. A big wind would come up and
they would capsize and all the men would be lost. Or they would
get lost in fog. The schooners would wait; though not only my
father's schooner but all the other ones would wait for them and
they would fire off a cannon to let these boat-pullers know where
they were. But they still lost a lot of men that way.

When the boat-pullers would go out, between the sealing
boats and the canoes, they would capture about a hundred skins a
day. They skinned them on board the ship and the Indians lived
on the seals' meat. Then the hides were all salted down. One thing
that I remember so clearly is this house on the wharf. My father
built a long shed alongside of this place and I can always see in
my mind's eye two hunters with rifles, one at one door, and one at
the other, guarding these valuable hides, salted down in barrels,
day and night. They were worth a tremendous amount of money.
But sealing ended as an industry on the west coast about 1913.

Because my father often hired west-coast Indians for the seal
hunt, we got to know some of their customs. On one occasion my
father was on the sealing schooner *Eva Marie*, waiting for some
Indian hunters to come aboard. Anyway, they were all invited to

a wedding in the village. Everybody had gone to the big party except for this one man who was lying in a canoe. So my father asked him why didn't he go to the wedding. Well, it seems he couldn't get up. He couldn't walk. And this was his story: He had had an accident and his people thought he was dead. Well, in those days they used to bury their dead in a box and put them up in a tree. Sometimes they couldn't always fit the body into the box so they'd break their legs and break their arms to get them in. The trouble was sometimes some of them were only unconscious. This had happened with this particular fellow. He had come to in the wooden box and although both his legs had been broken he had managed to get out and crawl down to the waterfront where he got into this canoe. The other Indians had found him there and used to come and feed him. They didn't want to move him you see. His legs finally did heal, but they stayed so stiff that he could never sit in a canoe for the rest of his life!

Mother told me that one time she saw a man swimming in the water off the coast, just out from one of these Indian villages on the west coast of Vancouver Island. They picked him out of the water and found he was in great pain because both his arms and legs were broken. He also had had them broken by the other Indians because he didn't fit in the box. But there had been a big wind that night and the box had been blown out of the tree and into the sea. He woke up and got out of the box and swam towards my father's schooner. So they got him up on board and gave him laudanum and looked after him.

The west-coast Indians also had some strange superstitions. If an Indian woman gave birth to twins, one was always killed. It was supposed to be a disgrace and the father of the twins was stoned until they killed him. Even if he lived he wasn't allowed back in the village again. I remember a story that Captain Heeter told me not so very many years ago. They were at an Indian village, and this chief's daughter had died and she had been put up in the tree in this box. All the dead person's belongings were piled around the trees around them, and it didn't matter if the rest of the family needed these things or not, they were always put with the body. Her father had bought her an organ, so that was put under the tree as well. My two brothers and Captain Heeter's son used to go up after dark and would bang away on this organ. Well, the Indians were absolutely terrified; they were sure it was the Devil come down who was playing the organ.

The old church that Father had fixed up for his family to live in while he was away at sea had only one thing wrong with it. It was built, according to the Indians, on top of an old Indian burial ground, and the Indians didn't like that at all. The chief of this Indian village was called 'Nookomas' and he was a very bad-tempered man. He had two wives, and one was a great big woman, and the other was a very small woman, and she was very nasty-tempered just like him. So he and his two wives lived on what they call 'Diana Island'. They had come across from their village and he told my mother he owned the village, he owned all the land, he owned the church, and he ordered her to get out. She refused to go. So he set his wives upon my mother. But she had the other Indians back her up and so he gave her until sundown to get out of the church and he went off with these two wives. Sure enough, by sundown back he came again, but in the meantime my mother had seen the priest, and told him the story. He said, 'All right, you go in and pretend that you've gone to bed. I will be in the other room. When Nookomas and his wives come back at sundown, invite them into the church.' Well, my mother was terrified of these two women, but she did as she was told. There was a long hallway between the two rooms that my father had built and the main church itself. Just as Nookomas and his two wives came in, our priest appeared. He walked down this long hallway and said to them, 'This is God's house, and if you don't get out immediately, God will strike you down dead.' Mother said that the three of them ran down the beach, into the canoe, and off they went. She never saw them again. They were *terrified*.

There was slavery on the west coast during those days, not between white and Indian, but among the Indians themselves. My father had on board one of his sealing schooners a hunter who was washed overboard and lost at sea. He was a chief and my father felt responsible for the wife. Now the wife had what they called a 'handmaiden'. So my father had the wife and her handmaiden, whose name was Martha, brought down to Victoria. They lived on the reserve down in Esquimalt and about once a month, Martha and Mary used to come to visit us. I'd come home from high school, and Mary and Martha would be sat at the kitchen table having a good meal. Then whatever was left they would take with them; the sugar bowl was emptied into a pocket and Mother would give them rice and all kinds of food. Well, as they were leaving, they used to say to my mother, 'We have a beautiful present for you. We're going to bring it one day.' We used to sort of snigger a little bit because we figured, 'Oh yes, that's Indian giver.' But about two years later Mary and Martha arrived with the present. It was a basket the size of a steamer trunk that they had made between them. In those days they used to bury the reeds to get their colour, and of course the mud was all impregnated with rotten clam shells and all that, so those reeds used to stink. Anyway, they brought the basket and we put it in the living room. When my father came home the stench that was in the room was terrible; it would knock you over. He insisted that it be put on the freight deck so it went down there and it was used for years for my brothers' and my father's tools. Someone, I don't know who, presented it to the museum and, as far as I know, that basket is in the museum today, behind a glass case.

It's all very different between the Indian and white people today. Now they even intermarry. My husband and I went up to Port Alberni two years ago to a wedding between my nephew's son and a girl from an Indian family at Nitinat. It was a very big wedding and there were fifty fish boats tied up at the dock. While the ceremony was going on all these Indian children were running up and down the aisles shouting, screaming, and playing tag and having a real good time. Then, every now and again, an Indian would jump up. He'd recognize a white fisherman and he'd call out, 'Well George, did you have a good catch this season?' and George would answer how many fish he'd caught and how much money he'd made. This was when the wedding ceremony was going on, you see. So the minister said, 'If you people don't keep quiet, there's going to be no wedding here.' One of the Indians jumped up and said, 'A wedding to us is a happy time and we are all very happy. You carry on with the wedding.' Well, it was just pandemonium. Then we went to the reception, and all the tables were laid out in this big hall and they had a very nice supper which was mostly Indian food, and these different Indians would get up and they'd do an Indian dance. Well anyway, there was an old Indian woman there, nearly 100, who was told that I was the daughter of Captain Jacobson. Her husband had been a hunter on a sealing schooner belonging to my father, so of course she wanted to meet me. So I went down and sat at a table with all these Indians. And I really enjoyed myself; we had a great time remembering the grand old days of the west-coast seal hunts."

JOHN G. DIEFENBAKER

John George Diefenbaker, the thirteenth Prime Minister of Canada, was born in this country to German-Scottish parents who homesteaded on the Prairies in the early part of this century.

The Prime Minister's Office and the leadership of the Conservative party were long gone from Mr. Diefenbaker when I talked with him on Parliament Hill in 1977. However, he was still the Member for Prince Albert, Saskatchewan, and he still had the same burning interest in Parliament and the parliamentary system that had carried him to the top political office in Canada in 1957. There was still the same sly wit and the messianic style of speech, the same piercing blue eyes; but there was warmth and less passionate ambition in this man of eighty-two than there had been in the brisk and businesslike new Prime Minister I had met only once before, in 1960. This time instead of the politician's firm handshake and half-smile, he squeezed my arm gently, asked about my family as though he really cared, and led me behind the desk to a chair alongside his own. He was prepared to talk with me, not to me. I liked this man very much.

Going Somewhere

"MY GREAT-GRANDFATHER'S PEOPLE came to Canada from the Baden-Baden area of Germany in the early eighteenth century. They started out in what was then York—it's Toronto today— around Yonge Street North, and they came to rest in Woolwich Township in Waterloo County. My great-grandfather's son, in turn, lived at Hawkesville, Ontario, and was a builder of buggies and small wagons and things like that. Both my grandfather and great-grandfather were highly skilled artisans. As a matter of fact, there is still one double sleigh in Saskatoon made by my grandfather in Hawkesville. When I was invalided home from the war in

1917, I went to Hawkesville and the wagon shop was still there. My grandfather passed away in 1907. I think my grandparents had about seven children altogether. That's a fairly large family but despite that, there are very few descendants today.

My father became a teacher. He went to Berlin High School and subsequently he took his teacher's course at the Model School in Ottawa, which is still in existence here on Cartier Street. He was there in 1890 and 1891.

No matter who came under Father's influence benefited. The last school he taught in Ontario was Todmorden Plains Road School about two miles from the centre of Toronto. It was then an area of market gardens. There were twenty-eight youngsters in that school in all grades and when I came into the House of Commons in 1940, four of those twenty-eight were MP's: George Tussens from Napanee, Joe Harris and R. H. McGregor from East Toronto, and me. Sitting opposite was Mackenzie King; Father had taught *him* in Primary. King always insisted after he was Prime Minister and all through the years that Father call him 'Willie'. The funny thing was, when King couldn't get elected in North York—he was defeated there—he came out to Prince Albert and defeated me!

Father seemed to exude his own love of politics to all those around him. He knew more about politics and the operation of Parliament than I know today. I don't think he could have been very attentive while taking his teaching course in Ottawa because he spent so much time in the Gallery of the House of Commons. In 1891 he was here in the month of May and saw Sir John Macdonald on the last occasion he was in the House. He wasn't a supporter of Macdonald, but when Sir John became ill and was bedridden at home, Father would go out to the Macdonald home and stand outside there. He developed a deep admiration, almost an adoration, for the British parliamentary system and the Crown. My own love of these things comes directly from him. When he went West, two or three of the books that we took along were bought at Britnell's Book Store on Yonge Street in Toronto: a book on Parliament, *Parliamentary Procedure and the History of the Development of Confederation*, and another dealing with the development of the province of Manitoba. It was that type of book that Father purchased for Elmer and me.

Father was kindness personified. Everybody liked him and he helped everybody. From the earliest days, no matter how small the salary no one who was poor didn't get help. As a matter of fact in Saskatoon the other day I was told how he used to be taken in by beggars. Most people then ignored people who begged, but they always considered Father to be an easy mark. He had a deep sense of justice. He was also a profound student. He went much beyond that formal Second Class Teacher's Certificate. He continued to study on his own through the years and at the age of seventy he took up calculus and astronomy while we were on the homestead. He was widely read in the classics, and Shakespeare and the Bible were daily companions. A couple of years ago that Todmorden Plains Road School in Toronto was to be renamed after me and I said, 'No. Call it Diefenbaker School after Father.'

We went West in the August of 1903 to the area of Fort Carlton on the Edmonton, Swan River, Winnipeg Trail. People were coming in from all over the world then. The Indians lived close at hand and the Battle of Duck Lake had taken place only twelve miles away. Many of the old Indians there at the time had participated in the Rebellion. From time to time Gabriel Dumont would pass by and teach me and my late brother, Elmer, how to shoot a rifle. Years later when I was at university, I wrote a thesis on Canada's greatest military commander, Gabriel Dumont, and I said there that he was the only superb tactician and guerilla warrior produced in North America. Beside him Red Jacket and Pontiac were amateurs. Incidentally, in 1947 Dumont's field notes were found; unable to read or write, unable to speak English, he had dictated them to someone else. Today, as a result of the discovery of those notes, the military schools say that he was the greatest of the great as military tacticians go.

As children, we were frightened of Dumont at first. But he took an interest in Elmer and me and after a while we weren't scared any more. He was a striking-looking person and a great buffalo hunter. He killed at least 100,000 buffalo and, as a matter of interest, his descendants still live near Duck Lake. About a year ago someone showed me a picture which they said was Dumont outside his tent after the Battle of Batoche. I said, 'That's not Dumont. After the battle he wouldn't have stood still long enough to have his picture taken.' Actually, he disappeared to the United States, to Montana, and I think it was in 1898 when he was granted the freedom to return to Canada.

You know as far as that whole thing was concerned—the

Rebellion—the Courts were absolutely right in finding Riel guilty, but he should never have been executed. He was obviously insane. I knew one man who was on the jury and about seven or eight of the old-timers who knew him when he came to Prince Albert in 1884, so I've thought about this and talked about it for many years. He was definitely insane and I've never thought of him as a martyr, because when he came over from the States originally he got in touch with Macdonald and said that if the Government would give him $135,000 or $125,000, I'm not sure which, he would go back to the United States and forget all about the Rebellion. Well, six weeks before the Rebellion broke out, he reduced the ante to $35,000. Now I've never regarded a person as a martyr who places his principles up for auction, and that's what Riel did. Now, there's no question that the Indians and the half-breeds were being treated unjustly, but as time went by Riel developed the concept that he had supernatural powers. In March of 1885 he announced, three weeks in advance, that the obliteration of the sun would take place on a certain date. Of course, it was just a predicted eclipse, but it convinced many of his doubtful followers, many of whom were illiterate, that he had magic powers.

Riel did have the two ablest lawyers that French Canada produced, Greenshields and Lemieux, but every time they raised the question of insanity, he'd scream blue murder from the dock. 'I won't have these lawyers,' he'd yell. 'They have no right to say that I am insane.' The jury's verdict was 'Guilty, with a recommendation for mercy'. Now I come into the picture this way. I've always concluded, and I had many defences before the Courts, that anyone who received a recommendation for mercy on a murder charge should be reprieved, for that recommendation indicates that there is a division in the jury. I remember one man who went to the gallows even though he had a recommendation for mercy. Six months after he was hanged, the star witness against this man broke down and admitted he had done it and put it on my client. So, the first day I became Prime Minister a case came up for consideration as to whether or not mercy should be given, and I said, 'As long as I sit here no one who has had a recommendation of mercy will be executed.' I followed that throughout my time as Prime Minister. I have always had this very strong concern about the rights of the individual going back as long as I can remember.

Our family was privileged to see the opening of the Canadian

The ice boats of Prince Edward Island were especially built to move across ice as well as open stretches of water. When the Northumberland Strait froze these ice boats were the islanders' only link with the mainland. "It was a real prize for a man to get a job on these ice boats." Captain Edwin McWilliams (The Public Archives of Canada)

A telegraph office with a machine similar to the one that Sue Lowther would have used when, in 1882, aged eight, she sent messages across to the mainland from Prince Edward Island. (The Public Archives of Canada)

Canadians across the country remember teachers like Julia Brewster and Laura Kidd. They were powerful figures in the lives of the children they taught. This school is in the Pouce Coupé District of Alberta. (The Public Archives of Canada)

Many Doukhobors arrived in Canada at the turn of the century and established colonies in Saskatchewan. Men and women would harness themselves to wagons to transport supplies from railway depots to their homes (*left*) or to plough their gardens (*above*). Elizabeth Popoff Bassiove remembers how often they would start with nothing and, in the space of a few years, have homes like the ones above. (The Public Archives of Canada)

People rush to file their claims for land at the Court House in Prince Albert, Saskatchewan. Around the time this picture was taken (1909), John Diefenbaker and his father sat for two days in front of the Land Office in Prince Albert so that they would be sure to get the land they wanted. (Saskatchewan Archives Board)

Arthur MacLeod Rogers would have often rested in a shell hole on his way to the front line in 1917, as these members of the 22nd Battalion are doing. (The Public Archives of Canada)

A group of flying trainees at Long Branch, Toronto, Ontario, in 1915 preparing to join Tom Williams and his colleagues fighting the Germans "man to man" over in France. (The Public Archives of Canada)

The collision between a Norwegian freighter and a French munitions ship in the Halifax Harbour caused an explosion that killed
an estimated 2,000 people and left major parts of the city in ruins.
"I don't think anybody who ... went through that could ever
forget it." Mrs. C. N. Brown. (The Public Archives of Canada)

The Dumbells, all Canadian soldiers, were formed in 1917 after the battle of Vimy Ridge and the next year they were amalgamated with the Princess Pats Concert Party (*left*). "The boys in the trenches really appreciated what we did and you'd hear them whistling the 'Dumbell Rag' going up the line." Jack Ayre (Both from the Public Archives of Canada)

The aftermath of the terrible fire of July 29, 1916, that swept through Matheson, Cochrane, Iroquois Falls, and other northern communities. "The fire just seemed to travel in great big balls . . . and then the balls would come down somewhere, explode, and start another fire there!" Amelia Veitch (The Public Archives of Canada)

West. Firstly, we were in a district where the people were mainly Germans from Prussia: High Germans and old-country French. Well, then we moved from there into a little village called Hague. Father was teaching all of this time. Then he decided he wanted to take up that 160-acre offer and become a homesteader on the west banks of the Saskatchewan River, west of Duck Lake. To do that, you had to file on the land and pay ten dollars; in effect you were betting ten dollars with the Government that you could stay for three years. If you did, you got a title.

Well, we went into Prince Albert where the Lands Office was. Father was going to file on a piece of land that he picked out three or four weeks before, and he took his position outside the Dominion Lands Office to wait for the opening on Monday morning. He sat on a milk stool from Friday evening till Monday morning and for those couple of days I slept wherever I could lie down, under a pool table one time; I would get Father tea to keep him going. On Monday morning he was in the number-one position in the line with about fifty behind him. A great big Swede was number two. He said to Father, 'You step back. You is first after me.' So he went first. But he didn't take the land that Father wanted and we went on to the homestead in June of 1905 and the three of us, Father, Elmer, and I, built the shacks. Mother was an indomitable soul. She was artistically minded, and while those shacks didn't look very attractive on the outside, they certainly were on the inside, thanks to Mother.

Mother's people came from the Highlands of Scotland. They had a great love for the land but they were driven off by greedy landlords. Her grandfather was driven out of Sutherland in 1812 by the Countess of Sutherland at a time when all of the people residing in the Kildonan Straths were being driven out. Their homes were torn down and burned and their cattle driven out. That was because the Countess could make more money by raising sheep on the land than she could by having people there. This was all part of what was called the 'Highland Clearances'. As a matter of interest, Sir John A.'s father and mother lived about twelve miles away and they left at the same time. Whether they were driven out I can't say, but certainly they left as a consequence of the Clearances. So if it hadn't been for the Countess of Sutherland, the first and thirteenth prime ministers of Canada wouldn't have been!

When we were on the homestead we lived seventeen miles

from the nearest village and, as was usual at that time in the West, doctors were not readily available. I remember in 1908, on the 11th of March, I was lost on the prairie in a storm with my late uncle Edward. We had started out for home about 9:30, after a concert at my uncle's school and just as a storm was coming up. We came over the hill and we could see the lantern Father put out whenever there was a storm. Five or six lives were saved as a result of that light—freezing to death was not uncommon on the Prairies at that time. Anyway, the storm got heavier and the horse left the road; he wouldn't put his face into the storm. Finally we came to rest in a snowbank in a slough about two and a half miles from home. All night long when I'd doze off, my uncle would wake me up. We would have been frozen to death if it hadn't been that the storm broke in the morning. It was thirty below zero and we were in an open sleigh. I got out to walk and went bumping along not knowing what was wrong with my legs. When we got home it was found that they were frozen from just below my knees up to my middle. For forty-eight hours Father and Mother worked to save me. Father would take a horse blanket filled with snow and keep it to me. At that time it was thought that was the proper treatment. I was in bed fifteen days and then gangrene set in. If it hadn't been for the great care my parents gave me, I never would have survived.

Life was hard, but it was good. I walked to school three and a half miles and back in the evening but nobody thought anything of that. Father was quite a hunter and in the proper season of the year we always had prairie chickens, ducks, wild geese, and jackrabbits. We lived exceptionally well and all the North West Mounted Policemen travelling between Edmonton and Prince Albert by way of Carlton dropped in at our home at mealtime. The travellers would come at mealtime, and the politicians would stay over a couple of days as well. Father and Mother would never permit anyone to pay anything and I never noticed the recipients of the meals object very much to this policy.

There was something happened in June of 1909 that I must tell you about; I failed my examinations for grades nine and ten. Those exams had to be written in Saskatoon, forty-five miles away, and I was on my own there. I was very fond of ice cream and I hadn't had any for a long time. There was a Maple Leaf Café on 20th Street W. in Saskatoon, so while I was there I never had less than a pint of ice cream for breakfast and more for lunch, and so on! In those days, if you failed one exam you were out and had to do the year over again. From all the ice cream I took sick on the last day of the examinations and had to leave. So I lost the year. It was a terrible blow to Mother, who believed greatly in education. She felt there was only one thing to do, move from the homestead to the city. So in February of 1910 Father managed to get a job as a clerk in the Land Titles Office and we moved into Saskatoon, where this fine new job paid him sixty dollars a month and we could go to school. Mother had great ambitions for her children and she would sacrifice anything for them.

I remember when I was nine years of age I announced to Mother that I was going to be Prime Minister when I grew up. She said that was fine but she also said that was pretty nearly an impossible dream. I said, 'Laurier was a poor boy, wasn't he?' She took it, I suppose, like all mothers do, but the thing was that I never deviated from that goal. In university they used to laugh when I said it. And when I entered politics I had four defeats in a row so that most people felt I was going somewhere but certainly not the House of Commons! But these defeats never discouraged me. I knew in my heart that someday I would be Prime Minister.

Ten days before the federal election of 1957, my first election as Leader of the Opposition, the press people said to me, 'You have no chance according to the Gallup Poll.' I replied, 'I've always been fond of dogs and they are the one animal that knows the proper treatment to give to poles.' Of course, you know what happened. We swept the country and I became the thirteenth Prime Minister of Canada."

ALEX BURNETT

Alex Burnett was born in 1890 to French-speaking parents in Montreal. He didn't see much future for himself in the city, so when he heard his friends talking about homestead land in Northern Ontario, he decided that that just might be the thing for a 6-foot, 5-inch, 230-pounder like himself. With little else but optimism, he soon found himself in the North and owner of 160 acres of virgin bushland near Cochrane, Ontario.

Alex worked his land for three years. He was young and strong and nothing could hold him back—nothing, that is, except fire. And in July of 1911 fire struck Cochrane. In three hours, Alex Burnett lost everything he had. The Burnetts survived by staying in a boat in the middle of the river, covered up with wet blankets, for eight hours. He didn't give up, though; he went back to Montreal for a while and then started over.

When I met Alex he was eighty-six years old and, despite protests from his children, he and his wife had made the decision to enter a senior citizens' home together if it could be arranged that they share the same room. It could, and it was, and there was a lot of laughter and love evident as they held hands for this interview. On the walls there were pictures of all of their children and a big one of them, reaffirming their marriage vows on the sixtieth anniversary of their wedding.

A Terrible Woman to Work

"MY WIFE, she was the one who helped me most at that time. I couldn't have started over without her. So she had to clean the land, take care of the horses, and run the farm. My job was running the ferry boat and sometimes I'd be away four or five months at a time. She milked the cows, six or seven of them, and sold the cream. She had a team of dogs too, and in the winter when there was too much snow for the horses, she would take eggs into town by dog team and sell them and come back with other provisions we needed. One time she went when it was fifty degrees below zero, and she said she never had time to get cold, because she went seven miles in forty-five minutes! That time she came back with food for us and three bags of feed for the chickens.

The only time my wife ever stopped work was to have a baby. And then that would only be for four or five days. Then she'd be right back at it again. She was always a *terrible* woman to work. I'd say, 'Stop for a while; take a rest.' But it was no use. She'd say, 'When I work I am happy. I don't get lonesome.'

The woman was the most important thing in those days for a man to make a go of the North. I don't mind saying that she was the most important. It was team-work all right, but without a good woman most men wouldn't have stood a chance!"

ARTHUR MACLEOD ROGERS

Grace D. MacLeod Rogers was a Nova Scotian housewife, who became famous in her time as an author. She wrote of her native province, and one of her books especially sticks in my mind, from my own school days, Tales from the Land of Evangeline. But to the four boys who were her sons, she was simply a wonderful and wise mother, who guided their footsteps with love. One of her boys, Norman, went on to become Minister of Defence in one of the Mackenzie King governments; another, Arthur Rogers, became a racket-busting lawyer with the Attorney General's Department in Ontario.

Scattered Far and Wide

"MOTHER WAS JUST A WONDERFUL WOMAN, who was so happy to have four boys to bring up, because she was one of five daughters—the middle one—and she had always wished to have been a boy. She had a marvellous memory for poetry particularly, and she could quote a line or two to suit just about any occasion that would come along in our home. I can always remember how she would use it to stop any quarrels that would arise with us four boys. Soon as the row would start she would say:

> They grew in beauty side by side;
> They filled one home with glee;
> Their graves are scattered far and wide,
> O'er hill and dale and sea....

She never got to the last couplet before the quarrel would stop. We just couldn't stand to hear that part about the graves being scattered far and wide!

She was the first woman to be made a governor of any university in Canada—Acadia University in Wolfville, Nova Scotia. She was also the first woman to run for the legislature in Canada.

She started writing as a young girl and she sent something to some magazine, and it was accepted. Well, it appeared in an issue that came to her home, and somehow she was able to control her emotions, and didn't let her mother know. You see, she had used a *nom de plume*. Well, her mother always chose a special story to read aloud to the family when they were gathered together. So this particular night she picked up this magazine, and read Mother's story, without knowing that her own daughter had written it. What a moment that must have been for Mother, who didn't let the secret out till the story was finished!

Our home was in Amherst, where you have the Bay of Fundy with the forty-foot tide fall on one side, and on the North Shore was the Northumberland Strait, so we had lots of water around us, and men of the sea, and sailing ships, and we loved it, but not one of us followed the sea when we grew up. Our home was full of books of all kinds, and reading was a great tradition in the family. We read every evening, and we also read after we went to bed, when we shouldn't have been. But I don't think Mother minded because she loved books so much herself. I'm sure that she was pleased to see us inherit that love.

The four boys were great fans of Rudyard Kipling, and it was out of that that we got the belief that war was romantic—all gallant men and magnificent horses. All four of us would get 'rigged' up in anything that looked military, and we'd recite alternate verses of Kipling, so it became very much a part of us.

I was about twenty-one when the First World War came along. When we heard that they were forming the Mounted Rifles of Nova Scotia, that was for me and my brother Norman! We trained at Valcartier, Quebec, in the hottest of weather, and dust, and then they put us on a cattle ship and sent us over.

We were with the Mounted Rifles of Nova Scotia, but we never had a horse. There were horses in the hold, but that's as close as we ever got to them. Norman and I ended up as signallers, and we used to work out from Ypres. One time it was my turn to get my hair cut—we'd take turns barbering each other's hair—and I was sitting on an upturned bucket when a German airplane came over. I guess he decided I needed a close shave too, so he dropped a couple of bombs. We could hear them coming, but we didn't know where they'd land. There was no point in running anywhere, because we might just as easily run into them. I dropped into a small shell hole about three feet across—enough to protect my stomach, and that's about all. Well, the bombs landed in this little pond, and we were very concerned because we thought they might have destroyed some of our cables which were running up to the front lines, so we went over to have a look. The cable was all right, but about two dozen nice fresh perch were floating on the surface, stunned by the concussion. We gathered them up, and one of our fellows proceeded to clean them and cook them, and this wonderful smell of frying fish was all over the area. Along came our Brigade Captain and he said, 'Oh, we're having fish tonight are we?' We said, 'You're not! We are.' So we told him how we got them, and he laughed and went away.

The next morning we were awakened by the sound of bombs going off. We went to investigate, and we caught the Captain throwing bombs in the same pond, right in there where we got our fish, but where our cables were too. I gave him hell, and he had to take it too! I guess it was the first time a buck private got away with talking like that to a captain, but he *knew* he was in the wrong. He just sneaked away from there with his tail between his legs, no fish, and a pretty red face too.

But just imagine! Fresh fish in the slime of that battlefield! The dugouts were not dug down there, because it was too gooey. They were built up, and my brother and I and two other signallers were sharing one of those built-up dugouts. The roof was only one sandbag thick, and over on the far side of the salient, the enemy could shoot right into the rear of us. Well, one night when all four of us were asleep in there, they dropped a shell right inside the doorway. If it had gone through the roof we'd all have been killed, but it just landed in the doorway, and exploded, and I didn't even wake up. It was a small shell—the kind they call a 'pipsqueak'—but it could have killed us with a direct hit. When I did wake up, the other boys had already dragged me outside by the heels. That was a close call. I still have that shell. I dug it out, what was left of it, after I woke up.

There was another time, a German machine gun was just cutting our company to pieces. They needed someone to run a message somehow across that deadly fire, and for some reason I was chosen. So I went over, and found one of the officers knocked out, and the machine-gun fire was still pouring in. So I found Jimmy Holland's platoon, and we decided to go after the Germans. One of our fellows was hit in the head, and I got a bullet through the rim of my steel helmet. How it missed my big nose, I don't know, but it did. I said to myself, 'If that's the best they can do, they won't get me.' But I was wrong! I got a bullet in the shoulder. It split the bone there, and my collarbone too. I was scared to death by this time, but we had to keep going, and the boys eventually got that machine gun.

Our commanding officer was Major Ralston, about the bravest man I ever met. I suppose if we all have a hero to admire in our lifetime, he would have to be mine. I remember one time, he was shot in both feet while he was trying to rescue two of our men who were caught in the German crossfire. He just kept on going, crawling along in the mud. He heard this man's groans, and he picked him up, out of the German wire, and brought him back to our side. The crossfire was going on the whole time, too.

When Ralston was recommended for the Victoria Cross for that action, what he got was a reprimand, because no CO was supposed to be out in front of his front line, because he knew too much, and the Germans might get it out of him. General McBrien, our Brigadier, took the reprimand and tore it up, and sent in another recommendation for the VC for Ralston. They sent back a second reprimand, only this time it was sent to the General directly. They just *wouldn't* change their minds. Of course, the troops loved Ralston even more after that, and they would have followed him anywhere. He was a wonderful soldier, who never thought of himself. He never got the Victoria Cross, but he *should* have.

A strange thing happened many many years later, during the *Second* World War. My brother Norman, by this time, was Minister of National Defence with the Mackenzie King government, and he was killed in a tragic airplane accident in 1941. The man appointed by King to be his replacement was this same Major Ralston who had been our CO during the First War. He was a wonderful man, and Norman would have approved of him as his replacement.

You know, when I got the news of Norman's death, those two final lines of Mother's little poem flashed through my mind:

Their graves are scattered far and wide,
O'er hill and dale and sea."

139

TOM WILLIAMS

Tom Williams flew his first plane during the First World War when he was thirty-one years old. That was considered old for a pilot at the time. He kept his pilot's licence until he was eighty-seven years old, and only gave it up then because his family was worried about his safety. When I met him at the Island Airport in Toronto he was wandering around touching other people's small planes; his licence to fly was gone but the love of flying that had kept him aloft for fifty-six years was as strong as ever.

Fighting Man to Man

"I WAS BORN ON A FARM in Ingersoll, Ontario, in 1885. Father wanted me to be a farmer, but I was more interested in machinery than in growing things. I was always tinkering with the bits of machinery we had on the farm in those days—taking them apart and putting them back together again. By the time the war came along I was getting pretty old—I was twenty-nine—but I made up my mind I was going to get in the war and fly airplanes. Canada didn't have an air force so I decided to join the army and get overseas quick so I could transfer over to the Royal Flying Corps.

To cut a long story short, pretty soon I was flying some of those old egg crates—as people called them in those days. Some were good and some I didn't like at all, especially one they called a 'Rumpitty'. It was what was called a 'pusher'. You sat out in front with a pair of spectacles on your face and looked out over the nose of the thing. The engine was an air-cooled 70 h.p. Renault, which was behind you. Anyway, that's the one they wanted me to fly the day it came for me to take my flier's test in France, but the RFC always let you choose your airplane, so I didn't take the Rumpitty. I chose an 80 h.p. instead and the officer in charge didn't like this at all. He said, 'What's the big idea?' I told him the other one didn't have enough horsepower for me, and he said, 'I wouldn't mind losing you, but I'd hate to lose that 80.'

Anyway, I took the one I wanted and made one circuit and I took it up higher than I had ever been—twenty-two hundred feet —and I shut the motor off and made my landing right inside the circle. One of the mechanics whispered to me, 'I wish our instructors could set 'em down like that.' After I did about five hours in the air, they picked me for a scout pilot and sent me to South Carlton, in Lincolnshire, to train. We had some great planes there —the Avro 504K, the Bristol Scout—one of the most beautiful planes I ever flew—the Nieuport, and the DH5, which I decided was useless for scouting. I ended up with a Camel in 45 Squadron, which was a Camel squadron.

Things went along fine until one day I got shot down. They say it was the Red Baron who got me, but I say it wasn't. The plane that got me didn't approach the way Richthofen did. They had the height on us and our leader, Arthur Harris, later Sir Arthur, head of Bomber Command, saw that they had us and he said to take evasive action. But I had too much confidence in my Camel and they got me—but two of our fellows stuck with me till I got down and the Germans didn't even know they scored a victory.

The other time I got shot down was when the Canadians took Passchendaele in Belgium on the 10th of November, 1917. Oh, that was a vicious battle. Down there on the ground the troops were just wallowing in mud and the whole Canadian Corps was involved. They took it from the Germans but it cost them sixteen thousand Canadian lives. I was up in the air in my Camel and my partner, John Firth, was in another, flying with me as a pair. He signalled that he was out of ammunition and so was I. But instead of going up around the barrage he played right through it. I had to follow him, and just as we got through the barrage, one of our own machine gunners on the ground mistook me for a Hun and put twenty bullets between me and the engine; I got down just as the engine started to seize up.

After Passchendaele some of us were sent down to help the Italians. The Italians had some funny ideas. They were fighting the Austrians and losing, but there were certain things they wouldn't do against the enemy, because they said it wasn't the gentlemanly thing to do. We had been fighting in France, where anything went, so that's the way we fought when we went to Italy

—we fought to win, and all's fair in war. The Italians couldn't see that at all. But they were good fighters, especially when they were winning.

I met some great fliers—Bill Barker and Bert Hinkler were outstanding. I don't like superlatives, but I think Bill Barker was the greatest flier in that war. He was dedicated to the proper use of aircraft against an enemy. He wasn't a head-hunter and would never come back bragging about how many he shot down. Some flyers scored more victories than Bill, but as an all-round man I would put him right up there with the very top Canadians. He won the Victoria Cross, you know, and if anyone ever deserved it he did.

What I liked about the Air Force was that you were on your own and you fought man to man—just you against him—and you couldn't help but admire real smart action on the other man's part, even if he was the enemy. You just couldn't hate him, because you knew it was a fight and a fair fight, as a rule. It was different from being on the ground. The air gave you a chance to use your own ingenuity. But believe me, none of us ever considered it a game between gentlemen. That other fellow was the enemy, especially after you'd seen one of your buddies go down in flames. Gentlemen don't kill each other.

After the war I kept right on flying airplanes because I loved it. The airplane broadened man's horizons so much. The car moved man a long way but the plane has moved him so much farther. My gosh, I've seen it all in my lifetime. I saw the bicycle with the big wheel in front, and that moved on to motorbikes, and then the car, the airplane, and after that man walking around on the moon. I would have loved to have gone on that rocket. I'm personally acquainted with James Lovell, one of the astronauts, and I told him that I was ready to go any time. So far he hasn't called."

JACK AYRE

The most popular and beloved group of entertainers in Canadian history was made up of a group of muddy soldiers plucked from the trenches of the First World War and dubbed "The Dumbells". They lifted the sagging morale of war-weary troops as they sang, danced, and joked their way through the fields of battle, putting their shows on right where the action was, just behind the front lines. Jack Ayre was the piano player, sometimes comedian, and composer of the group's theme song, "The Dumbell Rag". Born in 1895, Jack Ayre became a familiar and popular entertainer again around Toronto in his later years, right up to the time of his death in 1977. He was a youthful, roly-poly eighty-year-old when we had this talk— a few inches over five feet tall, still enthusiastic about the Dumbells although nearly half a century had passed since they entertained the troops in "the war to end all wars".

The Last Tune They'll Ever Whistle

THE DUMBELL RAG

Oh—The Dumbell Rag,
That Dummy Dumbell Rag,
Sing it high or sing it low,
Just sing it together and let her go.
Oh—The Dumbell Rag,
That Dummy Dumbell Rag,
What do you care if it shine or rain?
This way you'll feel you're home again.
The D-U-M-B-E-L-L,
That ever-loving Dumbell Rag.

"WE GOT TOGETHER OVER THERE in 1917 after the battle of

Vimy Ridge. The French had tried to take the Ridge, the English had tried, the Aussies had tried, but nobody could take it. We took it. Of course, there were great casualties, and we were in there ten or twelve days—no shaves, no baths, standing all the time in water. The only bright spot was the issue of rum. They'd pour it out for us in a shell case. That was a lifesaver after standing all night in a damp trench. I'll never forget Vimy.

Captain Merton Plunkett was the man who started us off. The war was going on all around us and he put on the variety show using soldiers right out of the trenches. None of us ranked higher than a sergeant but we all could do something, sing or play a mouth organ, or in my case, I played the piano. But we were the ones who were always clowning around. He picked us to do this show and as rough as it was, the boys in the trenches loved it. Then Cap Plunkett, he was an honorary captain, got permission to form the Canadian Army Third Division Concert Party. We were called 'The Dumbells' because that's what we had as the divisional insignia, dumbbells.

The reason I got into that first group was kind of funny. I was sitting there with the other troops after the battle was over, waiting for the show to start, and I had my steel helmet on and Captain Plunkett came out and asked the audience if anyone could play the piano. My pal said, 'Go on, Jack,' and he pushed me up on my feet.

The Captain said, 'Do you play the piano?' I said, 'Yes, sir.' 'Come on up,' he says, and that's how I started. After the show he said, 'Can you come again tomorrow?' 'Sure,' I said, because I'll tell you, the night before in the trenches, I said to myself, if I get through this night I think I'll make it through the war. I had a feeling something was going to save me . . . and here it was. I was being taken out of the trenches to play the piano. Funny how things happen.

When that show finished, Captain Plunkett said, 'Come on. There's going to be a show formed soon as the General gives me consent and I want you for the piano.' My Colonel agreed to let me go and in about two weeks' time I was back with the Captain. Al Plunkett, the Captain's brother, was there too, so Al and I were really the first two in the Dumbells shows. He said, 'We'll get Ross Hamilton and Alan Murray and some of the other boys.' We all got together and in the latter part of July 1917, we started rehearsals. We gave our first show in a little hut in a place we used to call

144

'Gooey Servants', that's as close as we could get to the real French pronunciation. We started the show off with a chorus number that started, 'Here's a toast to you and a toast to you.' I don't think I've played that number since those days. We had written away to English actresses asking for any old gowns they might have and the two 'girls' in our show, Ross Hamilton and Alan Murray, received back the most beautiful gowns from them.

A real genius of a guy in our outfit made a spotlight out of an old gasoline can and it even had a colour wheel on it. It was great. The fellows used to say that with all these colours and everything they really would forget they were in a shack behind the lines. For a while, anyway, it would seem like a theatre in the West End of London. The next day after the show, that's all you'd hear the troops talk about. 'Did you see the show last night?' 'Wasn't it wonderful?' It was a success from the very start. Of course, it was a wonderful bunch of talent that Plunkett had. Those boys wrote their own skits, they designed and painted scenery, designed costumes, and above all, they were good performers. The boys in the trenches really appreciated what we did and you'd hear them whistling 'The Dumbell Rag' going up the line. I used to think that maybe it's the last tune they'll ever whistle, my tune.

We used to get Sunday off but we worked, and worked hard, the other six days of the week. We didn't mind that, though. We loved it, and another thing, we were out of the trenches. Everybody was sick of the war by that time. We were sick of disease, sick of all the death, and morale was really low when Captain Plunkett organized the original eight of us and started entertaining the troops. No one can realize unless they were there how much that meant to the troops.

We had a quartet that was second to none and we had a couple of comedians and good character men. And, of course, we had the female impersonators, two of the best. Ross Hamilton was fantastic. If he were to walk in the door now I'd defy you to say that was a man. He was the most beautiful woman I ever saw and yet offstage he was totally male. His singing voice was wonderful, a high soprano voice that sounded exactly like a woman's.

We had one truck to carry our scenery and stuff and we always performed up in the forward area of the war. In fact, one of our shows had to be stopped when a shell came through the roof and went out the other side of the building. The idea was that we were up where we were needed. When the boys came out of the lines for a short breather we had a show ready for them. We weren't allowed to play in very big places because they didn't want too many men congregated in one spot because of shellfire or a bomb or something. So these huts built by our own engineers would hold maybe 250 or 300 men. They were just wood with sandbags around the outside. We all used to sleep on the stage after the show, just take a blanket and lie down on the hard board stage. I used to sleep close to the piano so if anything came in I'd have that extra protection. Anyway, it was better than a trench. I always figured that playing the piano saved my life because my battalion suffered great casualties after I joined the Dumbells. The company I had been in came out of one battle with 43 men; 215 had gone in.

The eight of us continued together for about a year and then they decided to amalgamate us with the Princess Pats Concert Party. They were a very fine group who had been going even longer than the Dumbells, but they had been doing it more on a part-time basis. It wasn't a permanent thing like our group was. So we got both groups together in 1918 to put on H.M.S. *Pinafore*. Boy, that was a good show. We borrowed the score from the D'Oyly Carte people and we stuck to the original plot and did most of the songs, but because some of the recitations were too dry for the troops, we added in some of the popular numbers of the times. For instance, in the second act, where Captain Cochrane is sitting on the deck singing 'Fair Moon to Thee I Sing', we thought, 'Oh gee, that's no good for the troops,' so we substituted one that went 'Give Me the Moonlight, Give Me the Girl, Leave the Rest to Me'. Altogether, it was a wonderful show. We put it on in Mons, Belgium, first and there was a reporter there from a paper in England called *The Referee*. He reported that although it was a lovely show he was sure that in some places Gilbert and Sullivan wouldn't recognize it. The D'Oyly Carte people saw this in London and sent a stiff note to Plunkett telling him to stick to the original score or they'd take it away. But they couldn't do anything. After all, it was wartime and we were at the front.

After the Armistice we played the show all the way down to Le Havre in France. We got to Paris and saw the Folies Bergères and sat in the front row, I remember. Then we went back to England and then home on the old *Olympic*. It was now March of 1919 and I had been away three years. Funny thing was, though, when the war was over and we wanted to continue the Dumbells in Canada, everyone said, 'Forget it. The war is over and all the people want to do is forget.' But Captain Plunkett got his uncle, who was in the fur business, to loan him some money and we got started in September of 1919.

The man who gave us our break was Ambrose Small, the big theatre operator in Toronto. He told Plunkett to take the show up to London, Ontario, where he had a theatre. The first night, the manager there, Mr. Minhinnick, phoned Mr. Small in Toronto and told him that we were the biggest success in years. The next day Small was there and saw the show and I heard him tell Plunkett, 'Toronto in two weeks.' So we played around Stratford and all those places and we came to Toronto and stayed one solid month and it was just sellout business. Never a vacant seat. Funny thing, it was while we were playing Ambrose Small's theatre in Toronto that he disappeared. He was a millionaire, you know, and they never found what happened to him to this day.

I think the secret of the thing was that the boys who saw us overseas would write home and tell their families they saw our show and now those families had a chance to see the same show that they saw. It was 1920 by the time we took the show on its first western tour and in the fall of that year we took it East and it was the same everywhere we went, people lined up for hours. I don't think we ever had an empty seat. The Dumbells became kind of a household word in Canada, everybody would be talking about us and wherever we went the papers were full of our pictures. I guess you could say we were the first full-fledged Canadian show-business stars.

Then we took the show to Broadway, to the Ambassador Theatre at 49th and Broadway. We started in May—the wrong time of the year because that was the end of the season and all the other theatres were closing down—but we still did extremely well. The contract was for six weeks but they kept us for nine. The papers raved about the show and they said, 'The female impersonators are the best we've ever seen and if that be treason— so be it.' We could have stayed all summer but the boys wanted their holidays and we had to start up in Canada again in September.

We met all the big names in show business at that time: Paul Whiteman, Mary Pickford and the Gish girls, Theda Bara, D. W. Griffith, and the big glamour girl of that era, Mae Murray. What a thrill for all of us rubbing shoulders backstage with all of those celebrities. It was prohibition time when we were there but it made no difference. Wherever we were invited there was always plenty to drink. I remember Red Newman one time at one of those parties. He was a great talent, a Cockney who was very proud of being a Canadian. Anyway, he was joking around and telling everybody he went to Cambridge University, speaking in his best Cockney accent. The London County Council School was all he went to. But at that party was a Lord Burley who had just won the Olympic hurdles. He heard Red say this and he turned around and said very seriously to Red in this very cultured English voice, 'I say, old chap, that's bully. I was at Cambridge too.' Red says, 'You was, was you?' Boy, that got quite a laugh.

We went back to Canada and the fall of that year, 1921, we started the tours again. They continued till 1929. The big mistake they made though was in '25 or '26, they put girls in it. See, it wasn't the same any more. It had been all men, with female impersonators. When they put real girls in it it became just like an ordinary revue. Ross Hamilton quit then because there was no way he could compete with the real thing.

I settled down after that. I was tired of living out of a suitcase. I became the piano player at Loew's Vaudeville Theatre in Toronto and I stayed in one form of show business or other all my life.

There is one thing I'll never understand though. Our group did a wonderful job in the war for the morale of the Canadian troops but we never received any kind of recognition for it from the Government, no medals or citations of any kind. I could never understand that, you know. People have been honoured for a lot less than we did."

NOTE: In 1975 *Voice of the Pioneer* held a reunion of the four remaining members of the Dumbell troupe in Toronto. Thousands of people wrote in for the 500 available seats at Lambert Lodge, a senior citizens' home that has since been torn down. We managed to have the Dumbells received by the Mayor of Toronto and presented on the floor of the Ontario Legislature, where they received a standing ovation. However, my suggestion that they be made Companions of the Order of Canada has met with silence from Ottawa.

Jack Ayre and Jerry Brayford died in 1977. As I write this, Bill Redpath and Jack McLaren are still very much alive.

MRS. C. N. BROWN

*On the 5th of December, 1917, the city of Halifax, Nova Sco-
tia, was devastated by explosion, and an estimated two
thousand people died. The Norwegian freighter Imo and a
French munitions ship, the Mont Blanc, collided in the harbour, and the resulting explosion, and its consequences,
ripped the city apart. An earthquake, air concussion, and a
tidal wave followed. Pavements split, and the whole city
trembled on its ironstone and granite base. In the north end
of Halifax, houses were lifted from their foundations; trees
were snapped off; and iron rails were twisted like so much
spaghetti. Windows shattered for sixty miles around, the
splinters flying like daggers, killing and blinding thousands
of people. Then came the tidal wave, followed by gale-force
winds, and a night-time blizzard to add to the misery.*

*For sixteen-year-old Isobel Shaw it started like any other
morning with school as usual.*

The Halifax Explosion

"I DON'T THINK anybody who ever went through that could
ever forget it. It happened during morning devotions as the principal was reading from the Proverbs. Suddenly the whole building
shook with an awful bang. We all thought that the furnace had
exploded. Well, that was soon ruled out, but as all the pictures on
the walls went sideways, there was panic in the class. For a moment everybody was screaming and running around, not knowing
what it was. We thought maybe it was a bomb, because the war
was on, and we had heard about air raids and zeppelins and that
sort of thing. And, of course, Halifax was very concious of those
things because we had the Navy there.

Finally, one of the boys got up and said, 'Now just a minute.
Let's calm down. Let's go to the fire escape and see.' Well, we
looked out and there was a cloud of white smoke in the sky and,

of course, that convinced us it was an airplane of some kind dropping something. Still not knowing what had happened, we left the building and decided to head for our homes. It was then that we began to meet people coming toward us, bleeding. It was a very cold, wintry day and we began to get more and more frightened, still not knowing what had happened. We moved on faster to our homes.

I got to our house and found that everyone was all right, but the front door had been blown in. Then we looked at some of the other houses and saw the same thing—the doors had been all blown in.

It wasn't long before we heard that two ships in the harbour had caused the explosion, but even then we had no idea of the damage.

Shortly after that, the police came 'round. They had a loudspeaker of some kind, telling the people to get out of their homes and make for an open space. A great many people went to Citadel Hill and the Commons, because they thought that there might be another explosion. We stayed there for most of the day, until we were told it was safe to go back. When we left our house in the morning we were told to take any valuables out. I don't know what I took, but my sister took the Bible and our uncle's picture. I've never forgotten that.

After we got back to our homes the more adventurous of us, some of the boys and a few of the girls, went up to see what was going on. By this time we began to see drays—those old-fashioned low wagons—piled high with bodies—just covered! My brother went up closer to look, and he came back sickened by what he had seen. It was then that we found that the north end of the city had got the full brunt of it. That night it stormed, and there was a very heavy snow-fall. That meant that a lot of the injured people who were trapped under something and who might have been saved just died of the cold. They froze to death.

There was a lot of fire too, because in those days people used stoves, and when they fell over, the houses burned. We didn't have radios, so the only news we were getting was word of mouth. It was the next morning, December 6, before we heard that help was needed at Camp Hill Hospital, which was new then, and still hadn't been officially opened. People were lying in the corridors, and the doctors were working frantically. Our job was to carry around bowls of hot water with blue tablets in them,

150

some kind of disinfectant to prevent blood-poisoning I think, because a lot of the wounds, aside from the broken and missing arms and legs, were skin wounds. These wounds were full of black dirt from all this exploding stuff and the nurses had to clean the skin off. Years later a lot of those people still had signs of those dirty wounds, because it was impossible for the doctors, under those circumstances, to do everything that should have been done.

We worked at the hospital all day and helped as best we could. The Halifax Station, the railway station, was completely destroyed and no trains could get in or out. The town of Truro, about forty miles away, had got word by this time and they sent down help on a train that came as close as it could get. The automobiles that were still running went out to meet them. Then the word came in by telegraph that the Massachusetts Relief Committee had been set up, and that help would be on the way—doctors, nurses, and medical supplies. The British Government responded too.

One of the problems that arose because of all the help coming in was that there was no place to house the volunteers. Some were put up in tents on the Commons, and those who had homes took some of them in.

The damage from the explosion was very erratic. One house might just have the front door blown in, while the house next door might be completely destroyed. And another might just have all the windows shattered. The explosion was just like a wave. It would skip one street and hit the next, all the way from the north down to the south end of the city. I know one man, in the business district of Barrington and Granville streets, who just got out after putting in a display behind his great big plate-glass window. It just shattered to pieces after he got out.

After my group left the hospital, we went up to the north end to a bank where we began to register people. That had to be done for the Relief Commission, so they would know where people were. It was *days* before they found out where some people were. Our job was to take names down, and where they lived, and if they were missing any relatives.

Many strange things happened. We had a milkman, and, of course, in those days they delivered with horses. Well, we never found his body, but we *did* find his coat, his milkman's coat with all his customers' bills in it. And that's how we knew Mr. Edmonds was gone. The rectory of St. George's Church, across the arm of Halifax harbour, had a piece of iron come right through the wall. It imbedded itself right above the fireplace. I was a member of St. George's, and this huge organ we had was just blown across the chancel—just like a feather—and almost completely destroyed. It happened in other churches too.

One of the worst things of all was the number of people who were blinded by flying glass. Working in the hospital, we did see a lot of people with bandages on their eyes, but we didn't know at the time how bad it was. We were too busy running back and forth, and being just high-school age we were very excited. It wasn't till later we took in the enormity of it. For days and days and days they couldn't find people. Often parents couldn't find the bodies of their children, and they didn't know if they were alive, or in the hospital, or if somebody had taken them in. That was one reason they started this registry thing, so they could at least find out where people were.

There was a Commission set up with the money sent by governments from all over the world, and they paid out compensation and gave pensions to people who were blinded by the Halifax explosion. The pensions were not enough though, but I guess it was something. That Commission wasn't disbanded until 1975, and even today there are blind people still getting those pensions, because some of the blinded were very young children in 1917."

CANON HARRY ALFRED SIMMS

Harry Alfred Simms was born in England in 1884 and he came to Canada as an Anglican minister in 1911 at the age of twenty-seven. For the next sixty-five years he served the people of Northern Ontario in parishes on Manitoulin Island and in Cobalt and New Liskeard. He fell in love with the North and the people who chose to live there. He called them the finest human beings in the world.

A Different Kind of Canadian

"I HAVE KEPT A RECORD which delights me now in my old age; I first started speaking in public in Portsmouth, England, sixty-eight years ago and I have never once failed to appear—and on time— through physical disability. I've always felt that if people could come to hear you on time, you could at least show them the courtesy of being there on time yourself!

When I landed in the silver boom town of Cobalt, Ontario, in 1915 I came into contact with the kind of Canadian I learned to appreciate very highly. I immediately found myself in the middle of all their activities concerning the war and soon was made Executive Secretary of the Soldiers' Patriotic Fund and Soldiers' Aid Commission. In that war, the wives were looked after by private contributions and there was no Canadian Legion either so I was responsible for all the contacts and care of the women and the children and also of the soldiers themselves when they returned and needed help.

When we started the Patriotic Fund and paid out our first cheques to the women, a few contributors complained because they heard that some of the women had gone down to Laing Street and bought themselves a new hat. So I asked Harry Browning of the *Cobalt Nugget* to put a notice in the newspaper the next day saying that as far as the Patriotic Committee was concerned, if any Cobalt wife of a soldier felt she could get more good from a

new hat than a noon meal, she was welcome to go and buy another new hat! It was nobody's business but her own.

It was a very happy and a very busy time. Everybody in Cobalt was giving a day's pay per month for patriotic purposes and
the idea was that no other collection would be made. At the end
of the war they figured out that they were just a few dollars short
of every man in Cobalt having given a day's pay for every month
of the war. And that's even more remarkable when you think that
a lot of those men in the mines were Eastern Europeans who
couldn't be expected to have the same kind of commitment to the
war as those with British backgrounds.

Cobalt was an extremely friendly place and everybody got
the maximum amount of respect no matter where you came from.
I remember at the end of the war, the Committee was having a
meeting to plan the celebration. There was a knock on the door
and a man was there who said that the Germans in the camp
wanted to know if they could join in the celebration. Bomber
Neilly, the manager at one of the mines, jumped up and said, 'Oh
hell, if those fellows think they've got anything to celebrate, let
them celebrate.' So they joined in and they marched up and down
Laing Street behind the band just as if they'd won the war. Oh
my, it was funny. You could only do that in Cobalt. What a wonderful town it was—totally, totally different.

Cobalt started when a prospector by the name of Fred LaRose
threw his hammer at a fox and accidentally struck a silver vein.
You'll hear people say that's not a true story but believe me, it is.
It was the biggest silver find that the world had ever known and
people flocked into Cobalt from everywhere. With all this going
on you might expect that the early Cobalt would be the kind of
place you see in the movies. It wasn't. It was a very respectable
place from the very beginning. There were no barrooms or sa-
loons. There were bars at the hotels, of course, but they were
quiet places carrying on in a normal way. The people in Cobalt
were isolated because there were no roads or railroads into town
from the outside and they made their own amusement. Soccer
was big. I played myself and so did most of the men, but the First
World War put an end to that; a lot of the men went over and
most of them never came back.

Hockey was also very big. Cobalt, as a matter of fact, belonged to the first National Hockey League. I said before that the
town was very well-behaved but things got pretty well excited at

hockey games. There was a fair amount of gambling and I'm afraid that was the main reason for having a professional hockey team. It was a good team, though, and they played against Ottawa, Montreal, and all the teams down there. And as far as gambling was concerned, the whole way of life there was a gamble. It was a silver boom and everybody, even those with just loose change in their pockets, was investing in the mines. Every prospector you'd meet on the street was convinced he had just struck the biggest and richest vein—and he had no trouble finding investors who wanted to believe in him. Stock certificates flooded the town and they weren't worth the paper they were printed on—but they looked good.

I used to go down to the Brokers' Office every day to get the war news on the telegraph. I was asked to be down on one certain morning because something was up, and when I arrived the office was packed and I was called to the front. The Chairman, John McKay, an insurance agent, said that the people of the town wanted to honour me for the services I was rendering. He pointed to one fellow and said, 'Joe, you're first.' Joe got up and said, 'I'll give him fifty shares in the Bluebird.' Well, the whole place burst out in a roar of laughter. Then Jim got up and said, 'I'll give him a hundred in the Golden Brick.' Another roar of laughter—and they kept that up for a long time. Of course they knew, and I knew, and they knew that I knew, that it was all worthless. They never bothered to even turn over the paper to me, but we had a great time that day!

The second day after I arrived there was a message asking me to come down to the mess, and so I went down. There were about ten men there and they said to me, 'Now, you're green to this kind of community,' and I said, 'Yes, very.' And they said, 'Well, we're a peculiar lot of people from all over the world but we're all a lot of optimists. We wouldn't be in mining if we weren't. We're just afraid that you might be carried away by all the optimism and we happen to know what your stipend is. We would like to warn you that a person in your financial position is in no position to be buying mining stocks.' Now I thought that was wonderful, although I had no intention of doing it in the first place, and I thanked them very much. That tells you, though, of the character of the people, to have thought of doing that for a stranger."

"CYCLONE" TAYLOR

Frederick Wellington Taylor was born on June 23, 1884, and
by the time the National Hockey League was formed in 1917,
he had already established a reputation for himself as the
fastest man who ever laced on a pair of skates. "Cyclone"
Taylor was what they called him because according to records of the time, he skated so fast he sometimes looked like
a blur.

There was no professional hockey when Cyclone Taylor
started to play, and he is rightly regarded as one of the true
pioneers of the game we know today.

The Best Game in the World

"I STARTED PLAYING HOCKEY when the family moved to Listowel, Ontario. I was about five years old. I stayed around there, playing in the Intermediate and the Ontario Hockey Association until
1904, when our Junior team cleaned up all the opposition in Western Ontario, and beat Barrie out for the northern districts. We
played off in Toronto in a sudden-death game against the King-
ston Frontenacs, who beat us 7-4 to win the Ontario Championship. The Listowel people were very annoyed at the OHA for making us come to Toronto to play a sudden-death game. If we had
had a home game our chances might have been better. It was just
that kind of thing that gave Toronto the name 'Hog Town' in those
days. They wanted the final game in Toronto so they could get a
big gate.

In the summer of 1904, some of the teams from as far away as
Portage La Prairie showed an interest in me, and I got offers to
play with them. It was then that the OHA came right out and told
me that if I would not come to Toronto and play for the Marlbor-
oughs, who were challengers for the Stanley Cup, they would
keep me out of hockey, which shows you that that kind of thing
was going on in sports even then.

Anyway, I decided to go to Portage La Prairie, in Manitoba, and that led to my joining the team in Michigan, and playing in the International League, the first *ever*. Michigan won the championship in 1905, and that was the first professional hockey in America. The League was suspended in 1907, because of a recession in that area of the States at that time, so the players, the majority of whom were Canadians, were released and allowed to go back to their homes. Soon as the hockey people in Canada heard about the suspension of that first professional league in the States, they jumped in, and started talking professional league—Quebec, Montreal, Ottawa, and Toronto—up here. They started signing us up fast, about sixty of us from that other league. So it was in the fall of 1907 that professional hockey got started in Canada. They called themselves the 'Eastern Canadian Hockey League'.

While all this was happening, the Renfrew team, which was tired of winning the Ottawa Valley League year after year, thought they would like to join the ECHL and play professional. The ECHL people just laughed at them and that made them so damn mad they said, 'We'll *form* a league.' See, Renfrew had lots of money behind them, six millionaires as a matter of fact. One of them, McBrien, already owned the national French team in Montreal, and they had big interests up in Northern Ontario; so they formed this league, which they called the National Hockey Association, with Renfrew, another team called the *Nationals*, Haileybury, Cobalt, and the Wanderers. Then Ottawa, Quebec, and Toronto fell in line and the ECHL was out, and the NHA was in! So the NHA went on till 1917, when the NHL was formed. I was one of the first players in the NHL, as I was in those other first professional leagues—more by good luck than good management I must say, but nevertheless, I was one of the first professional hockey players in North America.

In 1912 the Patrick boys organized their hockey empire on the Pacific coast. They had built three artificial ice rinks—one in Victoria, one in Vancouver, and one in Westminster. At the end of December 1911, they were ready to play and Frank Patrick came East to talk with the President of the Hockey League in the East at that time, and to ask him, in a nice way, if the NHL would lend him a few players, or sell him a few, or in some way give him a start, because there was no hockey at all in the West. But the President replied, 'Look here, Frank Patrick, if you've gone out there, and built artificial ice arenas, and you have no idea where you're gonna get your players from, you'll have to sink or swim yourself. You'll get no help from us.' And Frank said, 'That's all I want to know, Mr. President.' He walked out, and within two weeks he'd signed up thirty of the top-flight players in eastern Canada to fill his teams on the Pacific coast! And that caused as much trouble as any problems caused by Renfrew when they formed the ECHL! I was one of those thirty players Patrick signed. I went to the coast in the fall of 1911, and I stayed there.

There was seven-man hockey teams at that time. But I won't say whether it was better or not, because I remember when Ty Cobb—the greatest baseball player that ever played—was asked to comment, long after he'd retired, on the quality of modern baseball as compared to when he played the game. Well, he said so many cheap things that his prestige dropped down at least 100 per cent in the eyes of people who had always admired him. There he was, knocking the game that had made him the tiger of baseball history.

I've always remembered that, so for me to get out now and try to compare hockey today with when we were playing would be foolish. I'll defend them, but I won't say we were better. Certainly, we were as good, and I think any of our good players then would be the giants in today's National Hockey League.

In that seven-man hockey, there was an extra player, called a 'rover'. He was supposed to know where the weakness on his team was, and to fill up, and help wherever he was needed. That was the position I played. It made for an excellent game. We played sixty minutes of hockey, all of us! There was no two minutes on and two minutes off, and I've always contended that for any young man between the ages of eighteen and thirty who's taken care of himself and is in good health, sixty minutes of hockey would be no hard chore. I know it wasn't for me.

There was only one referee in the game when I played. There was violence then, too, though. I remember one game, back then, when the other team started clubbing ours with their sticks. Then they all left the ice, downed their hockey sticks, and picked up clubs—wherever they got 'em I don't know—and said to us, 'If you come out here, we'll finish you, before you get out of the rink.' Well, it calmed down after a while, and everything turned out okay. Things like that did happen occasionally, but not too often.

I recall another game in Sault Ste. Marie, where the referee, poor fella, was doing his best but the Sault team was behind in the score. The fans kept hollering what they were going to do with the referee when the game was over. About ten minutes before the game was to finish, this referee, who knew that some real trouble was afoot, called the game for some infraction or to fix his skate or something, and he left the ice for what people thought was just a minute or two. Well, he never came back, and we had to finish that game with a makeshift referee! The funny thing was, a more perfect ten minutes of hockey was played then than I ever saw before. The players went out there, and realized they had to do their best. There was no more fighting, or scrapping, and the 'Sault' won the game in overtime.

There were some great, great, great players at that time: men like 'Newsy' Lalonde, say, and Joe Hall, and Lester Patrick. Lester was a giant. 'Hods' Stewart was just immense. It's hard to pick one that I could say is the best I've seen over the years. There have been so many—Eddie Shore, Frank Boucher, the Conachers —the list is endless.

Hockey has always been Canada's game. We still play it better than anyone else in the world, and I wish I could lace up my skates right now, and get out there and help keep it that way!"

AMELIA VEITCH

Amelia Veitch was born in 1896 and went to Matheson, Ontario, in 1912. She remembers the great fire of July 29, 1916, vividly. That fire swept through Matheson, Cochrane, Iroquois Falls, and other northern communities, leaving thousands homeless.

Burnt Hands, Burnt Feet, Burnt Faces, and Burnt Hair

"THAT 1916 FIRE was the first one for most of the people in Matheson. They weren't here for the last big one before that, in 1911, so they didn't know much about forest fires or how bad they could be.

It was a real dry spell we were having, and there were lots of small fires everywhere. Most everyone was haying, and they already had it in the barns. It was beautiful weather for that and there was a real good crop that year. Somebody asked our neighbour, Mr. Brown, what he was going to do with all that hay, and he said, 'Oh, I don't know. I think I'll burn it.' He was joking, y'know, but that's what happened. He lost every bit of it the day of the fire.

The soldiers came before the fire, and made most of the people leave, y'know, even if they didn't want to go. There were two ladies, I remember, who didn't want to leave their homes, so the soldiers just picked them up bodily, and carried them to the train.

The freight cars were filled up with people and the train took them down to the river, and put them in the water there. Everybody took blankets with them to put over their heads. This helped them to breathe, y'see, because it was very, very hot. More people would have died if it hadn't been for those blankets. Most of the ones who did die were out in the woods when the fire came.

When the fire got bad it just seemed to travel in great big balls in the air, and then the balls would come down somewhere, explode, and start another fire there.

My father had a potato patch, and the crop was still in the ground when the fire came. For three or four days after, we'd keep running over to that patch and pulling the potatoes out and eating them. They were baked right in the ground from the heat. The forest came right up to the ends of our fields, you see.

It was the same with the chickens; they were just roasted and people used to pick them up and eat them because there was no other food. They weren't cooked real good, just partly, but they were better than nothing. The whole place was like an oven. Our house was the only place out there that didn't burn. All the neighbours' houses burned and they came over to our place, and when Mr. Pegg went out to look for his house, he couldn't find it, and no wonder—it was burnt to the ground.

We used to get our water in barrels at that time from Black River, and after the fire, the barrels were all there, but there was nothing left but the hoops—all in a bunch. They were full of water when the fire came.

People were good, though. When the relief came in after, there was food and clothes and everything, and lumber was sent in for people to build houses. Tents too, for people to stay in till the houses were built. The few people around here who had anything left at all shared it with everyone else. Mrs. Monahan had just got a bag of flour that morning, one hundred pounds, and that night they baked every bit of it up into biscuits to feed people.

I suppose it was pretty discouraging for a lot of the people because they were just gettin' started, y'know, and everything they had done in the last three or four years was all gone. But not many gave up that I can remember. The government gave enough wood for a house if you stayed. There was no insurance, of course. We couldn't get it, so there was nothing for people to do anyway except stay.

They had three undertaker tents in town to look after the bodies. They'd put five or six bodies in one casket because there was nothing left but bones, and they didn't know who the bones belonged to. Up in the Matheson cemetery, they dug a great big ditch and just laid all the coffins and rough boxes alongside each other and covered them up.

One family, the Robinsons, I knew very well. Mrs. Robinson's son was burned, but they never could tell his remains so they just took one body they found and buried it and told her it was her son, just to make her feel better.

The thing was though, you didn't have to look very far to see somebody worse than you; men with their feet burned because they had been too busy gettin' out of where they were to take off their burning shoes; and lots of people with burnt hands, burnt feet, burnt faces, and burnt hair. There was one little boy who had to go identify twenty bodies. He was the only one left of this family of uncles and brothers and children who all lived in the same place. They were out of town a bit, the flames were all around them, and when they'd run one way the fire was there. It caught them all, and they died right there. The little boy was away from home at the time, and that's why he lived. Other people smothered in root houses. In Val Gagné, a lot of people smothered in a railway rock cut; the fire took out all the oxygen and they just died with no air. It was a terrible, terrible time."

ARCHIE STERICK

Archie Sterick was a master mechanic in Winnipeg for the
CPR *during the First World War, and an officer with the rail-*
way unions. In this capacity he moved around the country,
and he was the man most responsible for keeping the Van-
couver railwaymen from walking off the job in sympathy
during the ill-fated Winnipeg General Strike of 1919.

Winnipeg was a rough-and-ready town in those days be-
fore and after the First World War, the prototype of the
Western frontier town. It had plenty of people in the push to
open the West, but there were few amenities.

Winnipeg Was a Rough, Tough Town

"I LIVED AT 377 LOGAN AVENUE IN WINNIPEG. There was no
water in the house, no toilet facilities, and practically no paved
roads. Alexander Street was the 'fast' street of the town, and a
mayor by the name of Tom Sharp got into power and he chased
these young 'ladies' out of the houses there. Well, they scattered
all over the city, and I got one of them living next door to me on
Logan Avenue. One morning my gate was covered with blood, so
I asked one of the roomers what happened. 'Well,' he told me,
'one of the guys trying to get in next door made a mistake, and
came into your house, and I had to handle him kinda rough to
throw him back over the fence.' Boy, oh boy, Winnipeg was a
rough, tough town in those days. I don't think you could get any
rougher in the western States. That's how Mayor Sharp got into
power, to see if he could clean it up. But he got into trouble, because instead of having that *one* street for prostitution, they were
distributed all over the city!

Winnipeg was also the leading union point in Canada then. I
think there was more union shops and union lodges in Winnipeg
than anywhere else. It got real bad during the 1919 General Strike,
which originated on the railroad. This strike tied up the railroad

and all of Western Canada just after the First World War. It was as serious as any strike before or since. Streetcars and buses were burnt and there was a riot every other day somewhere in the city.

My job was to travel all over the district and consult with all the union leaders, in order to keep them at work. When all this trouble started, I was sent to Vancouver to take charge of the CPR union in British Columbia. At Vancouver, especially, there was a lot of labour troubles and everybody in the larger shops were out on strike. I managed to keep the railroad unions in the province solid for staying at work. I kept the officers of the union and the management people in contact with each other every day.

At the same time, we had a boiler explosion at Revelstoke, and I was on my way up there, when I got a message to come back to Vancouver, because labour problems were piling up. At that time, the streetcar men were the main leaders in the labour movement there, and I remember advising them that if they joined this General Strike, they would start back to work when the strike was over as brand-new men, losing all the pension rights they had built up. As it turned out, that's exactly what did happen to hundreds of those men in that 1919 strike. And that's why I worked so hard to keep the men in Vancouver at work—so they wouldn't lose their seniority rights. I remember one meeting in the little garden behind the railroad shops in Vancouver; there were four or five hundred men there, and I was telling them the dangers of joining in this strike, and trying to persuade them to stay on the job. They were looking at me like a bunch of wolves, because they didn't much like what I was saying.

See, this whole strike was bad from the beginning, because the unions didn't have the know-how or experience to organize a general strike. The three levels of government—federal, provincial, and municipal—were convinced the whole thing was a communist conspiracy, mainly because of the fact that OBU was being formed at that time. OBU was what was known as 'One Big Union', and it was supposed to be Marxist. The strike was called for May 15, 1919, after the metals and building trades union had already gone on strike for union recognition and collective bargaining. So the General Strike was called in sympathy, and more than 22,000 workers in Winnipeg stayed off the job. Civil servants and everybody. The city came to a complete standstill. Only the essential services, like water and hospitals, were allowed to keep going, but with skeleton crews only. The government brought in the Royal

164

North West Mounted Police, because they knew the city police were sympathetic to the strikers. They even had the army on standby.

Well, the strike went on and on, and nothing much happened, because the union policy was a peaceful one, although that was hard to enforce. On the 21st of June, there was supposed to be a big parade of strikers, and they were gathering by the thousands in downtown Winnipeg. The police got frightened, because they figured they couldn't handle crowds like that, so they went to the mayor and told him. In the meantime, the crowds began attacking this streetcar that was being operated by 'scab' labour. The Mounties rushed in on their horses, and when one of the horses tripped, the crowd, which was in a frenzied mood by now, began to attack the rider, who was a Mountie. Then the rest of the Mounties started firing their guns into the crowd. Well, the result was that two men were killed, and about twenty others were injured. In fact, the whole thing has been known ever since as 'Bloody Sunday', because that's when it happened—Sunday, June 21, 1919. It was all downhill after that for the unions, and the strike was called off on June 26, five days later.

All the strike leaders were charged with seditious conspiracy, including Woodsworth, who was founder of the CCF. I think it may have been as a result of that strike that Woodsworth was elected two years later to the House of Commons in Ottawa. In fact, he was the first socialist ever elected, and after that, the CCF, and later the NDP, became a political force to reckon with in Canada. So as far as labour is concerned, there were some good things and some bad things that came out of it, but it was certainly a landmark in the annals of Canadian labour history."

ALFRED MILLER

The Gaspé Peninsula in the Province of Quebec is one of the great beauty spots in Canada. The people had a history of fishing, farming, lumbering, and little else, until the copper mines came. Before copper, just about everybody was poor, and they had come to accept poverty as their lot. Highways were limited to what were little more than wagon trails that followed the edge of the sea. Inland there wasn't much, except trees and rocks.

Alfred Miller was a typical Gaspésian. He fished a little, farmed a little, and did a bit of lumbering; but inside he carried the notion that all that rock must surely contain a wealth of minerals. So when he had nothing else to do, which wasn't often, he prospected. His persistence paid off in 1909, when he discovered copper, but it was many years later before anybody took his discovery seriously.

Gaspé Copper

"IN THE SUMMER OF 1909, I was with a party of timber cruisers on the York River and, as usual, I kept watching out for signs of minerals. We went ashore to have lunch where the gravel was, and when I got lookin' around at the rocks there, I noticed signs of copper in the loose gravel. I knew enough about minerals to know copper when I saw it. Anyway, I took some pieces home and they just sat there for the next twelve years before I *could* do anything about them. You see, prospecting was more or less a hobby; providing for my wife and family was my first responsibility. We had four girls and five boys, so I didn't have much time to prospect. I had to keep my nose to the grindstone just to feed and clothe everybody.

Well, by 1921, the children were growing up a bit, and for the first time I found myself with a little time on my hands. Times were really tough in 1921. Everything went flat for about a year, and there was no work at all so my brothers and I decided to go prospecting. Earlier that year my brother had gone with a party to blaze out a trail up at the head of York Lake, and I had told him about this copper I had found there years before. I said for him to watch out and see if he could pick up some more, because up until that time not more than a half-dozen men had ever been on that piece of ground in the whole of history. It was virgin ground. Well, when he came back, sure enough, he had some samples, and pieces he picked up at York Lake. So we decided to go and do some prospecting.

We gathered up some supplies in the town of Gaspé, and started up. We didn't have a tent, just a blanket to put up over us for shelter. Everything had to be carried on our backs because the York River gets so low you can't canoe on it. It took about five days, carrying about eighty pounds each, to get as far as York Lake. We thought because my brother found some stuff there, we'd try that branch of the river, but after a few days looking, we decided it wasn't there. So we tried another branch of the river, and by now our food was all gone and we had to go back to Gaspé for more. We hadn't found anything, but we figured we were on the right track. So we loaded up with more provisions, and started out on another five-day trip up there. One day, after we had lunch, we started up the brook again, breakin' rocks, of course, all the way. Then we saw a brood of partridges and we were gonna snare some of them, when my brother happened to look up, and see this big mound of rock, and he said, 'There's where we'll be.' We looked a little further north, and we could see the rocks were rusted around. We went over, and sure enough, that's where we found quite a good showing of copper. We spent a few more days lookin' over the country all 'round there, and we decided that was the best spot.

We started to stake, and we staked till our supplies ran out again, and we had to go back to Gaspé to get more. Between then and the new year of 1922 we made five trips up there. We couldn't carry enough, y'know, to last us very long. We could stake up to 200 acres—each of us. Then we climbed up this mountain, and my brother said, 'We'll call this "Needle Peak".' I remember that so well! Then, when we went up the other mountain we said, 'We'll call this "Copper Mountain".' And that's what they're called to this day.

After all our staking was done, we went home, and announced our find in the town of Gaspé. Nobody paid much attention and a lot just laughed at us. They said, 'Whoever heard of a mine down in Gaspé?' And, do you know, it was hard to get anybody outside Gaspé interested either.

In 1922, we had an inspector of mines come down from Quebec City to look at our stake for the Government. He said that it was quite a showing of copper, and it would be a reserve for the future. And then, it was in 1924 I think, Dr. Alcock, a geologist for the Canada Geological Survey, came down. He figured that further work might disclose larger bodies of low-grade ore, or a concentration of a higher grade. And then we had two or three parties that took options on it but nobody got very excited.

And then there was a party of brokers from Montreal that took an option in 1929. They did some work onto it too, but everything went flat in 1929, and the brokers went broke! They couldn't make their first payment so that ended that!

Anyway, we kept it up. We used to write to mining companies, trying to get them interested, but they didn't seem to care much, except for the ones that I already mentioned. The others didn't think there was much chance of anything in Gaspé anyway. I remember one company telling us not to waste our time in Gaspé, to go up in the Precambrian country, where we might find something.

Now, of course, the Depression was on, and most of the companies were having trouble just staying alive, let alone getting into new operations. In 1937, twenty-nine years after I made the strike, I was able to interest Dr. Dyer, of the O'Brien Mines, and just before we went up I got a letter from Dr. Bell of Noranda Mines saying that he'd like to look. I wrote and told him that I'd just made this appointment with O'Brien Mines, but I said if he turned it down I'd let him know. Anyway, Dr. Dyer went up, and he looked it over, and he said, 'Give us a week after I get back to decide what we'll do.' I had already told him about the letter from Noranda, you see.

Anyway, he wrote back and said, 'We've decided that it's too big a thing for us to handle just now.' He said for us to go ahead, and take in Dr. Bell of Noranda, but if he turned it down to come back to us.

So we brought Dr. Bell in, and he went back and not long after we heard from him that Noranda would take an option. It was 1938 by this time and they drilled there until 1940. The war was lookin' bad by then, so they quit. For the next seven years, nothing at all happened, except for the fact that in order to keep our claims to the property alive, we had to do so much work on it each year. Well, we did it and held onto the claim, though by now we didn't think much was ever going to happen.

And then, in 1947, Noranda came back and started drilling and exploration work again. By 1951 they had enough information to convince them that the property was worth while mining!

Dr. Bell came up to my home when my wife and I were there alone. He said, 'Well, Alf, I got some good news for you. The Company is going to exercise the option.' Well, y'know it's hard to tell you how I felt! I had made the first discovery in 1909, when I was twenty-nine years old, the second one with my brother in 1921 when I was forty-one, and here it was finally happening thirty years later, and I was seventy-one years old!

By 1955, the mine was in production. Sometimes I used to think that I mightn't live to see it, but I did, and it's hard to believe the changes that the mine brought about. When I went there first, it was just a forest, nothin' but animals and only a very few people had ever walked on that ground before. Now Murdochville is a big booming city and Gaspé copper is known all around the world. But you know, I never thought of wealth or fame or anything like that. What I used to picture in my mind, back in my earliest days, was a mine and a town there. And by gosh, it *did* come to pass. I got more of a kick out of *that* than anything else."

DR. CHARLES BEST

Dr. Charles Best, the co-discoverer of insulin with Dr. Frederick Banting, was only twenty-two years old at the time when they made the medical breakthrough which is credited with saving the lives of millions of diabetics around the world. I found it hard to persuade this extremely modest man to talk about himself when we met at his Toronto home in 1969. He was sixty-nine years old at the time, an amateur painter who could easily have turned professional, and he went daily to his work at the Banting-Best Institute at the University of Toronto.

Dr. Best collapsed and died in March 1978, after receiving news of the sudden death of his son from a heart attack.

What We'd Been Looking For

"I WAS BORN IN WEST PEMBROKE, MAINE, just south of the Canadian border. My father and mother were from Kings County, Nova Scotia. My father was a country doctor, a general practitioner with a very large area to cover. Some of the calls were forty and fifty miles away. To reach these patients he travelled by horse and carriage, changing horses twice and three times on the way. I went along with him on many of these calls and I learned to administer the anesthetics when I was very young. It would just involve pouring on a little ether and doing what Father told me, but I didn't think I had any real interest in medicine. I first enrolled in the arts course when I came to the University of Toronto. After two years of that I went overseas in the First World War. When I came back I decided I wanted to do medical research because somehow I was not satisfied to do the practice of medicine, so I started on a four-year course called 'Physiology in Biochemistry'. In the summers I worked in the laboratory and practised the techniques that I learned in the winter. Fred Banting and I started working on insulin the day after I took my final exams in that course, on the 16th of May, 1921.

What We'd Been Looking For

We had been working for some time on diabetic dogs and we knew that their blood sugar was sky high and they were very ill and likely to die. We had a lot of difficulties, of course, in getting to that stage but some time in the July of 1921, we gave quite a large dose of insulin, or what we hoped would be insulin, intravenously to this dog, and the blood sugar came down dramatically from 0.4 to 0.1, which is the normal. The animal got up and licked our hands. That was the actual moment of discovery.

Of course, we thought that might be an accident, so we had to repeat the experiment—actually we repeated it seventy-five times before we published our first paper. It was the miracle we had been hoping for but there was nothing accidental involved. We had simply found what we had been looking for.

On January 11, 1922, Fred Banting and I decided to take injections of insulin ourselves. After that we gave it to the hospital and they injected this fourteen-year-old boy, Leonard Thompson, and he got a lot better. Then there were seven or eight other diabetics who received the insulin, some of whom we were very much interested in personally. Those were the first to get insulin and they all seemed to improve.

Shortly after that we struck a bad batch or something, because the process seemed to fail us. Two of the diabetics who had been treated so successfully got ill again and died. That was a very hectic time for us, trying to get back on the right road. We never did know the cause of that failure and I don't think there was any single cause. It was a cumulation of consequences.

We used a lot of animals in our research and for a while they were supplied to us by the police, who used to be responsible for collecting stray animals. Then after the Humane Societies came into it, a lot of animal lovers started to protest, just like they do today. But, I must say this: I have never heard one mother or father of a diabetic child say that animals must not be used. I have always been an animal lover myself and I felt that these animals we were using should have the best care we could give them, that they shouldn't be made to endure any pain that you wouldn't want to endure yourself. Those were the criteria we operated under. I don't look on it as any different from abattoirs; we eat the flesh of animals, so I don't see why we shouldn't use them for experimental purposes, providing it's done in as painless a manner as possible. You'd condemn a lot of people to death if you took away animals in medical research.

The only alternative to using animals in research is to use human beings as guinea pigs. I mean, do all the same things to them, take the pancreas out and everything else. I don't think any sane person would recommend that human beings be used instead of animals.

Anyway, when it came to injecting humans I decided to inject myself to prove it wasn't poison. I always injected it in the leg, then when it works itself through the bloodstream to the face, the face gets red and you get a metallic taste in your mouth. One time when I did this, the student who had been working with me made the batch up a hundred times too strong, and when I gave it to myself I went into histamine shock and I nearly passed out of the picture. However, the students were bright. They got adrenalin and they brought me around and they began asking me questions about how I felt and so on and we ended up writing a little medical paper on the whole experience!

There hasn't been much change in insulin since Fred Banting and I discovered it. You add certain materials to it that makes it absorb more and more slowly, but it's been the same since it was purified in 1926.

Following the discovery, I was offered many good positions in the United States and in England, but after serious consideration we decided to stay here. . . . Canada is my home. After Fred Banting's death I felt there was a responsibility to the Banting-Best Institute here and I never seriously considered leaving after 1941. Canada has been very good to me.

It makes one feel very humble when I realize that there are millions of people around the world today *alive* because of our discovery. But I only think of that when I'm asked to speak at some Diabetic Association somewhere. I look out and realize the whole audience is made up of diabetics, the parents or relatives of diabetics, or just people who have some connection. I have three diabetics right now working in the laboratory who have been attracted to research in that field because of their own disability. These are the things that remind me sometimes of the enormity of our discovery, but believe me, I never think about it as a rule."

DOC CRUICKSHANK

*In 1924 Marconi was given a licence to broadcast messages
from England to other countries of the Commonwealth.
What a wonder radio was in those early days, back in the
twenties. There were very few people who knew anything
about it and what they did know they gained from magazines like* Popular Mechanics.

*One day back in 1926, Doc Cruickshank was leafing
through a copy of* Popular Mechanics *in Wingham, Ontario,
when he saw a plan for a radio transmitter. He had heard
about radio, but that's about all he knew about it at the time.
Using his mother's fifteen-inch breadboard as a base, he got
busy and built one.*

Doc Cruickshank's J.O.K.E.

"ONE TUBE WAS ALL I HAD in this transmitter, yet it was heard
nearly all around the world. At other times it couldn't be heard
fifteen miles outside of town. The trouble was that even though I
had a transmitter to send sounds out from, nobody had receivers
to pick those sounds up on. There were no receivers, in other
words, radios, available, so I had to make them myself if I was going to sell them. The first three or four I made I was able to sell in
just a few minutes, and that gave me the idea—why don't I repre-
sent some firm that manufactures radios? So I got a company in
Hamilton that was making them to supply me with these receivers
and I went out and sold them myself for one hour a day. That's
where I actually got it started.

Actually I could have sold a lot more of these things if I had
the time, but I didn't. I just had this one free hour a day. You see, I
worked in the foundry ten hours a day, seven days a week. And I
ran the projector in the picture show for about four hours a night.
There was one hour left over between seven and eight o'clock in
the evening where I had nothing to do. That's when I sold radios.

Nobody worried too much about studios in those days. Just about any place at all would do to put on a program. On Sunday we always did a service from one of the churches. At that time it meant that we had to connect up all the churches in town with a telephone line. We brought a great lot of wire and strung it on top of buildings and everything else, from the studio over to one of the churches. We did that for years before anyone thought there was any other way of doing it.

On Sunday, after church service, we had a little program for which I took the transmitter and everything down to my home. I had to do that in order to get a piano. I'd carry the transmitter under my arm down to my home and we'd do an hour broadcast, Sunday afternoon, from down there. There was a program of music—hymns and that sort of thing—with local people along for singing and playing the piano. There was recorded music available but it was of no use to me because I didn't have a turntable to play it on. I only had one microphone, and everything was done through that.

We didn't even know that you had to have a licence for broadcasting. Somebody tipped me off that I had to have one and, by golly, I enquired around and sure enough, I was supposed to have a licence. It was very simple to get it, though. All I did was write a letter and pay ten dollars. Before all this business of the licence I was calling the station J-O-K-E, because that's all it was to me up to this time, a private little joke and a lot of fun. But you know, depending on atmospheric conditions, that little station with one tube was being heard, some nights, all around the world. Of course, that was before the airwaves were all cluttered up with hundreds of thousands of stations. When you got a good night, why, my goodness, the world wasn't big enough for you. Lots of other nights, though, we couldn't even get outside of town.

One night we offered a prize for the one who telephoned in the longest distance. We heard from a fellow out here seven miles. That was it. That night was a very bad one you see. We didn't get anywhere. It was just five watts and two watts in those early days. It was just an ordinary receiving tube.

Up to this point I had been running the station with whatever little bit of money I had to spare out of my own pocket, but eventually I found I had no money at all. There were many times I became so discouraged about the station not bringing in money and taking so much of my time that I'd decide to quit—that today

174

would be the last day of broadcasting. Every time I'd say that, somebody would come along encouraging me to keep it going, and we'd try it again.

One day we hit on the idea of the spot advertisement and we found it wasn't a bit hard to sell them, not at the price we were charging—fifty cents! I would sell the ad and write it up and put it on the air and then go out and collect the money for it. I had to take groceries instead of money many times, but I was glad to get anything. Anyway, I survived and eventually the station, now called CKNX, became a vital part of the whole farming community. People started to depend on us for news of the world, farm market reports, and a great deal of their entertainment. In time our equipment improved and so did our programming. I was able to give up my job in the foundry and the other part-time jobs and give all my time to running the station.

I was full-time at the station for a while where I did everything from sweeping to announcing. Then one day I heard a recording of my own voice. I can tell you it was something of a shock! I couldn't believe that I was forcing people to listen to this kind of a voice. I said, 'That's it,' and I never went on the air again. I turned the job over to my son Bud, who was now old enough to take part in the business. Then my brother John came into it in 1935 and took over some of my duties, including some of the announcing.

We were all learning the whole business together as we went along. We weren't really teaching our early staff because many times we didn't know the answers ourselves. We made it possible for a lot of people to come in and try doing things *their* way."

OTTO KELLAND

When I went to meet Otto Kelland, I thought that I was going to meet a man who carved some of the best model ships
in the world. I found, indeed, a fine craftsman, but also a
poet with an intense love for the land he lives on, the wild
Atlantic that pounds its shores, and the sailing ships and
fishermen that have given Newfoundland a character that
no other province comes close to possessing. Otto Kelland
was born with a desire to be part of that tradition, but in the
end, he has become one of its most important chroniclers.

That Crackle of Old Canvas

"I WENT TO SEA MYSELF IN 1919, and my ambition was to become a sea captain. I used to see these old fellas up there on the
bridge with the four gold stripes, and I thought it would be a good
idea for me to get them somewhere along the road. So I got to get
some sea experience 'before the mast' before I could do that. Anyway, one time I was on a ship called *Sable Island*, and we came
into St. John's here on November 15, 1924. There was a longshoremen's strike in progress. Our captain told us he wanted to keep
the ship on time, and he wanted the crew to work cargo. Well,
you didn't go foolin' around and scabbin' longshoremen because
they were pretty rough customers. If you 'scabbed' one of them
fellas, you had it! That was it! Also we had some friends among
those men, and we didn't want to do anything to hurt them. Anyway, the captain told us to 'turn to' at two o'clock, and go to work.
Our spokesman said, 'I'm sorry, Captain. We're not going to
"scab".' The captain was a bit put out, but he asked if we'd recon-
sider. Our spokesman said no. So he said, 'You're all fired!' And
he put us all ashore! He fired the whole lot of us—six firemen and
six sailors y'know.

While this was goin' on, there was a British steamer called the
Liskeard County docked at the wharf just below us, and her crew

started to work cargo. Well, down comes the longshoremen, maybe a thousand, and that crew wasn't long in stoppin'. The bos'n had to go to hospital! Some fella socked him with his fist— they didn't use any weapons then and fists were the order of the day. Then a squad of police arrived, and the Newfoundland constabulary came down with fixed bayonets, and they lined up on the deck of the *Liskeard County,* and faced outwards with the bayonets at the ready. They were a semi-military force, you see, trained with the British Army, like the Irish Force was. We had no army, and no navy in Newfoundland, so they were not only the police, they were also the army and navy.

Well, about 1,800 longshoremen surged down, and they came up within three or four inches of the bayonet points and Inspector General Hutchings told his men, 'One more inch, and you *use* those bayonets.' We could hear him give that order. The longshoremen figured that discretion was the better part of valour, and they backed up.

Anyway, the strike meant that I was out of a job and my uncle was a member of the constabulary at the time and he said, 'Why don't you join the police force?' I intended just to stay on for the winter, and go back to sea in the spring, but I liked it so well, I stayed for nineteen years. After that they appointed me Chief Warder at His Majesty's Penitentiary. I went down there for a six-month trial, and I stayed there for twenty-three years. So I never got back to my first love, the sea, and I never got to be a captain of a ship, but I guess I spent more time wandering around the wharf talking to the old seamen than possibly any other man in St. John's. I loved those ships, and got to know every little nook and cranny of every one of them. I knew their names, where they came from, and all the boys who sailed on them. In the evenings I'd go back home, and work on ship models.

It was about 1950 I realized that the sailing vessel had almost had its day. Already, the ships were converting from all sail to part sail and diesel engines. The old-timers didn't want to put their trust in the engines alone, see? That was one reason they kept *some* sail. The other reason was that they just couldn't bear to part with it altogether. They liked that crackle of old canvas and squeakin' of ropes over their heads. They looked upon the engines with distaste. They couldn't stand the smell of gas and oil, but it was the time for change, and they had to go along with it. In time, as the engines became more and more reliable, they were forced to do away with sail altogether.

177

Actually, you know, the engines *were* a godsend! You take, if a vessel were caught on a lee shore, under all sail with a nasty storm blowin', in ninety-nine cases out of a hundred, she would go ashore on that lee shore, and become a total wreck, a loss with all hands, y'know. The engines eliminated that danger to a great extent because they could rev up and take the ship out of that trap. Eventually, the sails disappeared altogether as the old fellas died off, and the more modern seamen came along. They looked on the sails as a nuisance, gettin' in the way, the ropes frozen when they went to tie 'em up in the wintertime. So they got rid of them. But the *beauty* of the ships was gone too. There is nothing in the world as beautiful as a ship going on under full sail. My God, boy, it's enough to bring tears to your eyes.

Now, I didn't want these vessels ever to be forgotten. I knew every one of them like I know a person. Some I saw getting built, and some I got to be very familiar with, when they were launched and in operation. I knew the captains of them all, and I have photographs and measurements of all of them. I saw them in dry-dock and I saw them in the water. I know the boom gaff, and most measurements, even the cabin measurements. So, when I'm making the model, before I take the last shavin's off the hull, I call in the old skipper or someone who helped build the original. I'll say to him, 'Tell me if there's anything wrong there, and don't be scared to offend me, because I want to be offended. I want to get this thing *right*, because a lot of your crew members are still alive. I don't want them sayin', "We never had this, or we never had that, or that mast is too tall."' I said all this to Tom What's-his-name yesterday. He helped to build the *Stella and Kitty*. So Tom stood off, and he looked at her for a while, and he said, 'Boy, don't change yer hand. She's perfect.' So that's all I wanted to hear. 'If you say that,' I said, 'I won't have to worry 'bout anybody else.'

The pocketknife is the main tool for making these models. Nothing can cut out all these little things you have to do as neatly as a pocketknife. The bandsaw can cut some things out roughly, but the pocketknife is needed to make the finished job. Everything is built to scale, even the little oil and kerosene barrels, the row-boats and the oars, the cabins and bunks, and the wheelhouse—even the wheel itself. I make the brass fittings, and when I make the cog-wheels for the engine I cut a mould for it out of wood and then I run the molten metal into that.

Every piece has to be exactly like it was on the original—

scaled down, of course. Every sail, every rope, even the anchor. You never know when someone who sailed on the original is going to walk in, and say, 'Otto, that mast was never like that, or that anchor is not the kind we had.' I wouldn't want that, so everything has to be perfect. They're mostly about five, six, seven feet long, although some are bigger than that. I even check out the freight she was carrying because I put little models of that on board, and I put the addresses on the packages, of who they were goin' to.

There are many many things about the fishing industry that can be preserved in models. For instance, the fishermen on the Grand Banks fished in dories while the Labrador fishermen fished from their boats. There was what we call the 'fiddlehead' type of Labrador schooner, because there was a knee underneath her bowsprit which bore a similarity to a fiddle. This one has the old foghorn. And the kerosene torches. They used to use kerosene torches in the old days, for splittin' fish out there on the banks.

I had two 'grand' ladies from Toronto down visiting my workshop last week, and they were up in their eighties. I suppose when a woman gets that age, she doesn't mind tellin' her age any more. That's when they get *proud* of it. One of them picked up one of these little fife rails, and said, 'Look Shirley. He's even got little toilet seats aboard.' Well, I suppose it *does* look a bit like a toilet seat!

If I could do the whole thing without interruption, I could make a model like this in twelve months. There's so much detail, and as I said, I want everything exactly as it was. When I get finished, there'll be a complete record of what the Newfoundland fishing industry was like. But nobody will *ever* be able to show in models what the men who sailed them were like—grand, brave men who faced any kind of weather, and who were as at home on their ships as they were on land, more so. When the sails went so did they and my collection is as much a tribute to them as it is to the ships they sailed. I wrote a song one time about a Newfoundland fisherman, and the story of how I wrote it is this: I was a crew member of a steamer, and we were docked in East Boston, back in 1923. There was a young man came down, and he said to the captain, 'Do you want any crew members?' The captain said, 'No, I'm filled.' 'Well,' said the fella, 'can I work my passage home to Newfoundland?' The captain said, 'No. It's against the rules of the Company.' 'Well, can I stow away?' said the fella. 'If you stow away,' said the captain, 'I'll have to turn you over to the police. Why don't you stay here. A lot of Newfoundlanders are making good money up here.' 'No,' said the young man, 'I'd rather be back on my western boat, fishing off Cape St. Mary's, on one meal a day, than five meals up here.'

I thought about that young man many times over the years, because that's the way I feel about Newfoundland myself. I'd rather be poor here than rich anywhere else in the world. That's why I wrote this song:

> Take me back to my Western boat,
> Let me fish off Cape St. Mary's,
> Where the hang-down sail, and the fog horns wail,
> With my friends the Browns, and the Clearys
> Let me fish off Cape St. Mary's."

ALEX BERRY

*The poems of Robert Service brought the magic of the
Klondike Gold Rush camps to people all over the world,
and for some the magic was too much. It was like a siren
call and they couldn't resist. So they packed their bags,
and said their goodbyes, and away they went in search of
fortune perhaps, but mostly adventure. And that's a good
thing too, because that's all most of them got. The fortunes
went to perhaps as few as a couple of dozen.*

*But there's something about that northern land that gets
into the people who go there and it got into Alex Berry. He
went up there fifty years ago intending to stay a short
while. Now you couldn't get him out with a crowbar.*

Once a Prospector, Always a Prospector

"I WENT TO THE YUKON TERRITORY IN 1925. By the time I got there
the search for the Klondike gold was all over, but silver and lead
had brought a lot of prospectors back, some of the same ones who
didn't find gold when the Klondike was on. Once a prospector, always a prospector, I guess.

I knew lots of those old-timers, the '98ers, and that describes
them well. They worked hard, and they played hard. They
trapped animals and, of course, they prospected and they knew
how to get along alone in the bush. They cooked for themselves,
and all the rest that you have to do to stay alive. They didn't have
any training as a rule. I guess they just had it natural. There was a
famous character there, Bobby Fisher, who some people say
could smell gold.

Most of the mines, the big ones, were found by laymen using
sluice gates. They were placer miners, and they used these sluice
gates for washing the overburden away. They'd shovel tons of dirt
into these things, and watch for the gold as the water washed the

dirt down. A few, maybe a dozen or so, made good on it, really got rich. Somewhere between twelve and twenty, that's about all, out of the thousands who went up there. A lot died on the way, and those who did make it here found themselves working for somebody else, just making enough to stay alive.

Everybody has this picture of the Yukon as a place where all the prospectors were making big strikes, but that isn't true at all. The Yukon is just the same as any area north of Edmonton, or, say, Le Pas, Manitoba. It's always been an ordinary country, just a part of Northern Canada. But the thing that keeps you here is the chance that you *might* get rich. You always feel it's just around the next hill, or on top of it, or somewhere. But it's not, and never has been, sitting on a shelf waiting for you to grab it.

I think the reason we stay, too, is that it's kind of a semi-frontier country yet. One of the last. We all have this feeling up here that we're doing something together that not many others are doing anywhere else. I've been here half a century, haven't got anything to show for it, but nobody'll ever get me to leave the Yukon. I come out once in a while to meet old friends, but I can't wait to get back. And when I pass on, I still want to stay here."

LAURA KIDD

Laura Kidd started life in Southern Ontario, and her first years as a teacher were spent in a one-room school there. But a trial year in the undeveloped northland of the 1920s turned into a lifetime and a commitment to the people who lived there.

The Last of the One-Room-School Teachers

"I STARTED IN A ONE-ROOM SCHOOL in Southern Ontario and I stayed in that one-room school for eight years. My brother had gone to live at Sioux Lookout, away up in Northern Ontario, and all the time I was teaching in Southern Ontario he kept after me to come up there to teach. It was all bush then, and still pretty primitive country. There were no telephones, no cars—you had to walk everywhere—and only one road going down to the lake. A few of the stores were getting electricity from the CN, but none of the homes had it.

Sioux Lookout was really a railway centre, and most of the people were either conductors or engineers on the trains at that time. I liked it right away there, and I decided to give it a try for one school year. I thought that a year in the North would be interesting. As it turned out, I got along so well I decided to stay a second year.

One of the things that always bothered me in the North was that the schools didn't seem to understand that the Indian children needed special understanding. No allowance was ever made for the close bond that existed between the Indian parents and their children *and* the land. When the Indian children were first integrated into the white schools, they weren't allowed off at noon hour. In the spring, you see, they used to just disappear in droves because the call of nature was very, very strong. It was almost as if they couldn't help themselves. I used to say, 'I don't blame them. Why don't you send a teacher along with them and let them have their lunch on the hill. They're used to the outdoors and it's just as easy to supervise them on the hill as it is on the school ground. They feel nearer to home when they're up there.' But nobody listened. We had a high fence around our school ground, and at noon hour you'd see this Indian mother and father standing outside the fence, talking to their kids *inside* the fence. I always thought that was cruel!

The other sad thing was, the parents of these children would come to town to be near their children for two or three days, and the only place they could spend their time while the children were in school was the beer parlours. It's no wonder there'd be a problem with drinking among them.

Well anyway, that one year I was going to spend in the North turned into a lifetime. I never seriously thought about going back again. I became devoted to the North, and the people who lived in the North, especially the children. I taught so many children and so many different kinds of classes, but I still think the one-room school is the best of all. The teacher was in charge, and responsible for everything, and you felt you wanted to train those children to *do* something and *be* something. We used to put in a lot of effort. It would be something like taking a lump of clay, and fashioning something from it. If it turned out well, you felt good. If it didn't, you felt responsible. Those kids were just like my own. If they came to school in the mornings looking as if they just tumbled out of bed, I would just point my finger and tell them to get back home and wash their faces and comb their hair, and I wouldn't have any arguments about it either.

That's one thing we *did* have in the olden days—discipline! If we had to use the strap, we used the strap! I still have the strap that I started out with, and I'm going to put it in a museum. Maybe they'll want to put *me* in the museum too. There can't be very many one-room-school teachers left around now."

DR. MERTON WILLIAMS

Dr. Merton Williams, the man more responsible than anyone else for making the Department of Geology at the University of British Columbia tops in that field throughout the world, was born in a cheese factory in Bloomfield, Ontario, in 1882. His people were among Ontario's first cheese-makers, at a time when the factory and the house were one and the same thing. They had come to Ontario in 1785 after the American Revolution—United Empire Loyalist stock, as was everybody else in the area. Young Merton was a brilliant boy who took an early interest in the structure of the world around him: the rocks, the stones, and the strata of the earth. He went off on boyhood expeditions into the Ontario northland by canoe, always searching for new specimens. In university, he studied geology, and for his doctoral thesis he made the geological map of Nova Scotia which is still in use, and entirely accurate, today. From Yale University he went directly to the Geological Survey of Canada and started on the job of producing a fully accurate map of Canada. The boy from the Bloomfield cheese factory was to have a profound effect on the face of the entire globe.

Every Day Was a Discovery

"THERE WAS A BIG SHORTAGE OF OIL back in those days before the First World War. They had been depending on the oil produced in Western Ontario, around Petrolia, and they shipped a lot of the gas to the United States. So I was put on the search for oil.

The first thing I did on that job was to go to the old oil fields and get all the information I could from the men who were still there. They were pretty well gone, but there were a few around. From them I got the depths down to the oil formations, and then I levelled the country over and I found the altitude of the oil-bearing rock below the surface. Now, they had just struck a 3,000-foot well, a tremendously deep one for that time, down near Sarnia. They got quite a strike of gas there with a little oil. So I went down there and there were seven wells already under way—not one of them getting anywhere. Well, I went over all the charts and I found that they were going in the wrong direction. Oil has always been found in what we call 'anticlines', where the rocks come up into a crest and where the water below the oil, being heavier than the oil, pushes the oil up. But down there in that area there was no water in the oil. The oil had gone down and they were working in the anticlines when they should have been working in the incline. Well, I put them onto that, and sure enough, before the year was over they struck the oil in the incline. So they sank about thirty wells there and got the whole thing started again, only this time in the right way.

In 1921 I went out to the University of British Columbia, which was barely six years old at the time. The summer of 1921, I went right down the Mackenzie River in a fifty-foot scow with a fellow-geologist, Hume, and nine other men. We mapped the entire river—right from Great Slave Lake, down to the North. Then in 1923 I started in Southern Alberta. That Calgary sheet, the southern part, is all my mapping.

In 1924 I was asked to go out to Hong Kong for a year to make a geological map of the area. I'm very proud of the fact that the map we made at that time is the one they are still using today.

Of course we worked long hours and it was exhausting, but I didn't mind. Every day was a day of discovery. We got up at the crack of dawn when we were out in the field. We had a cook to get our breakfast, but most often we'd get our own. We'd be out on the job by seven o'clock, and we'd have our lunch with us. Sometimes we'd be on horseback, sometimes in canoes. We'd try to be back by six, and then after supper we'd spend the evening writing up all our notes. Sunday we'd always take off to do a bit of writing and get a bit of rest. The odd Sunday we'd work but for the most part one day off a week was important.

I taught at UBC for twenty-nine years, till I retired in 1950, but I never stopped enjoying my trips outside the university to do fieldwork. There is nothing to match the joy of discovery and of knowing that you are leaving records of that discovery for future generations."

FRANK BOUCHER

Frank Boucher spent most of his adult life in professional hockey. Born in Ottawa, in 1901, he breathed the sport from the time he could walk, and he never wanted to do anything else. He was a mainstay with the New York Rangers during the first twenty-nine years of their existence, first as a player, and then as coach and general manager. He was a Lady Byng Trophy winner, and a member of the Hockey Hall of Fame.

Feeding the Underworld

"I STARTED TO PLAY HOCKEY as soon as I could stand up on skates. Everybody did in those days. We made our own rinks in the schoolyards, or in the back yards, or if we couldn't find any room anywhere else, we'd just clean off a space on the river. We'd always make it near a bridge so we could get the benefit of the bridge lights for playing in the evening. Seems to me that when the winter rolled around we were continually either cleaning off the ice, or flooding it, or playing.

The hockey played then was very different from what it is now. We just gathered, one by one, on some rink and played for hours. When you got tired you simply went over and sat on the bank, cooled off a little bit, and got back in the game again. The hockey sticks in those days were one-piece sticks and they weren't laminated. We didn't often have a real puck; we used tin cans, coal, or a block of wood. It seemed like we were always looking for some kind of puck, and it never mattered to us what it was made of, or how it was shaped, as long as it would roll or slide or bounce!

I was thirteen when the war came and I took a job as an office boy. I played a lot of hockey, even though things were dampened a bit by the war, because a lot of boys who left from our neighbourhood didn't come back. After the war, though, I was out of a job, and a friend talked me into joining the Royal North West Mounted Police. I stayed in the force for about two and a half years but all the time I was there I had this thought in the back of my head that I was going to be a professional hockey player. So I bought my discharge for fifty dollars and went back to take a job in Iroquois Falls, Ontario. I was playing at Iroquois Falls for a while when Tommy Gorman invited me to turn pro and play for Ottawa.

Prior to turning pro, it was Frank Nihbor that I always wanted to be like. He played for Ottawa for years, and he was the first player who ever won the Lady Byng Trophy. All my life as a hockey player, I was guided by his influence—how he played and how he behaved.

When I began to play for Ottawa, my early training in those pickup games back home really helped. I really had to use all that skill playing with fellas like Frank Nihbor, Eddie Gerrard, and later, when I went to Vancouver, Mickey McKay, Roy Cook, and Alf Skinner. I got a great thrill out of playing with and against these men that I had admired for so long.

Going back to, say, around 1912, '13, '14, '15, they had a seven-man game. You had the goalkeeper, point, double-point, right wing, left wing, centre, and a rover. All passes had to be on-side. That meant when you passed the puck to a team-mate, he had to be even with you or behind you to accept it. It was very difficult, skating at full speed, to judge if you were making a proper pass, and there was an awful lot of whistle-blowings; it slowed up the game a lot. There were no blue lines or spots or circles, so as a result, it became sort of an individual game, and you had to be a very good stick handler in order to prove your worth. Those never-ending games back when we were kids had developed us into stick handlers and a good thing too; if you couldn't stick-handle you didn't have too much fun because someone would take the puck away on you.

It was Lester and Frank Patrick, the guys who started professional hockey on the west coast, who were most responsible for getting the rules changed so that the forward pass was permitted. This made a wonderful change in the game, because it encouraged more team play.

After playing for Ottawa I spent about four years with the Western League in Vancouver. When it folded, around 1926, most of the stars from the prairies and the coast moved over to the National Hockey League. I was chosen to play for the New York Rangers; they were just starting up that year of 1926-7. Our training camp was held at a little rink out in western Toronto, and we were kind of a motley crew. Only about four or five of us had ever played pro hockey before; all the rest were amateur players. I can still remember, as we were training, a lot of the old pros from around Toronto came out to the rink to watch us, and the general opinion was that we'd be chased out of the League. Strangely enough we played our first game against the previous year's champions, the Montreal Maroons, and we won it, 1 to 0.

The highlight of my career with the Rangers came in the spring of 1928, when we won the Stanley Cup. It was a very unusual series. Each year, around Eastertime, the circus comes to New York, and up till a few years ago, it chased the hockey team out of town. The result was that, when the Rangers were in the playoffs, they always had to play on foreign ice. Well, that year we were in the playoffs against the Montreal Maroons and we had to play all of our games in the three-out-of-five series on Montreal ice. And that was only the beginning of our troubles! In the second game our goalkeeper got hit in the eye and couldn't continue. We didn't have a spare goalkeeper and the Maroons wouldn't allow us to use any of the fellows who were goalkeepers from other teams who happened to be sitting in the stands so we wound up using our coach, Lester Patrick, who had never played goal in his life! Believe it or not, we not only won with him in goal, but we went on to win the Stanley Cup! I was fortunate enough, in those three games out of five, to score all of the goals but one. And since all of my goals were winning goals, I had a lot of personal satisfaction out of that series. And don't forget, this was only our second year in the League. For a team that had looked like—well, I don't know what you could've called us when we were training in Toronto—we had developed very very fast.

I always remember how naive we were when we first went to New York. Our poor little wives weren't used to these big cities, and going into New York was a terrific experience for them. That first year we went there, they were building the 8th Avenue subway, and at each corner there was a hole in the pavement where they went down underground to work. One day, my wife and Mrs. Cook were walking down 49th St. towards 8th Ave., and Mrs. Cook had been reading a lot of stuff about the underworld, and that sort of thing. Anyway, as they were walking—it was around noontime—there was a young fella with an armload of lunch boxes going down into the hole. And Mrs. Cook said, 'Look at that fellow. He's going down to feed the underworld.' The thing was, she was *serious!* The rest of us weren't much better, though. I remember people used to look at us kind of funny, because we were all wearing peak caps. About the only people in New York wearing caps in those days were thugs and some taxi drivers. I guess we were an odd-looking sight!"

DR. HUGH MACKINNON

Hugh MacKinnon was born in 1882. He was one of nine children of Gaelic-speaking Cape Breton parents, who managed to give their children enough to eat, enough to wear, a respect for God, and a thirst for knowledge. As was usual in those days, the girls married, and the boys did other things. Five became Presbyterian ministers, and the other two became doctors.

In rural areas of Cape Breton, up until, and shortly after, the Second World War, the Scots there lived in much the same way that their ancestors had done in the Outer Hebrides. They farmed, they fished, and they bartered at the store. And because these people seldom saw anyone from the outside, their culture remained intact. God was someone to fear; the language, of course, was Gaelic; and English was a foreign tongue.

Great Believers in Education

"MY MOTHER BELIEVED STRONGLY IN EDUCATION. She spent all her spare time reading everything she could get her hands on and then she'd tell us about the things she'd read. On Sundays we were never allowed to lift our hands to any kind of work. We'd have the sermon in church, and then Father would read out loud to us from some religious book, most times in Gaelic, sometimes in English. The Sydney papers had Gaelic stories in them in those days, too. He'd read us Sherlock Holmes stories, too, for hours and hours till his eyes would give out.

Our parents were great believers in education. All the Scotch in Cape Breton were. As each one of us got old enough, we would move off to work somewhere to get enough money to go to college. Then, the older ones would help the younger ones, and make sure they got a good education, too.

Our minister, whose name was Grant, was a Scotchman, and

he was dictator of the whole area for miles and miles around. He used to teach my older brothers Greek and Latin before they went to college. And he kept preaching this education—*education,* all the time just like our parents. Every day before we went to school the Bible was read, and prayers were offered, and then we'd get up off our knees, and skit off to school. There was never any singing or dancing in our home either. That was considered wasting time. It was always lessons and books. Later on, as we got older, we went to dances, and enjoyed them too, and I loved to listen to the bagpipes. Lots of people played them around Lake Ainslie where we lived. I remember a man named Farquhar MacKinnon, a tall man, 6 feet 6 inches, who played the violin. He could teach any kind of music: pipes, singing, everything. We'd walk three miles to his house just to hear him play the violin. And then when he finished, we'd walk next door to hear his son, little Farquhar, play the pipes!

Politics was serious business then. One time the Liberal and Conservative candidates for Lake Ainslie came to address this big meeting and they were both on the same stage. Well, things got pretty hot, and before you knew what was happening, the two of them were in a big fist fight up there on the stage. It was a terrible fight, and it took a lot of men to get them apart, but that's the way politics were in Cape Breton. A lot of people got their jobs that way in those days. The parties that got elected gave the jobs out to the people who supported them. When the Conservatives were in we got the job of delivering the mail from Whycocomagh to Lake Ainslie, and from Lake Ainslie to Strathborn. It was with the money they earned there that my older brothers managed to get to university. That was about the only money in circulation in those days.

Five of my brothers became Presbyterian ministers, and that came about because the Principal of Queen's University, Dr. Grant, used to go around the countryside recruiting boys for the church. The university would give them the tuition fee, but they would have to pay the room and board themselves. When they asked me if I wanted to go I'd say, 'I'm going to be a doctor.' I don't know why I said that, but I knew I wasn't going to be a minister!

After my Grade XI, I went to the Normal School. In the summers then, the students were sent out by the university to teach the foreigners in Alberta and Saskatchewan, so I spent my summers out there earning the money for my fees in the fall. That would be about 1907-8. I still remember how those foreign children wanted to learn. They strained to hear every word, and we were able to communicate even though there was a language barrier.

One time, it must have been when I was studying for medicine at the university and was home, the sky turned as black as night, and nobody knew what was happening. It turned out to be a cyclone, and it tore the roofs off many houses in Lake Ainslie and just devastated our whole house. There was one man caught under a roof that had fallen on the lawn, and one of my brothers, who was a minister by then, came along and bent down to talk to the man. He said to him, 'The Lord must have been with you.' And the man said, 'If He was, He was going pretty fast.'

I graduated in medicine in 1913. I was in the First World War as a doctor at Vimy Ridge and the Somme. The injuries were frightful, and I had some terrible experiences, that I don't like to talk about. But, I must say, the worst thing was Prohibition.

Now, I never drank or smoked in my life, but the liquor, or the lack of it, was a terrible plague. I was working in the town of Inverness then, and every hour of the evening there'd be queues of people lined up outside my office looking for prescriptions. You see, the only way they could get alcohol legally was with a prescription. They'd say, 'If *you* don't prescribe for it, somebody else will.' One doctor there had an office, and he didn't do one other thing except sign prescriptions for liquor. Then these people would take the prescription to the drug store, and get a bottle of alcohol. There was a terrible demand for cough medicine, too, because it had some kind of a kick, if you drank enough of it. People during Prohibition would do anything to get liquor, anything at all!"

J. W. (WES) MC NUTT

Wes McNutt of North Bay, Ontario, has been a professional forester all his life. He started in the woods as a stump-counter in the summers of his university days and rose to Chairman of the Board of a large Canadian lumber company. He has witnessed the startling changes in lumbering that have brought about the disappearance of lumberjacks, and remembers with great affection the old-time lumber camps and river drives of the late twenties and early thirties.

True Lumberjacks

"THE MEN IN THE WOODS in the late twenties and thirties were true lumberjacks. They had very little formal education, often none. The first camp that I lived in was on a tributary of the Saguenay River in Quebec in 1927 and I was the only person in the whole camp who could read or write—French or English. Every letter that anybody got was taken to me to read and while I'd be reading one man's letter to him, all of his buddies would gather round and hear whatever his girlfriend or his wife had to say. Now these letters had, in turn, been written by either the parish priest, the doctor, or the schoolteacher, the only people who *could* write in that community. For my part, I not only had to read their letters, I had to write their replies. I didn't bargain for that job when I hired on for the summer, but I'll tell you it made my job a lot more interesting.

A foreman in those days was always considered to be a much better foreman if he could lick any man in camp, preferably any two or three, and to a large degree, companies picked foremen with this in mind. Fights in camp didn't happen too often, mostly because the foreman *could* suppress any insurrection, but there were still a fair number of fights.

When I think of the early days on the Montmorency in Quebec, I think of the shock I had one night when we were caught by

Frank Boucher, one of the all-time greats of Canadian hockey. "I started to play hockey as soon as I could stand up on skates." (The Public Archives of Canada)

The ONE BIG UNION is
Bolshevism Pure and Simple
NOTE THE STRIKING PARALLEL

The fly-sheet of the *Winnipeg Citizen* gives a good idea of the paper's position on the issues involved in the 1919 Winnipeg General Strike. (CBC, Winnipeg, Manitoba)

C.A.S.C. trucks with Lewis machine guns, on June 21, 1919, Winnipeg's "Bloody Sunday". "It was all downhill after that for the unions." Archie Sterick (United Church Archives)

After the great northern forest fires of the early twentieth century, people who had the courage to stay and start again from scratch found themselves making do with anything they could find, even a Toronto streetcar. (The Public Archives of Canada)

Doc Cruickshank of Wingham, Ontario, one of Canada's radio pioneers, with the first radio transmitter he built back in 1926 using his mother's fifteen-inch breadboard as a base. (Photo courtesy of the Cruickshank family)

Photographs from the history of lumbering in Canada: a square-timber raft lies in the Ottawa River (*above*), and (*below*) a skidway of waney timber at a lumber camp on the Jocko River around 1912. (Ontario Forest Industries Association)

"Sandhill men" kept the icy hills covered with just the right amount of sand, so that sleighs hauling timber would not stick or run over the horses. "A good sandhill man was hard to find...." Jake Stewart (Ontario Forest Industries Association)

A fire pump on a launch on Lake Nipigon in 1919. Fire pumps were installed to provide protection to camps and settlements along the shore before the modern portable fire pump was developed. (Ontario Forest Industries Association)

Bush pilots, flying rickety planes like this, caught the public's imagination very quickly after the First World War. "Punch" Dickins made Canadian aviation history by being the first man to fly the length of the Mackenzie River in 1929. "We seldom thought of ourselves as pioneers." (The Public Archives of Canada)

Clearing stones from the land was necessary but back-breaking work for pioneers in Saskatchewan. Some of them, like Harry Hennig, were grateful for the work. "It was hard ... but I was glad to be in Canada, instead of Poland." (The Public Archives of Canada)

This picture of Dr. Norman Bethune was taken in China around 1939. Jean Ewan worked with Bethune in China and accompanied him on his first meeting with Mao Tse-tung. "I knew, even then, that I was taking part in a momentous occasion." (Courtesy of the Norman Bethune Homestead, Gravenhurst, Ontario)

Herman Smith-Johannsen, better known as "Jackrabbit", is, at 103, one of Canada's most famous skiers. He has recently been made a member of Canada's Skiing Hall of Fame. "Sometimes I think I would like to live forever." (Sport Canada)

a blizzard on the way home to camp. There were seven or eight men there and when supper was over everybody climbed into the same bed with a girl of about fifteen! Now this sounds a bit salacious, I'm sure, but the fact was that everyone was in their underwear and, in those days, lumberjacks got into their underwear in the fall and got out again in the spring. So believe me, there was nothing went on in that bed except sleeping. I'd come from a Methodist family and on the face of it, it didn't seem right at the time but it was better than sleeping out in that blizzard!

We were all under one roof there—the seven men and the girl, the four horses, myself, and the job contractor. At mealtime the contractor was at the head of the table. I was in what I suppose was the position of honour, on his right, and from time to time in the course of the meal, he would reach under the table and pull out a handful of hay and pass it across the stove to the horses, who had their heads towards the dining-room part of the shack. This way he could feed them without actually getting up from his own meal of beans and sowbelly.

Another feature of that shack was the underwear and socks hanging up from one end to the other. These boys had been working out in the wet snow and there was no other place to dry this stuff except inside. They didn't wash it, of course, so you can imagine the air inside was rather fragrant. It was hung all over the place, including the area around the stove where the big pot of pea soup was always bubbling.

The diet was beans and sowbelly, bread, pea soup, and prunes in all the camps at that time. We never saw beef from one year's end to the other. It was all sowbelly in 200-pound oak barrels.

We used to drive the pulpwood off streams into the main Montmorency River by a series of post-dams or splash-dams, and the rate at which you drove off the pulpwood which was piled alongside these streams during the winter was pretty well related to the rate at which you could throw it in and open and close those dams so that they would forward these four-foot sticks of pulpwood en masse down to the next dam. All along the creek men would be throwing in wood and opening and closing dams.

Well, this got to be quite competitive. We would load up each stream during the winter with what we thought in our wisdom it could carry, and then they would turn loose a foreman and his gang on each of the streams in the spring.

Anyway, our standard schedule at that time was breakfast at 3:30 in the morning, first lunch at 10:00, second lunch at 2:30, and supper at 7:30, and working all the time in between. Those meals were pretty short affairs, too, lasting twenty minutes to half an hour at the most. One evening after supper a fellow named Louis Arnbeau came to see me and he said he was falling behind Joe La Rochelle who was on the next creek. He wanted permission to have breakfast at 2:30 instead of 3:30 so as to get the drop on the other fellow. The warming thing about this kind of competition was that he wasn't going to get a nickel more for working those extra hours. All he would get would be the satisfaction of beating Joe La Rochelle at the main river so he could lord it over him in the beer parlours of Lower Town, Quebec, after the drive was over. There was no talk of overtime or anything like that in those camps, but I think the companies recognized the need for there to be a limit on the hours that a man should work but there was this incentive for a man to do a better job than the next fellow.

In those old camps there was one man who was more important than anyone else . . . and that was the cook. He ruled his domain like a king and one of the things he wouldn't permit was talking in the cookhouse. He figured that if there was talking between men, they were criticizing the quality of the food or the cooking, and it wasn't unusual for a cook to beat a man up and throw him out just for talking. I remember one cook up in Kapuskasing in Northern Ontario whose name was Napoleon. He used to stroll in a very leisurely and significant fashion within three feet of the backs of the men sitting on the benches in the cookhouse, swinging his cleaver back and forth in a very meaningful way. The people in his camp gained the reputation of being the quietest bunch in the entire organization, which had many logging camps. The cook was definitely the boss in the cookhouse—over everybody.

I remember once when I was a foreman, I had some visitors in from the U.S. who insisted on chattering away at the table. The cook came over and tapped me on the back and said, 'No talking at table.' He didn't care who I was or who my visitors were, even if it was the president of the company. His rules applied to one and all.

In the big camps at that time there would be upwards of 3,000 men. But all the camps weren't big in those days. There was what was called the 'shacker' or 'batcher' camps where three or four men would live together logging a small patch of timber which was remote from the main road arteries. There were lots of those.

In Quebec in those days there was an operation called 'chien te' from the word for 'dog' in French. This is where a man fitted himself between two shalves and piled several sticks of four-feet-long pulpwood across the base of the shalves, either in a chain or on a little platform—a sort of sleigh arrangement—and he hauled it himself as a substitute for the horse. These operations were only in areas where it was just about impossible to get a horse in. That was hard, hard work for a man.

The men thought a lot of their horses in the bush. On their own time on Sundays you'd see them out combing and grooming their horses and putting the little red, white, and blue celluloid rings in their noses and prettying them up in all kinds of ways. Those teams of horses were wonderful, and there is no comparison to be made at all with the tractors of today. There was lots of singing in the camps, too. That was a big pastime and you'd always hear a chanty coming from somewhere. There was always a great feeling of being part of a team or a group.

I can recall the great significance that a Christmas midnight Mass had down in Quebec—the combination of the frosty air and the snowflakes, the tinkle of sleigh bells, and the priest with his vestments all set out on the table in the cookhouse. There's a distinction between Quebec and Ontario in that in Quebec most people would work on Christmas Day, while almost no Quebecker would work on New Year's Day. That was the great festival and even though they might be confined to the logging camp, it was the big day of the year. That might be one of the very few days of the year that booze might enter into the picture at a lumber camp. There was always a special meal too—chicken or beef—something other than salt pork in the early thirties. In the late thirties turkey became the Christmas and New Year's meal. Now in Kapuskasing in Ontario, on the other hand, New Year's was not a special day.

We always started hauling as soon as we got our dumps on the lake and river ice rolled and hardened and strong enough to accept loads of logs. We'd start out on snowshoes if we were in a hurry to compact the first layers of snow depending on the thickness of the ice; if it were up to four inches of blue ice we could put a team of horses on it. This was our rule of thumb. Then we'd drag a log of about four inches thick sideways with a horse. This

197

would compact it further. After that we used a roller which weighed a good deal more than the pole, so by this time we knew that the ice was strong enough. Then we'd haul our logs out there and pile them up and we'd keep piling them up all winter and when spring came and the ice melted they were there in the water ready for the river drive.

This was just a way of transporting the logs by water down to the mill. It was relatively simple where you had a good river, but occasionally the logs would get all jammed up to the point where dynamite would have to be used to get it clear. This was a last resort because dynamite shattered a lot of timber. There was always a key log in a jam and if you could find that and get it clear, the logs would start moving again. Some of the men were very good at finding this log and clearing it, but that as you can imagine was a very dangerous job. But you had to keep those logs moving because if a drive lasted too long there was a lot of sinkage—logs would absorb too much water and they would just sink.

Enormous numbers of logs would be moved in this way—sometimes as many as ten thousand logs in one raft—a million feet of timber. It was only about a mile an hour or three-quarters of a mile an hour, but we were moving so much volume that it was extremely economical. The river drive has pretty well disappeared now but I still think it was the best way to move large amounts of timber.

The whole industry has changed so much in recent years you wouldn't recognize it. You wouldn't find an axe or even what we used to call a lumberjack in the woods any more. There are some of us around who can remember what it was like, but our numbers are fast disappearing. It was a hard, tough life, very lonely at times, but it did have many satisfactions and compensations, too. I wouldn't have missed that whole era for anything."

A. Y. JACKSON

When I met A. Y. Jackson, he was eighty-six years old, and crippled by a stroke that had impaired his speech. Although I chose not to put that recording on the air, the transcript proves that what he wished to say was clear in his head. It serves to remind us all how the Group of Seven changed our way of looking at our country.

A Starting Point for the Group of Seven

"I'M A MONTREALER BY BIRTH. I was born there in 1882. There were six children in all. My father left home when I was very young, so we just had to get out and work as soon as we were able. I got a job as an office boy, but it was a very hard thing for my mother, trying to keep a family together. I had all kinds of other jobs around Montreal and I even spent some time in Europe —worked my way over on a cattle boat. After I came back, I worked for the Chicago Commercial Art Company and I suppose this is where I first started thinking about art seriously. I wanted to get back to Europe to study, but that takes money, and I had none.

I started to save what I could and after a couple of years, I felt I could manage. I studied over there for a couple of years and after I came back I started to paint down around Sweetsburg, Quebec. There was one painting I did there called *The Edge of Maple Wood* that a lot of people seemed to like. I had forgotten about it pretty much for a couple of years, until MacDonald wrote me in 1911, and he wanted to know if I still had it. MacDonald said that that picture represented, more than any other he had seen, the idea he had of the kind of Canada we should be painting. Thomson always said it was the most *Canadian* picture he had ever seen.

At that time there were lots of artists, and good ones too,

199

painting in Canada, but they were all painting like European artists. They were making Canada look like England or Holland, or some other country. Well, Canada is not like those countries. It has a kind of beauty that we all found distinctive, and we felt it was time that Canadian artists started to paint Canada the way that Canadians saw it, and not the way the Europeans wanted it to be.

Anyway, when MacDonald wrote me about that picture I had painted, and asked if I still had it, I said, 'I suppose so. I'll look around.' What had started all this was that MacDonald and Harris had become excited about a show of Scandinavian paintings they had seen. Now, the north of that country is much like Canada, and these fellows from over there were painting their north country the way that MacDonald and Harris thought we should be painting ours. So, I guess if there was a starting point for the Group of Seven, that would be it.

Then MacDonald and Harris started asking others, artists like myself, who were searching around at the time for a Canadian style, if we would be interested in forming a group. Tom Thomson, Frank Johnson, Lismer, and Carmichael were the ones then who liked the idea, and we painted along together until 1914. The war put a crimp in things, and we didn't get formed officially until early 1920. Poor Thomson had died in Algonquin Park while the war was on, so by the time we got started as a group, we were MacDonald and Harris, Carmichael, Lismer, Johnson, Varley, and myself. That was the original Group. But then later, Casson, Holgate, and Fitzgerald joined in with us.

We all felt then that there was a very definite colour about the Canadian North, and that's what we tried to put on canvas. A lot of people didn't like what we were doing, especially some of the European people living in Canada, who didn't necessarily want to be here. They were the ones who would look at our paintings and say, 'It's bad enough to live in this God-forsaken country, without having pictures of it hanging on your walls.' That's the kind of opposition we ran into at the start."

"PUNCH" DICKINS

Canada's contribution to the history of aviation was a great one. Not only did we have men like Alexander Graham Bell and J. A. D. McCurdy working on flying machines at the same time as the Wright brothers made their first historic flight, but our Canadian boys made further steps forward in those early planes of the First World War.

After the war, those same fliers took to the air in the same flimsy aircraft and they proved that, with the airplane, the North country could be opened up. The lessons these Canadian bush pilots learned were of immense value to other pilots all over the world.

Bush Flying

"AS FAR BACK AS I CAN REMEMBER, I always had this desire to be doing something. That's why I got into the bush-flying thing after coming home from overseas after the First World War. From 1919 onwards I had this urge to start an air service from Edmonton down the Mackenzie River. It took me ten years to actually do it. It was a question of getting enough commercial business out of that whole northern area so we could keep going and, at the same time, showing people in Canada what the airplane could do for them. We wanted to prove that we could fly in the wintertime as well as in the summer.

Bush flying caught the public's imagination very quickly. Very soon people looked on us as some kind of heroes, or adventurers heading off into the great unknown. We didn't promote this idea. To us, flying was a job, an exciting one sometimes, but mostly it was hard work, and often dangerous.

You were too busy analysing each flight, having to make up your mind about the weather—about whether you'd fly or not—and about where you were going to land, to think about much else. Hundreds of the places you would go to, you'd never been to before, and neither had the fellow you were taking!

And then when you got wherever it was you were going, you had to figure where to set down. There were no landing fields; the planes had floats and skis so you used the water in the summer, and the snow and ice in the winter.

Every flight would be different. Conditions would have changed—the water gone down, or gone up—there'd be ice on the shoreline—heavy snowdrifts, or something—and you'd have to go somewhere else and land. And there'd be nobody anywhere to give you any information in advance. You had to find it all out the hard way.

We seldom thought of ourselves as pioneers, but I must admit there was one time it did occur to me; the time I was making the first flight ever to Aklavik at the very mouth of the Mackenzie River.

I flew in from Edmonton, the whole length of the Mackenzie, and I arrived at Aklavik, where the Mackenzie runs into the Arctic Ocean, by the light of the midnight sun, on Dominion Day 1929. It was eleven o'clock at night. I was greeted by the howling of maybe a hundred dogs tied to stakes up on this muddy bank, twenty to thirty feet above the river, and by the gaze of maybe fifty or sixty Eskimos—men, women, and children. A small group of RCMP, a missionary or two, and a couple of traders from the Hudson's Bay and the Northern Trading companies were there. Maybe seventy people in all.

I got the airplane ashore and scrambled up this muddy bank and stood there talking to some people for a few minutes. Then, I looked one way and there was the Mackenzie running into the Arctic. I looked the other way, from where I had come, and I thought about the source of this Mackenzie River, almost 2,000 miles away in the Columbia Ice Fields of the Rocky Mountains. And I began then thinking about this fellow Mackenzie, who had traversed only part of the way I had come. He did it in two birch-bark canoes with eight Indian paddlers. It had taken him nearly six months to get there, and he had all the flies and mosquitoes, the heat and the cold, and sometimes slightly hostile Indians. He'd had to live off the country, and never knew what might be around the next bend of the river. As all this went through my mind I thought to myself that I was *pioneering!* Then I started wondering how long ago it was that Mackenzie was here. I did some fast arithmetic and discovered that it was 140 years before I got there. I had come in three days on a journey that Mackenzie would have been unable to accomplish at that time, including the trip back, in less than two years! That took me right back to earth and made me feel pretty humble!

The engines in those planes at that time left a lot to be desired, and for that matter, so did the planes themselves. After all, aviation was barely twenty years old, and not many people knew very much about it, and what was required. It was really pretty presumptuous of the early bush pilots to be venturing up into that northland, which was, after all, some of the most forbidding country in the world.

In the summer, I usually flew without a mechanic. Wintertime I didn't fly very often without a crewman because it was just too much of a chore. You couldn't do everything that you had to do to look after that airplane overnight. You see, the engines were air-cooled in those days and the lubricating oils weren't developed to the stage they are today. We had only one grade of oil which would freeze solid in the airplane when it was left outside overnight. Then the pistons would stick in the cylinders, because the oil was congealed, so you'd have to heat the whole apparatus up with blowtorches and so on to unstick them. And, of course, we had to drain the oil the moment we stopped, and take it inside so it would be warm all night. That was if you were at a trading post, or something; if you weren't you had to put the oil over the blowtorches that you used to heat up the engines so you could get it warm enough to pour it back into the engine!

I went down on crash landings in the wilderness many times; sometimes alone, sometimes with another man, but we were always able to patch things up in some way and get going again. That was part of the game, and that's why it was necessary to know your plane inside and out.

Looking back on it all now, my feelings are more clearly defined than they were at the time. Flying these planes was a great thrill and I knew the moment I landed at Aklavik that the airplane was going to make a tremendous difference in the lives of those people who lived and worked on the remote regions of the Arctic coast."

HARRY HENNIG

Harry Hennig was born to Jewish parents in a small Polish village in the Carpathian Mountains. His childhood was one of grinding poverty, anti-Semitic pogroms, hunger, and, worst of all, hopelessness. He dreamed continually of a better world somewhere and he found it, through an uncle who lived on a homestead in Hirsch, Saskatchewan.

My First Meal in Canada

"I WAS SORT OF A DREAMER BY NATURE. As a child in Poland I remember sitting on top of a hill just next to our little clay hut and looking out at the towering mountains and saying to myself, I wonder what it's like on the other side of the mountains. Is there anything there? I had never been any place outside that little village that was down in the valley below and that was my world. A little brook running through the length of the village.

I had always wondered what it might be like in other places. I kept hoping that one day I would be able to leave our village and see. Most of the village was made up of totally uneducated Ukrainian peasants. They couldn't read or write but they did know how to be anti-Semitic. That they could do very well. There were pogroms every so often—and you'd never know when. A bunch of hoodlums would go on the rampage and smash into our home and break everything. We just took it because it just got to be a way of life and all the Jewish families knew it was going to happen every so often. It was expected, because that's the way our parents and grandparents grew up and we knew that's what was in store for us. That was our lot as Jews. But outside of that, the children were my best friends. We played together, and yet there was that anti-Semitism. They didn't know why any more than we did.

When the First World War broke out, the Jewish men went to war the same as the non-Jews. They fought side by side and they got killed just like everybody else, but when the war was over, the friends who were in the trenches together returned home and once again it became Jew and non-Jew, and they started hating each other again. The pogroms started all over, and you might say that life returned to normal. Who can understand it? It seemed that what they achieved in death with the war on, they could never achieve in life during the peace. That was my life over there. We never had enough to eat. We were very, very poor.

I had an uncle who had gone to live very far away in a place called Canada. I wrote to him in Hirsch, Saskatchewan, hoping that by some miracle he would take me over. The miracle did happen and he sent me the money to come across by ship. You can imagine how I felt!

The journey over was terrifying. I was on the ocean, alone, without one word of English, just like a piece of luggage with a pin on my lapel saying where I was going to. It was in November when I came across the Prairies by train and they looked so desolate and so sad. The cold wind was blowing and these little, dry bushes were shaking. When I got off the train in Hirsch, on a wooden platform, it was pitch dark, late at night, and there was not a single light to be seen anywhere. I thought, 'My God, where did I come? What kind of a world is here?' Then, out of the darkness, figures appeared with lights. It was my cousins searching for me.

They had a 1927 Ford and they piled me and my luggage in there and they drove across the fields. There were no roads, and I thought, 'How do they know how to get there, wherever they're going? There's no road; there's nothing.' But we did get there and went inside the house—I'll never forget that meal, my first meal in Canada. They put a pot of meat on the table and I thought, 'My God, I must be in a land of plenty; look at all that meat!' I had never seen anything like that in all my life. I was forever hungry in Poland, and my aunt was there insisting, 'Come on, Harry. Take some more. Take some more.' And that was my introduction to Canada and my uncle's homestead.

I'll never forget that first winter. My chores would begin at four o'clock in the morning when I would feed the horses and water them. Pull water out of the well with a rope that was frozen with ice to a thickness of three to four inches. By the time I got the water from the well to the trough for those ten horses, it was already frozen in the bucket, and it took a lot of buckets. I had to

205

milk the cows, too! I'd milk and milk and milk until the fingers got so numb it was happening automatically and you couldn't feel that you were doing it. It was hard work but I was glad to be in Canada, instead of Poland."

HANS POLKOLM

The Red Lake Gold Rush in Northwestern Ontario was trig-gered by the find of the two Howie brothers in 1925. Men with gold fever descended on Red Lake from all over the world. They went in by foot, boat, canoe, and dogsled. Often, they were men who had nothing and who were willing to en-dure the worst that nature could throw at them just to be given the chance to get a little.

Hans Polkolm was a youngster from Europe, born to pov-erty. He heard about Canada's Gold Rush and, one way or another, he made it to Canada. He got as far north as the railroad would carry him and he still had another 160 miles to go. It was the dead of winter, sixty degrees below zero, and there was only one way to get there and that was to walk!

Streets Paved with Gold

"WE HAD NO MAP, no compass, no snowshoes, and we were carrying two suitcases each! I think I had an overcoat. An old-timer there looked at us and just shook his head. He lent us snow-shoes, and a toboggan; somebody else gave us a compass and a packsack and we started out. We could only get two of the suit-cases into the pack so we ended up carrying the other two. We had our snowshoes on backwards—I never saw a pair before in my life—so after a while we carried them too, because as soon as we'd take two or three steps we'd take a header into the snow. The first day I think we made around thirty miles.

We got to this big lake, and by that time we were lost. It was dark, but we could see these five or six animals, and they were in a line, and they were howling. I said to my partner, 'Those are wolves.' We figured that was the end of us. We stood there shiver-ing with fright and cold for a long, long time. Then we heard the very faint tingle of bells in the distance coming closer and closer to us.

This fella had seen us and when he got close, the wolves ran away. I can never put in words how we felt when he came over to us. We asked him where we were, and he told us that this was the Red Lake we were lookin' for. So I said, 'Where's the town?' And he said, 'This is it.' When I asked where the buildings and the people and the streets were he pointed down around the lake to where we could just make out a log trading post, and another big building, and he said, 'That's it. That's all there is.'

My God, I can never tell you the disappointment I felt at that moment. If it had been humanly possible, I would have turned around and started walking back right then. But this fella with the sleigh took us down to the trading post. There were lots of men inside and it was warm. They gave us something to eat, and we slept there that night. In the morning, we found out from the men that this wasn't gold-nugget country, and they explained about how gold was mined, and the rock crushed, and refined, and all the rest of it.

Now, I had read all about the gold strike at Red Lake in 1925 over in my small village in Europe and I had started dreamin' about these streets paved with gold in Canada. I thought you could just walk around and pick it up until you had enough. I thought the lumps would be about the size of hens' eggs! Instead I found a couple of log shacks, a frozen lake, wolves, and everything buried in snow; and far from there being any gold in the streets, there were no streets!

Well, we thought about going back, but it was 160 miles through all that snow, with wolves, in the middle of winter, so we decided to stay. We got a job cuttin' wood, intending to leave in the spring.

The favourite pastime for everybody at Red Lake was drinkin', more drinkin', and gamblin'. There was nothin' else to do. But things never got rowdy or boisterous. You never had to lock your door or anything like that, and everybody shared whatever they had with everybody else. We were away up there in the northland together, without even a road to the outside, and we felt very close to each other, because of that. It was kind of like us against the world. By the time spring came around, we were used to everything, and decided not to leave.

Jobs underground were paying 60 cents an hour, which was good money in those days. Then the Company put up more buildings, and the town started to look like a town. They built a dance hall, and brought in some dance-hall girls. There were no women up till then, maybe one or two wives, but no girls, and you must remember that most of the men were young, and full of spirit. So the dance-hall girls—we'll call them that—sort of kept things under control. I must say, though, the men never ever molested or badly treated any woman up here. And after a while some families came up and we had schools and the boom town became a real town. We even got a town hall, and churches.

I started prospectin' and although I never made any fortune, I always had enough to supply my needs; and I still love that Scotch whiskey I learned to drink my first winter in Red Lake, Ontario."

CHARLIE PETERSON

By the time young Charlie Peterson got to Red Lake, the year was 1933, and there were mines all over the place; prospectors were out discovering new and promising showings every other day. After working around the mines for a while, Charlie decided to become a prospector. After more than forty years, he's still looking. But he's not discouraged, not at all.

Some Prospectors Can Smell Gold

"THERE WILL BE ANOTHER MINE FOUND HERE if people have enough initiative. I remember when the people who operated the Howie Mine said there was no more gold in Red Lake, and yet after they said that the finest mine in Canada, the Campbell, was discovered.

I've been working in an area just the other side of the Campbell and I've got a little mining company set up called 'Peterson Red Lake Mines'. We've spent a lot of money in there and I'm still working on it and I believe there's another mine in there. It takes work and more work and more work. In this mining it's a game of elimination. You're eliminating ground. But the whole thing is, are you eliminating it well enough? Maybe you should have another look at it, a fresh look. It's like the Campbell, y'know. I remember Joe Primo carrying rock off that little glory hole he had there for ten years, and there was nothing. The best sample he ever had was two dollars and some odd cents. And then, when George Campbell and Colin, his cousin, went in there and they put a flat diamond-drill hole in and they blew it up, well then, that's when the whole thing started. Do you know they drilled nine thousand feet and they had absolutely nothing? The last hole they had, in that last thousand feet, is when they found the thing that started the Campbell Red Lake off. The gold was in with the iron and it was very spotty so you'd just get a little bit of it here and a little bit of it there. And do you know that very hole, that very glory hole of Joe Primo's, is still there today. I spoke to Joe Chisholm, who's manager of the place, and I said, 'Joe, did you ever follow up that showing?' He said, 'Yeah we did, Charlie. It was very spotty. We never worked it.' And only eight hundred feet away from there is one of the finest mines in Canada. So you never really know, do you?

That's what keeps a prospector going—the stories of all the near misses. This dome land we're sitting on here now; it has to be explored, explored as good as possible. There could be some base metals but there could be another gold mine.

The thing is that gold mining is a rough life. Today the underground miner has someone to tram the muck for him, he has these little donkey engines, he has mucking machines. In the early days this was all done by hand. You mucked and you shovelled. If you were mucking in a drift you went in there and you mucked by hand about twenty-seven tons of rock, over one of these boots with a big pad on it, and then over the top into boxes, and after that you trammed it down out of the way. All by yourself.

Today you talk to some of these young fellas about that, and they say, 'You're crazy. That's impossible.' It's *not* impossible. This is the way it was. I remember one time in 1935, down at the fifth level, they burst into a water seam and the water was coming in so darned fast into that hole in the ground that we had to lower a canoe down there—down the shaft—and put a Cameron pump into it. They took this pump into the end of the drift about five or six hundred feet away—hooked her on to an air line—and they blew eighty bags of cement in that hole, and plugged her up. Then they pumped the darn hole out and went at it again.

That must have been the first canoe that ever went down a gold mine! I was the hoist man there then, and I lowered her down.

We had a lot of characters around here in those early days. I remember one in particular, and I'll never forget him as long as I live. They called him 'Copper Pipe John', a great big fella. I think he was a Russian or something. Whenever you'd see him he had a roll of this copper pipe. Y'see, he had a little still in the bush, and he'd be making moonshine.

The Howie Mine was operating at that time, and they would save all their bullion in this big building. Well, I wasn't very big in those days, so Copper Pipe said to me one day, 'Charlie, you're a small fella. You go in that hole and give me all the gold bricks out, and then I'll pull you out.' Can you imagine what he'd a done to me after? Me, a young kid, and him with all them gold bricks? I shudder every time I think of even knowing him. Most of those kinds of characters are gone now. They're prospecting no more.

They say some prospectors can smell gold. I don't think they can smell gold as much as they have sort of an intuition, an undying sort of drive to work at a certain spot where they think it is. But the smelling of it. I don't believe they can smell it.

For the past few years I've been working with a John Deere tractor. I just go along and scrape off the earth from the rock as good as I can and I leave it like that till the next year. In the meantime the good Lord helps me out and washes away the rest of the silt with rain and so on. Then I can look at that rock. But y'know, you've got to get right down there and eyeball that rock; get your nose right next to it. There's no other way. This geophysics is all right for some things, but in the end it's only the hardnose prospector with his pick who can really find gold. But for gold . . . geophysics is not nearly as good for gold as it would be for base metals—iron, copper, and nickel—because gold is not conductive. It doesn't read on the meter. You take the Campbell Mine for instance. You could go over that ground and do geophysics day and night for the rest of time and all it would show is your base metals. And that's why the prospector keeps at it.

We do need more prospectors. Despite all these fine instruments we still need people who will go out and prod around in that ground. I know I'll never stop. It's not so much the money I'm after any more, although in my younger days, of course, I was looking for that pot of gold at the end of the rainbow. But now, well it's not like that; it's just that I'd like to leave something behind which says 'Charlie Peterson made his mark.' George Campbell did it. So can I."

JEAN CAMPBELL

One of the richest gold mines in the world was developed during the Depression from a find in Red Lake, Ontario, by George Campbell. The Campbell Mine became a symbol of riches for all prospectors and they are sure that another "Campbell" is there in those rocks in Northern Ontario, just waiting for the right man to come along.

One of the ironies of the discovery of the Campbell Mine was that George Campbell's share amounted to very little. But then he hadn't expected much. His wife, Jean, explains why.

And Campbell Mine Was Born

"GOLD PINES WAS A VERY BUSY LITTLE TOWN, because it was the focal point of all the prospectors going North. It had about three stores, two hotels, a laundry, that sort of thing. All through the northeast, there were tiny little mines that the prospectors had started and Gold Pines was their supply point.

There were two or three houses of ill-fame in Gold Pines, and each one had a fancy name. There was the 'Western Front' and the 'Back Flats', and so on. These girls were brought in by the mine owners because they felt it was necessary. The men used to be out in the bush for maybe three months at a time, working in these small mines. They were making good money and when they came in for a breather, they'd want to spend that money. It wasn't placer mining, like the Klondike, you see, so there was no gold nuggets to be found. It was wages they earned, working for mine owners, but good wages. Gold Pines had the booze that they wanted, and the girls, and the gambling! It was a real frontier town. I met a man named George Campbell there and we got married. Everybody in town came to the wedding, because they wanted to see what kind of an old bag George had got for himself. I was green as grass and scared! I was brought up on the Prairies,

213

so the environment was completely different here, but it was exciting and romantic.

We headed up to Red Lake where George had built a beautiful log cabin. Gold had been discovered there by the Howie brothers and everybody was rushing up there to get in on it. There was all kinds of prospecting going on, and George had started a little transfer business there with his cousin. So we headed up there to start our married life.

We arrived there on the first day of October 1928. It was pretty well solid bush but our log cabin was beautiful. George had selected all the logs very carefully, and there wasn't a quarter-inch difference in the size of any of them. It was lovely and cozy and warm, and that's where we set up housekeeping.

A year later, George sent me back to Dauphin, Manitoba, to have my baby, and while I was there, a forest fire hit the Red Lake area. Our home was destroyed, and I didn't get back for a year and a half. By that time, the Depression was on, and we had to start out from scratch. George had originally come in as a prospector in 1926, so when everything collapsed he went back to that and we managed to get by. He had a very bad heart then, but he never told me about it. The baby stayed back in Manitoba with my mother. Red Lake was no place for babies.

George wanted to be prospecting and that's what he did. I used to go with him into the bush all the time and many's the bag of rock samples I carried home. We were happy. We managed to get enough to eat, clothes to wear, and to stay warm.

Red Lake was picking up by this time. More mines were starting—the MacKenzie, the Matheson—and the town was spreading out. George kept saying, 'Some place there's a big mine here—you can't have all these little mines without having the "Mother Lode".' He was working on this particular vein, and he'd come back very disgusted because it wasn't showing much.

One evening we were out on the veranda of the log shack and George was saying how he might have to give up prospecting and find a job, because our finances were really low. He was very very down. Then this fella came along and said, 'George, I did something I shouldn't have done. I picked up some rocks on your claim, and had them assayed.' Now that's something you don't do, pick up samples on somebody else's claim, but all George said was, 'I hope you had better luck than I did.' 'Well,' says the fella, 'I don't know what you found, but I got seven and a half ounces to the ton.' Well, George nearly jumped out of his skin. It seems he had been looking in veins, while this other fella found it in the walls. I don't know that much about rocks, but the excitement was on! George's cousin came in and the arrangements started.

George staked three claims. A fella by the name of Kenny McLeod put up fifteen dollars and I put up seventy-five cents to pay for recording them. Colin Campbell came in, and staked nine more, and they made it a group of twelve, and Colin, George, and Kenny became a third partner in each. Then they got a company to take an option, and the Campbell Mine was born, just like that! It turned out to be one of the richest gold mines in the world, and the people who took the option on the property decided to call it 'the Campbell'.

Well, the mine may have been rich, but *we* weren't. The first money we got was a thousand dollars, so we ran around paying our bills. I think we had enough left over after that to buy a bottle of ginger ale! They also gave us some free stock and some in escrow, which means you can't sell it unless they take up the option. We sold most of our stock, some of it for 5 cents a share, because George never thought it would really be a mine.

All kinds of options were taken up by companies from prospectors at that time because you never knew, one of them *might* become a mine. The companies tried to get as many options as they could and it didn't really cost them that much. So we spent the thousand paying bills, and sold the free stock, and then we lived it up for a while. George had always dreamed of having a small airplane, so he got one. He got a nice car and a boat. He was forty-six years old by this time, and he felt he deserved a little fun and a few luxuries. We had a wonderful time for three years, making up for all the lean ones. He took flying lessons, ran around in the car and the boat, and do you know something, I still didn't know he had a bad heart. I didn't find out until his pilot's licence came through. He told me then how bad his heart was, and that it was getting worse, so he'd decided he'd better not fly. One day, about six months later while the doctor was here talking to me in the kitchen, George just died in that bed right there. He was just forty-nine years old.

Well, when we started to figure out what was left, there wasn't much. The Campbell Mine people didn't owe us anything. We could have been rich if we hadn't sold the stock. Check your newspaper, and see what Campbell stock is worth today. It would make a strong man cry—but not me! I look at it this way. George could never have developed that claim himself. It takes a lot of money to do that, the kind of money that only big companies had. Most of the prospectors knew that some company would give them money and stock for a rich claim and *that* was their dream: to find a rich claim and sell it to some company. I have no regrets because George and I were happy together. I've got three dogs, my log house, and enough memories to last me three lifetimes. What else do I need?"

FREDERICK SNYDER

In 1927, while Hitler was stamping his feet and thirsting after power in Germany, a group of far-sighted people there seemed to sense the horror of what was to come. They pooled their resources and made plans to emigrate to the New World. One hundred and fifty of them landed in Canada with their leader, a man named Frederick Snyder. With high hopes they took over a tract of land north of Winnipeg that had never been settled before. They had broken the land and built their shelters when the weather turned against them for two years in a row. By 1929 and the start of the Depression, they had used up all of their resources, and they were almost ready to give up. Their only asset was their leader, Frederick Snyder.

The Milk War

"WHEN WE FIRST LANDED IN CANADA I chose about three or four of the best farmers in the group, the most intelligent and better educated men, as my advisors. At that time I knew very little about farming, and I knew I would have to depend very much on their judgment. In the beginning we were a co-operative. Each member of the group had put in a thousand dollars and all of the money was in one account. It was very like a socialistic enterprise except that there was one man at the head.

The first years were very hard. The price of wheat tumbled at the start of the Depression from $1.60 to 60 cents a bushel; barley went from 70 cents to 34 cents; and oats went from 60 cents to 18. We got 5 cents a dozen for eggs, and so on. It was a disaster for us, but we pulled through, and this is how: we decided to go into things that did not depend so much on the weather. We had lots of land, 3,500 acres, so we bought fifty Holstein cows to milk, and we were able to sell the milk to a wholesale dairy in Winnipeg. The price was $1.92 for a hundred pounds and at first that was enough to keep us going. It kept going down though, and within a few weeks it was down to 92 cents. We didn't know what to do!

We had become very friendly with a certain Mr. Crerar who was President of the Prairie Farm Growers. He said one day, 'I believe that milk could be declared a public utility.' That meant that milk, like gas, water, and electricity, would be declared necessary for the economy and the life of the people. We went to the Premier of Manitoba, John Bracken, with our plan and he told us to go to the Public Utilities Commission. We went first to the Milk Producers' Association and I ended up as Secretary-Treasurer because they thought that because I had been a lawyer in Germany, I could best present the case. Of course, law is much different here, so that didn't help me much! The big dairies were very much against the proposal of milk as a public utility, and they employed fifteen of the country's best lawyers to fight it. The case went on for six months with those fifteen lawyers on one side and just me on the other. Then the decision came down, and our side won! Milk was made a public utility, and that not only saved our poor struggling colony of farmers, but it saved 1,100 milk producers in Manitoba. Afterwards our legislation was copied in almost every state in the United States, and in every province in Canada. After we won, whenever my fellow German immigrants spoke of that time, they would say, 'We lost the Kaiser's war, but we won the milk war.' "

GREG CLARK

Gregory Clark, one of Canada's most beloved writers, was also one of the kindest and most gentle of human beings. It was the hardest thing in the world to get Greg to talk about himself; he'd always end up praising someone else.

The Funny Little City Guy

"MY FATHER WAS ANXIOUS FOR ME to follow in his profession. He was Joseph Atkinson's right-hand man from back in 1899 when Toronto was a Tory-Orange stronghold. My dad, with his gentle, laughing, humorous approach to editorial direction, structure, and appeal, was as responsible as any man I ever knew for the conversion of Toronto from what it was to what it is today, whatever that is.

After I got my feet into this newspaper thing, I found I liked it very much. The *Star* sent me all over the place, not just Canada but to countries all over the world. I was most interested in the human side of the stories I was sent to cover, in how these world events affected the people who were caught up in them. It was round about this time that I decided I would write in a way that anybody, no matter who they were or how educated they were, could understand me. I wrote about the usual wars and pestilences and famine but I always felt there was room, too, for stories that would ordinarily never make it into a newspaper. That's the way I went and people seemed to accept what I did.

In February of 1930, John R. Bowen, who was then the Managing Editor of the *Star,* called Cranston, the Editor of the *Weekly,* into his office and he had this fresh-off-the-press copy of the *Star Weekly.* 'Now,' he said, 'Cranston, just let's look at this,' and he turned the pages. Page after page was full of the Depression, full of its causes and its effects. Irvin S. Cobb, even, was analysing and writing about the Depression. When they finished the two sections—it came in two sections in those days—Bowen said,

'There is only one light, happy thing in this paper, Cranston, and that is Jimmy Frise's "Bird's-eye Centre".' Now, 'Bird's-eye Centre' was sort of everyman's Canada as seen through the eyes of a cartoonist by the name of Jimmy Frise, and it had been appearing for years.

Cranston said, 'Yes.' 'Well then,' says Bowen, 'on the other back page I want another piece of Frise's art. Find something that Jimmy can illustrate.' So Cranston walked back down the hall in a state of great indecision and some alarm. He called the whole staff together, all of us, and after a period of debate, I was elected to be the guy to provide the material for another piece of Frise's art. It was Jimmy who had the inspiration to use me as this funny little city guy in contrast to Jimmy, the quiet country boy. In fact, Jimmy Frise created a personality and I had to fit into it.

Jimmy never drew an unkind line in his life. He never drew a dumb character except Eli Doolittle, this useless fat man who had Ruby, his wife, doing all the work. The only letters we'd ever get would be maybe fifty letters, the week after Eli appeared, complaining to Jimmy Frise about this Eli character. But you know in every town and village in the world there is an Eli Doolittle. The funny thing is, it was all the Rubys who wrote to protest."

BILL "TORCHY" PEDEN

During the Depression years of the 1930s, the six-day bicycle race helped millions of people forget the misery of their own existence, for a little while. The race was a battle of endurance between a group of highly trained athletes, and for the best man there was acclaim, glory, and monetary reward.

"Torchy" Peden of Victoria, B.C., was one of the biggest racers at 6 feet, 2½ inches, and 217 pounds, and there are record books to prove that he was the best in the world. His account of the six-day races paints an unforgettable picture of a forgotten sport.

The Bike Marathon

"UP TILL THE AGE OF FOURTEEN, I was the skinny kid who couldn't do anything right! The folks got me into as many things as they could, like running, swimming, and bike riding, but I wasn't good at any of them. Then one day I said to myself, 'It's only the *best* at *anything* that makes the money, so you must dedicate yourself to it.' So I dedicated myself to the bicycle and first thing you know, I was winning. Then in 1929, I won four championships in the spring in Montreal. That did it! I went from there to Toronto and turned pro. There was a place there, called the 'Cycledrome'—six laps and four tracks, and it was there I started to race in earnest—for money!

In September of that year, I won my first six-day bicycle race in Montreal. The way they worked was this. There was a two-man team—one of them always had to be on the track—and they would relay each other over the whole twenty-four hours for six full days. They were supervised, too, so that there'd be no falling down on the job. The policeman on the beat had it as part of his job to report to the precinct every hour as to how many of the contestants were still on the track. You'd see him come in, and make his notes, three, four, five o'clock in the morning. Then he'd go back to the telephone and report in. They didn't have the radio communication that they have today.

There was a real marathon craze on at that time—walking, running, snowshoe, roller-skating, and dancing. All kinds of marathons. The bike marathon was the one they were all patterned after, because we were drawing the biggest crowds. Our races had all the atmosphere that could make for a good show. Two people could leave the office and grab a sandwich, and go into the Mutual Street Arena, and later on, Maple Leaf Gardens, in Toronto, for very little money, and they could stay as long as they wanted. There were some who stayed the whole time. Money was very tight in those days and this was a way you could have complete entertainment. Different bands around town would stop in and play a few numbers. The hot-dog stands would be there, and there'd always be something going on. The bicycles, of course, just kept going around and 'round. People would stay too long for their own good. They'd be moping around on their jobs—if they had jobs—the next day, saying, 'Gee, I couldn't leave those races till two or three o'clock in the morning,' or whatever time they left. It was fun for everybody, and we were providing some kind of diversion for a lot of people who spent their time lining up for a bowl of soup and a slice of bread. For a little while they could forget some of the misery that was a daily part of their lives.

As I said, there were two riders on a team. When the biggest crowd was there, from around eight in the night till eleven, everyone would be riding consistently steady and fast. At eight, they could have probably ten two-mile sprints. Then again, at ten o'clock, another ten. Same thing at midnight, and two in the morning. One driver would take one sprint for five or six minutes, then the other fella on the team would ride one. One guy would be trying to gain a lap on some opponent who wasn't a good sprinter. When they were trying to gain a lap, both riders from a team would be out there, relaying each other, top speed all the time. By the time my partner was to relieve me, he'd have the bike up to speed, and I'd give him a push and away he'd go. I've seen it go as long as two hours like that at top speed. Very exciting for us, and the crowd.

The track in Maple Leaf Gardens was only sixteen feet wide, but they'd have twelve to fourteen teams in there, each one with both riders on the track. It could be a real madhouse when teams were trying to gain a lap—jockeying for position, riding each other down, and every once in a while a tire would blow, and the bike would slip away from underneath you, or you'd hook your handlebars on somebody as you went by, and down the two of you would go. Occasionally, there'd be a hole and two drivers would head for it at the same time, which was equally disastrous. There were certain dangers in it, I suppose, but for a body in good physical condition it's almost unbelievable how much it can take.

Along about 4:30 or 5 o'clock in the morning there were very few people in the building. Most of them had gone home to bed, and there was no promoter in the world who would want his drivers tiring themselves out when there were no paid admissions. So one of us would be off the bike for about three hours, while the other one just rode around slowly. Quite often for that period, we'd put on a more comfortable seat and turn the handlebars up for just coasting around. There was no *agreement* to abandon the chase during this time but all the drivers just had an unspoken agreement to take it easy then. Occasionally, some team would put both their drivers on at this time, but then the other drivers would get together, and run into one or both of them, and neutralize the race.

On the last day, if you were in a contending position, you made sure you got yourself in the front of the field and, instead of your partner going away from the track to sleep, you'd have him sleeping on the inside of the track in a little cubicle there, so that he was readily available if a challenge for a lap came up. But usually one partner would sleep from five to eight in the morning, and the other from eight to eleven, and we'd also take an hour apiece for a shower, a change of clothes, and a real good meal. This would take us to about one o'clock, and the pace would start picking up, and everybody would be out then, trying to improve their position throughout the rest of the day. It was hard and gruelling, and exciting most of the time, and we were paid like other athletes. We might have a contract for, say, $200 a day for each of the six days, and one partner could be getting more or less than the other. It was up to each man to get as much as he could, and it was based on each man's ability to draw people into the building.

It was gruelling I suppose, but all I wanted to do was win and I thought of nothing else—the money or the acclaim or anything. I went out to *win*, and I didn't care how hard it was on me. My brother and I went to Madison Square Garden in 1938, and won there. The only brother team to win a major six-day race in the world. I'll never forget how proud our parents were of that!"

MONSEIGNEUR ATHOL MURRAY (PÈRE)

This is the story of one of the most remarkable men Canada has ever produced, a country priest who became the shaper of leaders and a friend to some of the world's most powerful people. Monseigneur Athol Murray of Wilcox, Saskatchewan, was a Catholic priest who didn't believe in sectarianism. He believed in one God, and he believed in people and the ultimate goodness of humanity. Father Murray, or "Père" as most people called him, was a chain-smoking, hard-drinking, hard-swearing doer of things. He set his objectives high because he believed that was the only way to reach the impossible dream. His own impossible dream was to build a college out of nothing, a college that would accept boys, regardless of race, colour, creed, or the ability to pay. This then is the story of not only Father Murray but of his dream —Notre Dame College in Wilcox, Saskatchewan.

A Guy That Really Loved the Other Guy

"I'LL TELL YOU how I came to be what I am. I was born in 1892. My mother died when I was four and my father sent my brothers to college at Antigonish, Nova Scotia, and put me on a farm at Bayfield, nearby. Do you know that I sat on the knees of old Alexander Graham Bell when he was working on his telephones at Baddeck, Cape Breton? I remember well the Boer War. I got into trouble with my father for putting on a soldier suit and trying to walk to South Africa when I was five. I had heard somewhere they were calling for volunteers. They all thought I'd gone mental. When I was seven years of age Dad put me with the Jesuits at Loyola in Montreal. I was much too young for a college course but they did have a Jesuit who happened to be an Indian. Now at that

225

time, although he was a man of great culture, the sense of discrimination barred him from the classes. So he took me on, and I got a lot of education from Father Quirk, an old Indian priest who's long since dead. He gave me a terrific love of the Jesuit martyrs. This all impressed my mind tremendously—had a great role in my life.

After I left Loyola, when I was around eleven or twelve, I was up in the Kawartha Lakes and the very first day I broke my arm. They paddled me down to an American doctor who was camping alone to have it fixed. He had a great laugh. He wasn't a medical doctor, but he was perhaps the world's greatest chemist from the Johns Hopkins University in Baltimore. He said, 'If there's no doctor I'll fix your arm.' And when I whined about having to go back to Toronto the very next day, he said, 'Well, I have a little silk tent here. If you're ready to wash dishes and catch bait for me, you stay right on.' I jumped at the chance and that meant that we camped together for the next twenty-five years till he retired from everything and later died in Bermuda. But he had a wonderful library, and when we used to tour the northern lakes of Ontario he always carried great books with him, Francis Parkman's story of the Jesuit martyrs, for example. Old Doc Reynolds was more or less an agnostic, but he insisted that I read all this stuff and, of course, my imagination leaped. I went on eventually to be educated in Quebec, but I took a couple of years at Osgoode in Toronto and I did newspaper work on the *Toronto Star* and worked under Bill Hewitt, the father of Foster.

While I was at Osgoode I went into a second-hand book shop on Yonge Street where I found a little book on the confessions of Augustine and in there I found the words, in Latin, 'To him who does what within him lies, God will not deny His grace.' Now, the flyleaf said that this book had belonged to the Archbishop of Paris who died on the barricades in 1848 and the book had fallen from his pocket. Well, I cherished it. It changed my life.

I grabbed a streetcar and went to see old Archbishop Neil McNeil of Toronto and asked to be accepted in the seminary. I wanted to go to the old seminary in Montreal among the French but he said, 'Come up and see the one we're building here.' And I had supper with him and we drove out and I didn't change my mind until I asked him, 'Who are you dedicating it to?' and he said, 'St. Augustine.' And I said, 'St. Augustine of Canterbury?' 'No,' he said, 'St. Augustine of Africa.' The same Augustine of my

226

little book. And I said, 'I'm coming here. That decides it.' You must remember, this old fellow Augustine played quite a role in my life. He wrote an extraordinary book called *The City of God*. Anyway, after many ramifications I landed in Wilcox, a little deserted parish without a padre in it, where the church turns out to be the Church of St. Augustine, the only one in the diocese. Now that's more than coincidence. Old Augustine had something to do with guiding me there.

It was because of Monseigneur Matthew, the Archbishop of Regina, and the old rector of Laval University, where I'd gone, that I came to Regina. He asked me to be his chancellor at the Diocese in Regina and I jumped at the chance, of course. I'd only been there about a week when I came in off the street and found a group of men with the Archbishop and apparently there was trouble. I recognized these men. One was the mayor of the city and the rest of them were distinguished Protestant chaps, and it seems that their sons were being brought to court. Here's what the trouble was: There used to be a field beside the Catholic cathedral; it's still there as a matter of fact, but at that time it was just a wilderness field and the boys used it to play ball. Well, one night they discovered that the ladies of the cathedral had left, after the bazaar, a lot of cartons of cigarettes and candy and pop and what have you in the basement, right beside the window where you could see it. So the inevitable happened. The boys broke the windows and got in. And they were eventually caught and they were going to be dragged before the courts and their fathers wanted them exempted from a record. They said they'd pay anything the Archbishop wanted, a thousand dollars or anything, if he just dropped the charges. Well, the Bishop would if he could, he said, but it was out of his hands. It was a cathedral matter and the only one who could do anything was a new priest arriving there that day, Father Frank Healey from Toronto. So, the Bishop said to me, 'You go over and see him and tell him I'd like those charges dropped. Don't let him take any money, just drop the charges.'

I went over and Healey had just arrived by train. He was wild Irish and a bit of a bigot; he was a Tory so I won't say too much, I am one too, and I got him at a bad time because he had just read a book which claimed that most of the juvenile delinquents in Saskatchewan were Roman Catholics. Now this was really quite true because all Europe had poured into Saskatchewan and these kids were almost in the position of our Métis of today, the thing was inevitable, but Healey, with his Irish blood, was saying, 'I'm going to show you chaps that the Protestant boys can be just as delinquent as the Catholics.' Well, I had quite a time with him. And I said, 'Now you're a new arrival here. So am I. Let's work together.' Well, I laid it on. I went far beyond what the Bishop told me. I told him I was Chancellor and it was the decision of the Archbishop that this thing should be dropped, and it had to be dropped. So he finally backed down. When we left the rectory, the boys were out there, all the culprits, playing catch. And they all rushed over and said, 'What's the score?' Their parents said, 'This young padre got you off the hook.' Well, I became their hero. They offered to drive me back to 13th and MacIntyre and I said, 'No, I'm walking over there, and I'm taking you fellows with me.' So we walked over and I took these little Protestants into our Catholic premises and showed them around. What really caught their eye was this really splendid billiard table there. So I told these boys, 'Look fellows, my father was the actual founder of the Argonaut Club in Toronto, at that time a rowing club. But the motto is "Pull Together" and I want you chaps to help me form a Regina Argo Club. I want all the better young athletes of the town up to 100. I'll rent a clubhouse. But you're all a bunch of Protestants, I want some Catholics in.' Well it was great. They brought in a bunch of Catholics, and we had the best damn athletes in the province of Saskatchewan. Later on, they proved it. There was Eddie Wiseman and Don Deacon and Angie Mitchell and Harry Wood, oh, so many wonderful fellows. And for five years we operated football, hockey, and baseball. We went right across Canada three times.

I loved those boys but I wanted to move on, to get out of the city to some place where we could have more than just a club. I asked the Archbishop to let me take over Wilcox, thirty miles from Regina, which was empty. I came out here and there was a little rectory, the rectory that was the Church of St. Augustine. I brought out about fifteen of my boys. In Wilcox at that time there were only two Catholic families in the village, and Catholics and Protestants wasn't talkin', and the Catholics couldn't understand how that new padre had his house full of Protestant kids (who eventually married several of their daughters). But it did an awful lot to change the complex, the sectarian complex, of the whole province. All those fellows eventually became great, great athletes. Out of that little group grew this college of Notre Dame which is completely non-sectarian . . . and doing a hell of a good job.

When I got to Wilcox I asked the nuns if they'd let my boys attend the high school courses which, of course, they did for two years and then later I got the University of Ottawa to grant us affiliation with an arts course. I remember in the early thirties, I think it was '31, Al Ritchie came out to see me and he said, 'Père, they've made me the coach of the Regina team but, damn it all, I've only got two men. All the better hockey players, you've got them out here. Now Father,' he said, 'you've got a Memorial Cup team here whether you know it or not. You can't afford to operate on the scale that they've got to operate for that. Let these Regina boys come back to Regina and play for the Pats.' And I put it up to the boys and they agreed. And you know, they won the Memorial Cup that year. I have their picture here somewhere. They beat Toronto at Winnipeg, and old Al was vindicated.

When the Second World War came on, I suffered like any father, because I knew and loved every one of those boys in that school. They rushed out like all young people to join up, and do you know, we lost sixty-seven boys in that war. I keep reminding René Lévesque of that, and these Separatists. These boys died not for Saskatchewan, they died for Canada. Those war days were tough days.

There was one little fellow, a great little chap, Dreamy Dwyer. He was a goalie, and I took care of him. He became like a little son to me. And when he was sent overseas, he had his photo taken in Regina, in colour, and at that time that cost a fortune. He brought it out and gave it to me and I didn't like it because in the picture he looked distressed, as if he knew what was gonna come. But none the less, I put it up on my wall and he wrote me all through the war, every week; and he finally wrote and said, 'Next week I'm making my last mission and I'll be back in Wilcox within a week. I'll be seeing you.' A day or so later I came into my room and that damn picture was smiling. And I knew that was it. That same day came the cable, he was missing. So now, of all the pictures, the only one I keep up is Dreamy Dwyer. And the boys all know about it. We have a wonderful cup, a hockey cup, in his name and we have a placard for the greatest player every year from '27 down till now. And it's the ambition of every Notre Dame boy to get his name on that cup. I don't think there's any cup in Canada, apart from the Stanley Cup, that has so much history, because remember, there's forty-three names on that cup. Forty-three years. And all wrapped around the memory of that sweet-faced little boy, Dreamy Dwyer.

I love a boy. Oh, gosh, a boy of sixteen, seventeen is wonderful. And the girls are all right. I was talking the other day to a connoisseur of women on the plane and I was complimenting the girl, the stewardess, and I said to this guy sitting next to me, 'You know, that's a beautiful girl.' And he said, 'Do you ever realize that all girls are beautiful?' And I think he was right. Taken by and large, a girl's face is beautiful, as a girl. But it's boys I know best.

Here at Notre Dame we've had great boys. Marvellous fellows. And they're so damn loyal to the college. There was a Jewish boy whose father was dead. I put him through for free. Do you know, he never forgot it. After he graduated and went into business he was giving us about $5,000 a year towards keeping the school alive. Then one time he took me down to Mexico and gave me a wonderful time and about a month ago he phoned me, he was phoning me all the time, he was going to get all his assets together and move permanently to North Mexico. He was building a bungalow and he said, 'Père, I'm going to fly you down to see it.' About three or four days later, on Easter Sunday, his wife called me and said, 'Ken died in his sleep this morning.' You can never tell, you know; it happens to us all. The thing is to live life greatly.

We have as a motto here at Notre Dame that every human is insignificant until he himself makes himself great. The boys all know that. And I have St. Augustine's 'To him who does what in him lies, God will not deny His grace'. When things are dark, well, somehow it gives you power to dive in there. I had a kid in my room here this morning, and I was telling him, for heaven's sakes, keep your faith in God, not churchy stuff. Realize that God is a fact, just like that magnetic field around us is a fact. You can't see it, you can't feel it, but it's there. And we've gotta co-operate. We're all accidents, but God is no accident, He's the great necessary thing we've got to work with.

People have been wonderful in the way they have kept this school going. They bring turkeys at Christmas till you can't eat them any more. Once they brought me one that was about 35 pounds, all wrapped up, and they put it on the veranda and I forgot about it, leaving it out, frozen. About three months later the boys came to me and said, 'Père, we're overdrawn at the store, we can't get any meat. We've got the gang to feed tonight. What are we going to do?' I was looking out the window while all this was going on and there on the veranda was this great big turkey all wrapped up. Well, to me it was almost as if God was laughing at us. What a feed we had that night! And it's been that way all down the years, over and over again. Wonderful fellows who are now dead came through when we needed it. There was old R. B. Bennett. Now you can throw all the mud you like at R. B. but he had a heart of gold. He was a millionaire and he didn't really break himself, but do you know, he sent us a cheque every month for fifty dollars all through the Dirty Thirties. That was a lot of money in those days. And other fellows, they'd see we had coal. Without that kind of help, we couldn't have carried on. How these fellows would love to come breezing out here in the days of the grasshoppers, everybody's forgotten that, but we had grasshopper afflictions where the sun was actually darkened by grasshoppers. I can remember old St. John, the man who founded our village, walking out, he was about eighty, and picking up a handful of the dry soil, it was just like the Sahara Desert, and dropping it, and saying, 'You know, Père, just give it a little water and it's the greatest soil in the world.' And he was right.

These are the days I like to look back to. And the wonderful characters. All kinds of 'em. Old Dr. Singleton in Rollo, he was a wonderful old character, you know. I remember once some poor old French Canadian was dying and I went out and gave him the last rites, and he looked up at Doc Singleton and he said, 'Doc, do you think there's a Hell?' Doc said, 'You wait fifteen minutes and you'll see.' Well, that frightened the poor man enough to pull him through. He lived for many years afterwards.

My life has been rich and if I'm going to be remembered at all, I'd like to be remembered as a guy that really loved the other guy. That's all.''

NOTE: Monseigneur Athol Murray died in December 1975 at the age of eighty-three.

DAN SARRAZIN

The birch-bark canoe may look frail but it played a major part in Canada's story. The Indians taught the first white men how to build and use them, and the voyageurs used that knowledge to paddle their way into the uncharted wilderness. Building a birch-bark canoe is a real skill, one known to very few people today. In 1972 I met Dan Sarrazin from the Algonquin Reserve at Golden Lake in Ontario. He was born in 1902, and learned the skill from his father, who had learned it from his father. Nothing has changed over the years. There's only one proper way to build a birch-bark canoe, and that's the way the Indians do it.

Mix It with Bear Grease

"FIRST THING I DO is get the material. I go in the bush, look for a birch big enough, smooth enough, and clean enough to take a sheet off about fifteen feet or sixteen feet long, as big as you can get it around in circumference; fifteen or sixteen inches in diameter would make about forty-eight inches in circumference. From about the first of June till the end of July, for about two months, is the only time for you to get that bark.

After that, you get the good cedar, clear, and free of knots. Then you pick out a good place on the ground where you're going to build your canoe. You make a mound of earth about fourteen feet long and you place a board on top of the mound, making sure it's steady. Then you put your bark on this board, and your form for the canoe on top of the bark. You cut the seams on each side, and you get the sticks ready; there's outside sticks, and inside sticks to hold the bark upright.

Next you'll need hot boiling water for softening up the bark. Fold the sides, and bring them up after you make the seams; then the sticks goes in. For binding those sticks together you have to use basswood string. Lots of that around here.

Then comes sewing seams, and getting the gunwales ready; you whittle the guns out, measure them, and put them on. After that, you go back someplace where it's sandy and you get the spruce roots. Don't get them where there's cattle, because they generally tramp the roots down, and make them crooked. If you go where there's light soil you can get roots about a half-inch in diameter, about fifteen to twenty feet long, and straight. They hold their shape very good. After you bring them in, you split them and clean them up and if they're a little bit too big you can split them again to get the size you want. Then you're ready to start binding the gunwales and whatever sewing you may have to do on the sides. Sometimes the bark is not wide enough to reach from one gunwale to the other. You have to add maybe five or six inches on each side, but make sure it's in proportion.

Next, you measure the wood for the gunwales; ten-inch wood is good for a twelve-foot canoe. On a fourteen-foot canoe—ten and a half or eleven inches. Then you go get more cedar wood for your lining; it should be four inches wide. Five inches is even better. Make your seating out of that. From the same tree you get the ribs. They got to be free of knots, number one! Select cedar; no knots or nothing. Otherwise you have trouble when you're steaming and bending them. You don't use cedar for crossbars though. You use white ash, if possible. You find this wherever there's basswood. It's quite plentiful.

You seal all the seams on the outside and all the sewing on the sides with spruce gum. We get it off the spruce tree, and mix it with bear grease to make it pliable. Make sure when you take that canoe out of the water always to pull it in the shade, because the sun will melt gum.

That's how Indians always build birch-bark canoes. Only difference for me now is that I don't build outside in woods. I have a place inside, and it's not so damp as crawling around grass in the woods. I am teaching young people 'round here how to do it, because I don't think we should forget how."

LEO CORMIER

Leo Cormier's story is really the story of a town and an area. The town is Baie Comeau and the area is the north shore of the Gulf of St. Lawrence in Quebec. Mr. Cormier was there in 1936 when it was just a construction camp, and he watched it grow from nothing but a pile of rocks and a stretch of timber to a thriving community of fifteen thousand people and good, solid homes.

A Little Canada

"WHEN I FIRST ARRIVED IN BAIE COMEAU there was two houses, one car, and a row of camps with about three thousand men working on the construction of the paper mill. It was in the middle of nowhere and there wasn't one woman in the whole place. Some women of the night tried to sneak in, pretending they were selling magazines, but the Company police force would very gallantly escort them down to the boat and tell them there was no room for them. The entire camp would stop work and everybody would try to get a look.

Not having our women wasn't the only thing that was tough. The climate was very very harsh, forty and fifty below in winter, and, don't forget, our homes were tents! The summers were very short and we were eaten alive by great clouds of mosquitoes. But back in 1936 and '37 you didn't have to worry about recruiting people for jobs in the bush, even in these conditions, because there was unemployment all over the place.

The whole thing, the building of Baie Comeau, came about because of one man, Colonel Robert McCormick of the *Chicago Tribune*. He wanted a paper mill for his newsprint but he also had this dream of making an ideal Company town, a perfect place for his workers to live. And he had the power and the money to do it. He only picked the kind of workers he wanted: so many Catholics, so many Protestants, no troublemakers or rowdies of any kind. He was *particularly* firm about those prostitutes not getting in there! So for two long years, while they were building the mill, the men had a bachelor life.

Colonel McCormick made it known that he wanted the employees to build their own homes because the Company only had money enough for the mill. A million dollars was a lot of money in 1937 and the whole town of Baie Comeau cost the Company thirty million dollars. That included the mill, the townsite, blasting the rock, and everything.

The men at that time were working ten hours at 25 cents an hour, $2.50 a day, with straight time for overtime. I remember if I was asked to work two or three hours after dinner, which gave me fifty or seventy-five cents extra, I was only too glad to do it. That extra money was valuable and we all looked for it.

There was no labour unions at the time . . . but I remember one time when the General Manager announced a ten-cent-an-hour increase for everybody. Everyone was overjoyed. It was like Christmas and New Year's rolled into one. That was big money in those days. You bet it was. At the time I was living at the Staff House and the cost was $1.20 a day for the three meals, my room, laundry, janitor, everything. So I was getting more than half my money free and clear. There was no income tax either. If the gross amount of your cheque for a month was $125, that's the amount you took home. There was no deduction for income tax, pension, union, medical, or anything. I don't know if it was better then or not, but I do know you could buy an *awful* lot for a dollar.

The whole area around Baie Comeau was solid rock. There was no heavy machinery for construction back then so everything had to be blasted; all the rest was pick and shovel. Shipload after shipload of dynamite came to the dock. It was all very hard work and it meant a lot of twenty-five-cent hours for the labourers. All the roads had to be blasted out too and that's why, for a long time, we only had one car; there were no roads to put cars on.

Although it was a closed town it was very well run. We had a mayor—the first one was the general manager of the Company—and we had a town council which set up very strict regulations. When we were building our homes, for example, we had to put in regular concrete foundations as well as sewers and water pipes. You couldn't build just anywhere. They didn't want a shack town. The whole thing had been planned right from the start and the company, the Ontario Paper Company, took care of all the town's deficits at the end of the year.

235

The change from construction camp to organized town came about gradually, month after month, once the mill got into operation. It was late 1938 by the time the men started bringing in their families. Before too long we had 15,000 people here. The mill had about 2,000 men working in it at the start and a lot of them were the same ones who had come here to work on the construction of the area.

Baie Comeau was like a little Canada, full of people from all across the country. The big difference, though, was that we were like one big family. I don't know why we got along so well, maybe we were joined together by hardship. We all came looking for a little better way of life. We all had the same goal. And the fact that it was the Depression and we had gone through the same sorrows and the same problems created a kind of friendship. I never in my life, for one second, ever regretted coming here.

In a way it was nice being isolated; there was hardly any crime and it was always peaceful. But you paid in other ways. If you wanted to go on vacation or see your folks outside the only way out was by boat or by small three-seater airplanes called 'Rapids'. They'd carry you across the river, for a price. But in the spring of the year, when the field was all muddy, these Rapids couldn't take off or land, so there was no way out until the boats started running.

They used to drop our mail in bags with a flag on them so we could see them. I remember one time they didn't find the bag until three months later. It had landed on top of a spruce tree!

We had no problems of any kind till about 1943, when they opened a highway into the area. That's when we started to get a different kind of person coming to Baie Comeau. There was no way to stop them either. By 1945 we had a regular airport and bigger planes and the isolation went completely. The road was kept open all year long, too. But it's still a good town. You won't find many people who want to leave Baie Comeau."

JEAN EWAN

The world's first mobile blood-transfusion service was organized by a Canadian doctor, Norman Bethune, while he was working for the Loyalists in Spain during the Spanish Civil War. Early in 1938, he joined Mao Tse-tung's forces in the hills of Yenan Province and formed the world's first mobile medical unit; and he died in China in 1939 from a disease he contracted while performing an operation.

Chairman Mao himself wrote an essay in praise of Bethune, who emerged as a leading hero of Communist China. Near his tomb the Chinese have erected a huge statue of Bethune, a pavilion, a museum, and the Norman Bethune Hospital; all for the Canadian doctor from the tiny town of Gravenhurst, Ontario.

Working alongside Bethune as his nurse was a young girl from the Canadian Prairies named Jean Ewan.

Tea with Mao Tse-tung

"I WAS ACTUALLY IN CHINA BEFORE DR. BETHUNE. I had gone out after graduation in March of 1932, mainly because I didn't relish the thought of staying on the hospital floor. I came from a kind of roving family and I wanted to see the world.

I stayed in China, except for holidays of course, for five years and I met up with Dr. Bethune in New York in the last days of 1937. I knew then that I would go with him back to China. I knew Chinese, you see, and he didn't. Although this irritated him sometimes, because he didn't like to be dependent on anyone, we got along fine.

I used to go out with him right to where the fighting was going on, and that could be terrible. There were all kinds of casualties—some you could help, and some you couldn't—but the biggest problem was food. When the Japanese advanced, all the crops were burned, and all the wells were filled up. So not only were our soldiers being killed, they were starving to death as well.

Dr. Bethune was continually frustrated because he didn't have the wherewithal to do what he wanted to do. He was a master at improvising, though. He made splints out of whatever he could find. We didn't have narcotics, but you could buy opium tar and he would dilute that for injections as a sedation because it was very important when you had so many casualties to keep them sedated.

Those who were operated on had to suffer some pretty severe pain under very poor conditions. We had no hospitals or operating rooms so Dr. Bethune would operate in any old shack or lean-to that was out of the weather. There were no other doctors besides Bethune in the area that we were in and I was the only nurse, but there was no time to feel alone, because we were always so darn busy.

While I was working with Dr. Bethune in China Mao Tse-tung expressed a desire to meet him. Mao Tse-tung had heard about the work he had done in Spain, for Bethune was a world figure even at that time. Dr. Bethune asked me to go along to the meeting with Mao as his interpreter. When we got there we heard that Chairman Mao's secretary spoke fluent English, so they ended up with two interpreters.

We went to see Chairman Mao at about 11 o'clock at night and the sun was coming up before the meeting ended. It wasn't what you'd call a secret meeting, because everybody around there knew about it. It was just a meeting to plan some of Dr. Bethune's future work with the Chinese.

They mapped out plans for hospitals, and for crossing the Japanese lines. They could only cross these lines with mule trains and when there was no fighting. They they'd take across maybe 800 animals and as many supplies as they could manage.

The meeting took place in a cave with an oval-shaped roof and an earth floor. It was Mao's headquarters at the time. There was a bookcase carved out of the stone wall and there was hardly any furniture. His batman brought us tea and peanuts. There were no cakes because there was no flour to spare for things like that. I do remember that we ate endless peanuts and dozens of cups of tea. I knew, even then, that I was taking part in a momentous occasion."

ANNETTE BRUNELLE

When Trans-Canada Air Lines was started on April 1, 1939, Annette Brunelle of Montreal was chosen to be stewardess on the first leg of the Montreal–Vancouver inaugural flight. Stewardesses were as new as commercial airlines, and the ten-seater "giant" she flew in was considered an eighth wonder of the world. The stewardess was a glamorous heroine, and all heads turned as she strolled along the streets of Montreal, casually wearing her uniform, and trying to look as though she didn't notice the stares. She was a final beautiful antidote to a Depression that would soon be ended by the Second World War. The days of innocence were drawing to a close.

Only a Ten-Seater Aircraft

"I THINK WE FIRST STEWARDESSES probably *did* feel like celebrities. There were interviews all over the place, all the radio stations and newspapers in Montreal, and, of course, our pictures in the papers, and all that. We had to be a certain size, a certain personality, and also bilingual. Those of us chosen could only think of how lucky we were to have the package that they wanted. Also, we had to be registered nurses. I think this may have been because so many of the passengers in those days were taking their first flight, and there was a fair amount of air sickness, because at that time we didn't have oxygen, and the cabins were not pressurized. Of course, on those early flights between Montreal and Toronto, we weren't flying that high, except when the weather was bad, and then we'd have to go above the clouds. People would really feel the pressure then. Then, of course, everybody was nervous about flying, and they'd say, 'What if anything happens to me, and I get sick on the airplane?' Nurses gave them some kind of security in that way. Also, nurses were used to dealing with people anyway, and they knew how to make the passengers comfortable. We could spot symptoms, too, and if we saw anything we would tell the Captain, who would radio ahead for a doctor to be at the airport when we landed. I do think it was important for the stewardess to be a nurse at that time. It was all so new to everybody.

That first flight was April 1, from St. Hubert Airport in Montreal, at nine o'clock. I'll never forget the crowd of people who came out to see us off. It was beautiful weather, and we arrived in Ottawa, where we were told we'd be delayed, because the weather was not good in North Bay, so we consulted with the passengers, and asked them if they wanted to wait, or be 'trained' to Toronto, because they were all Toronto passengers. They all decided to go by train, and the crew stayed overnight until four o'clock in the morning, when we headed out for North Bay. Then we found out we couldn't land, so we went to Kapuskasing, and we refuelled there, and landed in Toronto about nine o'clock in the morning—so it was really twelve hours from Montreal to Toronto.

That was the first leg of the trip, the only part that our crew was assigned to do. There was no such thing as one person flying the whole distance from Montreal to Vancouver. It was all done in legs. The first from Montreal to Toronto, *should* have been four hours. The second, from Toronto to Winnipeg would be eight hours, and from Winnipeg to Vancouver would be another ten hours. So it would mean twenty-two to twenty-three hours on duty for a crew member to go the whole distance. That would be impossible, and that's why it was broken up into three legs.

We had passengers on that first flight who were used to flying, like C. D. Howe, Maurice Lamontagne, who was with the Department of Transport, and C. P. Edwards of the Post Office Department. Then, we had executives of some of the larger stores, and a few first-flighters. You could always tell the first-flighters, because they called you so much, and asked so many questions, and they wanted you to be with them all the time. So we'd talk to them, and not leave them to themselves too much. C. D. Howe was a very nice man, and he found out my name and called me Annette all the time. I liked that.

It always got to be like a little family on these first flights. We'd only have ten passengers, and everybody got to know everybody else. The men would ask us to their homes, to meet their wives and children, and so on. It really was nice—and it was exciting because there was this feeling that you were part of the future of Canada. We were, too, because we were pioneers of aviation.

The planes were really very tiny and funny, as I look back now. Our seat—the stewardess's jump seat—was on the door, and if anyone was in the washroom, which was *really* tiny, you couldn't sit down, because they wouldn't be able to get out!

It was only a ten-seater aircraft, but it was thought to be a giant in those days. It was the first commercial aircraft, and I remember how people would look at it, and wonder how it would ever get off the ground. Even the passengers who flew in it were looked at like some kind of heroes by most people. Remember that in 1939, very very few people had ever been up in a plane.

I stayed a stewardess for three years, and I loved every minute of it, but I felt that it was time to go back on the ground after the three years. You never could be sure, then, when you were going to get home. Planes were grounded a lot, and I was going around with the man who became my husband, and he was always being disappointed when I didn't get back. It was a very very thrilling three years, but after a while, I felt that it was time to get back with the rest of the world."

JOEY SMALLWOOD

Christmas Eve 1900 was a fateful day in the history of Canada. It was on that day that a new voice was heard in the land as Joseph R. Smallwood came screaming his way into the world. A future Father of Confederation, a future premier of a brand-new province that he would create almost single-handedly, Joey Smallwood's story is the story of Newfoundland, and we begin that story in the outport of Gamble.

The Barrel Man

"ANYTHING IN NEWFOUNDLAND AWAY FROM ST. JOHN'S at that time was an outport. All the settlements, all the villages around the coast, were seaports, and Gamble was an outport in Bonavista Bay. There were very few places in Newfoundland in 1900 that were served by roads. The province had virtually no roads and there was no way of getting in touch with each other, except by boat. A lot of people don't realize this, but the Atlantic coastline of our province is longer in miles than the coasts of the United States on the Atlantic Ocean. So, if you have 6,000 miles of coastline and 1,300 different outports, you can imagine how far apart the places were; how isolated and how remote, especially since they were not connected by road. You'd get from one place to the other by boat or schooner or sailing vessel.

This was the only contact people had with each other, except that we had what were called coastal boats and steamers that were really part of the railway system. See, there was a railway *across* the island, but it went across the interior of the island where no one lived, and that railway was between 500 and 600 miles long, and it went through an area where the population consisted entirely of birds and rabbits and moose, caribou, and trout. It began at St. John's and ended at Port aux Basques, which was on the Newfoundland side of the Cabot Strait. On the other side of the Strait was North Sydney, Cape Breton, so a lot of the freight from Canada came to Newfoundland by rail—down to North Sydney and by boat across to Port aux Basques, and then by rail from Port aux Basques to St. John's. That was the only railway we had, except for a couple of very short branch lines which served only a very few outports or settlements. The great majority of settlements along the coast of Newfoundland and Labrador were served only by sailing ships and these coastal boats.

It was entirely possible for people in these outports to never see a strange face in their lives, or hardly ever. Now, Gamble was a bit different in that it was one of the few places that the railway touched, and that happened, incidentally, just around the time I was born. That was the time, too, that the railway was completed. It snaked its way across the island, avoiding hills, going around curves to avoid the more expensive business of trying to go in a straight line. This added at least a hundred miles, making it more like 600 miles than the 500 it should have been. It was, and still is, a narrow-gauge railway, one of the few left in North America, but the fact that Gamble had the railway made it a metropolis compared to some of the other outports. We had a population of two or three hundred people and it was unlike the typical Newfoundland outport because it was not really a fishing settlement. You see Newfoundland consisted of a lot of great bays with long indraughts and the codfish, which was the main fish, would be found in greatest numbers out by the headlands. As you went up farther inside the bay away from the entrance, there was less and less fish and Gamble was exactly at the inner end of that part of Bonavista Bay where there was precious little fishing done. The principal occupation of its people from the very beginning in the first half of the nineteenth century was logging. There were sawmills there. As a matter of fact my grandfather David, who was born near Charlottetown, Prince Edward Island, and went to Newfoundland when he was twenty-one years old, was the first man to build a sawmill in Gamble and one of the very first to build one operated by steam engine. The first sawmill was typical of all the others in Bonavista then in that it was powered by a water-wheel. That burned down and then he built the steam-powered mill—which may also have been the first of its kind in Newfoundland.

My father went to live in St. John's about a year after I was born so that's where I was actually raised. The first thing I can remember of St. John's is sliding down Garrison Hill in the winter-

243

---

time. I was sliding down with my sister Marie and I remember bumping into a stone wall and cracking my head. I got two or three stitches and if you look carefully at my forehead now, you can still see them. I was three or four at the time. At about that time, too, my father got this great big Newfoundland dog and he got a baby carriage made big enough for my sister and me, and he had shalves made so the dog could fit in there and pull us around. We got an awful lot of attention in that, and I guess that's the first public attention I attracted.

The merchants were the important class of people in St. John's in those days. The merchant in Newfoundland meant something different than what it would mean for example in Toronto or Montreal. Timothy Eaton would be a great merchant up there buying and selling goods. In Newfoundland, the word 'merchant' had a much narrower meaning and it meant 'a man who dealt in codfish' because codfish was to Newfoundland even more than what wheat ever was to the Prairies. Codfish was the one great commodity that constituted the economy. Now there were other fish like salmon, too, but codfish was the mainstay of everything. There were lobsters then, too, but the fishermen considered them a pest when they got them in the nets. They'd throw them away! There was also some herring, and don't forget the great seal hunt! In March every year from about 1800, instead of just the inshore fishermen venturing about a mile or two off to capture seals, schooners began going out looking for them, until there was a fleet of seal hunters that ran up to 400 or 500 vessels. Then the steamers and the steel ships came and it became a very great industry indeed. For a short few weeks every year the seal hunt became an important part of the economy too! But the merchants who dealt in salt codfish also dealt in those other kinds of fish, and also the biggest of them dealt in seals. So merchants in Newfoundland were basically salt-codfish merchants and they supplied the fishermen who caught it and salted it and cured it in the sun with the things they needed. They were the ruling class of Newfoundland. Those Water Street merchants controlled the trade of the island.

They exported to countries all over the world dealing in all sorts of foreign currency. They also owned the retail shops and the wholesale shops, so they supplied all the small shops scattered over those outport communities around the island's coastline. They were the ruling class and, as such, they were the Tories. The

Liberals were 'the ragged-arse artillery'—the fishermen, the labourers, and so on, who made up ninety-eight per cent of the population. Historically that is the case.

When the merchants formed the Government—it was called just that, the Merchant Government—a lot of people felt it was better to *have* a merchant government, because after all, they had the money, they had the business interests, they had the influence, the authority, and the power, so it was just as well for them to rule. The people of Irish and Scottish descent, on the other hand, had that small-'l' liberal tradition, and they put up the opposing part. Because they came, usually, from the 'raggle-taggle', they won most of the elections. So what you had was the working class in power in the government, but the *real* power—the power of money—lay with the merchants.

Everything was carried on on a credit basis. It was barter. In a settlement of say, three hundred men, women, and children, the only occupation—aside from a schoolteacher and a clergyman, a merchant and a small shopkeeper—was fishing. In the spring of the year, as the season was about to start, the fisherman would go to the merchant and the merchant would agree to outfit him on credit. He'd give him salt, and gasoline to operate his boats, a pair of rubber boots, oilskins and Cape Ann, and some food. He'd give this to each of the fishermen on a boat. See, these men on each boat wouldn't be working for wages, they would share. The owner of the boat got the largest share. It was the owner who would get the gasoline and salt. The men got the other things that they needed for themselves. So, every fisherman would start the season in debt to the merchant.

Then the fisherman was expected to turn his fish in, and as the season went on, he'd be back to the merchant, getting more supplies all the time until 'settling-up' time came in the fall of the year. Each man would go into the merchant's office, and the bookkeeper would open the great big ledger, six or eight inches thick, and turn to the man's account. He'd have it there, that the man owed for this and that, and that his share of the fish came to so many kentles and pounds. The merchant decided whatever price he wanted for the goods he gave on credit, and when it was all added up, the bookkeeper would announce that the fisherman would have a dollar coming to him, or fifty dollars, or whatever— or he might *still* be in debt!

Now, the merchant would only carry over the fishermen he

considered loyal and honest, the ones who didn't sneak their fish away to another merchant. The temptation to do that was terrific because these men were living on a shoestring. It was natural for them to want to sell some fish to the 'barter-shops', where they could get some things that the fisherman wasn't able to get from his own merchant—a little tobacco, extra food, or things like that. He'd sneak down in the night with an armful of salt cod, and the barter-shop man would weigh it on the scales and pay at a rate rather lower than the going price mostly. So the barter-shop man was getting fish that the supplying merchant should have got to pay off the fisherman's debt. The occasional fisherman, therefore, ended up in debt, because he didn't deliver all his fish to his merchant—some of it went to the barter-shop. That whole system of merchants was called 'the truck system'—not cash transactions. Any fisherman caught going to a barter-shop was blacklisted and cut off from further credit.

There's a classic story of the fisherman who ended the season without squaring his account. He asked the merchant for a bit more credit and the merchant said, 'No sir, not a nickel's worth will you get. It's not my concern how you live. You shoulda thought of that before.' 'But sir, I can't believe you'd deprive me of a chance to live through the winter.' 'Yes I would,' said the merchant, 'after the way you treated me, and if you had anything I could take for the debt I'd take it.' 'Well,' said the fisherman, 'the only thing I got is me bed. You wouldn't take that would you?' 'Yes,' the merchant said, 'I'd take your bed!' 'If you took that,' said the fisherman, 'I'd have to go down and mow meself another one.' In other words, he was so down and out anyway that all he had to sleep on was dried grass. Under that system a lot of fishermen were as badly off as that.

That whole system came to an end, I would say, during the Second World War. There was more cash around than Newfoundland had ever seen. The Americans had bases in Newfoundland—Canada had bases here, and we had more employment and more cash than we ever dreamed of. It was fantastic!

When the war was ended, we were still prosperous, but after a year or so the British Government came out with a big announcement. They said it was time for the Newfoundland people to decide their own future. Of course, Britain was then on the verge of bankruptcy itself, so the British Government were going to hold a referendum by secret ballot among all the Newfoundland people. On the ballot would be the names of different forms of government and you were to mark an 'X' across from the form of government you wanted for your country for the future. This referendum would be preceded by a National Convention, with the representatives elected by the Newfoundland people. There would be 48 people elected from across the island, and the purpose of the convention was to recommend the forms of government that should go on the ballot paper which was to follow; also to decide whether we were, indeed, ready to be self-supporting again—or was our prosperity only due to the war, and we'd soon be back in the doldrums where we were before—on our backside.

Now I had thought and written and broadcast about these very things for years. In my radio show *The Barrel Man*, I had talked about these things, and tried to give Newfoundlanders a true picture of their own worth. I wanted them to cast off their inferiority complex and show the world they were as good as anybody else—which indeed they were. And now here was the chance. Now that the time had arrived I said to myself, 'What in God's name is it that I favour? This Commission government we've had since 1934 with six men, not elected by the people and not answerable to the people? Could I go for that? On the other hand, are we ready to go back to what we had before we went bankrupt—self-government?' Neither of these appealed very much to me, to tell you the truth. I came to the conclusion that Newfoundland just couldn't go on as it was. Either we would have to hang on the skirts of England, or find some other skirts to cling to. We needed somebody else to cling to, or we couldn't make it!

England wasn't in very good shape herself, so that left only Canada and the United States. A lot of middle- and upper-class people and some fishermen felt secure with the British connection, others said, 'Oh God, let it be the United States, because they're rich!' 'They're wealthy. They're the land of milk and honey. They're powerful.' And virtually every family in Newfoundland, including mine, had relatives living in the United States. Most Newfoundlanders knew very little about Canada, but they knew all about the United States, but I made up my mind that I should find out what this Confederation thing was all about. What would it mean? I wrote a letter to every Premier across Canada. There were nine of them, and I had to find out their names first, and I even had to find out the names of the capital cities. I knew Halifax was the capital of Nova Scotia, and Charlottetown was the capital of Prince Edward Island. I thought the capital of Quebec was Montreal, when of course, it was Quebec City, and so on. I didn't know the names of the Premiers, even! I just wrote 'The Honourable the Premier' in each of the provinces and I wrote the Premier of Canada, who at the time was Mackenzie King, and I said in the letter—the same letter to all of them—'As you may be aware the people of Newfoundland are shortly to elect a National Convention to consider the possible future of Newfoundland in a National Referendum. I propose to offer myself as a candidate for this National Convention, and I would like to know what Confederation means and what it would mean to Newfoundland should we become a Province of Canada. Would you be so kind as to send me any documents, budget speeches, and other speeches that you may have which would throw some light on this?'

A few weeks later the stuff began to pour in on me. Armfuls of it. And I began to read and study it. That's right up my alley anyway. I love that kind of thing. I've been doing that all my life. I got at it for weeks at a time, all night long, and I'd have to pull down the shades to keep the sun out in the morning so I could shut my eyes for a few hours' rest. I'd get up again at seven, have some breakfast, and go right back at it again and I made a tremendous study of the whole Confederation set-up. I probably knew more when I finished studying than anybody in the Canadian Government at that time because I had gone through those stacks of material from every one of the provinces and it was all very fresh in my mind. Then every day for thirteen days, I wrote a letter for the newspapers in St. John's, which appeared serially, in which I explained what Confederation meant. That was the introduction to the people of Newfoundland of what Confederation was about.

Then it struck me like a lightning bolt. I didn't know even if Canada wanted us, or whether they'd touch us with a forty-foot pole! I said to myself, 'I better find out,' because the Convention was starting in a few weeks, and if I were going to recommend Confederation, I'd better be darn sure that they'd take us. I went to see Scott MacDonald, the Canadian High Commissioner, in St. John's. He said he'd been fascinated by my letters in the newspaper, and he said he was all for Newfoundland joining Canada. He arranged for me to get to Ottawa, and scout around.

When I got there I met Frank Bridges of New Brunswick, who was then the federal Minister of Fisheries, and through him, I saw ministers and deputy ministers, and also the leader of the Tory party, who was then John Bracken, a former Premier of Manitoba, who was a very knowledgeable provincial man. I talked with M. J. Coldwell, who was then leader of the CCF and Solon Low, leader of the Social Credit Party. For two weeks it was work, work, work. Night and day. Meeting and study sessions, and I ended up with a great amplification of what I had already learned from those documents. After all that, I talked with the Acting Prime Minister, Louis St. Laurent—King was in Europe at the time—and from it all I gathered that Newfoundland would be most welcome to join the Canadian Confederation.

Then, I went back and when the Convention opened I launched my campaign for joining Canada.

I had the greatest fun of my life outwitting them and playing games. Every word of the Convention was broadcast—*every word!* The Convention met at three o'clock every day to six o'clock, and at nine o'clock that night those three hours which had been taped would be broadcast. The entire population of Newfoundland listened. The *entire population!* Those who didn't have radios went to houses that had them. Every nook and cranny, every little cove, every harbour and every little village in Newfoundland was listening. In all the outports twelve or fifteen people would be crowding into kitchens at nine o'clock with the battery radios turned on to hear that day's debate. I heard about one man who said, 'I can't understand that Mr. Smallwood. He keeps on gettin' up and demandin' a pint o' water. He must be an awful thirsty man!' This is where I'd be saying, 'Mr. Speaker, a point of order.' He heard that as a 'pint o' water'.

But anyway, they listened for a year and a half for five nights a week from nine to midnight. A tremendous debate—a tremendous educational process. Now I had spent years broadcasting, and I knew the magic of broadcasting. The sheer, sheer magic, especially in a place like Newfoundland with so many isolated people. I always said that God created radio just for Newfoundland and having done so, He graciously allowed it to be used in other parts of the world. It was *meant* for an isolated people who never met or saw each other. I knew how to use radio and I never let my mouth turn away from that microphone. *Never!* So my voice came through always clear while some of the others disdained this contemptible modern contraption. I was always heard, therefore, on the radio broadcasts throughout the island, while many of the others were not. Of course, I had to have solid arguments. I did! The Newfoundland people agreed with me. I found this out by travelling everywhere trying to meet each and every one of them—presenting my case in person.

The long and the short of it was that the people agreed with me. Newfoundland became a province of Canada in 1949. I'd be a hypocrite to deny that I am not proud of my part in bringing that about."

LORNE BERRY

*In the summer of 1940, Lorne Berry and his partner, Phil
Gauthier, spent the months of July and August prospecting
the area of Ungava in Northern Quebec. They spent the evening of September 8 celebrating. Their work was done for
the season and they planned to spend a week just taking it
easy. The plane they had contracted at the beginning of their
two-month stint in the bush would pick them up on the 15th.
These two old friends—bush buddies—didn't have a care in
the world.*

The Closest of Friends

"WE WERE IN THE BUSH ALL SUMMER and we had so many problems because of weather and that sort of thing, but now it was all
over and, boy, were we happy. They were going to fly us out from
Breece Lake, where we were, directly to Seven Islands or Ri-
mouski. In our packsacks we had a forty-ounce bottle of whiskey
that we'd taken off the ship and we were looking forward to having it that night because no matter how good friends you are, after
you spend two or three months in the bush with just one other
man, you kind of wear off each other. But we were actually the
closest of friends—great chums.

Anyway Phil was roaring around there with a few shots into
him and I was the cook because he didn't like cooking too much.
But he'd eat anything. Phil was a great man to eat—a terrible man
to eat. If you cooked him poplar bark or spruce gum or anything,
he'd eat that as long as it filled his belly. So this night I'm hungry
and he's hungry and we're going out in a week and we're happier
than hell. We had caught a couple of trout that day—and we had
all these damn old dried vegetables, you know, desiccated potatoes and onions and turnips, which always gave you indigestion.
The only way to get rid of that indigestion was to walk and walk
and walk and get rid of it. So, I cooked Phil up a big mess of this
stuff after we had a couple of big shots out of that bottle.

It's a funny thing you know. If you like a man and you're in the bush with him you'll do anything in the world for him and he'll do anything in the world for you. If you're not feeling too good one day, he'll pick up the heavy load that day and never say a word about it. Tomorrow it may be his time. Anyway, by gosh, I filled him up real good that night. I cooked him a whole big frying pan of trout and a whole frying pan of those damned old desiccated vegetables. We had a hell of a feast. He was singing and I was singing. We were going out in a week and we were happy—to hell with Ungava—we were going out, and so on.

Phil and I had taken an oath that we were going to join the commandos when we came out and we were going to beat the hell out of Hitler. There was no doubt about it. Soon as Gauthier and I got over there Hitler was going to quit. By gosh he was a good partner. It's pretty hard to find a good fellow to stay in the bush with you for three or four months you know.

After a while I couldn't hear Phil singing so I figured he'd gone to bed. I was cleaning up the plates and stuff and had a couple more shots. So I walked into the tent and here he was sitting with his head kinda down over his chest and a bit to one side. I thought, 'He's been sick a little bit,' you know. I shook him and said, 'Phil, come on. Go to bed. I'll pull your boots off, and your pants off and you go to bed.' He never answered me. Not a sound. I shook him and his head flopped around like it was on a stick. I gave him a shove and he fell back onto the bed and it kinda struck me then that there must be something seriously wrong with him. I thought, 'You bugger. You're dead.'

So I listened to his heart, I felt his pulse, and he wasn't breathing. There was nothing going on with that fellow. He was dead. I rolled him over on his back and tried to give him artificial respiration. I blew in his mouth and I banged at him and everything but it was no use. Phil was dead and I couldn't do a thing about it. I didn't know what to do. Here's old Phil dead and me alive and we're going to be together for another week till that plane arrives. What to do?

I dug a trench down in the permafrost, wrapped Phil up in his sleeping bag, took a silk tarry, and sewed it all up. You know this is a hell of a thing to have to do with your best friend and your partner. I dragged him out of the tent—I couldn't carry him, he weighed 200 pounds—and I put him down in that damned grave and I said, 'Well Phil, damn you to hell, what did you go and do that for?' I gave him the last rites or whatever the hell you call it. Then I tied a bunch of tin cans together and put them all over the grave, in case any of these brown bears came around. That way I'd hear them if I happened to fall asleep.

So we sat there, Phil and I. I must have drunk a million gallons of coffee. In a week the airplane came in to pick us up and we flew to Seven Islands with old Phil, the greatest man to be in the bush with you could imagine, and here I was in Seven Islands feeling glad to be rid of his body. So Joe Reddie came along and said, 'Lorne, you've had a tough time.' I said, 'Joe, if I never see a Frenchman or the Ungava or prospecting again in my life I'll be happy.' Joe said, 'Here's forty ounces of whiskey. Go and get yourself good and drunk.'

I did."

"JACKRABBIT" JOHANNSEN

Herman Smith-Johannsen *was one hundred and one years old when I visited him. He was born in Norway in 1875 but he lived most of his life in Canada. He's an amazing man. He lives alone in the Laurentian Mountains of Quebec where he does all his own housekeeping, chops his own wood for his fireplace, and in the winter skis every day. In the summer he paddles his own canoe. The world knows Herman Johannsen by one name only and that name is "Jackrabbit".*

Jackrabbit

"THE NAME 'JACKRABBIT' really originated among some skiers. We had 'hare' and 'hound' races, and I was the 'hare'. That's the way it really originated. Anyway, it's a good name. The rabbit is at home in the snow—so am I. Most people who come from Scandinavia feel that way.

I left Norway in 1894 and I was in the United States before I came to Canada somewhere around 1900. The company that I worked for in Cleveland, Ohio, had to send a man to Canada to do a job and they sent me. That's the best thing they ever did for me. I was an engineer, a construction man. There was a big railway boom going on in Canada, the Transcontinental was being built and I was selling machinery to the Grand Trunk up north, pushing from North Bay up into Cobalt, where we found silver, and later on gold at Timmins. My job was to get out back in the country, where they were running the line. It was just exactly what I wanted. It was wonderful. I love the out-of-doors and I was glad to get away from Cleveland and that whole industry down there. I got back to Canada, eventually, where I wanted to be. I've spent most of my life in this wonderful country and most of that time in the bush . . . in the wilderness. That's the real Canada. You know, people who live in Canada . . . most of them, live in the towns—

Montreal, Toronto, Vancouver, and so forth. They don't know their own country. Right now, in February and March, this is the best time of the year up north. There's a dry cold; you can sleep out in the snow anyplace. Build a big fire, and you're nice and warm down in the snow. If you're down in the snow, you're nice and warm. You may have thirty below zero in the air but down in the snow it's just a little bit below freezing. Just like being in your own living room, if you're in a good sleeping bag.

People spend too much time today worshipping money and worrying about it. I was like that for a little while. I had a good business and had the satisfaction of making money, but I also had the good fortune of losing the money. I was wiped out in 1930 at the Depression and I considered that one of the greatest blessings that I've had. It brought me back into the right way of living. It cleared up my thinking. I stopped trying to be rich in dollars and I used that energy enjoying life in God's outdoors.

Of course, having the right mate in life is important. I met the right woman. She followed in line with all my adventures. She was with me in hardship, in pleasure, and everything. And when I was wiped out in 1930 financially, she considered it an adventure. We found out money wasn't everything. I went out hunting and I had moose and deer hanging in the woodshed every winter. I cut my own wood and did everything that was really healthy. Losing the money was a blessing in disguise; ever since then I've had a very happy life, and that's forty-five years ago. My wife and I bought this little house in the mountains before we went broke. It was supposed to be a country vacation place but we moved in and made it our home.

Fifty years we were married. I have a ski trail right back of the house, you know. It's only two miles long now but we skied every day when there was snow. She was on skis, on that ski trail, two weeks before she died, at the age of 82.

Most of my forefathers have lived long . . . all my family. I still have one brother and one sister alive. My youngest brother is only eighty-five. He's just a young fellow. My sister's about ninety. One other sister died a year ago. She was ninety-two. Another brother of mine died last year. He was ninety-four.

I've always had a cheerful disposition. I've always believed that time will fix up everything. If you try to do the right thing you'll come out all right. I try to live one day at a time. Sometimes I think back with pleasure on the past and I'm thankful for all the blessings I've had. But most of the time I live in the present and in the future and I have a lot of friends, lots of young friends who come in here to see me. It keeps me going. I'm always doing something. That's the only way. I'm always trying to do something for other people. I think that's the main thing. If you can manage to do something for other people you get happiness yourself. I really think that I must be one of the happiest people on earth. I'm thankful. I'm cozy here. I have my fireplace going all the time. It's difficult to handle everything but I think that's part of my blessing —that I'm able to do it.

I get up before sunrise. In summer I get up at five o'clock but in winter I sometimes stay in bed until dawn, whatever time that is. Then I'll tend to the chores, and as soon as I can possibly get out, I put my skis on and take a little trip, back on my trail, back of my house there.

My life is outside. The house is really a place that's very handy to have when the weather is so bad outside that you can't be out in it. Then the house is all right. But I love the outdoors. The other thing I like is reading but I don't get a chance to read as much as I like because the day is too short. But I like reading. I don't hear very well on the telephone. Then there's the TV and the radio, but I don't hear very well. But my eyes are good. I can see a good-looking girl way back in the hill without any glasses.

I also like to eat well. I usually have breakfast between six and seven—porridge and a cup of coffee. In the old days, I used to have a heavy breakfast that kept me going all day. Today, I can't make the long trips any more, so instead I get a big meal in the middle of the day. I usually come home for that. Then at night I have a light supper, early, and I try to get to bed by nine or ten o'clock to get a good night's rest and be ready for the next day.

But the whole of last year I've been having celebrations . . . celebrating my one-hundredth birthday. I think they were trying to kill me off with cocktail parties and everything else. All the time, the whole year. Actually I've always been very moderate in everything I do. Cocktail parties don't bother me in that way. I believe in a drink, but I don't believe in taking too much. I enjoy my pipe and I enjoy my drink. But always in moderation. I don't think I've been living in too moderate a way during the last year on account of all the cocktail parties. But when I get to a cocktail party now, I try to find a place to sit down, instead of standing up with a glass in my hand listening to a whole lot of talk that no-

Jackrabbit

body hears anyway. But it's not every year you get to be one hundred years old. I'm thankful. I'm thankful that I can still carry on. I get a great kick out of life. I'm interested in everything. I'm interested in sports. I'm interested in seeing that the ski sport is being developed in the proper way, because I believe that there are two sports that Canada is particularly suited to develop—canoeing in summer and skiing in winter. Those two sports are better than anything else. Football and hockey are all right, but the people who play football and hockey quit it when they're thirty years old. Then they get fat and retire behind the TV and then they go to Florida in winter. They should have gone canoeing in summer and skiing in winter and then they could carry on until they are at least one hundred years old. Maybe even longer than that. You can't carry on with hockey and football until you're one hundred years old. When I'm not skiing or canoeing I like to go fishing and hunting. I do all my own housework. I make my own meals and that way I know what I'm getting to eat. I chop my own wood. I have a good woodpile and I split the wood and bring it in every day. I have the fireplace going and I sit down and smoke my pipe when I want to rest.

I live alone and although I'm happy most of the time, you can't help feeling a little lonesome once in a while. But, I have time to sit down and think it over and pick out the right thoughts, the right way of living. I get a great kick out of life. I'm thankful, very thankful, that I can still carry on alone, without bothering anybody. I have a lot of friends who offer to help. I take advantage of it at times, because I like to keep my friends. I like to accept what's being done for me but not unless I need it. I've no thought of when I want to die. I'm thankful, thankful for every day. Sometimes I think I would like to live forever but that's asking too much.

When the time does come to leave this world I can't think of any better way to go than the way the Eskimos and the Indians do. They disappear in the bush and they're gone. That's what Jackrabbit would like to do."

THIS PRAYER was sent to me by a listener who found it displayed in the historic Convenanters' Church in Grand Pré, New Brunswick. She said that on reading it she immediately thought of the people she listened to on *Voice of the Pioneer* because the words relate so perfectly to them and to the reasons why we should not forget them. I agree.

Father God:

We keep forgetting all of those who lived before us.

We keep forgetting those who lived and worked in this community.

We keep forgetting those who prayed and sang hymns in this church before we were born.

We keep forgetting what our fathers have done for us.

We commit the sin, Lord, of assuming that everything begins with us.

We drink from wells we did not find, we eat food from farmland we did not develop, we enjoy freedoms which we have not earned, we worship in churches which we did not build, we live in communities that we did not establish.

This day, make us grateful for our heritage.

Turn our minds to those who lived in another day and under different circumstances, until we are aware of their faith and work.

Today we need to feel our oneness, not only with those of a recent generation who lived here, but those of every generation in every place, whose faith and works have enriched our lives.

We need to learn from them in order that our faith will be as vital, our commitment as sincere, our worship as alive, our fellowship as deep, as many of the devout and faithful who lived in other times and places.

AMEN.